John Ashton

Humour, Wit & Satire

of the seventeenth century

John Ashton

Humour, Wit & Satire
of the seventeenth century

ISBN/EAN: 9783337386931

Printed in Europe, USA, Canada, Australia, Japan

Cover: Foto ©Andreas Hilbeck / pixelio.de

More available books at **www.hansebooks.com**

HUMOUR, WIT, & SATIRE

of the

SEVENTEENTH CENTURY

Collected and Illustrated by

JOHN ASHTON

AUTHOR OF "CHAP-BOOKS OF THE EIGHTEENTH CENTURY,"
"SOCIAL LIFE IN THE REIGN OF QUEEN ANNE," etc.

London

CHATTO AND WINDUS, PICCADILLY

1883

Printed by R. & R. CLARK, *Edinburgh.*

Preface.

OUR forefathers delighted to call their country "Merrie England;" and so, in very truth, it was. All sorts of sports and pastimes, such as no other nation can show, were then in use; and even the elders, in their hours of relaxation, were wont to exchange a merry jest with one another.

Perhaps some of their jokes lacked the refinement of the present age, but they denoted a keen sense of humour. Many, nay most, cannot be reproduced at the present day, and much has this book suffered therefrom; and it is for this reason that the jest-books and ballads of this century are so little known. Some few have been printed in small editions, either privately, or for dilettante societies; but they are not fit for general perusal, and the public at large know nothing of them. This is specially the case with the ballad literature of the century, which is unusually rich. The Pepys, Roxburghe, Bagford, Luttrell, and other collections, are priceless treasures; but I know no publisher who would be bold enough to reproduce them, in their entirety, for the use of the general public. By this I do not wish to cast any slur, either on the modesty, or morality, of our ancestors; but their ways were not quite as ours.

The Bibliographical Reference, which forms an Appendix, will show the wide range that the humour of this century takes; and this does not exhaust the store by any means. In it I have given, for the use of students, the British Museum Catalogue number of every authority (to save trouble, should they wish to refer to the books); and, to avoid the multiplicity of footnotes, I have placed against each paragraph a number, by means of which (on turning to the reference) the work from which it was taken can at once be seen.

Political satire ought to be a work in itself, so that I have but sparingly used it; and as religious satire hardly comes within the scope of such a book as this, I have but just glanced at it.

In every instance that I have found possible, I have given the tunes of the ballads, taken from the books in which they first appeared, such as *The Dancing Master*, and *Wit and Mirth;* also, in two instances, where I could not thus find them, I have taken them from *The Ballad Literature and Popular Music of the Olden Time*, by W. Chappell, Esq., F.S.A.

If the perusal of this book gives a tithe part as much pleasure and amusement to the Reader, as it did to me when compiling it, I am more than content with my labour.

JNO. ASHTON.

Humour, Wit, and Satire

of the

Seventeenth Century.

[1.] THERE was a man that had been drinking so hard that he could scarse stand upon his feet, yet at night he would go home, and as he went through a green Meadow, neer a hedge side the Bryers held him by the cloaths and the legs, and he had thought that one had holden him, and would have had him to drink more, and he said, Good fellow, let me go, by my troth I can drink no more, I have drank so much already, that I cannot go home; and there he abode all the same night, and on the morrow went his Ways.

[2.]   When *Marcus* hath Carrowst March beere and sacke,
And feels his head grow dizzy therwithall.
Then of Tobacco he a pype doth lacke,
Of Trinidade in cane, in leafe, or ball,
Which tane a little he doth Speet and Smacke,
Then layes him on his bed for feare to fall
And on Tobacco layes the blame of all,
But that same pype that Marcus brain did lade
Was of Madera not of Trinidade.

[3.]   I had a love, and she was chaste,
      Alack the more's the pity,
But wot you how my love was chaste,
      She was chaste right through the City.

4. A Justice of Peace overtaking a Parson upon the Road, between *London* and *Bow*, told his Company that he would put a Trick upon him : and so, coming up to him, said, *Sir, You don't follow your Master's Rule, for he was content with an Ass, but you have a very fine Horse.* The Parson replyed, the reason was, because the King had made so many Asses Justices, that a Clergyman could not get one to Ride on.

On a drawer drunk.

[5.]   Drawer with thee now even is thy wine
      For thou hast pierced his hogs-head, and he thine.

Upon the weights of a Clock.

[5.]   I wonder time's so swift, when as I see,
      Upon her heeles such lumps of lead to bee.

Nonsense.

[3.]   Oh that my Lungs could bleat like butter'd Pease ;
      But bleating of my lungs hath Caught the itch,
      And are as mangy as the Irish Seas,
      That doth ingender windmills on a Bitch.

I grant that Rainbowes being lull'd asleep,
Snort like a woodknife in a Lady's eyes ;
Which makes her grieve to see a pudding creep,
For Creeping puddings only please the wise.

Not that a hard row'd herring should presume
To swing a tyth pig in a Cateskin purse ;
For fear the hailstons which did fall at Rome,
By lesning of the fault should make it worse.

For 'tis most certain Winter woolsacks grow
From geese to swans, if men could keep them so,
Till that the sheep shorn Planets gave the hint,
To pickle pancakes in Geneva print.

Some men there were that did suppose the skie
Was made of Carbonado'd Antidotes;
But my opinion is, a Whales left eye,
Need not be coyned all King *Harry* groates.

The reason's plain, for Charons Westerne barge
Running a tilt at the subjunctive mood,
Beckoned to Bednal Green, and gave him charge
To fasten padlockes with Antartic food.

The end will be the Mill ponds must be laded,
To fish for white pots in a Country dance;
So they that suffered wrong and were upbraded
Shall be made friends in a left handed trance.

[1.] There was three young men going to Lambeth along by the Water side, and the one plaid with the other, and they cast each others Cap into the water, in such sort as they could not get their Caps again: but over the place where their Caps were, did grow a great old tree, which did Cover a great deale of the Water. One of them said to the rest, Sirs, I have found out a notable way to come by them. First I will make myself fast by the middle, with one of your girdles unto the tree, and he that is with you shall hang fast upon my girdle, and he that is last shall take hold on him that holds fast on my girdle, and so with one of his hands he may take up all our caps and cast them on the sand. And so they did; but when they thought that they had been most secure and fast, he that was above felt his girdle slack, and said, Soft, sirs, my girdle slacketh; make it fast quickly, said they, but as he was untying it to make it faster they fell all three into the water, and were well washed for their pains.

Of Lynus borrowing.

[6.] *Lynus* came late to me sixe crownes to borrow,
And sware G— d— him, hee'd repai't to morrow.
I knew his word as current as his band,
And straight I gave to him three crownes in hand;
This I to give, this he to take was willing,
And thus he gain'd, and I sav'd fifteene shilling.

𝕿𝖍𝖊 𝖂𝖔𝖒𝖆𝖓 𝖙𝖔 𝖙𝖍𝖊 𝕻𝖑𝖔𝖜

and

The Man to the Hen Roost.

Or, a fine way to cure a *Cot Quean*—.

The Tune is, *I have for all good Wives a Song.*—

[7.]

Both Men and Women listen well,
A merry Jest I will you tell,
Betwixt a Good man and his Wife,
Who fell the other day at strife :
He chid her for her Huswivery,
And she found fault as well as he,
With him for's work without the door,
Quoth he (*we'l quarrel thus no more*)
Sith you and I cannot agree,
Let's change the work.   Content, quoth she,
My Wheel and Distaffe here take thow,
And I will drive the Cart and Plow.
This was concluded 'twixt them both,

To Cart and Plow the good-wife goeth,
The Good man he at home doth tarry,
To see that nothing doth miscarry.
An apron he before him put,
Judge, was not this a handsome slut.
He fleets [1] the Milk, he makes the Chese,
He gropes [2] the Hens, the Ducks, & Geese,
He Brews and Bakes as well as he Can,
But not as it should be done, poor man :
As he did make his Cheese one day,
Two Pigs their Bellies broke with whey ;
Nothing that he in hand did take,
Did come to good ; once he did Bake,
And burnt the Bread as black as a stock,
Another time he went to Rock
The Cradle, and threw the child o' th' floor,
And broke his Nose, and hurt it sore.
He went to milk one Eventide
A Skittish Cow on the wrong side,
His pail was full of Milk, God wot,
She Kickt and spilt it every jot.
Besides she hit him a blost o' th' face
Which was scant well in six weeks space.
Thus was he served, and yet too well
And more mischances yet befell.
Before his apron he'd leave off,
Though all his neighbours did him scoff.
Now list and mark one pretty jest,
'Twill make you laugh above all the rest,
As he to churn his Butter went,
One Morning with a good intent,
The Cot [3] Quean fool did surely dream,
For he had quite forgot the Cream,
He churn'd all Day with all his might,
And yet he could get no Butter at night.
'Twere strange indeed for me to utter

---

[1] Floats, *i.e.* skims the cream floating on the milk.
[2] Feels whether they have eggs.
[3] One who meddles in women's business.

That without Creame he should make Butter.
Now having shew'd his huswivery,
Who did all things thus untowardly,
Unto the good-wife I'll turn my Rhime,
And tell you how she spent her time ;
She us'd to drive the Cart and Plow,
But do't well she Knew not how,
She made so many banks i' th' ground,
He been better have given five pound
That she had never ta'ne in hand
So sorely did she spoil the Land.
As she did go to Sow likewise,
She made a Feast for Crows and Pies,
She threw away a hanful at a Place,
And left all bare another Space.
At the Harrow she could not rule the Mare
But hid one Land, and left two bare.
And shortly after, one a day,
As she came home with a Load of Hay
She overthrew it, nay, and worse
She broke the Cart, and Kill'd a Horse :
The good-man that time had ill luck,
He let in the Sow, and Kill'd a Duck,
And being grieved at his heart,
For loss on's Duck, his Horse and Cart,
The many hurts on both sides done,
His eyes did with salt water run ;
Then now, quoth he, full well I see
The Wheel's for her, the Plow's for me,
I thee intreat, quoth he, good-wife,
To take thy Charge, and all my life
I'll never meddle with huswivery more,
Nor find such faults as I did before ;
Give me the Cart Whip and the Frail,
Take thou the Churn and Milking pail.
The good-wife she was well content
And about her Huswivery she went ;
He to Hedging and to Ditching,
Heaping, Mowing, Lading, Pitching,

He would be twatling [1] still before,
But after that ne'r twatled more.
I wish all Wives that troubled be
With Hose and Doublet Huswivery,
To serve them as this Woman did,
Then may they work and ne'r be chid.
Though she i' th' intrim had some loss,
Thereby she was eased of a Cross;
Take heed of this you husband men,
Let Wives alone to grope the Hen,
And meddle you with Horse and Ox.
And keep your Lambs safe from the Fox,
So shall you live Contented lives,
And take sweet pleasure in your Wives.

FINIS.

Printed for J. Wright,[2] J. Clarke,[3] W. Thackeray,[4] and T. Passinger.[5]

[8.] The Marquess of *Worcester*, calling for a glass of Claret wine, it was told him by his Physician, that Claret wine was naught for his gout; What, said the Marquess, my old friend Claret? nay, give it me in spight of all Physicians and their books, it never shall be said that I forsook my friend for my enemy.

On a cowardly Soüldier.

[5.] *Strotzo* doth weare no ring upon his hand,
Although he be a man of great command;
But gilded spurs do jingle at his heeles;
Whose rowels are as big as some coach wheels,
He grac'd them well, for in the Netherlands,
His heels did him more service than his hands.

---

[1] Chattering. [2] Published from 1670 to 1690.
[3] From 1650 to 1682. [4] From 1660 to 1680.
[5] From 1670 to 1682.

On a fly in a glasse.

[5.]   A fly out of his glasse a guest did take,
'Ere with the liquor he his thirst would slake,
When he had drunk his fill, again the fly
Into the glasse he put, and said, though I
Love not flyes in my drink yet others may,
Whose humour I nor like, nor will gainsay.

Upon a Churle that was a great usurer.

[9.]   A Chuffe that scarce hath teeth to chew his meate,
Heares with deafe ears, and sees with glassy eies,
Unto his grave his path doth daily beate,
Or like a logg upon his pallett lies :

Hath not a thought of God, nor of his grace,
Speaks not a word but what intends to gaine,
Can have no pitty on the poore Mans case,
But will the hart-strings of the needy straine :

Cries not till death, and then but gives a groane,
To leave his silver, and his golden bags,
Then gapes and dies, and with a little moane
Is lapped up in a few rotten ragges :
      What will this Clunch fist leave upon his grave ?
      Here lies the Carkasse of a wretched Knave.

[4.] An Arch Wag speaking of the late dreadful Fire of *London*, said Cannon Street roared, Wood Street was burnt to Ashes, Bread Street was burnt to a Coal, Pie Corner was over bak'd and Snow hill melted down.

[4.] A Highway man being to be hang'd in a Country Town, Order was sent to the Carpenter to make a Gallows ; which he neglecting to do, the Execution was forc'd to be defer'd, for which the Judge was not a little angry, who sending for the Carpenter, asked him why he had not done it ? Why Sir, said he, I have done two or three already, but was never paid for them ; but had I known it had been for your Worship, I would have left all other business to have done it.

[3.] Sir *Egley More* [1] that Valiant Knight,
  With his fa, la, lanctre down dille ;
  He fetcht his sword and he went to fight
  With his fa, la, lanctre down dille ;
  As he went over hill and dale,
  All cloathed in his coat of Male,
  With his fa, la, lanctre down dille.

A huge great Dragon leapes out of his Den,
  With his &c.
Which had kill'd the Lord knowes how many men,
  With his &c.
But when he saw Sir *Egly More,*
Good lack had you seen how this Dragon did roare
  With his &c.

This Dragon he had on a plaguy hide,
  With his &c.
Which could both sword and speare abide,
  All the trees in the wood did shake,
  With his &c.
Stars did tremble and man did quake,
  With his &c.
But had you seen how the birds lay peeping,
  'Twould have made a mans heart to a' fallen a weeping.
  With his &c.

But now it was too late to feare,
  With his &c.
For now it was come to fight dog, fight beare,
  With his &c.
And as a yawning he did fall,
  He thrust his sword in, hilts and all.
  With his &c.

But now as the Knight in coller [2] did burne,
  With his &c.
He ow'd the Dragon a shrewd good turne ;
  With his &c.

---

[1] For tune see Appendix.   [2] Choler, anger.

In at his mouth his sword he bent,
The hilt appeared at his fundament.
With his &c.

Then the Dragon like a Coward began to fly,
With his &c.
Unto his Den that was hard by.
With his &c.
And there he laid him down and roar'd ;
The Knight was vexed for his sword,
With his &c.

The Sword it was a right good blade,
With his &c.
As ever Turk or Spaniard made ;
With his &c.
I for my part do forsake it,
And he that will fetch it, let him take it.
With his &c.

When all this was done to the Ale house he went,
With his &c.
And by and by his two pence he spent ;
With his &c.
For he was so hot with tugging with the Dragon,
That nothing could quench him but a whole Flagon.
With his &c.

Now God preserve our King and Queen,
With his &c.
And eke in London may be seene,
With his &c.
As many Knights, and as many more,
And all as good as Sir *Eglemore*.
With his &c.

[1.] There was a Fryer in *London*, which did use to go
often to the house of an old woman, but ever when he came
to her house, she hid all the meat she had. On a time this
Fryer came to her house (bringing certain Company with him)
and demanded of the Wife if she had any meat. And she

said, Nay. Well, quoth the Fryer, have you not a whetstone? Yea (qd. the Woman) Marry, qd. he, I would make meat thereof. Then she brought a whetstone. He asked her likewise if she had not a Frying-pan. Yea, said she, but what the devil will ye do therewith? Marry (said the Fryer) you shall see by and by what I will do with it; and when he had the pan, he set it on the fire, and put the whetstone therein. Cocks body, said the woman, you will burn the pan. No, no, qd. the Fryer, if you will give me some eggs, it will not burn at all. But she would have had the pan from him, when that she saw it was in danger; yet he would not let her, but still urged her to fetch him some eggs, which she did. Tush said the Fryer, here are not enow, go fetch ten or twelve. So the good Wife was constrayned to fetch more for feare lest the Pan should burn; And when he had them, he put them in the Pan. Now, qd he, if you have no butter the pan will burn, and the eggs too. So the good wife being very loth to have her pan burnt, and the eggs lost, she fetcht him a dish of butter, the which he put into the pan, and made good meat thereof, & brought to the table, saying, Much good may it do you my Masters, now may you say, you have eaten of a buttered Whetstone. Whereat all the Company laughed, but the woman was exceeding angry because the Fryer had subtilly beguiled her of her meat.

The Devill and the Fryar.

[5.] The Devill was once deceived by a fryar,
Who though he sold his soul cheated the buyer.
The devill was promist if he would supply,
The Fryar with Coyn at his necessity,
When all the debts he ow'd discharg'd were quite,
The Devill should have his soul as his by right;
The Devill defray'd all scores, payd all; at last
Demanded for his due, his soul in haste:
The Fryar return'd this answer, if I owe
You any debts at all, then you must know
I am indebted still, if nothing be
Due unto you, why do you trouble me?

On Battus.

[5.] Battus doth bragge he hath a world of bookes
His studies maw holds more than well it may,
But seld' or never he upon them looks,
And yet he looks upon them every day,
He looks upon their out side, but within
He never looks nor never will begin :
Because it cleane against his nature goes
To know mens secrets, so he keeps them Close.

The
Unconscionable Batchelors of DARBY,
or the
Young Lasses Pawn'd by their Sweethearts, for a large
Reckoning, at *Nottingham* Goose Fair ; where
poor Susan was forced to pay the Shot.

To the Tune of *To thee, To thee &c.*

[10.] You lovers of mirth attend a while,
a merry new ditty here I write,
I know it will make you laugh and smile,
for every line affords delight :
The Lasses of Darby with young Men,
they went to Goose Fair for recreation,
But how these Sparks did serve them then,
is truly worth your observation,
Truly, truly worth your observation,
therefore I pray observe this Ditty ;
The Maids did complain they came there in vain
and was not, was not that a pity.

So soon as they came into the Fair,
The Batchelors made them conjues [1] low,

---

[1] Congées, low bows.

And bid them a thousand welcomes there,
　　this done to a tippling school they go ;
How pleasant was honest Kate and Sue,
　　believing they should be richly treated,
But, Neighbours and Friends, as I am true ;
　　no Lasses ever was so cheated ;

Cheated, cheated, very farely cheated,
　　as you may note by this new Ditty ;
They were left alone, to make their moan,
　　and was not, was not that a pity ?

The innocent Lasses fair and gay,
　　concluded the Men was kind and free,
Because they pass'd the time away,
　　a plenty of cakes and ale they see ;
For sider and mead they then did call,
　　and whatever else the House afforded,
But Susan was forc'd to pay for all,
　　out of the mony she had hoarded,

Hoarded, hoarded, mony she had hoarded;
  it made her sing a doleful Ditty,
And so did the rest with grief opprest,
  and was not, was not that a pity?

Young Katy she seemed something Coy,
  because she would make them eager grow,
As knowing thereby she might enjoy
  what beautiful Damsels long to know,
On complements they did not stand,
  nor did they admire their charming features;
For they had another game in hand,
  which was to pawn these pretty creatures,
Creatures, creatures, loving, loving Creatures,
  which was so charming, fair, and pretty;
The Men sneak'd away, and nothing did pay,
  and was not, was not, that a pity?

Though out of the door they enter'd first,
  and left them tipling there behind,
Those innocent Maids did not mistrust,
  that Batchelors could be so unkind.
Quoth Susan, I know their gone to buy
  the fairings which we did so require,
And they will return I know, for why,
  they do our youthful charms admire;
Therefore, therefore, stay a little longer,
  and I will sing you a pleasant Ditty,
But when they found they were catch'd in the pound,
  they sigh'd and weep'd the more's the pity.

Now finding the Men return'd no more,
  and that the good People would not trust,
They presently call'd to know the Score,
  it chanc'd to be fifteen shilling just:
Poor Kate had but five pence in her purse, ,
  but Sue had a crown besides a guinney;
And since the case had happen'd thus,
  poor Soul she paid it e'ry penny,

Penny, Penny, e'ry, e'ry penny,
  tho' with a sad and doleful Ditty
Said she, for this I had not a kiss,
  and was not, was not that a pity ?

Printed for J. Bissel,[1] in West Smithfield.

[1.] There was a Priest in the Country, which had christned a Child ; and when he had christned it, he and the clark were bidden to the drinking that should be there, and thither they went with other people, and being there, the Priest drunk and made so merry that he was quite foxed,[2] and thought to go home before he laid him down to sleep; but having gone a little way, he grew so drowsie, that he could go no further, but laid him down by a ditch side, so that his feet did hang in the water, and lying on his back, the Moon shined in his face : thus he lay till the rest of the Company came from drinking, who as they came home found the Priest lying as aforesaid, and they thought to get him away, but do what they could he would not rise, but said, Do not meddle with me, for I lie very well, I will not stir hence before morning, but I pray you lay some more cloathes on my feet, and blow out the Candle, and let me lie and take my rest.

In Getam.

[5.] *Geta* from wool and weaving first began,
  Swelling and Swelling to a gentleman ;
  When he was gentleman, and bravely dight,
  He left not swelling till he was a knight ;
  At last forgetting what he was at first,
  He swole to be a Lord . . . and then he burst.

On Button a Sexton making a grave.

[5.] Ye powers above, and heavenly poles,
  Are graves become but *Button* Holes.

---

[1] James Bissel lived at the Bible and Harp, by the Hospital Gate, and published between 1685 and 1695.   [2] Drunk.

[4.] Two Sparks standing together in the Cloysters, seeing a pretty Lady pass by, says one of them, *There goes the handsomest Lady that I ever saw in my Life;* She hearing him, turned back, and seeing him very ugly, said, *Sir I would I could in way of Requital say as much of you.* Faith, says he, *so you may, and Lye as I did.*

On Jack Wiseman.

[3.]   *Jack Wiseman* brags his very name,
Proclaims his wit, he's much to blame,
To doe the Proverb so much wrong,
Which sayes he's wise that holds his tongue;
Which makes me contradict the Scooles,
And apt to thinke the wise men fools,
Yet pardon *Jack*, I hear that now
Thou'rt wed, and must thy wit allow,
That by a strange œnigma can,
Make a light Woman a *Wiseman.*

Of a Woman's Kindnesse to her Husband.

[6.]   One that had lived long by lewdest shifts,
Brought to the Court that Corne from Cockle[1] sifts
Adiudged, first to lye a yeere in fetters,
Then burned in his forhead with two letters,
And to disparage him with more disgrace,
To slit his nose, the figure of his face.
The prisoners wife with no dishonest mind,
To shew herselfe unto her husband kind,
Sued humbly to the Lords, and would not cease,
Some part of this sharp rigour to release.
He was a man (she said) had serv'd in Warre,
What mercy would a Souldiers face so marre.
Thus much said she, but gravely they replied,
It was great mercy that he thus was tried:
His crimes deserve he should have lost his life,
And hang in chaines; Alas, reply'd the wife,
     If you disgrace him thus, you quite undo him,
     Good my Lords, hang him, pray be good unto him.

---

[1] The *Agrostemna githago*, Linn.

[1.] There were once too men that were both masterless and moneyless, & one said to the other, What remedy canst thou now find out, that we may either get some meat or money? By my troth (qd. the other) I do know a very fine shift, (& being very early in the morning they espyed a man coming with Hogs). Lo, yonder cometh a man with Hogs, and I will tell him that they be sheep, and I will cause him to lay a Wager with me, whether they be Sheep or Hogs: & I will cause the matter to be judged by the next man that cometh, but then thou must go another way & meet with us; when we demand of thee whether they be sheep or hogs, thou must say that they be sheep. Then they separated themselves the one from the other, and the one went to meet the man that had the Swine, bidding him good morrow; the man doing the like to him again. Then he said to the old man, Father, where had you your fair sheep. What sheep qd the man; these sheep that you drive before you: Why, qd the old man, they are swine. What (qd. the other) will you make me a fool? think you I know not Sheep from Swine? Marry (qd. the old man) I will lay one of my Swine against what thou wilt, that they be no Sheep. I hold thee my coat against one of thy sheep qd. the other. I am content qd the old man, by whom shall we be tryed? By the next man that meets us. Content, said the old man; and then they perceived the man coming being the fellow of the young man. And when he came to them the old man requested him to tel them what beasts those were? Why (qd. he) they be sheep, do you not know sheep? I told him so (qd. the other young man) but he would not believe me, so I laid my Coat upon a Wager that they were sheep, and he laid me one of his sheep against my Coat that they were Swine; and I won it have I not? Yea (qd. the old man,) but God help me, I bought them for Swine. And then the young man took one of the fattest hogs he could find amongst them all, & carryed him away, and his fellow went another way, as though he had not known him, and the poore man returned again to the place where he had bought them.

What became of him afterward I cannot tell: only thus much I know, that he was deceived by those two crafty fellows

of one of his hogs.   But they immediately met one the other
again, and sold the hog for Money, and rejoyced that they
fared so well (not knowing how to have otherwise sustained
their wants).

Of Marcus.

[5.]   When *Marcus* fail'd a borrowed sum to pay,
  Unto his friend at the appointed day :
  'Twere superstition for a man he sayes,
  To be a strict observer of set dayes.

[11.]   The industrious Smith wherin is showne,
  How plain dealing is overthrown,
  That let a man do the best that he may,
  An idle huswife will work his decay,
  Yet art is no burthen ; tho ill we may speed,
  Our labour will help us in time of our need.

To the Tune of *Young Man remember delights are but vain.*

There was a poor Smith liv'd in a poor town,
That had a loving wife bonny and brown,
And though he were very discreet and wise,
Yet he would do nothing without her advice ;
His stock it grew low, full well did he know,
He told his wife what he intended to do,
Quoth he, sweet wife, if I can prevail,
I will shoo horses, and thou shalt sell Ale.

I see by my labour but little I thrive,
And that against the stream I do strive
By selling of Ale some money is got,
If every man honestly pay for his pot :
By this we may keep the wolf from the door,
And live in good fashion though now we live poor,
If we have good custom, we shall have quick sale,
So may we live bravely by selling of Ale.

Kind husband, quoth she, let be as you said,
It is the best motion that ever you made,

A Stan[1] of good Ale, let me have in,
A dozen of good white bread in my Bin ;

Tobacco likewise we must not forget,
Men will call for it when malt's above wheat.
When once it is known, then ore hill and dale,
Men will come flocking to taste of our Ale.

They sent for a wench, her name it was *Besse*,
And her they hired to welcome their guesse,[2]

---

[1] A Stand of Ale was a beer barrel set on end.　　　　　[2] Guests.

They took in good Ale, and many things mo,
The Smith had got him two strings to his bow :
Good fellows came in, and began for to rore,
The Smith he was never so troubled before,
But quoth the good wife, sweet hart do not rayl,
These things must be, if we sell Ale.

The Smith went to his work every day,
But still one or other would call him away,
For now he had got him the name of an Host,
It cost him many a Pot and a Toste.
Beside much precious time he now lost,
And thus the poor Smith was every day crost,
But quoth the good wife, sweet hart do not rayl
These things must be if we sell Ale.

Men run on the score, and little they paid,
Which made the poor Smith be greatly dismaied,
And bonny *Besse* though she were not slack
To welcome her guesse, yet things went to wrack ;
For she would exchange a pot for a kisse,
Which any fellow should seldom times misse.
But quoth the good Wife, sweet hart do not rayl,
These things must be if we sell Ale.

The Smith went abroad, at length hee came home,
And found his maid and man in a room,
Both drinking together foot to foot,
To speak unto them he thought was no boot :
For they were both drunk and could not reply,
To make an excuse as big as a lye.
But quoth the good wife, sweet hart do not rayl,
These things must be if we sell Ale.

He came home again and there he did see
His Wife kindly sitting on a man's knee,
And though he said little, yet he thought the more,
And who can blame the poor Wittall therfore.
He hug'd her and kist her though Vulcan stood by,
Which made him to grumble, and look all awry.

But quoth the good wife, sweet hart do not rayl,
These things must be, if we sell Ale.

A Sort of Saylers were drinking one night,
And when they were drunk began for to fight,
The Smith came to part them, as some do report,
And for his good will was beat in such sort
That he could not lift his arms to his head,
Nor yet very hardly creep up to his bed.
But quoth the good wife, sweet hart do not rayl,
These things must be if we sell Ale.

The Smith by chance a good fellow had met,
That for strong Ale was much in his debt,
He ask't him for money; quoth he, by your leave,
I owe you no money, nor none you shall have.
I owe to your wife, and her I will pay;
The Smith he was vext and departed away.
Alas who can blame him, if now he do rayl,
For these things must be if we sell Ale.

.   .   .   .   .   .

A flock of good fellows, all Smiths by their trade,
Within a while after a holiday made,
Unto the Smith's house they came then with speed,
And there they were wondrous merry indeed,
With my pot and thy pot to make the score hier,
Mine Host was so drunk he fell in the fire.
But quoth the good Wife, sweet hart do not rayl,
These things must be if we sell Ale.

.   .   .   .   .   .

But men ran so much with him on the score,
That Vulcan at last grew wondrous poor,
He owed the Brewer and Baker so much,
They thretned to arrest him, his case it was such;
He went to his Anvill, to my pot and thine,
He turn'd out his Maid, he pul'd down his Signe,

But O (quoth the good Wife) why should we fail,
These things should not be, if we sell Ale.

The Smith and his boy went to work for some chink,
To pay for the liquor which others did drink
Of all trades in London few break as I heare,
That sell Tobacco, strong Ale and good Beer,
They might have done better, but they were loth
To fill up their measure with nothing but froth.
Let no Ale-house keeper at my Song rayl,
These things must be if they sell Ale.

Humfrey Crowch.[1]

FINIS.

London.   Printed for RICHARD HARPER[2] in Smithfield.

[8.] *Jack Roberts* was desired by his Taylour, when the reckoning grew somewhat high, to have a Bill of his hand. *Roberts* said, I am content, but you must let no man know it; when the Taylour brought him the Bill, he tore it as in choler, and said to him, *You use me not well, you promised me that no man should know it, and here you have put in: Be it known unto all Men by these Presents.*

[1.] A Certain Butcher was flaying a Calf at night and had stuck a lighted Candle upon his head, because he would be the quicker about his business, and when he had done, he thought to take the same Candle to light him to bed: but he had forgot where he had set it, and sought about the House for it, and all the while it stuck in his Cap upon his head, and lighted him in seeking it.   At the last one of his fellows came and asked him what he sought for? Marry, (quoth he) I look for the Candle which I did flay the Calf withal.   Why, thou

---

[1] Of Humphrey Crowch or Crouch little is known, but we know he published many ballads and books of the chap-book order; among the former is the Mad Man's Morrice, and among the latter is England's Jests refin'd.   He certainly wrote from 1637 to 1687.

[2] Richard Harper published from 1635 to 1642.

fool, qd. he, thou hast a Candle in thy Cap: and then he felt towards his Cap, and took away the Candle burning, whereat there was great laughing and he mocked for his labour, as he was well worthy.

[12.]   A rich man, and's Wife,
Were every day at strife,
And each wisht t'other in the Grave;
But their good Son and Heir
Begg'd God grant their Prayer,
That both their desires they might have.

[12.]   One *Hart*, that was Wild
Got a woman with Child,
But the Justice did take his part;
Then she cry'd and did mumble,
Sayes the Justice de'e grumble?
No, I grieve, Sir, and lay it to *Hart*.

[4.] Just after the late Kings Restauration, when going to Church came to be in fashion, an old Woman was advised by her Neighbours to go to Church; for fear of being Presented, she was resolved to go once a month to save her Bacon: So Dressing herself very fine, she came into the Church, just at the Expiration of the Letany, and the Parson having said, *Lord have Mercy upon us*, and then the People Responding thereto, she Cryed out aloud, *I never was here before in my Life, and since you make such a Wonderment at it I will never come again.*

On Sextus.

[5.]   Sextus doth wish his wife in heaven were
Where can shee have more happines than there?

The Rurall Dance about the May-pole.[1]

The Tune the first Figure dance at Mr Young's Ball *in* May 1671

[13.]   Come lasses and ladds,
Take leave of your Dadds,

[1] For tune see Appendix.

And away to the *May-pole* hey ;
 For every he
 Has got him a she
With a Minstrill standing by.
For *Willy* has gotten his *Jill*,
And *Jonny* has got his *Jone*,
To jigg it, jigg it, jigg it, jigg it,
Jigg it up and down.

Strike up sayes *Wat*
Agreed sayes *Kate*,
 And I prethee Fidler play,
 Content sayes *Hodge*,
 And so sayes *Madge*,
For this is a Holliday.
Then every man did put
His Hat off to his Lasse,
And every Girle did curchy,
Curchy, curchy on the Grasse.

Begin sayes *Hall.*
[1] I. I says *Mall*
Wee'l lead up *Packingtons*[2] pound
 No, no, says *Noll*
 And so says *Doll*
Wee'l first have *Sellengers*[3] round :
Then every man began
To foot it round about,
And every Girle did jet it,
Jet it, jet it in and out

[1] Ay, ay.

[2] This tune certainly was known in Queen Elizabeth's time, for it occurs in her Virginal book, and Chappell says, "It probably took its name from Sir John Packington, commonly called 'lusty Packington,' the same who wagered that he would swim from the Bridge at Westminster, *i.e.* Whitehall Stairs, to that at Greenwich for the sum of £3000. 'But the good Queen, who had particular tenderness for handsome fellows, would not permit Sir John to run the hazard of the trial.'"

[3] Or St. Leger's round, was thought by Sir John Hawkins to be the oldest country dance now extant, and is to be found in Queen Elizabeth's Virginal book.

Y'are out, says *Dick*,
'Tis a lye, says Nick,
The Fidler play'd it false ;
 'Tis true says *Hugh*,
 And so says *Sue*,
And so says nimble *Alice ;*
The Fidler then began
To play the 'Tune agen,
And every Girle did trip it,
Trip it, trip it to the men.

Let's kiss says *Jane*,
Content, says *Nan*
And so says every she
 How many says *Batt*,
 Why three says *Matt*,
For that's a maiden's fee ;
But they instead of three
Did give 'em halfe a score,
And they in kindnesse gave 'em,
Gave 'em, gave 'em as many more.

Then after an hour,
They went to a bower,
And play'd for Ale and Cakes,
 And kisses too
 Untill they were due,
The Lasses kept the stakes.
The Girles did then begin
To quarrel with the men,
And bid 'em take their kisses back
And give 'em their own agen.

Yet there they sate
Until it was late
And tyr'd the Fidler quite,
 With singing and playing
 Without any paying,
From morning untill night.
They told the fidler then,

They'd pay him for his play,
And each a 2 pence, 2 pence, 2 pence,
Gave him and went away.

[4.] A Minister finding his Parishioners to be Ignorant,
was resolv'd to Examine and Instruct them at home ; so
going to an Ancient Womans House, amongst other Questions,
he asked her how many Commandments there were ?   She
told him she could not tell : he told her there were Ten :
Whereat she replied, *A Jolly Company !   God Bless you and
them both together.*   Well, but, Neighbour, (says he) Do you
think you can keep these Commandments?   *Ah ! God bless
you, Sir,* (said she) *I am a poor Woman, and can hardly keep
my self ; I hope you will not put me to the Charge of keeping
any of the Commandments for you.*

On Charismus.

[5.] Thou hast compos'd a book, which neither age
Nor future time shall hurt through all their rage,
For how can future times or age invade
That work, which perished as soone as made.

[12.]   A man did surmise
That another mans eyes
Were both of a different frame ;
For if they had been Matches,
Then, alas, poor wretches,
His Nose would a set 'em in a flame.

[8.] Master *Mason* of *Trinity* Colledge, sent his Pupil to
another of the Fellows to borrow a Book of him, who told him
*I am loath to lend my Books out of my Chamber, but if it please
thy Tutor to come and read upon it in my Chamber, he shall as
long as he will.*   It was winter, and some daies after the same
Fellow sent to Mr *Mason* to borrow his Bellows, but Master
Mason said to his Pupil, *I am loath to lend my Bellows out of
my Chamber, but if thy Tutor would come and blow the Fire in
my Chamber he shall as long as he will.*

Of a drunken Smith.

[6.] I heard that *Smug* the Smith for Ale and Spice,
Sold all his tooles, and yet he kept his Vice.

[6.] When Lynus meetes me, after Salutations,
Curtesies, complements, and gratulations,
He presseth me unto the third deniall,
To lend him twenty shillings or a ryall;[1]
But, with his curt'sies, of his purpose fayling
Hĕ goes behind my backe cursing and railing.
Foole, thy kind speeches cost thee not a penny,
And more foole I, if they should cost me enny.

[4.] A Minister going to one of his Parishioners he asked her, who made her? She reply'd, She did not know: A Child standing by, he asked him the same Question, who Answered, God; whereupon the Parson Reproving the Old Woman, told her it was a shame that she should be so Ignorant, who had lived to those Years, and that little Child could tell. *Marry*, quoth she, *I am an old Woman, and have been made a great while, and he was made but t'other day, he may well tell who made him.*

[13.] I went to the Tavern, and then,
I went to the Tavern, and then,
I had good store of Wine,
And my Cap full of coyne
And the world went well with me then, then,
And the world went well with me then.

I went to the Tavern agen
When I ran on the score
And was turn'd out o' th' door
And the world went ill with me then, then, &c.

When I was a Batchelor then,
I had a Saddle and a Horse,
And I took my own Course,
And the world went well with me then, then &c.

1 Value ten shillings.

But when I was marry'd, O then
My Horse and my Saddle
Were turn'd to a Cradle,
    And the world went ill with me then, then, &c.

When I brought her home mony, then
She never would pout,
But clip me about,
    And the world went well with me then, then, &c.

But when I was drunk, O then,
She'd kick, she'd fling,
Till she made the house ring,
    And the world went ill with me then, then &c.

So I turn'd her away, and then,
I got me a Miss
To Clip and to kiss,
    And the world went ill with me then, then &c.

I took my wife home agen,
But I chang'd her note
For I cut her throat.
    And the world went well with me then, then, &c.

But when it was known, O then,
In a two wheeld Charret
To *Tiburn* I was carry'd,
    And the world went ill with me then, then, &c.

But when I came there, O then,
They forc't me to swing
To heaven in a string.
    And the world went well with me then, then &c.

[1.] There was a man in the Country, who had not been
any far Traveller, and dwelt far from any Church except a
Church that was seven or eight miles from his house, and
there they never sung Mass nor Even song, but did ever say
it. And on a time he came to *London*, having never been
here before, & being in *London* he went to *Pauls* Church, &
went into the Chappel, where they sung Mass with Organs,
and when he heard the melody of the Organs and the singing

together, that he never heard before, he thought he should
have gone to Heaven by and by, and looked, and said aloud
that every one heard, O Lord, shall I go to heaven presently?
I would thou wouldest let me alone till I might go home and
fetch my white stick and black hood, and then I would go
gladly with thee. Where at all the people laughed heartily.

Sorte tuâ contentus.

[5.] If adverse fortune bring to passe
    And will that thou an asse must bee,
    Then be an asse, and live an asse,
    For out of question wise is hee
        That undergoes with humble mind
        The state that chance hath him assign'd.

[12.] A Fellow told his Friends,
    That a Pudding had two ends;
    But that's a lye, sayes another;
    Do but think agen,
    And you'l find it begin
    At one end, and ends at t'other.

[14.] If that from Glove you take the letter G
    Then glove is love, and that I send to thee.

[15.] THE JOLLY WELSH WOMAN

Who drinking at the Sign of the *Crown* in *London*, found a
    Spring in her Mugg, for Joy of which hur Sung the
    praise of Old *England* resolving never to return to *Wales*
    again.

Tune of, *Hey brave* Popery &c.   Licensed according to Order.

There was an Old woman came out of North Wales,
And up to fair London her merrily Sails,
It was for her pleasure Cuts-plutter-a-nails
    Sing O brave Welsh *Woman, Jolly brave* Welsh *Woman,*
    Delicate Welsh *Woman.* O.

As soon as hur came into fair *London* town
Hur went to an Alehouse the sign of the Crown,
In order to tipple hur streight did sit down.
     Sing O brave &c.

Hur being a weary and willing to rest,
Hur would not be one of the worst of the guest,
But call'd for a Pitcher of Ale of the best.
     Sing O brave &c.

The Tapster then giving the Jugg in her hand,
The *Welsh* woman streight on hur feet she did stand,
And drank a good health to hur King of England.
     Sing O brave &c.

Now while she had gotten the jugg at her snout,
And being both lusty, courageous and stout,
Hur gave it a tug, till hur swigg'd it half out.
     Sing O brave &c.

The Tapster he see her to be of that strain,
And how she did tipple the Liquor amain,
Thought he, I will fill up thy pitcher again.
     Sing O brave &c.

The jugg hur had plac'd on the Bench by her side,
To which the young tapster did cunningly slide,
And fill'd it as if it had been a full tide.
    Sing O brave &c.

Now hur did not know how her pitcher did fill,
Therefore hur did say with a merry good will
Here's Tipple and drink, and her Pitcher full still.
    Sing O brave England &c.

The praise of this Nation Cuts-plut her will sing,
Hur never had known such a wonderful thing,
The juggs in this land has a delicate Spring.
    Sing O brave England &c.

Once more she saluted the lips of her Mugg,
And gave it a hearty and dextrous tugg,
The Tapster once more he did fill up her jugg.
    Sing O brave England &c.

The Liquor up into her Noddle did steel,
The Floor with her feet hur hardly could feel,
So that hur began for to stagger and reel.
    Sing O brave England &c.

Hur swore hur would never to *Wales* any more,
For hur has tasted Rich liquor good store,
The like in all *Wales* hur had neer drank before,
    Sing O brave England &c.

Hereafter hur never will honour the Leek,
This was the best Nation as e're hur did seek,
Here's liquor of life that will make a Cat speak.
    Sing O brave England &c.

In praise of this liquor, hur Cap up she flung,
For why, it Created an Eloquent Tongue,
Besides it will make an Old Woman look young,
    Sing O brave Nappy Ale, Delicate Nappy Ale,
    Dainty fine Nappy Ale.

[1.] In the country dwelt a Gentlewoman who had a French man dwelling with her and he did ever use to go to Church with her, and upon a time he and his Mistresse were going to Church and she bad him pull the doore after him and follow her to the Church, and so he took the doore betweene his armes, and lifted it from the hooks, and followed his Mistresse with it: But when she looked behinde her and saw him bring the doore upon his back, Why, thou foolish knave, qd. she, what wilt thou do with the door? Marry Mistresse, qd. he, you bad me pull the doore after me. Why, qd. she, I did command thee that thou shouldest make fast the doore after thee, and not bring it upon thy back after me. But after this, there was much good sport and laughing at his simplicity and foolishnesse therein.

On a Watch lost in a Tavern.

[14.]　A Watch lost in a Tavern? that's a Crime,
You know how men in drinking lose there time :
A Watch keeps time, and if time pass away,
There is small reason that the Watch should stay.
The key hung out, and you forgot to lock it,
Time scorns to be kept tame in any pocket.
Hereafter if you keep't, thus must you do,
Pocket your Watch, and watch your pockets too.

Of a Precise Taylor.

[16.]　A Taylor thought a man of upright dealing,
True, but for lying, honest but for stealing,
Did fall one day extreamly sicke by chance,
And on the sudden was in wondrous trance.
The Fiends of hell mustring in fearfull manner,
Of Sundry Coloured silkes displayed a Banner,
Which he had stolne, and wish't as they did tell
That one day he might finde it all in hell.
The man affrighted at this apparition
Upon recovery grew a great Precisian.

He bought a Bible of the new Translation,
And in his life he shew'd great reformation;
He walked mannerly, and talked meekely,
He heard three Lectures, and two Sermons weekely:
He vowed to shunne all companies unruly,
And in his speech he used none oath, but truly.
And zealously to keepe the Sabboths rest,
His meat for that day, on the e've was drest,
And least the custome that he had to steale,
Might cause him sometime to forget his zeale,
He gives his journeyman a speciall charge,
That if the stuffe allow'd fell out too large,
And that to filch his fingers were inclin'd,
He then should put the Banner in his minde.
This done, I scant can tell the rest for laughter,
A Captaine of a ship came three daies after,
And brought three yards of Velvet, and three Quarters
To make Venetians [1] down below the garters.
He that precisely knew what was enuffe,
Soone slipt away three quarters of the stuffe.
His man espying it, said in derision,
Remember, Master, how you saw the vision.
     Peace (knave) quoth he, I did not see one ragge
     Of such a coloured silke in all the flagge.

[8.] A Notorious Rogue being brought to the Bar, and knowing his case to be desperate, instead of pleading, he took to himself the liberty of jesting, and thus said, *I charge you in the Kings name to seise and take away that man* (meaning the Judge) *in the red Gown, for I go in danger of my life because of him.*

On a gentleman that married an heire privately at the Tower.

[5.]   The angry Father hearing that his childe
        Was stoln, married, and his hopes beguild;

---

[1] Trunk hose.

D

('Cause his usurious nature had a thought
She might have bin to greater fortunes brought :)
With rigid looks, bent brows, and words austere,
Ask'd his forc'd son in law how he did dare
Thus beare his onely daughter to be married ;
And by what Cannons he assumed such power ?
He sayd, the best in England, sir, the Tower.

Of Galla's *goodly Periwigge.*

[16.] You see the goodly hayre that *Galla* weares,
'Tis certain her own hayr, who would have thought it ?
She sweares it is her owne ; and true she sweares,
For hard by Temple-barre last day she bought it.
So faire a haire, upon so foule a forehead,
Augments disgrace, and showes the grace·is borrow'd.

[17.] Several Gentlemen were at dinner together, and one
of them was a Parson ; among the Dishes one was a Pig, but
'twas very lean ; Then they concluded that it was only fit
for the Parson, being a spiritual Pig, for it had no flesh upon it.

An Invitation to Lubberland.

with

An Account of the great Plenty
of that Fruitful Country.

There's all sorts of Fowl and Fish,
with Wine and store of Brandy,

Ye have there what your Hearts can
wish,
the Hills are Sugar Candy.

The Tune of *Billy and Molly* Or, The Journey-man Shoe maker

This may be printed R. P.[1]

[19.]   There is a ship we understand
now riding in the river,

1 Richard Pocock, who licensed from 1685 to 1688.

'Tis newly come from *Lubberland*
  the like I think was never;
You that a lazy life do love,
  I'd have you now go over,
They say land is not above
  two thousand leagues from Dover.

The Captain and the Master too,
  do's give us this relation,
And so do's all the whole ships crew,
  concerning this strange nation.
The streets are pav'd with pudding-pies
  nay powder'd [1] beef and bacon,
They say they scorn to tell you lies,
  who thinks it is mistaken.

The king of knaves and queen of sluts
  reign there in peace and quiet;
You need not fear to starve your guts,
  there is such store of diet:

    [1] Salt beef.

There may you live free from all care,
  like hogs set up a fatning,
The garments which the people wear
  is silver, silk and sattin.

The lofty buildings of this place
  for many years have lasted,
With nutmegs, pepper, cloves and mace,
  the walls are roughly casted,
In curious hasty-pudding boil'd,
  and most ingenious Carving.
Likewise they are with pancakes ty'd,
  sure, here's no fear of starving.

The Captain says, in every Town
  hot roasted pigs will meet ye,
They in the streets run up and down,
  still crying out, *come eat me :*
Likewise he says, at every feast
  the very fowls and fishes,
Nay, from the biggest to the least,
  comes tumbling to the dishes.

The rivers run with claret fine,
  the brooks with rich Canary,
The ponds with other sorts of wine,
  to make your hearts full merry :
Nay, more than this, you may behold
  the fountains flow with Brandy,
The rocks are like refined gold,
  the hills are sugar candy.

Rosewater is the rain they have,
  which comes in pleasant showers,
All places are adorned brave
  with sweet and fragrant flowers :
Hot Custards grows on e'ery tree
  each ditch affords rich jellies
Now, if you will be rul'd by me,
  go there, and fill your bellies.

There's nothing there but holy-days,
    with musick out of measure ;
Who can forbear to speak the praise
    of such a land of pleasure ?
There you may lead a lazy life,
    free from all kinds of labour,
·And he that is without a wife,
    may borrow of his neighbour.

There is no law, nor lawyers fees,
    all men are free from fury,
For e'ery one do's what he please,
    without a judge or jury :
The summer-time is warm they say,
    the winter's ne'er the Colder,
They have no landlords rent to pay,
    each man is a free-holder.

You that are free to cross the seas,
    make no more disputation,
At *Lubber land*, you'll live at ease,
    with pleasant recreation :
The captain waits but for a gale,
    of prosperous wind and weather,
And that they soon will hoist up sail,
    make hast away together.

Printed for *J. Deacon*,[1] at the Angel in *Gilt Spur Street.*

[4.] An ignorant Country Fellow coming along *Paternoster Row*, had occasion to change a Half-Crown into small money, and looking over a Grate which stood on the Stall, there sate a large Monkey, whom he prayed to change his Money ; the Monkey took it and put it into the Till of the Compter, where he had observed to be put, and then came and Grinn'd at the Man, who, being in a passion, made a noise at the Door, whereat the man of the Shop, coming into the Shop, asked him what was the matter ? *Sir*, said he, *I gave your Son half*

    [1] Jonah Deacon published from 1684 to 1695.

a Crown to change,' and he will not give it me again, but laughs at me, and will not give me one word of answer, tho I have asked him for it many a time.

[13.]   The old name of Robbing,
       Is now call'd Padding,
   For when the Padders have done,
      Their Lodgings are ta'ne
    At the Rope in Tyburn Lane
  In the Parish of *Paddington.*

Epitaph

On an usurer.

[14.]   Here lies at least ten in the hundred,
  Shackled up both hands and feet,
  That at such as lent mony *gratis* wondred,
  The gain of usury was so sweet ;
  But thus being now of life bereav'n
  'Tis a hundred to one he's scarce gone to heav'n.

[8.] In Chancery, one time, when the Councel of the parties set forth the boundary of the Land in question, by the plot, and the Councel of one part said, we lie on this side my Lord, and the Councel of the other part said, we lie on this side.   The Lord Chancellor *Hatton* stood up and said, *If you lie on both sides, whom will you have me to believe?*

In praise of the Black Jack.[1]

[13.]   Be your liquor small, or as thick as mudd.
  The Cheating bottle cryes, good, good, good,
  Whereat the master begins to storme,
  'Cause he said more than he could performe.
    And I wish that his heires may never want Sack,
    That first devis'd the bonny black Jack.

---

[1] A bottle made of leather. Sometimes they were ornamented with silver rims, and a silver plate with the owner's coat of arms thereon ; but generally they were very rough.

No Tankerd, Flaggon, Bottle nor Jugg
Are half so good, or so well can hold Tugg,
For when they are broke or full of cracks,
Then they must fly to the brave black Jacks,
    And I wish &c.

When the Bottle and Jack stands together, O fie on't,
The Bottle looks just like a dwarfe to a Gyant ;
Then had we not reason Jacks to chuse
For this'l make Boots, when the Bottle mends shoes.
    And I wish &c.

And as for the bottle you never can fill it
Without a Tunnell, but you must spill it,
'Tis as hard to get in, as it is to get out,
'Tis not so with a Jack, for it runs like a spout.
    And I wish &c.

And when we have drank out all our store,
The Jack goes for Barme to brew us some more ;
And when our Stomacks with hunger have bled,
Then it marches for more to make us some bread.
    And I wish &c.

I now will cease to speak of the Jack,
But hope his assistance I never shall lack,
And I hope that now every honest man,
Instead of Jack will y'clip him John.
    And I wish &c.

[18.] A melting Sermon being preached in a Country
Church, all fell a weeping, except a Country man, who being
ask'd why he did not weep with the rest? *Because* (says he)
I am not of this Parish.

[18.] A Country-man admiring the stately Fabrick of S.
Pauls Cathedral, asked *Whether it was made in* England, *or
brought from beyond Sea.*

The invincible
PRIDE of WOMEN
or
The *London* Tradesman's Lamentation

For the Prodigality of his Wife, which doth daily
pillage his Purse.

To the Tune of the *Spinning Wheel.*   Licensed according to orders.

[20.]   I have a Wife, the mores my Care,
    who like a gaudy Peacock goes,
In Top Knots, Patches, Powder'd Hair,
    besides she is the worst of shrows;
This fills my Heart with grief and care
To think I must this burthen bear.

It is her forecast to Contrive
    to rise about the hour of Noon,
And, if she's Trimm'd and Rigg'd by Five
    why this I count is very soon:
Then goes she to a Ball or Play
To pass the pleasant night away.

And when she home returns again
    conducted by a Bully Spark,
If that I in the least complain,
    she does my words and actions mark:
And does likewise my Gullet tear,
Then roars like Thunder in the Air.

I never had a Groat with her
    most solemnly I here declare,
Yet she's as proud as *Lucifer*,
    and cannot study what to wear:
In sumptuous Robes she still appears
While I am forc'd to hide my Ears.

The lofty Top Knots on her Crown,
   with which she sails abroad withal,
Makes me with Care alas ! look down,
   as having now no hope at all :

That ever I shall happy be
In such a flaunting Wife as she.

In debt with ev'ry Shop she runs
   for to appear in gaudy Pride,
And when the Millener she duns,
   I then am forc'd my Head to hide :
Dear Friends, this proud imperious Wife
She makes me weary of my Life.

Sometimes with words both kind and mild
  I let her know my wretched state,
For which I streightways am Revil'd :
  says she, I will appear more Great
Than any Merchants *London* Dame,
Tho' thou art ruin'd for the same.

'Tis true she is both fair and young,
  and speaks *Italian*, *Greek, and Dutch*,
Besides she hath the scolding Tongue,
  which is, in faith, a Tongue too much :
I dare not speak nor look awry,
For fear of her severity.

My worldly glory, joy and bliss
  is turn'd to sorrow, grief and care,
He that has such a Wife as this,
  needs no more torment I declare :
To buy those Trinkets which they lack,
Both Stock and Credit goes to Rack.

There's many more, as well as I,
  in famous *London* City fair,
Whose Wives with prodigality
  doth fill their Husbands hearts with care ;
I pity those with all my Heart,
Since I with them do bear a Part.

[4.] Two Persons who had been formerly acquainted, but
had not seen each other a great while, meeting on the Road,
one ask'd the other how he did ; he told him He was very
well, and was Married since he saw him : the other reply'd,
That was well indeed : not so well neither, said he, for I have
Married a Shrew. That's ill, said the other. Not so ill
neither, said he, for I had 2000 Pounds with her. That's well
again, said his Friend. Not so well neither, for I laid it out
in Sheep, and they died of the Rot. That was ill indeed,
said the other. Not so ill neither, said he, for I sold the
Skins for more money than the Sheep cost. That was well,

indeed, quoth his friend.   Not so well neither, said he, for I
laid out my money in a House and it was burned.   That's
very ill, said the other.   Not so ill neither, said he, *for my
Wife was burned in it.*

On a little Gentleman and one Mr Story.

[5.]   The little man, by t'other man's vain glory,
It seems was roughly us'd (so says the story)
But being a little heated and high blown,'
In anger flyes at *Story*, puls him down ;
And when they rise (I know not how it fated)
One got the worst, the *Story* was translated
From white to red, but ere the fight was ended
It seems a Gentleman, that one befriended,
Came in and parted them ; the little blade,
There's none that could intreat, or yet perswade,
But he would fight still, till another came,
And with sound reasons councel'd gainst the same.
'Twas in this manner ; friend, ye shall not fight
With one that's so unequall to your height,
Story is higher ; t'other made reply,
I'd pluck him down were he three *Stories* high.

[18.]   A Tradesman that would never work by Candle
light, was asked the reason why?   *To save Candles*, says he ;
a Peny saved is a Peny got.

Epitaph on a Scrivener.

[13.]   Here to a period is a Scriv'ner come ;
This is his last sheet, full point and total sum.
Of all aspersions, I excuse him not,
'Tis plain, he liv'd not without many a blot ;
Yet he no ill example shew'd to any,
But rather gave good coppies unto many,
He in good Letters alwayes had been bred,
And hath writ more, than many men have read.

He Rulers had at his command by law,
Although he could not hang, yet he could draw.
He did more Bond men make than any,
A dash of's pen alone did ruine many.
That not without all reason we may call
His letters, great or little, Capitall ;
Yet 'tis the Scrivner's fate as sure as Just,
When he hath all done, then he falls to dust.

[8.] One was saying that his great Grandfather, and
Grandfather, and Father died at Sea. Said another that
heard him, and I were you, I would never come at Sea.
Why, saith he, where did your great Grandfather, Grandfather
and Father die? He answered, where, but in their beds?
saith the other, *And I were as you, I would never come to bed.*

These following are to be understood two ways.

[13.]   I saw a Peacock, with a fiery tail.
I saw a blazing Comet, drop down hail.
I saw a Cloud, with ivy Circled round.
I saw a sturdy Oak, creep on the ground.
I saw a Pismire,[1] swallow up a Whale.
I saw a raging Sea, brim full of Ale.
I saw a Venice Glass, sixteen foot deep.
I saw a Well, full of mens tears that weep.
I saw their Eyes, all in a flame of fire.
I saw a House, as big as the Moon and higher.
I saw the Sun, even in the midst of night
I saw the Man that saw this wondrous sight.

[12.]   One writ *Olivarius*
Instead of *Oliverus*,
In *Oliver's* time ; 'twas his will,
And his reason was good,
If well understood,
'Cause he varies from *verus* still.

[1] An ant.

[12.] A man he did say
    To his friend t'other day,
'That his sow had lost her life;
    Sayes one Mr *Howes*,
    Now you talk of Sowes,
Pray, Neighbour, how does your wife?

[18.] *John Scot* so famous for his Learning, sitting at 'Table with a young Gallant, was by way of Jest, asked by him what Difference there was between *Scot* and *Sot.* To which he presently reply'd *Mensa tantum*, that is the Tables breadth; for the other sat just over against him.

The Devil's Oak:

or, his

Ramble in a Tempestuous Night, where he hapn'd to Discourse with Men of several Callings, of his own Colour and Complexion.

To a very pleasant new Tune.

[21.] And the Devil he was weather-beat,
    and forc'd to take a tree,
Because the tempest was so great,
    his way he could not see:
But under an Oak, instead of a Cloak,
    he stood to keep himself dry,
And as he stood, a Fryer in his hood,
    by chance came passing by.

And the Devil he made the Fryer afraid,
    with that he crost his breast;
Then up the Devil started, the Fryer was faint-hearted,
    you may wink and choose the best:

For I am the Fryer, and thou art the Lyar,
  therefore thou art my father ;
I am a Doctor of Evil, and thou art the Devil,
  the worser I hold thee rather.

A Collier and his Cart came by,
  which coals he did use to carry.
And as soon as the Devil he did him espy,
  he caused him awhile to tarry :
For why, I do think that with thee I must drink,
  and he called for a glass of claret ;
Now I find by thy smell, that thou camest from hell,
  and I fear thou hast stole my chariot.

The next that came by was a Chimney Sweeper,
  with poles, his brooms, and shackles,
What meanest thou, Man, the Devil he said,
  that thou usest all those tackles ?
I pry thee gentle Blade, tell me thy trade,
  thy face it is so besmeared,
Hadst thou been so black, and no tools at thy back,
  thou'dst have made me sore afraid.

Sir, a Chimney Sweeper I do profess,
  although my trade's but mean,
It is for to sweep all dirty holes,
  and to keep foul chimneys clean :

Then go to Hell, where the Devil doth dwell,
   and he will give thee a piece,
God a mercy, old Dog, when I sheer my hog
   then thou shalt have the fleece.

The next that came by was a tawny Moor,
   and the Devil bid him see,
And he fleered on his tawny skin,
   crying, Friend, art thou any kin to me ?
For sure your skin doth resemble our kin,
   therefore let us walk together,
And tell me how you do allow,
   of this tempestuous weather.

Then the next that came by was a Gun-powder man,
   which coales and brimstone sifted,
That in three quarters of a year,
   himself had hardly shifted :
Then up the Devil rose, and snuffed his nose,
   he could indure it no longer,
Cry'd, Away with this fume, 'tis not fit for the room
   it will neither quench thirst, no, nor hunger.

I pre thee, gentle Blade, tell me thy trade,
   as thou hast so strong a smell,
It is for to make gunpowder, he said,
   for to blow the Devil out of Hell :
And if I had him here, his joynts would I tear,
   he should neither scratch, no, nor bite,
I would plague the Devil, for all his evil, ·
   and make him leave walking by night.

Then a Tinker worse than all the rest,
   although he was not so black,
By chance as he came passing by,
   with his budget on his back :
He cry'd, Yonder is the Devil's tree
   let us see who dar'st go thither,
For it will sustain, from the wind and the rain,
   or any tempestuous weather.

That shall be try'd, the Devil then he cry'd,
   then up the Devil he did start,
Then the Tinker threw his staff about,
   and he made the Devil to smart :
There against a gate, he did break his pate,
   and both his horns he broke :
And ever since that time, I will make up my rhime,
   it was called *The Devil's Oak.*

Printed for C. Bates,[1] at the Sun and Bible, in Pye Corner.

[4.] A Wine Cooper in *Mark Lane* taking a Gentleman down into his Cellar to Treat him, he, finding no Seat there for him to sit on, asked him the reason of it ; *Why*, says the Wine Cooper, *I will have no Man here Drink longer than he can stand.*

[16.] *To Doctor* Sheerhood *how Sack makes one leane.*
I marveld much last day what you did meane,
To say that drinking Sack will make one leane ;
But now I see, I then mistooke you cleane,
For my good neighbour *Marcus*, who I tro,
Feares fatness much, this drinke hath plyde him so,
That now except he leane he cannot goe.
Ha, gentle Doctor, now I see your meaning,
Sack will not leave one leane, 'twill leave him leaning.

[12.]   *Tom's* Ears being lost,
     For fear of the frost
The haire very long he wears ;
    Then ask him why he will
     Not cut it ; he still
Says he dares not for his ears.

[8.] A debaucht Seaman being brought before a Justice of Peace upon the account of swearing, was by the Justice commanded to deposit his Fine in that behalf provided, which

[1] Charles Bates, at this address (there were three contemporary C. Bates), published in 1685.

was two shillings, he thereupon plucking out of his pocket a half crown, asked the Justice what was the rate he was to pay for cursing, the Justice told him six pence, quoth he then, A Pox take you all for a company of Knaves and fools, and there's half a crown for you ; I will never stand changing of mony.

The Long Nos'd Lass

is evidently traceable to Miss Tannakin Skinker, who was born in 1618 ; but it is astonishing how widely spread is the belief in "Pig faced Ladies." No doubt but there has been some foundation in fact for it, for I am credibly informed that not long since,[1] a child, whose face bore a singular likeness to a pig, was born in the City of London Lying - in Hospital in the City Road—and not only survived its birth, but is in all probability still living. In 1815 a pig-faced lady, elegantly dressed, used to drive about London in her carriage ; but whether people were being hoaxed by one wearing a mask is not known. George Morland painted a portrait of the "Wonderful Miss Atkinson Born in Ireland, has £20,000 fortune and is fed out of a Silver Trough," and Fairburn published an engraving of her. Miss Steevens, who founded Steeven's Hospital at Dublin, is also credited with being pig-faced ; whilst pig-faced ladies used commonly to be shown at fairs. But these were fictitious, as a quarrel in a caravan at Plymouth, some years since, brought to light, when it was shown that her ladyship was a bear whose face and neck had been carefully shaved, whilst its head was adorned with a wig with ringlets and a cap with artificial flowers. The bear was securely fastened in a chair, and draped to imitate a fashionably-dressed lady.

It is, however, with the contemporary monstrosity that we have chiefly to deal, and a very rare tract in the Bodleian Library[2] gives "A certaine Relation of the Hog faced Gentlewoman called Mistris *Tannakin Skinker*, who was borne at *Wirkham* a Neuter Towne betweene the Emperour and the

---

[1] Some time between 25th June and 29th September 1881.

[1] A wonderful lithographic facsimile by Francis Compton Price, Esq., is in the British Museum, 12205. h., catalogued under the heading *Skinker*.

Hollander, scituate on the river Rhyne. Who was bewitched
in her mothers wombe in the yeare 1618, and hath lived ever
since unknowne in this kind to any, but her Parents and a
few other neighbours.   And can never recover her true
shape tell she be married &c.   *Also relating the cause, as it is
since conceived, how her mother came so bewitched.   London.*
Printed by *J. O.* and are to be sold by *F. Grove,*[1] at his shop
on *Snow-hil* neare *St Sepulchers Church."* 1640.

This veracious history gives an account of various remarkable births.   " But I come now to humane Births, beginning
with those forraigne, and ending with the domesticke ; about
the beginning of the Marsick Warre, one *Alcippe,* a woman of
especiall note, at the time of her childing, was delivered of
an Elephant ; and another (whose name is not left unto us)
of a Serpent.   In *Thessaly,* one was brought to bed of an
infant which had the shape of an Hypocentaure, and expired
the same day that it received breath," etc.

After thus paving the way for his own particular marvel,
the writer goes on : " I fall now immediatly upon the party
before propounded.   In a place in *Holland* called *Wirkham,*
being a neuter Towne ; as lying between *Holland* and those
parts belonging to the Empire, on the River *Rhine,* lived one
Ioachim Skinker, whose wife's name was *Parnel,* a man of
good revenue, but of a great estate in money and cattle ; these
two having very loving lived together without any issue to
succeed them in their goods and inheritance : it being no
small griefe unto them, that either strangers, or some of their
owne ungrateful kindred should after death enjoy those
meanes, for which they had so laboriously travail'd : When
they were in their greatest despaire, it hapned thus, she found
herselfe conceived with childe, which was a greater joy and
comfort to her and her husband : But whether they were
unthankful for such an unexpected blessing, or what other
thing was the cause, I am not able to determine ; but it so
hapned, that in the yeere 1618, she was safely delivered of a
Daughter, all the limbes and lineaments of her body well
featured and proportioned, only her face, which is the orna-
ment and beauty of all the rest, had the Nose of a Hog, or

---

[1] Francis Grove published between 1620 and 1655.

Swine : which was not only a stain and blemish, but a deformed uglinesse, making all the rest lothsome, contemptible and odious to all that lookt upon her in her infancie.

"If the joy of the parents was great in the hope of a Childe, how much greater may wee conjecture their sorrowes were, to be the parents of such a monster : but considering with themselves what Heavens would have, they had not power to hinder, and studying (as farre as in them lay) to conceale their shame, they so farre mediated with the Midwife and the other women that were present at the delivery, that they should keepe it as close and secret as it was possible to doe : and they called the name of it *Tannikin*, which is as much in English as *Anne* or *Hannah.* . . . .

"This prodigious birth though it was knowne to some few, yet it was not made popular & spoken of by all, which the Father and Mother for their owne reputations and credits were very carefull to maintaine; so that it was never seene by any (being an infant bare-fac'd) but vail'd and covered, and so brought up in a private Chamber, both fed and taught by the Parents onely; and her deformity scarce knowne to any of the Servants : and as the daughter grew in stature, so the Father also increased with wealth, so that he was accounted to be one of the richest men in all that Country. . . . .

"It is credibly reported, that this Burgess wife having conceived, an old woman suspected for a Witch came to begge of her an Almes, but she being at that (time) busied about some necessary affaires gave her a short and neglectfull answer; at which she went away muttering to herselfe the Divell's *Pater noster*, and was heard to say ; *As the Mother is Hoggish, so Swinish shall be the Child shee goeth withall* : which is a great probability that the infants deformity came by the malitious Spells and divelish murmurations of this wicked woman; who, after, for the like, or worse practises both upon men women and children whom she had bewitched unto death, being brought within compasse of the Law; and after to suffer at the stake; amongst many other things confessed as much as I have before related; yet either out of her perverse obstinacy would not, or else (the Devill forsaking her in extreamity, as he doth all his other servants) in her deficiency

of power, could not uncharme her : yet by this means that
which was before kept so private, was now publickly discovered to the World ; insomuch that much confluence of
people came to see the progedy, which wearied the Father,
and cast a blush upon the cheekes of the good woman the
mother : some desirous to heare her speake, whose language
was onely the Dutch Hoggish Houghs, and the Piggs French
Owee, Owee, for other words she was not able to utter ; which
bred in some, pitty, in others laughter, according to their
severall dispositions.

"Others were importunate to see her feede, then milke and
the like was brought unto her in a Silver Trough ; to which
she stooped and eate just as a Swine doth in his swilling Tub ;
which the more mirth it bred in the Spectators, increased in
the Parents the more Melancholy."

From this part the tract gets more and more romantic.
An astrologer was consulted, and he advised her being married,
when her cure *might* be effected.   So the parents gave out
that she would have a dowry of £40,000 paid down on her
marriage.   Then follows a list of her suitors, and after an
episode which has nothing to do with the matter in hand, the
tract winds up : "I should have spoken something of her
residing in or about *London*, as of her being in *Black Friers*,
or *Covent Garden*, but I can say little : onely abundance of
people doe resort to each place to enquire the truth : some
have protested they have seene her, by the helpe of their
acquaintance and give this reason why she will not as yet be
Constantly in one place, because the multitude is so great that
doe resort thither that they dare not be knowne of her abiding,
lest by denying the sight of her, they that own the house should
have it pulled down about their eares.   Her portion is very
large, it being 40,000 pounds ; she likewise goeth very gallant
in aparrell, and very courteous in her kind to all.   And whoever shall in Pamphlet, or Ballad, write or sing otherwise than
is discoursed of in this small Tract, they erre from truth : for
what is here discovered, is according to the best and most
approved Intelligence."

The Long-Nos'd LASS

or

The *Taylors, Millers, Tinkers, Tanners,* and
Glovers; with a great number of other
Tradesmen, dash't out of Countenance by a Sow-
SHIP'S Beauty, to their great discontent, and
her perpetual trouble.

Tune of *The Country Farmer.*   This may be printed R. P.

[22.] O did you not hear of a Rumor of late,
Concerning a person whose Fortune was great ;
Her portion was Seventeen thousand good pound,
But yet a good Husband was not to be found :
The reason of this I will tell to you now,
Her visage was perfectly just like a Sow,
And many to Court her came flocking each day,
But seeing her, straight they run frighted away.

Amongst all the rest, a fine *Taylor* also,
Resolv'd to this person a Suitor to go ;
Quoth he, at the present, alas I am poor,
Of Silver and Gold I shall then have good store :
Tis *Cowcomber*[1] time, and I now have no Trade,
But if I do get her, I then shall be made,
Therefore I will put on the best of my Cloaths,
My Hat, with my Band, and my *Holyday* Hose.

The hopes of this Fortune his fancy did feed,
And therefore to her he did hasten with speed,
When coming, he straight for this person did ask,
She came her own self in a fine Visor, Mask ;
And said, I am she, Sir, pray what would you have ?
I'm come, quoth the *Taylor*, your Love for to crave ;
She open'd the door, and bid him welcome in,
And then to his Courting he straight did begin.

The *Taylor* went on with a noble good grace,
Like one of much Courage his Love to Embrace ;
Thought he, with a Fortune I now shall be blest,
But, listen, I pray, to the Cream of the Jest :
She pull'd off her Vizor, and turn'd her about,
And straightway the *Taylor* beheld her long Snout ;
Ah ! how he was frighted and run out of door,
And vow'd he would never come near her no more.

The next was a Miller who to her did Ride,
Resolved he was for to make her his Bride ;
Quoth he, as I now am a right honest Man,
I'le Wed her and Love her as well as I can ;
For Beauty, O let it be now as it will,
As long as she brings me good Grist to the Mill ;
Both Silver and Gold I shall have at Command,
With which I will Purchase me Houses and Land.

I now in conceit am as great as a Lord,
What pleasures soever the World can afford,

---

[1] *i.e.* People had their summer clothes, and business was slack until the autumn.

I'le have it, and likewise in Silver will shine,
Then *Gillian* will wonder to see me so fine :
To *Robin* my Servant, i'le give my great Bowl,
With which I was formerly us'd to take Toll,
And likewise the Mill, if I marry this Maid,
For never no more will I follow the Trade.

As he was a riding to her on his Mare,
He thus was a building Castles in the air ;
But when he beheld her most amiable Face,
Alas ! he was soon in a sorrowful Case ;
His hopes were confounded, away he did run,
Saying, should I have her, a thousand to one.
But I shall be frighted, when her I behold,
Therefore I'le not have her for Silver or Gold.

Both *Tinkers* and *Tanners* and *Glovers* also
Came to her, the Money encouraged them so ;
Nay, thousands came to her then every day,
Each striving to carry this Beauty away :
But when they beheld this most ordinary stuff.
The sight of her Visage did give them enuff ;
Yet if she be Marry'd while here she does live,
A perfect account of the Wedding I'le give.

Printed for *P. Brooksby*[1] at the *Golden Ball* in *Pye Corner*.

[17.] Says one, why is thy Beard so brown, and thy head so white ? *Cause*, says he, *my head is twenty years older than my beard.*

[4.] A Tinker coming through *Cornhill*, and sounding briskly on his kettle, *Have you any Work for a Tinker?* A Grocer that thought to put a Jest upon him (there being a Pillory near his door) bid him stop those two Holes, pointing to the Pillory : to whom the Tinker smartly replyed, *Sir, if you will lend me your Head and Ears, I will find a Hammer and Nails, and give you my Work into the bargain.*

<hr>

[1] He published from 1672 to 1695.

A Dialogue concerning Hair, between a Man and a Woman.

M.

[13.] Ask me no more why I do wear
My Hair so far below my ear :[1]
For the first Man that e're was made
Did never know the Barbers Trade.

W.

Ask me no more where all the day
The foolish Owl doth make her stay :
Tis in your Locks ; for tak't from me,
She thinks your hair an Ivy tree.

M.

Tell me no more that length of hair
Can make my visage look less fair ;
For how so'er my hair doth fit,
I'm sure that yours comes short of it.[2]

W.

Tell me no more men wear long hair
To chase away the Colder air ;
For by experience we may see
Long hair will but a back friend be.

M.

Tell me no more that long hair can
Argue deboistness[3] in a man ;
For 'tis Religious being inclin'd
To save the Temples from the wind.

---

[1] Prynne was especially exercised in his mind about this fashion, and wrote a book called "The Unlovelinesse of Love Lockes, or a Summarie discourse, proving the wearing and nourishing of a locke or love locke to be altogether unseemly and unlawfull unto Christians" (1628), and also "A Gagge for Long Hair'd Rattle Heads &c." (1646).

[2] An allusion to the curly crops and fringe over the forehead then worn by ladies.   [3] Debauchedness.

W.

Ask me no more why Roarers wear
Their hair extant below their ear ;
For having morgag'd all their Land,
They'd fain oblige the appearing Band.

M.

Ask me no more why hair may be
The expression of Gentility :
'Tis that which being largely grown
Derives its Gentry from the Crown.

W.

Ask me no more why grass being grown,
With greedy Sickle is cut down,
Till short and sweet ; So ends my Song,
Lest that long hair should grow too long.

[12.]   Some did ask *Tom Gold*
             What's Latin for Cold ;
Why truly, says he, my Friends,
      I know it full well,
      And I feel I can tell,
For I hav't at my fingers ends.

[18.] A Papist asked a Protestant, as 'tis their usual Way, where his Religion was before *Luther*. *In the Bible*, says he, *where yours never was.*

[8.] A witty Rogue coming into a lace shop, said he had occasion for some lace, choice wherof being shewed him, he at last pitched upon one pattern, and asked them how much they would have for so much as would reach from ear to ear, for so much he had occasion for, and they told him for so much ; so some few words passing between them, he at last agreed, and told down his money for it, and began to measure .

on his own head, thus saying, *One ear is here, and the other is nailed to the Pillory in* Bristoll, *and I fear you have not so much of this Lace by you* at present as will perfect my bargain; therefore this piece of Lace shall suffice at present in part of payment, & provide the rest with all expedition.

MARK NOBLE'S FROLLICK;

who being

Stopp'd by the Constable near to the Tower, was examin'd where he had been; whither he was going; and his Name and Place where he dwelt: to which he answered, Where the Constable would have been glad to have been, and where he was going he dared not go for his Ears, as likewise his Name, which he called *Twenty Shillings;* with an Account of what followed and how he came off.

To the Tune of *The New Rant.*   Licensed according to order.

[23.]   One night at a very late hour
           a Watchmaker home did repair;
         When coming along by the Tower,
           was stopp'd by the Constable there.

         Friend, come before Mr Constable,
           to see what his Worship will say,
         You'd have me do more than I'm able,
           I fear I shall fall by the way.

         Sir, tell me, and do not deceive me,
           where have you been playing your part?
         Kind Mr Constable, believe me,
           where you'd have been with al your heart.

Sweet Bacchus in Bumpers were flowing,
  which Liquor all mortal Men chears,
And now, after all, I am going,
  where you dare not come for your Ears.

Your Words they are sawcy and evil,
  this may be a Charge to your Purse ;
For why? you are something uncivil,
  to answer a Constable thus.

Oh, where do you dwell with a whennion?[1]
  cross Humours we will not allow,
Sir, out of the King's own Dominion,
  pray, what can you say to me now?

[1] "Wanion," with a vengeance, with a plague.

Pray what is your name you cross Villain ;
   be sure that you answer me true ;
Why, Sir, It is just *Twenty Shilling,*
   I think I have satisfied you.

What Trade are you, Brewer or Baker ?
   or do you a Waterman ply ?
No, Sir, I'm an honest Watch-maker,
   my Trade I will never deny.

Have you e'er a Watch you can show, Sir,?
   we'll see how it sutes with our Clocks ;
Yes, faith, and a Constable too, Sir.
   I wish you were all in the Stocks.

You Sawcy impertinent Fellow,
   because you have answered me so,
Although your mad Brains they be mellow,
   this Night to a Prison you go.

Therefore without any more dodging,
   the Lanthorns was lighted streightway ;
They guarded him to his strong Lodging,
   to lye there while Nine the next day.

Next Morning the Constable brought him.
   before a Justice to appear,
And earnestly then he besought him,
   a Sorrowfull Story to hear.

Of all the Transactions he told him,
   to which the good Justice reply'd,
From Liberty he would withold him,
   till the Naked Truth should be try'd.

The Tradesman returned this Answer,
   the Truth I will never deny ;
If I may speak without Offence, Sir,
   I scorn to be catch'd in a Lye.

I said nothing which was unfitting,
   as solemnly here I profess ;

The King, he is King of Great Britain
and I live in Britain the less.[1]

The next thing that causes the Trouble,
my Name he would have me to show,
The which is right honest *Mark Noble*,[2]
and that's Twenty Shillings you know.

Then asking me where I was going,
and I being void of all Fears,
Right readily made him this Answer,
where he dare not go for his Ears.

I rambl'd all day, yet the Centre,
at night was to lye by my Wife,
Instead of his Ears, should he venture,
i' faith it might cost him his Life.

Now when he had given this Relation,
of all that had past in the night,
It yielded most pleasant Diversion,
the Justice he laughed outright.

It seems that a Glass of Canary,
conducted the Gallant along :
I find that he's nothing but merry,
intending no manner of wrong.

Therefore I will free him from Prison
without any Charges or Fees,
It being no more than right reason,
you watch not for such men as these.

Printed for *B. Deacon* at *the Angel* in *Giltspur Street.*

[17.] A Gentleman ask'd a Shepherd, whether that River
was to be passed over or not : Yes, says he, but going to try,
flounc'd over head and ears. Why thou Rogue, says he, did
you not tell me it might be past over ? Truly, Sir, says he, I
thought so, *for my Geese go over and back again every day.*

[1] Little Britain, by Aldersgate Street.
[2] A mark was a coin worth 13s. 4d., and a noble 6s. 8d.

[12.]   One did ask why B
               Was set before C,
         And did much desire to know ;
               Why, a man must be,
               Before he can see,
         And I think I have hit on't now.

Against Swearing.

[6.]   In elder times an ancient custome was
       To sweare in weighty matters by the Masse.
       But when the Masse went downe (as old men note)
       They sware then by the Crosse of this same grote.[1]
       But when the Crosse was likewise held in scorne,
       Then by their faith, the common oth was sworne.
       Last, having sworne away all faith and troth,
       Only God damn them is the common oth.
             Thus custome kept decorum by gradation,
             That losing Masse, Crosse, Faith, they find damnation

One fighting with his wife.

[24.] *Meg* and her husband *Tom*, not long agoe,
       Were at it close, exchanging blow for blow.
       Both being eager, both of a stout heart,
       Endured many a bang ere they would part.
             Peter lookt on & would not stint the strife,
             He's curst (quoth he) that parteth man and wife.

The Welch Mans Inventory.

Han Infentory of the Couds of *William Morgan*, ap *Renald*, ap *Hugh*, ap *Richard*, ap *Thomas*, ap *Evan*, ap *Rice*, in the County of *Clamorgan*, Shentleman.

Imprimis. In the *Pantry of Poultry* (for hur own eating) One

---

[1] Queen Elizabeth's groats were the last bearing a cross on the reverse. James I. coined none.

creat Pig four Week old, one Coose, one Cock Gelding, two Black puddings, three Cow-foots.

Item. In the *Pantry of Plate*, one Grid-iron, one Fripan, one Tripan, three Wooden Ladle, three Cann.

Item. In the *Napery*, two Towel, two Table Cloath, four Napkin, one for hurself, one for hur Wife *Shone*, two for

Cusen *Shon* ap *Powell* and *Thomas* ap *Hugh*, when was come to hur House.

Item, In the *Wardrope*, one Irish Rugg, one Frize Sherkin, one Sheepskin Tublet,[1] Two Irish Stocking, two Shooe, six leather Points.

Item. In the *Tary*,[2] one Toasting Shees, three oaten Cake, three Pint of Cow Milk, one pound of Cow Butter.

Item in the *Kitchen*, one Pan with white Curd, two White pot, two Red Herring, nine Sprat.

Item. In the *Cellar*, one Firkin of Wiggan, two Gallon sower

[1] Doublet. [2] Dairy.

Sider, one Pint of Perry, one little Pottle of *Carmarden*
Sack, *alias* Metheglin.

Item, In the *Armory of Weapon,* to kill her Enemy, One
Pack Sword, two edge, two Welsh-hook, three long Club
one Cunn, one Mouse trap.

Item. In the *Carden,* One Ped Carlike, nine Onion, twelve
Leek, twelve Worm, twelve Frog.

Item. In the *Leas-way.* Two Tun Cow, one Mountain Calf.

Item. In the *Common-field,* Two Welch Nag, twelve long
leg'd Sheep, fourteen and twenty Coat.

Item. In the *Proom Close,* three Robin Run-hole, four Hare,
hur own Coods if hur can catch hur.

Item. In the *Parn* one half Heblet of Oate, seven Pea, two
Pean.

Item. In the *Study* (*py Cot hur was almost forgot hur*) One
Welch Pible, two Almanack, one *Erra Pater,*[1] one Seven
Champions[2] for St *Taffy* sake, twelve Pallat,[3] one
Pedigree.

Item. In the *Closet* Two Straw hat, one louse.

Item. In the *Ped.* Two naked Pody, one Shirt, one Flannel
smock at hur Ped's head.

Item. More Cattle about the House. Two Tog, three Cat,
twelve Mouse (*pox on hur, was eat hur tost Cheese*) 1000
White Flea with black Pack.

Item. More Lumber about the *House.* One Wife, two Shild,
one call hur Plack *Shack,* and t'other little *Morgan.*

Item. In the *Yard* under the Wall, one Wheel, two Pucket,
one Ladder, two Rope.

This Inventory taken Note in the presence of hur own Cusen
Rowland Merideth *ap* Howel *and* Lowellin Morgan *ap* William
in Anno 1849,[4] *upon the Ten and Thirtieth of Shune.*

The above named *William Morgan* dyed when hur had
threescore and twenty years, thirteen Months, one Week and
Seven days.

---

[1] An astrological almanac.
[2] Chap-book of the "Seven Champions of Christendom." [3] Ballads.
[4] Probably antedated two centuries to make it more comical.

A NOTE of some LEGACY of a creat deal of Coods, bequeathed to hur Wife and hur two Shild, and all hur Cusens, and Friends and Kindred in the Manner as followeth.

Imprimis.   Was give hur teer Wife, *Shone Morgan,* awl hur Coods in the Ped, over the Ped, and under the Ped.

Item.   Was give to hur eldest Son *Plack Shack,* 40 and 12 Card to play at Whipper Shinny 4 Try to sheat hur Cusen : besides awl her Land to the fule value of 20 and 10 shillings 3 groats per Annum.

Item.   Was give to hur second Son, Little *Morgan* ap *Morgan,* hur short ladder under the Wall in the Yard and two Rope.[1]

Item.   Was give to hur Cusen *Rowland Merideth* ap *Howell* and *Lewellin Morgan* whom was made her Executor, full power to pay awl hur Tet, when hur can get Money.

Seal'd and deliver'd in the Presence of *Evan* ap *Richard,* ap *Shinkin,* ap *Shone,* hur own Cusen the Tay and Year above written.

Licens'd and Enter'd.

London.   Printed by and for W. O.[2] and sold by the Booksellers.

Upon one Day *that ran away, and laid the Key under Door.*

[25.] Here *Night* and *Day* conspire a cheating flight,
For *Day* they say, is run away by *Night.*
The Day is past, why, Landlord! where's your rent,
Cou'd you not see the Day is almost spent.
Had you but Kept the Watch well, I suppose,
'Twas no hard thing to Know how the *Day* goes?
Day sold and pawn'd and put off what he might,
Though it were ne'er so dark, *Day* would be light :
That he away with so much Rent should get,
Though *Day* were light, 'twas no light matter yet.

---

[1] Is this legacy a gentle intimation to his son that he may hang himself?
[2] Is this William Onley, who published from 1650 to 1702?

F

You had one Day a Tenant, and wou'd fain
Your Eyes might one day see that Day again.
No, Landlord, No ; you now may truly say,
And to your cost too, you have lost a Day,
By twy-light *Day* is neither Day nor Night ;
What then ? 'twixt both, he's an *Hermaphrodite.*
Day is departed in a Mist, I fear,
For *Day* is broke, yet does not Day appear :
His pale face now does Day in Owl light shrowd,
Truth is, at present *Day's* under a Cloud.
If you wou'd meet with *Day* you must be wiser,
And up betimes, for Day's an early riser.
Broad Day is early up, but you begin
To rouze, and then broad Day is shutting in.
From Sun to Sun are the set times of Pay,
But you should have been up by break of Day :
Yet if you had ? you had got nothing by 't.
For *Day* was Cunning and broke over Night.
Day like a Candle is gone out, and where,
None knows, except to th' other Hemisphear.
You must go look the *Day* with Candle light,
This *Day* was sure begotten in the Night.
The Lanthorn-looker,[1] if he now began,
Might find the *Day*, but scarce the honest Man.
Well, *Day* farewel ; be't spoke to thy small praise
There's little honesty found now a Day's.
In vain you do yourself this trouble give,
You'l never make an even day while you live ;
And yet, who trusted him for any Summe,
Might have their mony, if the *Day* were come.
And when will that be ; when the Devil's blind ;
You will this *Day* at the *Greek* Calends find.
For, if the Sun doth hang *behind* the Change,
If you can find the *Day before* 'tis strange.
 Then to the Tavern, Landlord, let's away,
Chear up your heart, hang't, 'tis a broken Day.
And for your Rent, never thus Rent your Soul,
E're long you'l see *Day* at a little hole :

[1] Diogenes.

Look at the *Counter*[1] when you go that way,
Early enough, and you'l see peep of *Day*.
But how now Landlord? what's the matter pray?
What, can't you sleep, you do so long for *Day?*
Have you a mind, Sir, to arrest the *Day?*
There's no such Sergeant as a *Joshua*.
Why, Landlord, is the Quarter out I pray;
That you Keep such a quarter for the Day?
Put off your passion, pray; true, 'tis a Summe:
But don't you know that a Pay-day will come?
I'le warrant you, do you but banish sorrow,
My life for yours, *Day* comes again to morrow.

[26.] A Person of Quality in this Kingdom, was one night at Supper at *Pickadilly house* which was then an Ordinary and great Gaming House, where he had bowled all day; and after Supper he call'd for some Cheese, which it seems was very thin and lean; then he ask't the Master of the House, where those Cows went, of whose Milk that Cheese was made? He told him they graz'd not far off; then he swore a great Oath that he was Confident that they never fed in any other place than his Bowling Alley, which was made good by the fatness of the Cheese they now tasted of, for it cries *Rub, rub*, in the eating of it, when 'tis so long a going down.

Another person of Quality also, in this Kingdom, amongst other Gentlemen, did often meet at a Bowling Ally, which stood next to the Church-yard; and the Parson of that Church had this Benefit, That if any did swear there, he was to have 12d for every Oath: This Person aforesaid, happened to swear a great *Goliah* Oath, upon which the Parson demanded 12d. which he gave him; and after that swore many others, for which he paid 12d a piece; and then swearing another, he demanded 12d as before; then he pluckt out of his pocket a 20 Shilling piece and bid him give him 19s. again. *Sir*, says he, *I cannot. Why then*, says he, *take it for I intend to swear it out.*

---

[1] One of the city prisons.

THE GREAT BOOBEE.[1]

To a pleasant New Tune or *Sallenger's Round.*

[28.]   My Friend, if you will understand
      my Fortunes what they are,
  I once had Cattell, House and Land,
      but now I am never the near;
  My Father left a good estate,
      as I may tell to thee,
  I couzned was of all I had,
      like a great Boobee.

  I went to School with a good intent,
      and for to learn my Book,
  And all the day I went to play,
      in it I never did look :
  Full seven years, or very nigh,
      as I may tell to thee,

            [1] For tune see Appendix.

I could hardly say my *Christ Cross Row,*[1]
    like a great Boobee.

My Father then in all the haste,
    did set me to the Plow,
And for to lash the Horse about,
    indeed I knew not how :
My Father took his Whip in his hand,
    and soundly lashed me,
He call'd me Fool and Country Clown,
    and great Boobee.

But I did from my Father run,
    for I will plow no more,
Because he so had slashed me,
    and made my sides so sore :
But I will go to *London* Town
    some Vashions for to see,
When I came there, they call'd me Clown
    and great Boobee.

But as I went along the street,
    I carried my Hat in my hand,
And to every one that I did meet,
    I bravely bust[2] my hand :
Some did laugh, and some did scoff,
    and some did mock at me,
And some did say I was a *Woodcock,*
    and a great Boobee.

Then did I walk in hast to *Paul's*
    the Steeple for to view,
Because I heard some people say,
    it must be builded new ;

[1] The alphabet, so called because in the old Horn books the letters, which were of course in a row, commenced with a Cross. In Morley's *Introduction to Practical Music* (printed 1597) is the following : " Christes Crosse be my speed, in all vertue to proceede A. b. c. d. e. f. g. h. i. k. l. m. n. o. p. q. r. s. and t. double u. v. with y, ezod & per se, con per se, tittle, tittle est. Amen. When you have done begin again, begin again ! "
[2] Kissed (bussed).

Then I got up unto the top,
  the City for to see,
It was so high, it made me Cry
  like a great Boobee.

From thence I went to Westminster
  and for to see the Tombs,
Ah, said I, what a house is here,
  with an infinite sight of Rooms?
Sweetly the Abby bells did ring,
  it was a fine sight to see,
Methought I was going to Heaven in a string
  like a great Boobee.

But as I went along the Street
  the most part of the day,
Many gallants did I meet
  methought they were very gay:
I blew my Nose and foul'd my Hose,
  some people did me see,
They said I was a Beastly Fool,
  and a great Boobee.

Next day I through *Pye Corner* past
  the roast meat on the Stall
Invited me to take a taste
  my Money was but small:
The Meat I pickt, the Cook me kickt
  as I may tell to thee,
He beat me sore, and made me rore,
  like a great Boobee.

As I through Smithfield lately walkt
  a gallant Lass I met
Familiarly with me she talkt,
  which I cannot forget:
She proferr'd me a pint of Wine,
  methought she was wondrous free,
To the Tavern then I went with her,
  like a great Boobee.

She told me we were neer of kin,
    and call'd for Wine good store,
Before the reckoning was brought in
    my Cousin proved a —— :
My Purse she pickt, and went away,
    my Cousin couzned me,
The Vintner kickt me out of door,
    like a great Boobee.

At the *Exchange* when I came there,
    I saw most gallant things,
I thought the Pictures living were
    of all our English Kings :
I doft my Hat, and made a Leg,
    and kneeled on my knee,
The people laught, and call'd me Fool,
    and great Boobee.

To *Paris Garden*[1] then I went,
    where there is great resort,
My pleasure was my punishment,
    I did not like the sport :
The Garden Bull with his stout horns
    on high then tossed me,
I did bewray myself with fear,
    like a great Boobee.

Then o're the Water did I pass,
    as you shall understand,
I dropt into the Thames alas
    before I came to Land :
The Water-man did help me out,
    and thus did say to me,
Tis not thy fortune to be drown'd
    like a great Boobee.

But I have learned so much wit,
    shall shorten all my cares,
If I can but a License get
    to play before the Bears :

[1] A place at Bankside, Southwark, famous for bull and bear baiting.

'Twill be a gallant place indeed,
    as I may tell to thee
Then who dare call me Fool or Ass˙
    or great Boobee.

Printed for *F. Coles*,[1] in *Wine Street*, on *Saffron Hill* near
Hatton Garden.

[18.] A pleasant Fancy of an Italian by name *Trivelino*,
Who falling asleep one Day, with his Horse's Bridle twisted
in his Arm, another came who unbridled his Horse and got
away. *Trivelino* being awaked, and missing his Horse began
to feel himself about, saying *Either I am* Trivelino, *or not: If
I am* Trivelino *my Horse is lost; If not, I have got a Bridle,
but know not how.*

[12.]   A simple Fellow lookt
    On a dish that was cookt,
Wherein was a Calves Head by name ;
    One told him, 'twas so clear,
    If he lookt very near,
He might see his face in the same.

Ad Johannuelem Leporem, *Lepidissimum ;*
Carmen Heroicum.

[24.] I sing the furious battails of the Sphœres
    Acted in eight and twenty fathom deep,
    And from that (*a*) time, reckon so many yeares
    You'l find (*b*) *Endimion* fell fast asleep.

a. There began the *Utopian* accompt of years. *Mor: Lib* I. *circa
finem.*

b. Endimion was a handsome young Welshman, whom one *Luce
Moone* lov'd for his sweet breath ; and would never hang off his lips ; but
he not caring for her, eat abundance of toasted cheese, purposely to make
his breath unsavory ; upon which she left him presently, and ever since
'tis proverbially spoken (as inconstant as Luce Moone). The *Vatican*
coppy of *Hesiod* reades her name *Mohun*, but contractedly it is *Moone.
Hesiod. lib* 4. *tom.* 3.

---

[1] Francis Coles published between 1646 and 1674.

And now assist me O ye (*c*) Musiques nine
That tell the Orbs in order as they fight
And thou dread (*d*) *Atlas* with thine eyes so fine,
Smile on me now that first begin to write.

c. For all the Orbes make Musick in their motion. *Berosus de Sphera,*
lib 3.

d. Atlas was a Porter in *Mauritania,* and because by reason of his
strength, he bore burthens of stupendious weight, the Poets fain'd that he
carried the Heavens on his shoulders. *Cicero de nat Deorum. lib.* 7.

(*e*) *Pompey* that once was Tapster of *New June,*
And fought with *Cæsar* on th' (*f*) *Æmathian* plaines,
First with his dreadful (*g*) *Myrmidons* came in,
And let them blood in the Hepatick veines.

e. There were two others of this name, Aldermen of *Rome.* *Tit.*
Liv. hist. lib. 28.

f. Æmathia is a very faire Common in *Northampton shire.* *Strabo.*
lib 321.

g. These *Myrmidons* were *Cornish-men* and sent by *Bladud,* sometime
king of this Realme, to ayd *Pompey.* *Cæsar de bello. civili. lib.* 14.

But then an *Antelope* in Sable blew,
Clad like the (*h*) Prince of *Aurange* in his cloke,
Studded with Satyres, on his Army drew,
And presently (*i*) *Pheander's* Army broke.

h. It seemes not to be meant by *Count Henry* but his brother *Maurice,*
by comparing his picture to the thing here spoken of. *Jansen. de præd.*
lib 22.

i. Pheander was so modest, that he was called the Maiden Knight ;
and yet so valiant, that a French Cavaleer wrote his life, and called his
book *Pheander* the *Maiden Knight. Hon. d'Urfee. Tom* 45.

(*k*) Philip for hardiness sirnamed *Chub,*
In Beauty equall to fork bearing (*l*) *Bacchus,*
Made such a thrust at (*m*) *Phœbe* with his Club,
That made the (*n*) *Parthians* cry she will —— us.

k. This seems not to be that king that was Son of *Amintas,* and king
of *Macedon ;* but one who it seems was very lascivious.

l. Bacchus was a drunken yeoman of the Guard to Queen *Elizabeth*
and a great Archer ; so that it seems the Authour mistooke his halbert for
a forke.

m. This was *Long-Megg*[1] of *Westminster*, who after this conflict with *Phillip* followed him in all his warres. *Justinian. lib* 35.

n. These were *Lancashire-men* and sent by King *Gorbadug* (for this war seemes to have been in the time of the *Heptarchy* in *England*) to the aide of *Cæsar.* Cæsar. lib. citat. prope finem.

A subtle Gloworme lying in a hedge,
And heard the story of sweet cheek't (*o*) *Apollo*,
Snatch'd from bright (*p*) *Styropes* his Antick sledge,
And to the butter'd Flownders cry'd out (*q*) *Holla.*

o. *Apollo* was *Cæsars* Page, and a *Monomapatan* by birth, whose name by inversion was *Ollopa :* which in the old language of that Country, signifies as much as faire youth : but *Euphoniæ Gratia*, called *Apollo. Gor. Bec. lib.* 46.

p. *Styropes* was a lame Smith's-man dwelling in *St. John's Street ;* but how he was called Bright I know not, except it were by reason of the Luster of his eyes.

q. *Holla*, mistaken for *Apollo.*

Holla you pamper'd Jades, quoth he, look here,
And mounting straight upon a Lobsters thigh,
An *English* man inflam'd with (*r*) double Beere,
Swore nev'r to (*s*) drink to Man, a Woman by.

r. Cervisia (apud Medicos, vinum hordeaceum) potus est Anglis longè charismus ; Inventum Ferrarii *Londinensis*, Cui nomen *Smuggo. Polydor. Virgil. de Invent. rerum. lib.* 2.

s. Impp. Germaniæ, antiquitus solebant, statis temporibus, adire *Basingstochium ;* ubi, de more, Jusjurandum solenne præstabant, de non viro propinando, præsente muliere. Hic Mos, jamdudum apud *Anglos*, pene vim legis obtinuit ; quippe gens illa, longe humanissima morem istum, in hodiernum usque diem, magna Curiositate, pari Comitate conjuncta, usurpant. *Pancirol. utriusque imperii. lib.* 6. cap 5.

By this time grew the conflict to be (*t*) hot,
Boots against boots, 'gainst (*u*) Sandals, Sandals fly,
Many poor thirsty men went to the pot,
Feathers lopt off, spurrs every where did lie.

Cætera desiderantur.

t. It seems this was a great battail, both by the furie of it, and the aydes of each side ; but hereof read more in *Cornel. Tacit. lib. de moribus German.*

u. This is an imitation of *Lucan.* "Signis Signa & pila" &c. *Pharsalia. lib.* 1. in principio.

---

[1] A virago who lived temp. Henry VIII.

Of Treason.

[16.] Treason doth never prosper; what's the reason?
For if it prosper, none dare call it Treason.

    [12.]   A miserable *Jack*
             Gave a little glass of Sack.
    To a Lass that liv'd at the *Spittle;*
         'Tis old wine, says he,
         That's a wonder, says she,
    To be old, and yet so little.

[18.] 'Tis said of one who well remembred what he had lent, but forgot what he had borrowed, that *he had lost one half of his Memory.*

On the word intollerable.

[5.] Two gentlemen did to a Tavern come,
And call'd the drawer for to shew a room,
The drawer did, and what room think ye was't?
One of the small ones, where men drink in haste;
One gentleman sat down there, but the other
Dislik'd it, would not sit, call'd for another :
At which his friend, rising up from the table,
Cryes, friend, let's stay, this room is tollerable :
Why, that's the cause (quoth hee) I will not stay,
Is that the cause, quoth th' other? why, I pray?
To give a reason to you, I am able,
Because I hate to be in—Tollerable.

[26.] A Gentleman coming drunk to Bed over night, in the morning could not find his breeches : then he knock'd for the Chamberlain : *Sir*, says he, *if you are sure you brought them in with you, you had best search your pockets for them, for you lost all your Money last Night out of your Pockets, it may be your Breeches are got in there.*

THE CUNNING NORTHERNE BEGGER

Who all the By-standers doth earnestly pray
To bestow a penny upon him to day.

To the Tune of *Tom of Bedlam*.

[29.]   I am a lusty begger,
And live by others giving,
        I scorne to worke,
        But by the highway lurke,
        And beg to get my living :
I'le i' th' wind and weather,
And weare all ragged Garments,
        Yet though I am bare,
        I am free from care,
        A fig for high preferments.
For still will I cry good, your worship, good sir,
Bestow one poor denier, sir ;
        Which when I've got,
        At the Pipe and Pot,
        I soon will it casheere, sir.

I have my shifts about me,
Like *Proteus* often changing,
　　My shape when I will
　　I alter still,
　　About the country ranging :
As soon as I a Coatch see,
Or Gallants by come riding,
　　I take my Crotch,
　　And rouse from my Couch,
　　Whereas I lay abiding.
And still doe cry, &c.

Now as a wandring Souldier,
(That has i' th' warres bin maymed
　　With the shot of a Gunne)
　　To Gallants I runne,
　　And begg, sir, helpe the lamed :
I am a poore old Souldier
And better times once viewed,
　　Though bare now I goe,　　·
　　Yet many a foe,
　　By me hath been subdued.
And therefore I cry &c.

Although I nere was further,
Than Kentish-street in Southwarke,
　　Nor ere did see
　　A Battery
　　Made against any bulwarke ;
But with my Tricks and Doxes,
Lay in some corner lurking,
　　And nere went abroad,
　　But to beg on the road,
　　To keep my selfe from working :
And alwaies to cry &c.

Anon I'm like a saylor
And weare old Canvas cloathing,
　　And then I say
　　The Dunkerks away,
　　Took all and left me nothing :

Sixe ships set all upon us,
'Gainst which we bravely ventur'd
  And long withstood,
  Yet could doe no good,
 Our ship at length they enter'd
And therefore I cry &c.

Sometime I like a Criple
Upon the ground lye crawling,
  For money I begge,
  As wanting a legge
 To beare my corps from falling :
Then seeme I weake of body,
And long t' have beene diseased,
  And make complaint
  As ready to faint,
 And of my griefs increased.
And faintly I cry &c.

My flesh I can so temper,
That it shall seeme to feister
  And looke all ore,
  Like a raw sore,
 Whereon I stick a plaister :
With blood I daub my face then,
To faigne the falling sicknesse,
  That in every place
  They pitty my case,
 As if it came from weaknesse.
And then I doe cry &c.

Then as if my sight I wanted,
A Boy doth walke beside me,
  Or else I doe
  Grope as I goe,
 Or have a dog to guide me :
And when I'm thus accounted,
To th' highway side I hye me,
  And there I stand
  With Cords in my hand,

And beg of all comes nye me.
And earnestly cry &c.

Next to some country fellow
I presently am turned,
    And cry alacke,
    With a Child at my back,
    My house and goods were burned :
Then me my Doxes follow,
Who for my Wifes believed,
    And along wee two
    Together goe,
    With such mischances grieved.
And still we doe cry &c.

What though I cannot labour,
Shall I therefore pine with hunger,
    No, rather than I
    Will starve where I lye,
    I'le beg of the money monger :
No other care shall trouble
My minde, nor griefe disease me,
    Though sometimes the flash
    I get or the lash
    'Twill but a while displease me.
And still will I cry &c.

No tricks at all shall scape me,
But I will by my maunding
    Get some reliefe
    To ease my griefe,
    When by the highway standing :
'Tis better be a Begger
And aske of kind good fellowes,
    And honestly have
    What we do crave,
    Than steale and goe to the Gallowes.
Therefore I'le cry &c.

FINIS.

Printed at London for *F. Coules.*[1]

[1] Same as Francis Coles (see " The Great Boobee ").

[26.] One coming into *New-Market* to buy some Butter, and there cheapened some; and the woman askt. 10d a pound: then he smelt to it; *What,* says she, *do you smell to it, it seems you do not like my Butter:* Yes, says he, *but 'tis no better than it should be.* *Then you'll buy none,* says she : *No,* says he, *for a reason best known to myself.* Then she askt him the reason, and with much importunity he told her, 'twas because he had no Money : *Well then,* says the Woman, *take it for nothing, so you'll pay me for it next time you come.*

<blockquote>

[12.]   Sirrah, you are base
To spit in my face,
That he vow'd, he wou'd him kill ;
Sir, I pray forbear,
I thought no hurt here,
Nay, I'le tread it out, if you will.

</blockquote>

A contest at the Hoop-Tavern *between two Lawyers.*

<blockquote>

[25.]   Two *Lawyers* had of late a *Tavern* Jarr
And as 'twas made, 'twas try'd at *Bacchus* Bar ;
The *Jury* Pints and Quarts, and Pottles were,
Each of a quick and understanding Eare,
Brought in their verdict, which no sooner pass'd
But that the Lawyers they themselves did cast.
Sir *Burdeux* Claret, White, Signiour Canary,
Sir *Reynold Rhenish,* with a tertiorary,
Whipt up my Youths (& they ye know were able)
This into th' Chimny, that beneath the Table.
Where They lay both, instead of a demur,
So foxt, that neither, in the case, could stir,
They might have else a *Writ of Error* got,
But, O the Error of the Pottle Pot !
Both over-thrown, and on their backs now laid,
Let the Sute fall, and their own charges paid.
    And thus, though *Westminster* makes *Clients* stoop,
    The *Lawyer's* Case was alter'd at the *Hoop.*

</blockquote>

[4.] A Conceited Scholar that was lately come from *Oxford*, drinking with two or three Gentlemen, at the *Mitre Tavern* in the *Poultrey*, was very brisk and airy, and would needs be forming of Sylogismes &c. One wise one was this, He bid them fill two Glasses of Wine, which they did : now : says he, I will prove those two Glasses to be three, thus, Is not here one, says he? Yes, says the Gentleman. And here another, that's two, says he ; Yes, says the Gentleman again. Why, then, says he, one and two is three, so 'tis done. *Very well,* says the Gentleman, *I'll have one Glass, and that Gentleman shall have the other, and you shall have the third for your pains in finding it out.*

Of inclosing a Common.

[6.]   A Lord, that purpos'd for his more availe,
To compass in a Common with a rayle,
Was reckoning with his friend about the Cost,
And charge of every rayle, and every post :
But he, (that wisht his greedy humour crost)
    Said, Sir, provide you Posts, and without fayling,
    Your neighbours round about will find you rayling.

[12.]   Some said, Sir, you keep
Such a gaping in your sleep,
He told 'em then they did lye all ;
For a looking glass he'd buy,
At his bed's-feet to lye,
On purpose to make a tryal.

[4.] A Scholar of *Oxford* having wore out the Heels of his Boots, brought them in his hands to a Cobler, and shewing him them, said, *O thou curious Artificer, that hast by no small pains and study, arrived to the perfection of that exquisite art of repairing the defects of old decayed Calcuments, affix me two Semicircles to my Suppeditors.* The Cobler stared upon him, as if he would have looked him through ; but a little recovering himself, said, *Before George, Sir, I understand not your hard*

G

Language: but if I put on two Heel pieces, I'll have a Groat for them.

The same Scholar being asked by a Porter for a Gentleman's Chamber in the Colledg, he directed him thus, *you must crucifie the Quadrangle, and ascend the Grades, and you will find him perambulating in his Cubicle, near the Fenester.* Pray Sir, says the Porter, what is that *Fenester ?* *It is*, replies the Scholar, *the Diaphonous part of an Edifice, erected for the Introduction of Illumination*, which so amazed the Porter, that at first he did not know what to think, till recovering himself, he went and enquired of another, who gave him plainer directions, in more intelligible terms.

A Caution for Scolds

or

A True Way of Taming a Shrew.

To the tune of *Why are my eyes still flowing.* . This may be printed R. P.

[30.] A Noble Man he Marry'd with a cruel Scold,
    Who in her humours would ne'r be controul'd,
    So that he was almost a weary of his Life,
    By the cross humours of his froward Wife :
    Although he shewed himself exceeding kind,
    Yet she was still of a turbulent mind ;
    Husband and Servants her Fury must feel,
    For in their Ears she would ring them a Peal.

    When any Friend approach'd the presence of her Lord,
    By this vile Shrew they were strangely abhor'd ;
    With cruel Frowns and Railings she would them salute
    Tho' they were Persons of worthy Repute ;
    All was a case for she woud have her Will,
    And the whole House with Confusion she'd fill ;
    So that for fear of the heat of her Fray
    They have been forc'd to run packing away.

It was his chance to make a worthy noble feast,
Inviting full forty Couple at least,
Both Lords and Earls, with vertuous Ladies of high fame,
Who in true Friendship accordingly came :
All sorts of dainties he then did prepare,
No cost nor charge in the least he did spare ;
But ere they could to their Banqueting fall,
Sirs, you shall hear how she welcom'd them all.

When she beheld the Costly Dishes of Rich Meat,
This Shrew had not the Stomach to Eat,
But did cry out, I shall be Ruined at this rate,
This is enough to consume an Estate :
Before she any more words did reply
She made both Bottles and Dishes to flye ;
Both Friends and Husband she there did abuse,
Asking him how he dare be so profuse?

Like Thunder loud, her voice she straight began to raise,
Which made the Guests to stand all in a maze,
Who never saw the like in all their lives before,
Dishes of Meat they lay strow'd on the floor ;
Thus in disorder they all went their way,
Each one was glad they were out of the fray ;
Then said her Husband did ever Man know,
Any poor Mortal so plagu'd with a Shrow.

Now the next day he to a skilful Doctor went,
Promising that he would give him content,
If he could cure the cause of a Distracted Wife
Which almost made him a weary of his Life ;
Yes, quoth the Doctor, i'le do it ne'r fear,
Bring her, for now 'tis the Spring of the Year ;
I'le take the Lunacy out of her Brains,
Or else I wont have a Groat for my pains.

Then home he went and sent her thither out of hand,
Now when the Shrow, she did well understand
All their intent, she cal'd the Doctor sneaking knave ;
Now when he see she began for to Rave,
Straightways the Doctor did bind her in Bed,
Leting her Blood, likewise shaving her Head ;
Sirrah, said she, I would have you to know,
That you shall suffer for serving me so.

Madam, said he, I know you are beside your Wits,
But I will soon bring you out of those Fits ;
I'le cut your Tongue, and when a Gallon you have bled,
'Twill cure that violent Noise in your Head ;
Pray Sir, said she, don't afflict me so sore,
I'le ne'r offend my sweet Husband no more ;
Thus by sharp Usage and keeping her low,
He had the fortune to Conquer the Shrow.

After some time, he came to see his Wife at last,
When she begg'd pardon for all that was past ;
Saying, her Fits for evermore she would refrain,
If he'd be pleas'd to receive her again ;
My former Follies I pray now forgive,
Ile ne'r offend you no more while I live :
Then in much love they both homeward did go
Thus has he made a sweet Wife of a Shrow.

FINIS.

[18.] One being set upon by Robbers at five a Clock in the
Morning, *Gentlemen*, says he to 'em, *you open Shop very early
to day.*

[12.] Mr *Hill* he did say
  H *non est litera,*
But a note of aspiration still;
  Now I think on't better,
  If it be not a letter,
With him it will go very ill.

On Galla *going to the Bath.*

[14.] When *Galla* for her health goes to the Bath,
  She carefully doth hide, as is most meet,
  With aprons of fine linnen or a sheet,
  Those parts that modesty concealed hath ;
  Nor only those, but even the breast and neck,
  That might be seen or shown without all check ;
    But yet one foul and unbeseeming place.
    She leaves uncovered still ; what's that ? her face.

[8.] There was one that died greatly in Debt, when it was reported in some company, where divers of his Creditors were, that he was dead ; one began to say in good faith, then he hath Carried five hundred ducates of mine with him into the other world ; and another of them said, and two hundred of mine ; and some others spake of several sums of theirs : whereupon one that was amongst them said, *Well, I see now, that though a man cannot carry any of his own with him, into the other world, yet he may carry other mens.*

[5.] A Welshman and an Englishman disputed,
  Which of their Lands maintain'd the greatest state,
  The Englishman the Welshman quite confuted,
  Yet would the Welshman nought his brags abate :
    Ten Cooks, quoth he, in Wales one wedding sees ;
    Truth quoth the other, each man tosts his cheese.

  [12.] 'Fore a Justice was brought
    One for a great fault ;

Y'are an errant Dog, Rogue, says he ;
   Sir, I am no Dog,
   Nor so errant a Rogue.
As your Worship ——— takes me to be.

[17.] A Western Lady was very Hospitable to many Gentlemen, and it happened a Knight came thither ; and being a great House-wife, early in the Morning she called to her maids, and ask'd whether the Pigs were served ; which the Knight hearing, said before the Gentlewoman at dinner, Madam are the Pigs served ? Sir, says she, *I know not whether you have had your breakfast yea or no.*

[5.] My love and I for kisses play'd
   She would keep stakes, I was content,
   And when I wonne, she would be payd ;
   This made me aske her what she meant,
   Sayth she, since you are in this wrangling vaine,
   Take you your kisses, and give me mine againe.

On a farmer knighted.

[5.] In my conceit Sir *John*, you were to blame,
   To make a quiet good wife, a mad dame.

[26.] Some Gentlemen were sitting at a Coffee-house together, one was asking what News there was ? T'other told him, There was forty thousand Men rose to day, which made them all stare about, and asked him to what end they rose, and what did they intend ? Why faith, says he, only to go to bed at Night again.

Of Milo the Glutton.

[6.] *Milo* with haste to cram his greedy gut,
   One of his thumbs into the bone had cut.
   Then straight, it noysed was about by some,
   That he had lost his stomacke with his thumbe.
      To which one said. No worse hap fall unto him,
      But, if a poore man finde it, 'twill undo him.

[18.] A Person of Quality owed a Gentleman a Thousand Pounds. Meeting together in a fair Road, where both their Coaches went a good rate; the first looking out of the Coach called to the Gentleman, and begged a thousand Excuses. *And I beg*, said the Gentleman presently, *a thousand Pounds.*

A **P**leasant new Ballad you here may behold,
How the Devill, though subtle, was guld by a Scold.

To the Tune of *The Seminary Priest.*

[31.]   Give eare my loving Country-men
       that still desire newes,
   Nor passe not while you heare it sung,
       or else the song peruse :
   For ere you heare it, I must tell
       my newes, it is not common,
   But Ile unfold a trueth betwixt
       a Devill and a woman.

   Tom Thumb is not my subiect,
       whom Fairies oft did aide,
   Nor that mad spirit *Robin*
       that plagues both wife and maid

Nor is my song satyricke like,
 invented against no man,
But onely of a pranke betwixt
 a Devill and a woman.

.   .   .

A woman well in yeares
 liv'd with a husband kinde
Who had a great desire
 to live content in minde,
But twas a thing impossible
 to compasse his desire
For night and day with scolding
 she did her husband tire.

With roughish, lowtish clowne,
 despight thee Ile be wilde,
Doest thou think I marryed thee
 to use thee like a childe,
And set thee on my lap,
 or humour what you speake?
Before Ile be so fond,
 thy very heart Ile breake.

Why, loving wife, quoth he,
 Ile never doe thee wrong,
So thoul't be rul'd by me,
 and onely hold thy tongue.
And when I come from worke,
 wilt please at board and bed ;
Doe this my loving wife
 and take all being dead.

Marke well, quoth she, my words
 what ere you speak me to,
By faire meanes or by foule,
 the contrary Ile doe.

According to her speech,
    this man led such a life,
That oft he wish't the Devill
    to come and fetch his wife.

Had he bid her goe homely,
    why then she would goe brave,
Had he cal'd her good wife,
    she cal'd him rogue and slave ;
Bade he, wife goe to Church,
    and take the fairest pew,
Shee'd goe unto an Alehouse,
    and drinke, lye downe and spew.

The Devill being merry
    with laughing at this mirth,
Would needs from hell come trotting,
    to fetch her from the earth ;
And coming like a horse,
    did tell this man his minde,
Saying, Set her but astride my backe,
    Ile hurry her through the winde.

Kinde Devill quoth the man,
    if thou a while will wait,
Ile bid her doe that thing
    shall make her backe thee straight
And here Ile make a vow
    for all she is my wife,
Ile never send for her againe
    whilest I have breath or life.

Content, the Devill cry'd,
    then to his wife goes he
Good wife, goe lead that horse
    so black and fair you see.
Goe leade, sir Knave, quoth she
    and wherefore not goe ride ?
She took the Devill by the reines,
    and up she goes astride.

The Devill neighed lowd,
   and threw his heeles i' th' ayre,
Kick, in the Devill's name, quoth she,
   a shrew doth never fear.
Away to hell he went,
   with this most wicked scold,
But she did curbe him with the bit,
   and would not loose her hold.

The more he cry'd, Give way,
   the more she kept him in,
And kickt him so with both her heeles,
   that both his sides were thin.
Alight, the Devill cry'd,
   and quick the bridle loose,
No I will ride (quoth she)
   whiles thou hast breath or shooes.

Again she kickt and prickt,
   and sate so stiffe and well,
The Devill was not so plagu'd
   a hundred years in hell.
For pitty light (quoth he)
   thou put'st me to much paine,
I will not light, (quoth she)
   till I come home againe.

The Devill shewed her all
   the paines within that place,
And told her that they were
   ordain'd for Scolds so base.
Being bereft of breath,
   for scolding tis my due,
But whilest I live on earth
   Ile be reveng'd on you.

Then did she draw her knife,
   and gave his eare a slit,
The Devill never felt
   the like from mortall yet.

So fearing further danger,
   he to his heeles did take,
And faster than he came,
   he poast hast home did make.

Here take her (quoth the Devill)
   to keep her here be bold,
For hell would not be troubled
   with such an earthly scold.
When I come home, I may
   to all my fellowes tell,
I lost my labour and my bloud
   to bring a scold to hell.

The man halfe dead did stand,
   away the Devill hyde,
Then since the world, nor hell,
   can well a Scold abide :
To make a saile of ships
   let husbands fall to worke,
And give their free consents
   to send them to the Turke.

Then honest wives and maides,
   and widdowes of each sort,
Might live in peace and rest,
   and Silence keep her court,
Nor would I have a scold,
   one penny here bestow,
But honest men and wives
   buy these before you goe.

FINIS.

Printed at London for Henry Gosson[1] dwelling upon London Bridge . neare to the Gate.

[32.]   He went to the wood and caught it,
      He sate him down and sought it,

[1] Henry Gosson published between 1607 and 1641.

Because he could not find it,
Home with him he brought it.

Solution.

That is a thorn; for a man went to the wood and caught
a thorn in his foot, and then he sate him down, and sought to
have pull'd it out, and because he could not find it out he
must needs bring it home.

[26.] A rich and covetous Councellor of this Kingdom,
that had an only Child, which was a Daughter and worth
£20,000. A young and handsome Gentleman of good Birth
though of no great Fortune; yet had so far insinuated himself
into the young Lady's Favour, that she promis'd him Marriage,
if he could get her Father's Consent. Immediately he comes
for *London*, and goes to her Father, and told him, That he
would give him £10 for a Fee if he could assist him in a
business which did much concern him : which was, That there
was a rich young Heiress in town, which had promised him
marriage if it could any way be made good by Law: Why,
says he, let her hire a Horse, and invite you to take her
away, and let her get up before, and you behind that it may
not be said that you rode away with her, but she with you,
and let her go to the Minister, and tell him, 'tis her desire to
be married to you, and to get a Licence accordingly; and
when you are married, then be sure to bed her, and I'll
warrant you she's your own. And this, says the Gentleman,
you'll avouch for Law? He told him, Yes. Well Sir, says
he, if you will set your Hand to it, I'll give you Ten Pounds
more; which he did. Immediately he goes into the Country,
and shews the young Lady what was done, and how 'twas
done; and she accordingly performed her promise, and
suddenly married and bedded; and having so continued a
week they both came to *London*, and came to her Father, and
fell down upon their knees to him, and craved his Blessing;
which made him at first fly into harsh Language; but the
Gentleman said, We have done nothing but what you avouch't
for Law, and have it under your hand. The Lawyer fearing

his Reputation might be brought in question, and seeing him to be a handsome and well bred Gentleman, and of a good family, clape both their hands together, and bid God bless them; and then gave them a subsistence for the present, and made over all to them after his death.

[12.]   Three had a contest
                Which grain was the best;
                The first said Wheat had the Quorum
                The second stood for Rye
                But the third did reply
                Hordea est farra forum.[1]

On one in debt.

[14.] *Don Pedro's* out of debt; be bold to say it;
      For they are said to owe that mean to pay it.

[4.] A Gentleman that had never been used to Wounds, received a small scratch with a Sword in a Tavern Fray; at which he was sadly frighted, and sent immediately for a Chyrurgeon, who coming, and seeing the Wound but slight, and the Gentleman in a great fear: for sport's sake pretended great danger, and therefore sends his Man with great speed to fetch him such a Plaister: *Why Sir*, quoth the Gentleman, *is the wound so dangerous?* *O Yes*, replyed the Arch Chyrurgeon, *for if he don't make great haste, it will heal of it self, before he comes.*

Scylla *toothlesse.*

[24.] *Scylla* is toothlesse; yet when she was young,
      She had both tooth enough, and too much tongue:
      What should I now of toothlesse *Scylla* say?
      But that her tongue hath worne her teeth away.

The extravagances of male attire in Charles the First's time justly called down the wrath of the Satirists, particularly of the

---

[1] Far afore 'em.

Puritan School. The Cavaliers, however, were only effeminate in their dress, their gallant conduct in the Civil war proving them to be men of mettle. The subjoined is so faithful in its representation of the then height of fashion as to be almost removed from caricature, still the letterpress evidently intends it to be a satire as bitter as could be made by the Roundhead who penned it, who naturally believed in "the Unlovelinesse of Love Lockes."

The

Ꝙicture of an Engliꞩꞩ Ꝗntick,

with a List of his ridiculous Habits and apish Gestures.

Maids, where are your hearts become? look you what here is!

[33.] 1 His hat in fashion like a close-stoolepan.

2 Set on the top of his noddle like a coxcombe.

3 Banded with a calves tail, and a bunch of riband.

4 A feather in his hat, hanging down like a Fox taile.

5 Long haire, with ribands tied in it.

6. His face spotted.

7. His beard on the upper lip, compassing his mouth.

8. His chin thrust out, singing as he goes.

9. His band lapping over before.

10. Great band strings, with a ring tied.

11. A long wasted dubblet unbuttoned half way.

12. Little skirts.

13. His sleeves unbuttoned.

14. In one hand a stick, playing with it, in the other his cloke hanging.

15. His breeches unhooked ready to drop off.

16. His shirt hanging out.

17. His codpeece open tied at the top with a great bunch of riband.

18. His belt about his hips.
19. His sword swapping betweene his legs like a Monkeys taile.

20. Many dozen points at knees.
21. Above the points of either side two bunches of riband of severall colours.

22. Boot hose tops, tied about the middle of the Calfe, as long as a paire of shirt sleeves, double at the ends like a ruffe band.
23. The Tops of his boots very large turned down as low as his spurs.
24. A great paire of spurres, gingling like a Morrice dancer.
25. The feet of his boots 2 inches too long.
26. Two horns at each end of his foot, stradling as he goes.

Nov. 18, 1646.

[12.] One desir'd, being dead,
      To have Hysop round his head,
  But Time is better I think ;
    For you'l find it a crime,
    If not buryed in time,
  For certain your Corps will stink.

[32.] What work is that the faster ye work, longer is it ere ye have done, and the slower ye work the sooner ye make an end ?
Solution. That is turning of a Spit ; for if ye turn fast, it will be long ere the meat be roasted, but if ye turn slowly, the sooner it is roasted.

A new married Bride.

[5.] The first of all our sex, came from the side of man,
    I thither am return'd from whence I came.

Of finding a hare.

[6.] A Gallant full of life, and void of care.
    Asked his friend if he would find a hare ?
    He that for sleepe, more than such sports did care,
    Said, Goe your waies, and leave me heere alone ;
    Let them find hares that lost them, I lost none.

The next illustration is from a single sheet broadside entitled "Englands Wolfe with eagles clawes, or the cruell

Impieties of Bloud-Thirsty Royalists, and blasphemous *Anti-Parliamentarians*, under the command of that inhumane Prince *Rupert*, *Digby*, and the rest. Wherein the barbarous Crueltie

of our Civill uncivill Warres is briefly discovered.   London :
Printed by *Matthew Simmons* dwelling in *Aldersgate* Streete.
1646."

   This broadside scarcely comes within the scope of this
work, dealing as it does with the alleged cruelties committed
by the Cavaliers ; but the engraving clearly is a political
satire, not only on the Cavaliers themselves, but on their extravagances in dress.

   [18.] If you ask why borrowed Books seldom return to
their Owners? this is the Reason one gives for it : *Because
'tis easier to keep 'em, than what is in them.*

   [8.] There was a Painter became a Physician, whereupon
one said to him, You have done well, for before the faults of
your work were seen, but now they are unseen.

> [12.]   A Lawyer said in jest
> A Taylor is the best
> Client in all the Land :
> And his reason is good,
> If well understood,
> 'Cause he has so many Suits in hand.

In Richardum quendam, Divitem, Avarum.

[24.]   Devising on a time what name I might
   Best give unto a dry illiberall chuffe,
   After long search on his owne name I light,
   Nay then (said I) No more, I have enough ;
      His name and nature do full well agree,
      For's name is *Rich* and *hard ;* and so is he.

The Dumb MAID,[1]

or, the

Young GALLANT Trappan'd.

A young Man did unto her a Wooing come,	*The Doctor's skill was likewise with her try'd;*
But she pretended much that she was dumb;	*The Doctor he set her Tongue on the Run,*
But when they both in Marriage bands were ty'd,	*She Chatters now and never will have done.*

To a New Tune, call'd, *Dum, dum, dum;* Or. I would I were in my own Country &c.

Licens'd and Enter'd according to Order.

[35.] All you that pass along,
Give ear unto my song,
Concerning a youth
    that was young, young, young;
And of a Maiden fair
Few with her might compare
But alack, and alas, she
    was dumb, dumb, dumb.

She was beautious, fresh and gay
Like the pleasant Flowers in *May,*
And her cheeks was as round,
    as a plum, plum, plum;
She was neat in every part,
And she stole away his heart,
But alack, and alas, she
    was dumb, dumb, dumb.

At length this Country Blade,
Wedded this prety Maid,
And he kindly conducted
    her home, home, home;

[1] For tune, see Appendix.

Thus in her Beauty bright,
Lay all his whole Delight
But alack, and alas, she
  was dumb, dumb, dumb.

Now will I plainly show
What work this Maid could do,
Which a Pattern may be,
  For girls young, young, young:

O she both day and night
In working took delight.
But alack, and alas, she
  was dumb, dumb, dumb.

She could brew, and she could bake,
She could wash, wring and shake,
She could sweep the house
  with a broom, broom, broom:

She could knit and sow and spin,
And do any such like thing
But alack, and alas, she
    was dumb, dumb, dumb.

But at last this man did go,
The Doctor's skill to know,
Saying, Sir, can you cure
    a Woman of the Dumb?
O it is the easiest part,
That belongs unto my Art,
For to cure a Woman
    of the Dumb, dumb, dumb.

To the Doctor he did her bring,
And he cut her Chattering-string,
And he set her Tongue on
    the run, run, run :
In the morning he did rise,
And she fill'd his house with cries,
And she rattled in his ears
    like a drum, drum, drum.

To the Doctor he did go,
With his heart well fill'd with woe,
Crying, Doctor, I am
    undone, done, done ;
Now she's turn'd a scolding Wife
And I'm weary of my life,
Nor I cannot make her hold
    her tongue, tongue, tongue.

The Doctor thus did say,
When she went from me away,
She was perfectly cured of
    the dumb, dumb, dumb.
But it's beyond the Art of Man,
Let him do the best he can,
For to make a scolding Woman
    hold her tongue, tongue, tongue.

So as you to me came
Return you back again
And take you the Oyl
   of Hazel [1] strong
With it anoint her Body round,
When she makes the House to sound,
So perhaps you may charm her,
   tongue, tongue, tongue.

[26.] A Schoolmaster did always dictate to his Scholars. *H non est Litera*, that is H is no letter; and on a time he call'd one of the Scholars to him, and bid him *heat the Cawdle*, and when he askt for it, the Scholar told him, *that he had done with the Cawdle as he bid him. What's that?* says his Master, *Why Sir*, says he, *I did eat it. Sirrah*, says he, *I bid you heat it with an H. Yes Sir*, says he, *But I did eat it with Bread.*

[32.] What is that that hath his belly full of man's meat and his mouth full of dirt? *Solution*. It is an Oven when it is full of bread, or pies, for that is man's meat, and the Ovens mouth is then closed with dirt.

[12.] What's an *Ace*, says one,
Dewce take me, says *John*,
The Tray will be up in a trice
You cater waule now.
And your wit sinks low,
Why friends, the jest is concise.

[24.] Death and an honest Cobler fell at bate
And finding him worne out, would needs translate;
He was a trusty so'le, and time had bin
He would, well liquord, go through thick and thin.
Death put a trick upon him, and what was't?
The Cobler call'd for All, death brought his last;

[1] A hazel switch.

'Twas not uprightly done to cut his thread,
That mended more and more till he was dead;
But since hee's gone, tis all that can be said,
Honest *Cut-Cobler* here is underlayed.

In political satire it was not to be expected that so prominent a person as Prince Rupert, the son of James I.'s own sister, could come off scathless; but it is somewhat singular, and it shows the bitterness of the parties, that even his pets, his poodle dog, and his monkey, should provoke the

satiric ire of the Roundhead writers. Both are historical, and, thanks to Thomason, whose wonderful collection, known as the "Kings Pamphlets," exists in the British Museum, the materials of their history are easily accessible to the student. The Prince's dog "Boy" was a white poodle, and it is somewhat curious to note that poodles, over 200 years since, were shaved so as to conserve the lionlike mane, although the dandyisms of tufts on the legs and tail seem to have been reserved for a later era.

His master must have had a special and peculiar affection for "Boy," as he, and a tame hare, "which used to follow him about & do his bidding with facility," were his solace when imprisoned at Lintz in 1641. According to a writer,[1] whose "Prince Ruperts diary" everybody would like to see, it was a "beautiful white dogge," was given him by Lord Arundell, and was "of a breede so famous that the Grand Turk gave it in particular injunction to his ambassador to obtaine him a puppie thereof." His nationality is given in a tract [36] as being either of German or Finland breed, and he must soon have become notorious, as Prince Rupert did not come over to England after his release from prison until February 1642; and we find from the accompanying engraving [36] that early the following year he was politically made use of for party purposes.

In this dialogue, which is too lengthy for reproduction here, it will be seen that he was already accredited with supernatural qualities.

"*Tobies Dog.* . . . I heare you are Prince *Ruperts* white Boy.

P. Rup. dog.   I am none of his White Boy, my name is *Puddle.*

Tob. dog.   A dirty name indeed, you are not pure enough for my company, besides I hear on both sides of my eares that you are a Laplander, or Fin land Dog, or truly no better than a Witch in the shape of a white Dogge.

.   .   .   .   .

Tob. Dog.   You are of *Brackley* breed, better to hang than to keep.

Pr. Rob. Dog.   No, Sirrah, I am of high Germain breed;

Tob. Dog.   Thou art a Reprobate, and a lying Curre; you were either whelpt in Lapland, or else in Fin land; where there is none but divells and Sorcerers live."

This supernatural idea seems to have had its rise in Boy's accompanying his master always, even on the battlefield, enjoying a marvellous immunity from harm. There is a very similar engraving to the accompanying, in a chap·book of "The History of the Blind Begger of Bednal Green" [38], where it does duty for "Young Monford Riding to the Wars,

---

[1] Memoirs of Prince Rupert and the Cavaliers, by Eliot Warburton. Lond. 1849.

where he unhapily lost his Eye sight." [1]   And I have no doubt but that in this present work the engraving to "The Poets Dream" is an old woodcut of Prince Rupert and his dog Boy.

[37.]

In another tract of the time [39] are plentiful allusions to his being a witch.   "Grumbling Sir, or counterfeit Lapland Lady, I admire thy impudence in calling thyself a Lady : Art thou a Lady and hast so much haire ?   .   .   .   Thou wouldst be a rough bed fellow for the Divell himself; if thou art not a Divell thyself, thou hast conditions sutable to thy shape, for thou doest snarle and bite at the Parliament, and hast learnt that quality from other Popish Dogs; good thou canst do

[1] This is reproduced on p. 360 of " Chap Books of the 18th Century," by John Ashton.   Lond. 1882.

none to the Prince, for that is contrary to the nature of a
Witch, which in some respects thou unjustly doest assume, but
in other conditions most fitly, for a Witch will dine or suppe
with a roasted crab squittering in the fire, or with a few boild
Onions and a draught of Buttermilke which one of her neighbours gave her for fear more than for love, but thou doest
fare most deliciously of the rumps and wings of Capons, and
Kidneys, and art indeed better fed than taught. Besides a
Witch will lie upon an old straw bed with her house Cat which
seems instead of her bed fellow.   But the Kings chair of state
and all the embroydered velvet stools are thy day couches,
where thou lyest and sleepest with thy malignant eyes half
open, and canst winke at small and great faults as thou doest
for occasion.   But then thou art a Witch again in some conditions, for they are overgrown with ugly gray hair which hangs
down about their shoulders, and so art thou, *Boy*.   Witches
are ready to doe mischief, but can do no good, and such are
thy malignant qualities, *Boy ;*   Pardon me, for though our
gracious King loves thee, it is not as thou art a Witch but as
thou art Prince *Robert's* dog."   And this attack on poor *Boy*
winds up with calling him " a very cowardly malignant cur,"
though he look like a lion.

Another tract [40] talks of " her cousen Prince *Ruperts*
with her white Tog, which as her Moderns hold is a Prince
disguis'd."   And Cleveland [41] in his ode " to Prince Rupert "
sings to poor *Boy's* disadvantage, and holds him up as a bug-
bear.

> " They fear the Giblets of his Train, they fear
> Even his Dog, that four legg-d Cavalier :
> He that devours the Scraps which *Lunsford* makes,
> Whose Picture feeds upon a Child in Stakes.
> Who name but *Charles* he comes aloft for him,
> But holds up his Malignant Leg at *Pym*.
> 'Gainst whom they've several Articles in Souse ;
> First that he barks against the Sense o' th' House.
> *Resolv'd Delinquent*, to the Tower straight ;
> Either to th' Lyons, or the Bishops Grate.

Next, for his Ceremonious Wag o' th' Tail;
But there the Sisterhood will be his Bail,
At least the Countess will, *Lust's Amsterdam*,
That lets in all Religions of the Game.
Thirdly, he smells Intelligence, that's better,
And cheaper too, than *Pym* from his own Letter :
Who's doubly pay'd (Fortune or we the blinder ?)
For making Plots, and then for Fox the Finder.
Lastly he is a Devil without doubt ;
For when he would lie down, he wheels about ;
Makes Circles and is Couchant in a Ring,
And therefore score up one for Conjuring."

In a contemporary tract [36] *Boy* is accredited with being invulnerable, and he had escaped the chances of war in a remarkable manner. It would be a pity to curtail the extract, as it shows well the political amenities of that age. "The Challenge which Prince *Griffins* Dogge called *Towzer* hath sent to Prince *Rupert's* Dog whose name is *Puddle*, daring him to meet him at the Parish Garden this present Lent to try a combate before the Worship full the Beares, who are appointed to be their Judges in that Case.——Thou worme of Wickednesse, fritter of Folly, spawne of doggednesse, and piece of mungrele stuffe ; in regard of thy base grumbling words and bawling against thy betters. Besides that, is honest *Pepper*. Tobies *Dogge* your match, no he is too milde for thee ; thou should have given notice of your Treaty and discourse to me who am thy equall, thou shouldst have found enough of me, for I will have thee know, that I eate as good Rumps and Kidneyes as ever thou, base Cur, dost ; when I have you at the place appointed I will so rump you, and so frump you, that I will leave you never a rumpe nor yet a kidney, no, not with a heart as big as a hen or chickins : I doe now with open mouth defie thee and all thy proceedings, and doe challenge thee to meet me at the place before mentioned, there will I fight, tug and teare thee in a single combate, where I mean to rend thee in pieces, and be revenged on thee, base cur. *And*[1] *although I hear thou art impenitrable and likewise besmeared*

---

[1] These italics are mine.

over with inchaunted oyle, so that no weapon, bullet nor sword can enter thee to make thee bleed; yet I have teeth which I have newly whetted shall so fasten and teare your German or Finland hide limb meale, and then flea thy skin and hang it on the hedg, and give thy pomperd flesh to those Iudges which we are to fight before, (namely the Worshipfull the Bears), to satisfie their hungry mawes this Lent; let me hear your dogged answer, or else I will proclaim thee Coward in print, and set thy name upon every whipping post &c. . . . Expect no favour from mee, nor will I from you ; I will end the difference

I will have no Outlandish cur domineer in our Land. *So saith your Surley foe* Towzer, and servant to Prince Griffin."

Long after poor *Boy's* death he was associated with Prince Rupert, for instance [42]—

> "See how the Sectists bustle now,
> The Independents sturre.
> London is tam'd say they ; as once
> Prince *Rupert* with his curre."

Boy at all events proved mortal, for he met with his death, after escaping in many battlefields, at Marston Moor, on 2d July 1644 ; and great rejoicings were made by the Puritan faction over his death. One of the " King's Pamphlets " is entirely devoted to him [43], and from this the accompanying engraving is taken. Here poor *Boy*, who is environed by a hail of bullets, is represented as being "killed by a Valliant Souldier, who had skill in Necromancy." And to keep up the idea of his supernatural birth a witch is standing by, lamenting. The "Elegie" commences with "P. *Ruperts* Sorrow."

> " Lament poor *Cavaliers*, cry, howl, and yelp.
> For the great losse of your *Malignant Whelp.*
> Hee's dead! Hee's dead: No more, alas, can he
> Protect you *Dammes*, or get Victorie.
> How sad that *Son* of *Blood* did look to hear
> One tell the death of this shagg'd *Cavalier,*
> Hee rav'd, he tore his Perriwigg, and swore.
> Against the Round heads that hee'd ne're fight more."

It goes on with a fabulous supernatural pedigree of *Boy.*

> " 'Twas like a *Dog*, yet there was none did know
> Whether it Devill was, or Dog, or no."

And after a long political diatribe it winds up thus—

> " To tell you all the pranks this *Dogge* hath wrought,
> That lov'd his Master, and him Bullets brought,
> Would but make laughter, in these times of woe,
> Or how this Curr came by his fatall blow,
> Look on the Title Page, and there behold,
> The Emblem will all this to you unfold.

> Morrall.
> The *World's* the *Witch*, the *Dogge* is the *Devill,*
> And *men* th' Actors, that have wrought this evill."

So famous was *Boy*, that the different newspapers gave his death as a special piece of intelligence [44]—"I may not omit to tell you that Prince *Rupert* lost his Bever, and his horse, and also his Dog was slain, and lay dead neere the Beanfield, where divers affirme the Prince hid himselfe, after a little service, till it was dark, and then he got to *Yorke.*" Again [45]—"As for newes from the North, I heare it further confirmed, that the rumour which was here about Towne concerning Pr *Ruperts* hiding himselfe in a Beane field, and for which act hee is almost quite out of the Malignants bookes, is acknowledged to be most certaine, Nay, and I myselfe have heard it confessed from the mouths of some notorious Malignants : It had beene brave, with a blood hound there to have found him out, the plunderings, cruelties, Massacrings, rapes, and bloodshed, which lie upon his conscience, and which he cannot but beare about continually, must needs have yelded a strong scent to betray him unto revenge.   But though his *Necromantick* Dogge, his *Mephistophiles*, was slaine, yet he seemes he made a shift to get secure into *Yorke*, and

there to sweare the Townesmen into an opinion of his Victory."   And in another newspaper [48] he is mentioned thus—" Amongst the dead Men and Horses which lay on the ground, wee found Prince *Ruperts* Dog killed.   (This is onely mentioned by the way ; because the Prince his Dog, hath been much spoken of, and was more prized by his Master than Creatures of much more worth.) "

   . A contemporary tract [46] (which is a dry political discussion, and has nothing whatever to do with the title-page) furnishes the accompanying engraving, which is exceedingly graphic.   Here we again see poor Boy, exactly as described, lying " dead neere the Beanfield," which is represented with preraphaelite fidelity.   It is also hinted at in the engraving which shows him being shot " by a Valliant Soulder, who had skill in Necromancy," but in this one is introduced the head of Prince Rupert, who is supposed to be there hiding.

His baggage fell into the hands of the victorious Parliamentarians, and the satirist cannot help having a fling at the Prince's Romish proclivities, as the contents of his sumpter horses' baggage shows bulls, crucifixes, images, a bell, etc. On this subject there is another satire [47]—"The Catholikes Petition to Prince Rupert," from which the accompanying engraving is taken.

But the Prince had another pet, a she monkey, and the satirist must needs make that inoffensive animal a mark at which to spit his spite, although nothing like the supernatural powers of *Boy* were attributed to her. There are two portraits extant of her, but I have only reproduced one, the dresses in both cases being precisely similar, and may probably represent her real costume [49]. In this tract she is described as—" I never saw such a strange fashioned creature in my life ; for she hath a kind of Round-head as smooth as an apple, and if there be any Round-head this Munkey is one, her brow is low and wrinkled hanging over her little eyes ; her nose thats flatt is very short, her cheekes are leane and lanke, and her thin lipps do hardly cover her teeth, the complection of her whole face is swarthy, cover'd with hayre greene as mosse, and lastly she

hides her head in a black begg, moreover she weares a greene or yellow gowne trimmed about with lace, & a girdle about her middle by the which she is fastned to the nave of a wheele, for the Prince is full of feares and Jelousies that if she were loose she would steale away into some wood and live there upon nutts and apples. . . . Thus P. *Ruperts* Monkey is a kind of old, little, wrinkled, old faced, petulant, wanton, and malignant gentlewoman . . . that sometimes rides upon the beast

that is Prince *Rupert's* dog . . .

Prince *Rupert's* Monkey is a toy,
That doth exceed his dog called Boy,
 Which through dogged folly,
  Both Barkes and Bites,
  But this delights
 The Prince when's melancholy.

He puts sweetemeats and sugar plumbs
Into his Monkey's toothlesse gums,
 Which open like an oyster,
  For he doth esteeme
  A wench I meane,
 More than a Nun in a Cloister.'

The colour of her dress is also described in a tract, before quoted from [39]—"And Prince *Roberts* Monkey dare not come thither, lest the Parliaments Bitch should tear her green coat off from her back."

Her food is described in another tract [50]—"She would eat no oatmeal, nor lome of walls to cure her infirmitie, but the longest whitest sugar plums she could put into her mouth, were most delightfull to her taste, and had such a ravenous appetite to fruit that she would swallow all but the stones, and having gotten a delectable bit in her mouth, she would onely suck the juice out of it and then spit out the rest. . . . Moreover this Monkey was and is by nature a notable plunderer not onely of studdies and closets, into which, if she got, she would teare the books, spill the ink, and eat the sweetmeats."

This is about all I dare reproduce about this pet of Prince Rupert's, the remainder of these tracts being filled with political allusions, which are somewhat hard to be understood now, and of no interest to this book, the remainder being written somewhat more coarsely than usual. But enough has been said about them to show how the satirists of that age seized upon any thing which they could turn to their purpose.

[51.]   A Citizen for Recreations Sake
To see the Countrie would a journie make,
Some dozen mile, or little more,
Taking his leave of friends two months before ;
With drinking healths, and shaking by the hand,
As he had travail'd to some new-found land.
Well, taking horse, with very much a doe,
London he leaveth for a day or two :
And as he rideth meets upon the way
Such (as what haste soever) bid men stay ;
Sirrah (sayes one) stand, and your purse deliver ;
I am a taker, you must be a giver.
Unto a wood hard by they hale him in,
And rifle him unto the very skin.
Masters (quoth he) pray heare me ere you goe,
For you have robbed more than you doe know :

I

My horse (in troth) I borrowed of my Brother,
The Bridle and the Saddle of another :
The Jerkin and the Bases[1] be a Taylers,
The Scarfe, I doe assure you, is a Saylers :
The Falling-band is likewise none of mine,
Nor Cuffes, as true as this good light doth shine :
The Sattin Doublet and the Velvet Hose,
Are our Church-wardens, all the parish knowes.
The Bootes are *John* the Grocers of the Swan,
The Spurs were lent me by a Serving-man :
One of my Rings, (that with the great red Stone)
Insooth I borrowed of my gossip *Joane.*
Her husband knowes not of it gentlemen,
Thus stands my case, I pray shew favour then.
Why (quoth the theeves) thou needst not greatly care,
Since in thy losse so many beare a share :
The world growes hard, many good fellows lack
Look not at this time for a penny back.
Goe tell at *London,* thou didst meet with four,
That rifling thee hath rob'd at least a score.

The Connicatcher[2] *and Priest of Paris.*

[52.] A lewd knave, a Cheater, espied a wealthy Priest, whose purse was full of money, lately arrived in the City of Paris out of the Countrey to buy necessaries, and with a bold face saluted him, requested his aid in a small matter concerning a man of his own calling. What's that, (quoth the Priest ?) It is, Sir, (quoth he) this. The Parson of our Towne hath given mee money to buy a Surplesse, and I, having small knowledge in it, would request your ayde in the Choyce of a good one, making no question of your good skill. With all my heart (quoth the Priest.)

Comming to the shop of sale, the Connicatcher called for some choyce Surplesses, and desired the Priest to choose out one of the best. Which done, intreated him to assay it,

---

[1] The exact meaning of these garments seems to be in doubt. They were probably some kind of skirt.   [2] A sharper.

whether it were in all points as it ought to be. The Priest was nimble at his game, for it was his dayly exercise, but the Cheater found fault with the making, bearing out such an uncomly bulke at his right side. Oh (quoth the Priest) my girdle and pouch is cause of that, and immediately loosed his girdle and pouch, willing the Connicatcher to hold it till he had better girded up the Surplesse as it ought to be. The Connicatcher having as much as he desired suddenly leapt out of the shop and ranne away as fast as he could with the Priests girdle and pouch full of money. The Priest turning about, and seeing his purse and money flying for religion (*sic*) made all the haste he could in the Surplesse after the Connicatcher, crying and calling Hold the Theefe, Hold the Theefe, The Connicatcher cried out. Hold the Priest, for he is mad, and will kill me: the shopkeeper followed as fast as he could and cried, Stop the Priest, for he hath stolne my Surplesse. The people halfe amazed at this accident, laid hold on the Priest, but before he could declare his misfortune, the Connicatcher was gone far enough, not to be caught again in haste. Which caused much good laughter, and the Priest payed for the Surplesse.

[12.]   One askt a simpleton,
       Pray what Countryman
Are you?` says he, from the West;
      By my troth says *Hugh*,
      I do think so too,
All the wise Men come from the East.

On Bond *the Usurer.*

[24.]   Here lyes a Bond under this tombe,
      Seald and deliver'd to, god knows whom.

[17.] One that had sore eyes, was jeer'd by another that was clear ey'd; who told him they were not so sore, but that he could see a knave: It may be so, says he, *but you must look in a Glass then.*

[18.] A Citizen telling a Courtier that he had just then eased himself of a great Burden by paying a Debt he owed, and that he could not apprehend how any Man could sleep that was in Debt; *For my part*, answered the Courtier, *I should rather wonder how my Creditors can sleep, well knowing that I shall never pay them.*

[4.] A certain Knave asking a virtuous Gentlewoman, jearingly, *What was honesty?* she answered, *What's that to you? Meddle with those things that concern you.*

THE POETS DREAM[1]

OR,

The Great Out-cry and Lamentable Complaint of the LAND *against* BAYLIFFS and their DOGS.

Wherein is Expressed their Villanous Out-rages *to poor* Men; *With a true Description of their Knavery and their Debauch'd Actions; Prescribed and Presented to the view of all People.*

To the Tune of *Sawny* &c.

[53.] As I lay Slumbring in a Dream,
    methought the world most strangely went;
The Bayliffs on High Seats was seen,
    which caus'd the Poor's great discontent.
They pluckt true Justice from the Throne,
    erecting Laws made of their own,
And burthen'd the Poor till they made them groan,
    And that's the cause that the Land Complains.

[1] For tune, see Appendix.

Their Meeting house was an Ale-wives Bench,
    fix'd in a Street that is termed Old ;
Their Speaker was a Play-house-Wench
    both —— and Thief, and a Devilish Scold.
Shee'd guzzel Brandy, Wine or Ale,
    and then she'd at her Neighbours Rail,
And send for the Bayliffs to have them to Jayl,
    And that's the cause &c.

Methoughts a mighty hunting-match,
    was made by Bayliffs and their Currs :
Poor men was the Deer they strove to catch,
    the Houses plac'd in the Room of Furrs :[1]
The Suburbs-Round, it was their Park,
    the Bayliffs yell, the Dogs did Bark,
The Poor kept as close as Noah in the Ark,
    And that's the Cause &c.

Then *Shephard* and his Dog wheel'd up to th' right,
    and thunder'd by a Cursed Lane,

[1] Fir-trees.

And there the Villains wrought their Spight,
    for by them, once, was a poor Man slain.
They Swear, before they'l ever lack,
    they'l go to Hell, a Pick-a Pack,
And thus poor Debters they go to rack,
    And that's the Cause &c.

There's Cursing *Will* and Damme *Jack*,
    and Robbin *Tanner's* alive agen,
And Paunchgut *Tom*, (a Hellish Pack).
    with perjur'd *Dick*, and bawdy Ben :
Which formerly on Earth did Dwell,
    and now they are return'd from Hell,
And doth against our Laws Rebell.
    And that's the Cause &c.

When I awaked from my Dream,
    methoughts the world turn'd upside down,
And in great haste, I Writ this Theam,
    for the Bayliffs Doggs of our Town ;
Who for their Pray each hour doe wait,
    like Death at every poor Man's Gate,
And brings the Realm to a Dismal fate.
    And that's the Cause &c.

When Poor men are out of Employ
    and have not a Farthing in the World,
The while there Wives and Children cry,
    there's many are in a Prison hurl'd :
Men are enticed by the Bumms,
    who swear they ne'r will pay their Summs,
Thus Poor in Flocks to the Jaylor comes,
    And that's the Cause &c.

The Tallyman, Curmudgeon, keeps
    a Baylif and his Dog to Bite,
If in their Books, men ever Creeps,
    they quickly swear they'l have their Right :

So soon as e're they do Back-slide,
   the Torturing Jale they must abide
Then *Toby* and Dog's employ'd;
    And that's the Cause &c.

When Rogues are at the *Old Bayly* Burn'd,
   and that their Pilfering Trades do fail;
From Thieves to Bayliff's Dogs have turn'd,
   to plague and hurry the Poor to Jayl:
How like Kid-nappers all the Day,
   in every Corner they Survey,
And quaff whole Bowls when they get their way.
    And that's the Cause &c.

Ten Groat's the Fees, and a Crown the arrest
   and three Round OOO's for a Writ beside,
Thus Laws are broken, and poor men opprest,
   such Racking torments they must abide.
And while the Prisoner sends for Bail,
   they Tope the Brandy, Beer and Ale,
And makes him pay, or they have him to Jail.
    And that's the Cause &c.

For Twenty Shillings, Ten or Five,
   they'l put a man to a Cursed Charge;
Or run him to Jayl they'l soon contrive,
   where other Bills are exprest at Large:
The Jayl Fees many are bound to Rue,
   the Garnish, Bed and Turnkey too,
Expects an unexpected Due,
    And that's the Cause &c.

Tis seldom a Bayliff or his Dog
   is ever known for to go to Church;
As soon as they here the Word of God
   they leave the Parson in the lurch:
They swear they'l come to Church no more,
   they lay their sins to *Adam's* Score,
And jaunt to *Moorfields* to a ——,
    And that's the Cause &c.

Thus I conclude and end my Song,
  desiring that you wou'd be content ;
There's Christian Peers that may right our wrong.
  when Heaven yields up a Parliament :
I hope true Reason will plead our Cause,
  while they'r erecting wholesome Laws
They'l keep us from the *Crocodils* paws,
  and cease the Poor of the Land's Complaints.[1]

Printed for *P. Brooksby* at the *Golden Ball* near the *Bear*
Tavern in *Pye Corner.*

The dumbe wife recovered her speech.

[52.] A certaine Farmer had taken to wife a dumb woman,
and hearing of a great Magician lately come into England,
he tooke horse and rode to him, and demanded if there were
no help for a woman that had lost her speech. The Magician
answered, Yes, it is an easie matter, and told him hee must
take an Aspen leafe, and lay it under her tongue, and it
would instantly help her. The Farmer was joy'd with this
tidings, and returned in haste homewards, suspecting in himselfe the vertue of his new receit, and therefore to make the
matter more sure, he tooke three Aspen leaves, and laid them
all three under his wifes tongue, who immediately began to
talk and prate very nimbly, and in the end, upon a very
small occasion to curse and raile downeright upon her husband, as if shee had beene mad. The Farmer was now in a
peck of troubles, and posted in all hast to the Magician,
certifying him of this unhappy accident. The Magician
demanded if hee absolutely followed his counsell. The
Farmer answered No, for (quoth he) instead of one leaf I
have used three, hoping to make the matter surer. Marry
then, God help thee, (quoth the Magician) for it is an easie
matter to make a woman speak, but to make her hold her
tongue is past my cunning. Nay, all the devills in Hell could
never worke such a wonder. Whereat the Farmer much
grieved, departed.

[1] 16th Dec. 1671. See the Kings Bench Prisoners Thanks to his
Majesty for their late Deliverance By his Majesties Most Gracious Act.
$\frac{82.\ 18}{53.}$ s. sh. fol.

[32.] What is that the more ye lay on, the faster it wasteth ?
Solution. That is a Whetstone, for the more ye whet the less
    is the Whetstone.

[51.] A Money Monger choyce of Sureties had ;
    A Countrey fellow plaine in Russet clad ;
    His doublet Mutton-taffety Sheep-skins,
    His sleeves at hand button'd with two good pins ;
    Upon his head a filthy greasie Hat,
    That had a hole eate thorou it by a Rat,
    A Leather Pouch that with a Snap-hance shut,
    One hundred Hobnailes in his Shooes were put :
    The stockings that his Clownish legs did fit,
    Were Kersie to the calfe, and t'other knit ;
    And at a word, th' apparell that he wore
    Was not worth twelve pence, at *Who gives more?*
    The other surety of another stuffe,
    His neck inviron'd with a double Ruffe,
    Made Lawne and Cambrick both such common ware,
    His Doublet set had falling Band to spare ;
    His fashion new, with last Edition stood,
    His Rapier Hilts imbru'd in golden blood :
    And these same trappings made him seeme one sound,
    To passe his credit for an hundred pound,
    So was accepted ; Russet coat deny'd,
    But when time came the money should be pay'd,
    And Monsieur Usurer did hunt him out,
    Strange alteration struck his heart in doubt ;
    For in the Counter [1] he was gone to dwell,
    And Brokers had his painted cloaths to sell ;
    The Usurer then further understands,
    The Clowne (refus'd) was rich and had good lands ;
    Ready (through rage) to hang himselfe, he swore
    That Silken Knaves should cozen him no more.

[8.] A seaman coming before the Judges of the Admiralty
for admittance into office in a ship bound for the *Indies*, was
by one of the Judges much sleighted, as an insufficient person

             [1] See footnote, *ante.*

for that office which he sought for to acquire; till the Judge telling him that he believed that he could not say the points of his Compass; the Seaman answered, better than he could say his *Pater Noster*: The Judge replyed, that he would wager twenty shillings with him of that; so the Seaman taking him up, it came to trial, and the Seaman began and said all the points of his Compass very exactly; the Judge likewise said his *Pater Noster*, and when he had finished it, he required the wager according to the agreement, because the Seaman was to say his Compass better than he his *Pater Noster*, which he had not performed: nay hold, quoth the Sea man, the wager is not finished, for I have but half done; and so he immediately said his Compass backward very exactly, which the Judge failing of in his *Pater Noster*, the Seaman carried away the prize.

[12.]   A Grave there was made
        For one *Aylet*, he said
    The Bell for him then did toul;
        But you lye like a Knave,
        It is not a Grave,
    But only an Aylet hole.

[17.] One having a very great Nose, and thin beard, was told the shadow of his Nose did hinder his Beard's growth.

[26.] An Apothecary in *Oxford* spoke to a Country man by way of Jeer to bring him some live Rats, and he would give him eighteen pence a piece for them; and a fortnight after he brought them; and then the Apothecary told him, *That he was provided the day before.* The Country Fellow seeing he was abused, was resolved to be quit with him, saying, *I am unwilling (seeing I have brought them) to carry them back again;* and told him he would take three pence out in Physick at some time or other; and so opened his Bag, and let them about the Shop, which did so whisk up and down the Shelves, that in a little space they broke him about forty Pots and Glasses, and could never get rid of them since. *Probatum est.*

A Courtier and a Scholler meeting.

[5.]   A Courtier proud walking along the Street,
Hap'ned by chance a Scholler for to meet,
The Courtier said, (minding nought more than place)
Unto the Scholler, meeting face to face,
To take the wall, base men Ile not permit,
The Scholler said, I will, and gave him it.

[4.] A Lady going to Mass to present her Tapers, fixed one to *St. Michael,* and another to the *Devil* that was at his Feet. The Clerk seeing her, told her she did not well to offer a Candle to the Devil. *No matter,* says the Lady, *'tis good to have Friends every where; for we know not where we shall go.*

[8.] There was a gentleman fell very sick, and a friend of his said to him, Surely you are in danger, I pray you send for a Physician; but the sick man answered, *It is no matter, for if I die I will die at leisure.*

[51.] A wealthy Misers sonne, upon a day,
Met a poore Youth, that did intreat and pray
Something of Charitie in his distresse;
Helpe Sir (quoth hee) one that is Fatherlesse,
Sirrah (sayd hee) away, begone with speed,
Ile helpe none such; thou art a Knave indeed:
Dost thou complaine because thou wants a Father?
Were it in my case I would rejoyce the rather;
For if thy Father's death, cause thee repine,
I would my Father had excused thine.

The little Barly-Corne.[1]

Whose Properties and Vertues here,
Shall plainly to the world appeare,
And make you merry all the yeere.

To the tune of *Stingo*

[55.] Come, and doe not musing stand,
　　　　if thou the truth discerne,
　　　But take a full cup in thy hand,
　　　　and thus begin to learne,

Not of the earth, nor of the ayre,
　　at evening or at morne,
But, joviale boyes, your Christmas keep
　with the little Barly-Corne.

It is the cunningst Alchymist,
　　that ere was in the Land,
Twill change your Mettle when it list
　　in turning of a hand,
Your blushing Gold to Silver wan,
　　your Silver into Brasse,
Twill turn a Taylor to a man
　and a man into an ass—

　　　　[1] For tune, see Appendix.

Twill make a poore man rich to hang
    a signe before his doore,
And those that doe the Pitcher hang,
    tho rich, twill make them poore ;
Twill make the silliest poorest Snake [1]
    the King's great Porter [2] scorne ;
Twill make the stoutest Lubber weak,
    this little Barley Corne.

It hath more shifts than *Lambe* [3] ere had,
    or *Hocus Pocus* too,
It will good fellowes shew more sport
    than *Bankes* [4] his horse could doe :
Twill play you faire above the boord,
    unless you take good heed,
And fell you though you were a Lord,
    and iustifie the deed.

It lends more yeeres unto old Age,
    than ere was lent by Nature,
It makes the Poet's fancy rage,
    more than Castalian water ;

[1] ? Sneak.

[2] William Evans, a Welshman in the service of Charles I. He was 7 ft. 6 in. high and at a masque at Whitehall drew Sir Jeffrey Hudson out of his pocket. There used to be a bas-relief over Bull's Head Court in Newgate Street, of "The King's Porter and Dwarf."

[3] Dr. John Lambe was an impostor who early in the 17th century practised fortune-telling, juggling, showing a magic crystal, and recovering stolen goods. He was indicted at Worcester for witchcraft, after which he removed to London, where he got into trouble, and he was finally pelted to death by an infuriated mob on 13th June 1628. There is a very rare pamphlet on this subject — "A brief description of the notorious life of John Lambe, otherwise called Dr. Lambe, together with his ignominious death, with a wood-cut of the populace pelting him to death in the City of London." 4° 1628.

[4] Banks was a Scotchman, and his performing horse had the rare honour of being alluded to by Shakspeare ("Love's Labour's Lost" Act i. s. 2). Moth says to Armado. "Why Sir, is this such a piece of study ? Now here's three studied, ere you'll thrice wink ; and how easy it is to put years to the word three, and study three years in two words, *the dancing horse will tell you.*" The horse was certainly wonderfully trained, and

Twill make a Huntsman chase a Fox,
    and never winde his Horn,
Twill cheere a Tinker in the stockes,
    this little Barly-Corne.

It is the only Will o' th' wispe
    which leades men from the way,
Twill make the tongue ti'd Lawyer lisp
    and naught but (hic-up) say.
Twill make the Steward droope and stoop
    his Bils he then will scorne,
And at each post cast his reckning up,
    this little Barly-Corne.

Twill make a man grow jealous soone,
    whose pretty Wife goes trim,
And raile at the deceiving Moone
    for making hornes at him :
Twill make the Maidens trimly dance,
    and take it in no scorne,
And helpe them to a friend by chance ;
    this little Barly-Corne.

It is the neatest Serving man
    to entertaine a friend,
It will doe more than money can,
    all iarring suits to end :

is spoken of in Tarlton's Jests, as having picked him out as being the
biggest fool in the company. His tricks were marvellous, but perhaps
his most noted feat was riding up the steeple of St. Paul's in the year 1600.
This feat is mentioned in the following books. Decker's Dead-Tearme—
Owle's Almanack, 1618—The Meeting of Gallants at an Ordinarie, or the
Walkes in Powles, 1604—The Blacke Booke, 1604—Northward Hoe,
1607—Rowley's Search for Money, 1609—Decker's Gul's Horn-book,
1609—and His Jests to make you merie, 1607. The horse afterwards
went a continental trip, where he excited great wonder, and his high
training was put down to witchcraft. Indeed a rumour was spread about
that both he and his master were burnt for sorcery ; but this was not so,
for in Charles I.'s reign mention is more than once made of Banks being a
vintner in Cheapside. The horse's name was Marocco, and there was a
very curious book printed in 1595, called "Maroccus extaticus or Bankes
Bay Horse in a Trance," etc.

There's life in it, and it is here,
   'tis here within this Cup,
Then take your liquor; doe not spare,
   but cleare carouse it up.

If sicknesse Come, this Physick take
   it from your heart will set it,
If feare incroach, take more of it,
   your heart will soon forget it :
Apollo and the Muses nine,
   doe take it in no scorne,
There's no such stuffe to passe the time,
   as the little Barly-Corne.

Twill make a weeping Widdow laugh,
   and some incline to pleasure ;
Twill make an old man leave his staffe
   and dance a youthfull measure :
And though your clothes be nere so bad,
   all ragged, rent, and torne,
Against the Cold you may be clad
   with the little Barly Corne.

Twill make a Coward not to shrinke,
   but be as stout as may be,
Twill make a man that he shall thinke.
   that *Jone's* as good as my Lady :
It will inrich the palest face,
   and with Rubies it adorne,
Yet you shall thinke it no disgrace,
   this little Barly Corne.

Twill make your Gossips merry,
   when they their liquor see,
Hey, we shall nere be weary,
   sweet Gossip, here's to thee :
'Twill make the Country Yeoman
   the Courtier for to scorne,
And talk of Law suits ore a Can,
   with this little Barly Corne.

It makes a man that write cannot
  to make you large Indentures,
When as he reeleth home at night,
  upon the watch he ventures :
He cares not for the Candle light
  that shineth in the horne,
Yet he will stumble the way aright,
  this little Barly-Corne.

Twill make a Miser prodigall,
  and shew himselfe kind hearted
Twill make him never grieve at all,
  that from his Coyne hath parted :
Twill make a Shepheard to mistake
  his Sheepe before a storme :
Twill make the Poet to excell,
  this little Barly-Corne.

It will make young Lads to call
  most freely for their Liquor,
Twill make a young Lass take a fall,
  and rise againe the quicker :
Twill make a man that he
  shall sleepe all night profoundly,
And make a man what ere he be
  goe about his businesse roundly.

Thus the Barly-Corne hath power
  even for to change our nature,
And make a Shrew within an houre,
  prove a kind-hearted creature :
And therefore here I say againe
  let no man tak't in scorne,
That I the vertues doe proclaim
  of the little Barly-Corne.

Printed in London for E. B.

The Tanner and the Butcher's dogge.

[52.] A Country Tanner that was runing hastily through Eastcheape and having a long Pike-Staffe on his shoulder, one of the Butchers dogs caught him by the breech. The fellow got loose, and ranne his pike into the Dogs throat, and killed him. The Butcher seeing that his Dog was kill'd tooke hold of the Tanner, and carried him before the Deputy, who asked him, What reason he had to kill the dogge? For mine owne defence (quoth the Tanner). Why, quoth the Deputy, hast thou no other defence but present death? Sir, quoth the Tanner, London fashions are not like the Countries, for here the stones are fast in the streets, and the Dogs are loose, but in the Country, the dogs are fast tied, and the stones are loose to throw at them ; and what should a man do in this extremity, but use his staffe for his own defence? Marry (quoth the Deputy) if a man will needs use his staffe, he might use his blunt end, and not the sharp pike. True, Master Deputy, quoth the Tanner, but you must consider, if the Dog had used his blunt end, and runne his taile at me, then had there good reason for me to do the like ; but I vow Master Deputy, the Dogge came sharpe at me, and fastned his teeth in my breech, and I again ranne sharp at him, and thrust my pike into his belly. By my faith a crafty knave, quoth the Deputy, if you will both stand to my verdict, send for a quart of wine, be friends, and so you are both discharged.

Cede majoribus.

[5.] I took the wall, one rudely thrust me by,
And told me the high way did open lye,
I thankt him that he would mee so much grace,
To take the worse and leave the better place.
For if by owners we esteem of things
The wall's the subject's, but the way the King's.

[32.] What is the most profitable beast, and that men eat least on? *Solution.* It is a Bee, for it maketh both hony and wax, and yet costeth his master nothing the keeping.

[12.] Mr. *Button* being dead,
He was so fat, one said

K

That his Grave was three foot o're ;
Why, you talk like a Fool,
'Tis but a Button-hole
To Graves I have made before.

[54.] Act 1. s. 6. Dame Purecraft. Win the fight
Littlewit (her daughter) John Little wit (a Proctor, Win's
husband) Zeal of the land Busy (a *Banbury* [1] man suitor to
Dame Purecraft.)

Purecraft. Now the blaze of the beauteous discipline, fright
   away this evill from our house ! how now *Win the fight*,
   Child : how do you ? Sweet child, speake to me.
Win. Yes forsooth.
Pure. Looke up, sweet *Win the fight*, and suffer not the
   enemy to enter you at this doore, remember that your
   education has bin with the purest ; what polluted one
   was it, that nam'd first the uncleane beast, Pigge, to you,
   Child ?
Win. Uh, uh.
John. Not I, o' my sincerity, mother ; she long'd above three
   houres, ere she would let me know it ; who was it *Win* ?
Win. A prophane blacke thing with a beard, John.
Pure. O ! resist it, *Win the fight*, it is the Tempter, the
   wicked Tempter, you may know it by the fleshly motion
   of Pig ; be strong against it, and its foule temptations, in
   these assaults, whereby it broacheth flesh and blood, as
   it were, on the weaker side, and pray against its carnall
   provocations, good child, sweet child, pray.
John. Good mother, I pray you, that she may eate some
   Pigge, and her bellyfull too ; and doe not you cast away
   your owne child, and perhaps one of mine, with your tale
   of the Tempter : how doe you, *Win* ? Are you not
   sicke ?

[1] A synonym for a Puritan, as Butler says in *Hudibras*—

"Through Banbury I passed, O profane one,
And there I saw a Puritane one
Hanging of his Cat on Monday
For killing of a Rat on Sunday."

Win. Yes, a great deale *John* (uh, uh).

Pure. What shall we doe? call our zealous brother *Busy* hither, for his faithfull fortification in this charge of the adversary; childe, my dear childe, you shall eate Pigge; be comforted, my sweet childe.

Win. I,[1] but i' the *Fayre*, mother.

Pure. I meane i' the *Fayre*, if it can be any way made, or found lawfull; where is our brother *Busy*? Will hee not come? looke up, Child.

John. Presently, mother, as soone as he has cleans'd his beard. I found him fast by the teeth, i' the cold Turkey pye, i' th' cupbord, with a great white loafe on his left hand, and a glasse of *Malmesey* on his right.

Pure. Slander not the *Brethren* wicked one.

John. Here hee is, now, purified, Mother.

Pure. O brother *Busy*! your helpe heere to edifie, and raise us up in a Scruple, my daughter *Win the fight* is visited with a naturall disease of women; call'd A longing to eate Pigge.

John. I, Sir, a *Bartholomew*[2] pigge; and in the *Fayre*.

Pure. And I would be satisfied from you, Religiously-wise, whether a widdow of the sanctified assembly, or a widdowes daughter, may commit the act, without offence to the weaker sisters.

Busy. Verily, for the disease of longing, it is a disease, a carnall disease, or appetite, incident to women: and as it is carnall, and incident, it is naturall, very naturall: Now Pigge, it is a meat, and a meat that is nourishing, and may be long'd for, and so consequently eaten; it may be eaten; very exceeding well eaten; but in the *Fayre*, and as a *Bartholomew*-pig it can not be eaten, for the very calling it a *Bartholomew*-pigge, and to eate it so, is a spice of *Idolatry*, and you make the *Fayre* no better than one of the high *Places*. This, I take it is the state of the question. A high place.

John. I, but in a state of necessity, *Place* should give place Mr *Busy*. (I have a conceit left, yet)

---

[1] I is frequently used for ay.

[2] It was the proper thing to eat roast sucking pig at Bartholomew fair.

Pure. Good brother *Zeale of the land,* thinke to make it as
lawfull as you can.

John. Yes, Sir, and as soone as you can ; for it must be, Sir ;
you see the danger my little wife is in Sir.

Pure. Truely, I doe love my child dearely, and I would not
have her miscarry or hazard her first fruites if it might be
otherwise.

Busy. Surely, it may be otherwise, but it is subject to con-
struction, subject, and hath a face of offence, with the
weake, a great face, a foule face, but that face may have
a vaile put over it and be shaddowed, as it were, it may
be eaten, and in the *Fayre,* I take it, in a Booth, the
tents of the wicked : the place is not much, not very
much, we may be religious in midst of the prophane, so
it be eaten with a reformed mouth, with *Sobriety,* and
humblenesse ; not gorg'd in with gluttony, or greedinesse ;
there's the feare : for should she goe there, as taking
pride in the place, or delight in the uncleane dressing, to
feed the vanity of the eye, or the lust of the palat, it were
not well, it were not fit, it were abominable, and not
good.

John. Nay, I knew that afore, and told her on't, but courage,
Win, we'll be humble enough ; we'll seek out the home-
liest Booth i' the *Fayre,* that's certaine ; rather than faile,
wee'll eate it o' the ground.

.   .   .   .   .   .

Busy. In the way of comfort to the weake, I will goe, and
eat. I will eate exceedingly, and prophesie ; there may
be a good use made of it, too, now I thinke on't ; by the
publike eating of Swines flesh, to professe our hate, and
loathing of *Iudaisme,* whereof the brethren stand taxed ;
I will therefore eate, yea, I will eate exceedingly.

Why women weare a fall.

[5.]   A question 'tis why women weare a fall,
The truth it is to pride they are given all,
And pride the proverbe saies must have a fall.

[12.]   A Gentleman did say
           On the last Twelf-day,
   That Cheese digests ev'ry thing ;
          Y'are dispos'd to jest,
          And will ne're be at rest,
   But at all will have a fling.
          I'le say't o're agen
          Nay, before any Men,
   That it causes a good digestion ;
          You'l jest on still,
          Let me say what I will,
   Though you ne're are askt the Question.

[32.] What is it that goeth to the water, and leaveth its guts at home? *Solution.* It is a pillow beer,[1] for when it goeth to washing, the pillow and the feathers be left at home.

[17.] Two Widdows sitting by the fire, were chatting together of their dead Husbands ; and one said, come, let us have another candle, for my poor Husband lov'd light, God send him Light ever lasting ; and says the other ; My poor Husband lov'd a good fire, I wish him Fire everlasting.

[26.] A Young Country Fellow went a Wooing to a Country Lass, and he had on then a speck and Span new Suit with Silver Buttons also ; and in all his Discourse with her, he used all the Art he could, to have her take notice of his Buttons ; at last when he saw she would take no Notice of them at all : *Well,* says he, *these Silver Buttons keep me so warm: Yes,* says she, *you had best lie in them all night, lest you should take cold this frosty weather.*

[1] Pillow case.

The poore man payes for all.

This is but a dreame which here shall insue,
But the Author wishes his words were not true.

To the Tune of *In slumbring sleepe I lay.*

[56.]   As I lay musing all alone
          upon my resting bed,
       Full many a cogitation
          did come into my head :
       And waking from my sleepe, I
          my dreame to mind did call,
       Methought I saw before mine eyes,
          how poore men payes for all.

I many objects did behold,
 in this my frightfull Dreame,
A part of them I will unfold ;
 and though my present Theame
Is but a fancy you may say,
 yet many things doe fall
Too true alas ; for at this day
 the poore man payes for all.

Methought I saw (which caused my care)
 what I wish were a fable,
That poore men still inforced are
 to pay more than they are able ;
Me thought I heard them weeping say,
 their substance was but small,
For rich men will beare all the sway, '
 and poore men pay for all.

Me thought I saw how wealthy men
 did grind the poore mens faces,
And greedily did prey on them,
 not pittying their cases :
They make them toyle and labour sore,
 for wages too too small :
The rich men in the Tavernes rore,
 but poore men pay for all.

Methought I saw an Usurer old
 walke in his Fox-fur'd gowne,
Whose wealth and eminence control'd
 the most men in the Towne :
His wealth he by extortion got,
 and rose by others fall,
He had what his hands earned not,
 but poor men pay for all.

Me thought I saw a Courtier proud,
 goe swaggering along,
That unto any scarce allow'd
 the office of his tongue :

Me thought wert not for bribery,
  his Peacocks plumes would fall,
He ruffles out in bravery,
  but poor men pay for all.

Me thought I met (sore discontent)
  some poore men on the way,
I asked one whither he went,
  so fast, and could not stay?
Quoth he, I must go take my Lease,
  or else another shall,
My Landlords riches doe increase,
  but poore men pay for all.

Me thought I saw most stately wives
  go jetting [1] on the way,
That live delightfull idle lives,
  and go in garments gay :
That with the men their shapes doe change,
  or else they'l chide and brawle,
Thus women goe like monsters strange,
  but poore men pay for all.

Me thought I was i' th' countrey
  where poore men take great paines,
And labour hard continually,
  onely for rich mens gaines :
Like th' Israelites in *Egypt*,
  the poore are kept in thrall,
The task-masters are playing kept,
  but poore men pay for all.

Me thought I saw poore Tradesmen
  i' th' City and else where,
Whom rich men keepe as beads-men,
  in bondage, care, and feare :
Thei'l have them worke for what they list,
  thus weakest goe to the wall,
The rich men eate and drinke the best
  but poore men pay for all.

        [1] Strutting.

Me thought I saw two Lawyers base
  one to another say,
We have had in hand this poore mans Case,
  a twelvemonth and a day;
And yet wee'l not contented be
  to let the matter fall,
Beare thou with me, & Ile beare with thee
  while poore men pay for all.

Me thought I saw a red-nose Oast,
  as fat as he could wallow,
Whose carkasse, if it should be roast,
  would drop seven stone of tallow:
He grows rich out of measure,
  with filling measure small,
He lives in mirth and pleasure,
  but poore men pay for all.

And so likewise the Brewer stout,
  the Chandler and the Baker,
The Mault man also without doubt,
  and the Tobacco taker,
Though they be proud and stately growne,
  and beare themselves so tall,
Yet to the world it is well knowne,
  that poore men pay for all.

Even as the mighty fishes still,
  doe feed upon the lesse;
So rich men, might they have ther will
  would on the poore man ceaze [1]
It is a proverbe old and true,
  that weakest goe to th' wall,
Rich men can drinke till th' sky looke blue,
  but poore men pay for all.

But now, as I before did say,
  this is but a Dreame indeed,
Though all dreames prove not true, some may
  hap right, as I doe reade.

[1] Seize.

And if that any come to passe,
I doubt this my Dreame shall;
For still tis found too true a case,
that poore men pay for all.

FINIS.

Printed at London for H. G.

A Witty answer of a Countrey fellow.

[52.] A Country fellow walking London Streets, and gazing up and down at every sight he saw, some mockt him, others pulled him by the Cloake, in so much he could not passe in quiet. He having as much wit, as the boyes knavery, thought hee would requite them for their kinde salutations, with something to laugh at, and to try their wits; and, comming to Paul's gate, where they sell pinnes and Needles, the boyes being very saucie, pulled him by the cloake, and one said. What lacke you friend? another, What lacke you Countryman? Quoth the fellow, minding to make himself some sport, I want a hood for a Humble Bee, or a payre of Spectacles for a blinde Beare: which so amazed the boy, that he had nothing to reply, and the Countrey Man went laughing away.

[32.] What is that which 20 will goe into a 'Tankard, and one will fill a Barn?
Solution. It is 20 Candles not lighted and one lighted.

[51.] A Sort of Clownes for loss which they sustain'd
By Souldiers, to the Captaine sore complain'd,
With dolefull wordes, and very woefull faces,
They Moov'd him to compassionate their Cases.
Good Sir (sayes one) I pray redress our wrong,
They that have done it, unto you belong;
Of all that eare we had we are bereft,
Except our very Shirts, theres nothing left.
The Captaine answer'd thus; Fellowes heare mee:
My Souldiers rob'd you not, I plainely see:

At your first speech, you made me somewhat sad,
But your last wordes resolv'd the doubt I had.
For they which rifled you left Shirts (you say)
And I am sure mine carry all away :
By this I know an errour you are in,
My Souldiers would have left you but your skin.

[4.] A brisk young Lady, seeing the Sheriff of a County who was a comely young Man, wait upon the Judge who was an old Man, was asked by one, which she had most mind to, the Judge or the Sheriff? She answered, the Sheriff. He asking the reason, she replied, *That she loved Judgement well, but Execution much better.*

[12.] One.did praise dead Beer,
Says his Friend, I fear
That you have a Worm in your Head ;
Why de'e praise dead Beer?
So must you too I swear,
We must all speak well of the dead.

[52.] It chanced, on a Bartholomew-day, when men keep Boothes in Smithfield, a Countrey Gentleman having some Store of money (and no lesse honesty) about him, comming to the Faire, would, amongst the rest needes view the pictures at that time hanging in the Cloysters, where was then much variety of postures, personages, stories, landskips, and such like, which carieth away the Senses, to a kinde of admiration for the present : and as he was thus gazing up and down, there comes a nimble diver (as at that time there resorts many) and closes with him, and quickly draws his purse forth of his pocket, and away he hies him presently : the Gentleman mist his purse, but knew not how to helpe himselfe. Going home to his lodging, and pondering in his minde how either to regain his losses, or to be revenged on the Pick-pocket, at length he bethought himself of this device : he caused an honest Taylor to sew a certain number of Fish hookes within, and round about the mouth of his pocket ; with the poynts of the hookes hanging downward, and the next day hies him to the same place, in another Countrey like habit, and baites his Pocket with more money, and there he stood gazing againe at the pictures, presently his former fish (or one of his fraternity) closes with him again, and dives, which the Gentleman being watchfull of, gives a slip aside and had presently strucke the nibling fish into the hand, and feeling him fast, begins to goe away, and the more he hastes away, the deeper the hookes went into the Divers hand, Oh, (quoth the Pick-pocket) how now Sir (quoth the Gentleman) what makes your hand in my Pocket? Pull it out I say : Oh Sir (quoth he) I beseech you be good to me : The people gathering together, imagined the Gentleman had an inchanted Pocket, and that the fellow had not power to pull forth his hand again, they would have him before the Justice. No (quoth the Gentleman) Ile carry him myselfe, so away he went (with the fellowes hand in his Pocket to a Taverne, with two or three of his friends, and told him what he had lost there the day before, and unlesse he would restore it, he would have him before a Justice : which match the fellow for feare of hanging, willingly condescended to surrender. And that ten pound, and ten shillings more towards the mending of his Pocket : so the Gentleman being well satisfied, ript forth his pocket, and away went the Cut-purse, who had so much picking worke to get out of his hands, he could not use his trade for a Moneth after.

[32.] I came to a tree where were apples, I eat no apples, I gave away no apples, nor I left no apples behind me : and yet I eat, gave away, and left behind me. *Solution.* There were three apples on the tree, for I eat one apple, gave away one apple, and left one. So I eat no apples, for I eat but one apple, which is no apples, and thus I gave away no apples, for I gave but one, and thus I left no apples for I left but one.

[5.]   When *Crassus* in his office was instal'd,
         For summs of money, which he yet doth owe,
         A client by the name of Clerk him Call'd,
         As he next day to Westminster did go.
         Which *Crassus* hearing, whispers thus in's eare,
         Sirrah, you now mistake, and much do erre,

That henceforth must the name of Clerke forbear,
And know I am become an Officer.
  Alas (quoth he) I did not so much marke,
  Good Mr Officer, that are no clerke.

[8.] When Sir *Thomas Moore* lived in the City of *London*, being one of the Justices of Peace, he used to go to the Sessions at *New-gate*, where it fell out that one of the ancientest Justices of the Bench was wont to chide the poor men whose purses had been cut, for not being more careful; telling them their negligence was the cause that so many cut-purses were brought thither, which when Sir *Thomas Moore* observed him so often to repeat at one time, especially; the night after, he sent for one of the chief Cut-purses that was in prison, and promised to save him harmless, and stand his friend too, if he would cut the aforesaid Justices Purse the next day as he sate on the Bench, and then presently make a sign of it to him : the fellow very gladly promiseth him to do it the next day ; therefore, when they sate again, that Thief was called among the first, who, being accused of his fact, said he did not doubt but that he could sufficiently excuse himself, if he were permitted to speak to some of the Bench in private. He was therefore bid to chuse one who he would, and presently he chose that grave old man, who then had his pouch at his girdle, as they wore them in those dayes; and whilst he whispered him in the ear, he cunningly cut his purse, and then solemnly taking his leave, returns to his place. Sir *Thomas* knowing by a private sign, that the business was dispatcht, presently took occasion to move the Bench to distribute some alms to a poor needy fellow that was there, and for good example began himself to do it ; when the old man came to open his purse, and sees it cut away, and, much wondering, said he was confident he brought it with him when he came thither that morning, Sir *Thomas* replied presently, *What ! will you charge any of us with felony ?* But his choler rising, and he being ashamed of the thing, Sir *Thomas* calls the Cut-purse and bids him give him his purse again, and withal advised the good old Justice hereafter *Not to be so bitter a censurer of innocent mens negligence, when as himself could not secure his purse in that open assembly.*

A merry Jest of *John Tomson* and *Jakaman* his Wife
Whose Jealousie was justly the cause of all their strife.

To the Tune of *Pegge of Ramsey.*[1]

[57.] When I was a Batchelour
    I liv'd a merry life,
But now I am a married man,
    and troubled with a wife,
I cannot doe as I have done,
    because I live in feare,
If I goe but to *Islington*,
    my wife is watching there
Give me my yellow Hose againe,
    give me my yellow hose ;
For now my wife she watcheth me,
    see yonder where she goes.

But when I was a prentice bound,
    and my Indentures made :
In many faults I have beene found
    yet never thus afraid.

[1] For tune, see Appendix.

For if I chance now by the way
    a woman for to kisse,
The rest are ready for to say
    thy Wife shall know of this.
        Give me my yellow Hose &c.

Thus when I come in company
    I passe my mirth in feare,
For one or other merrily,
    will say my wife is there.
And then my look doth make them laugh,
    to see my wofull case :
How I stand like *John hold my staffe,*
    and dare not shew my face.
        Give me my yellow Hose &c.

There comes a handsome woman in,
    and shakes me by the hand :
But how my wife she did begin,
    now you shall understand.
Faire dame (quoth she) why dost thou so?
    he gave his hand to me :
And thou shalt know before thou go,
    he is no man for thee.
        Give me my yellow Hose &c.

Good wife (quoth she) now doe not scould,
    I will doe so no more ;
I thought I might have beene so bolde
    I knowing him before.
With that my wife was almost mad,
    yet many did intreat her ;
And I, God knowes, was very sad,
    for feare she would have beat her.
        Give me my yellow Hose &c.

Thus marriage is an enterprise
    experience doth show ;
But scolding is an exercise,
    that married men doe know.

For all this while there was no blowes,
    yet still their tongues was talking;
And very fain would yellow hose
    have had her fists a walking.
          Give me my yellow Hose &c.

In comes a neighbour of our towne,
    an honest man, God wot :
And he must needes goe sit him downe,
    and call in for his pot.
And said to me, I am the man
    which gave to you your wife,
And I will doe the best I can,
    to mend this wicked life.
          Give me my yellow Hose &c.

I gave him thankes, and bad him goe,
    and so he did indeed,
And told my wife she was a shrow,
    but that was more than need.
Saith he, thou hast an honest man,
    and one that loves thee well;
Said she, you are a foole, good sir,
    It's more than you can tell.
          Give me my yellow Hose &c.

And yet in truth he loveth me,
    but many more beside ;
And I may say, good Sir, to thee,
    that I cannot abide,
For though he loves me as his life
    yet now, sir, wot you what,
They say he loves his neighbours wife,
    I pray you how like you that.
          Give me my yellow Hose &c.

Saith he, I hope I never shall
    seeke fancy fond to follow,
For love is lawfull unto all
    except it be too yellow.

Which lyeth like the Jaundies so,
   in these our Women's faces ;
That watch their husbands where they go
   and hunt them out in places.
     Give me my yellow Hose &c.

Now comes my Neighbour's wife apace,
   to talke a word or two,
My wife then meets her face to face,
   and saith, dame, is it you
That makes so much of my good man,
   as if he were your owne ?
Then clamp as closely as you can,
   I know it will be known.
     Give me my yellow hose &c.

Now when I saw the woman gone,
   I call'd my wife aside,
And said why art thou such a one,
   that thou canst not abide
A woman for to talke with mee,
   this is a wofull case,
That I must keepe no company
   except you be in place.
     Give me my yellow hose &c.

This maketh Batchelers to wooe
   so long before they wed,
Because they heare that women now
   will be their husband's head.
And seven yeare long I tarried
   for Jakaman my wife,
But now that I am married
   I am weary of my life.
     Give me my yellow hose &c.

For yellow love is too, too bad,
   without all wit or policie,
And too much love hath made her mad,
   and fill'd her full of Jelousie.

L

She thinkes I am in love with those
   I speake to passing by
That makes her wear the yellow hose
   I gave her for to dye.
        Give me my yellow Hose &c.

But now I see shee is so hot
   and lives so much at ease,
I will goe get a Souldiers coate,
   and sayle beyond the Seas ;
To serve my Captain where and whan,
   though it be to my paine,
Thus farewell gentle Jakaman,
   till we two meet againe.
        Give me my yellow Hose &c.

Quoth she, good husband, doe not deale
   thus hardly now with me,
And of a truth, I will reveale
   my cause of jealousie :
You know I alwaies paid the score,
   you put me still in trust,
I saved twenty pound and more,
   confesse it needes I must.
        Give me my yellow Hose &c.

But now my saving of the same,
   for aught that I doe know ;
Made Jelousie to fire her frame,
   to weave this web of woe :
And thus this foolish love of mine
   was very fondly bent,
But now my gold and goods are thine,
   good husband, be content.
        Give me my yellow Hose &c.

And thus to lead my life a new,
   I fully now purpose ;
That thou maist change thy coat of blew,
   and I my yellow hose.

This being done, our Country wives
 may warning take by me,
How they doe live such jealous lives,
 as I have done with thee.
 Give me my yellow Hose &c.

 M. L.

Imprinted at London for Edward Wright.[1]—

[17.] Two riding down a great hill together, one said, it was dangerous riding down : No, says t'other, I will not light ; for I have but one pair of shooes, and I shall spoil 'em : says the other, and I have but one neck, and I fear I shall spoil that, and therefore I'l. light.

[12.]   One hung a dirty sheet
    On a pale in the street,
  And there it did hang all the day
   But 'twas stole at Night,
   Says the Man, by this light
  They have stole it clean away.

[5.2.] Three loytring companions that fell in company together, domineered and swaggered so long, that all their mony was quite consumed and gone. So being pennilesse, and having little or no credit at all left, one of them said, Wee are now in a faire taking : for we may, if we please seek our Dinners with Duke *Humphry*, Nay, hold (quoth the second) If I come where any presse of people be, I can get mony enough for us all. And I (quoth the third) can as easily assemble people. They were at that time not much above two miles from a small Towne in Bark shire, where, when as thither they came, there was a new Pillory, newly set up, which the third of them seeing, steps to the Bailiffe,

1 Edward Wright lived at Christ Church Gate, and published between 1620 and 1655, at which date he assigns to W. Gilbertson.

and desires him to have the first turn at their new Pillory.
The Bailiffe, being a Butcher, was half amazed, and standing
a while musing, at the last asked counsell of his honest
neighbours, and they bad him set up the knave and spare
not.   So he makes no more a doe, but up he went, and
when he was up, he looked about, and saw his two fellow
Cheaters busie with their hands in the holes of the Butcher's
aprons, where they put all their money.   To it, to it (quoth
he) apace.   The people laughed heartily to see him stand
there.   At last, when he saw that his fellows had sped their
matters, and were going away, he said to the Bailiffe, Turn
the Pillory about, and now I will come down.   So he, laughing heartily, did.   And when he was come down, the Bailiffe
said, now art thou an honest good fellow, and because thou
hast made us some sport, I will give thee a Teaster to drink ;
and, thinking to take some money out of the hole of his
apron, he found there never a penny.   Cockes armes, quoth
the Bailiffe, my money is picked out of my apron ; and then
the rest of the Butcher's besides swore they had lost theirs
also.   I hope, quoth the fellow, you do not think that I have it.
No, certainly, quoth the Bailiffe, I know well enough thou
hast it not ; for thou wert on the pillory all the while.   Why
then no harm, for I did it to make you merry, quoth the
fellow, and so went his wayes.

[51.]   Gentlemen that approch about my Stall,
        To most rare Phisicke I invite you all ;
        Come neere and harken what I have to sell,
        And deale with mee all those that are not well.
        In this Boxe heere, I have such precious stuffe,
        To give it prayse, I have not words enuffe :
        If any Humour in your Braines be crept,
        I'le fetch it out, as if your heads were swept.
        Almost through *Europe* I have shewne my face
        In every Towne, and every Market-place—
        Behold this salve, (I do not use to lye)
        Whole Hospitals there have been curde thereby.
        I doe not stand heere like a tattar'd slave,
        My Velvet, and my Chaine of Gold I have :

Which cannot be maintained by mens lookes;
Friends, all your Towne is hardly worth my Bookes.
There stands my Coach and Horses, t'is mine owne;
From hence to *Turkie* is my credite knowne:
In sooth I cannot boast, as many will,
Let nothing speake for mee, but onely skill.
See you that thing like Ginger-bread lies there.
My tongue cannot expresse to any eare
The sundrie vertues that it doth containe,
Or number halfe the Wormes that it hath slaine.
If in your Bellies there be crawlers bred
In multitudes like Haires upon your head,
Within some howers space, or there about,
At all the holes you have, I'le fetch them out,
And ferret them before that I have done,
Even like the Hare that foorth a Bush doth run.
Heere is a wond'rous Water for the Eye;
This for the Stomacke: Maisters will you buy?
When I am gone, you will repent too late,
And then (like fooles) among yourselves will prate,
Oh that we had that famous Man againe,
When I shall be suppli'd in *France* or *Spaine:*
Now, for a *Stater*,[1] you a Box shall have
That will the lives of halfe a dozen save.
My man has come, and in mine eare he sayes
At home for me at least an hundred stayes,
All Gentlemen; yet for your Good, you see,
I make them tarry, and attend for mee.
If that you have no Money, let me know,
Phisicke of almes upon you Ile bestow.
What Doctor in the world can offer more?
Such arrant Clownes I never knew before:
Heere you doe stand like Owles and gaze on mee,
But not a Penny from you I can see.
A man shall come to doe such Dunces good,
And cannot have his meaning understood?
To talke to senselesse people is in vaine,

---

[1] A "façon de parler;" a stater really was a tetradrachm in silver,
and was worth about half a crown.

I'le see you hang'd ere I'le come heere againe :
Be all diseas'd as bad as Horses be
And die in ditches like to Dogges, for me !
An Old-wives-medicine, Parseley, Time and Sage,
Will serve such Buzzards in this scurvey age :
Goose grease and Fennell, with a few Dog-dates,
Is excellent for such base lowzey mates :
Farewell, some Hempton [1] halter be the Charme,
To stretch your neckes as long as is mine arme.

The following is a satire on card-playing, which, doubtless, was carried to excess by the Cavaliers in Charles I.'s time.

[58.]

Pafs my aple gainſt thy mouſe jle lay
The gams miſne jfth aſt n ēr a tramp to play
Miſter apes ſace th art deceiud in mee
Thaue many trumpshers ons duſt ſee

For a pint of wine the drawer call
I come oprittie d'ye ſee this ſquall
Apes and Catts to play at cards are fitt
Then & women ought to heue more witt

[59.] A Continuation of a Catalogue of Ladies to be set up by AUCTION, on *Monday* the 6th of this Instant *July.*

Catalogues are distributed by the Booksellers of *London*
& *Westminster.*

---

[1] Hempen.

Conditions of Sale.

First. He who bids most is the Buyer, and if any Difference arises, she is to be put up again.

Secondly. That no Person shall bid less than £500 the first Proposal, and always advance £100.

Thirdly. That all of them shall be bound up in Silks; and if any shall happen to be otherwise, the Party that buys them shall be at Liberty to take them away or leave them.

By *E. Cl——r* Auctioneer that sold the young Heiress in *Q—— Street.*

		£
1.	One brisk Underbuilt young Widdow near *Temple Bar*	1000
2.	A Buxome young Maid of 19 years of age, who stinks of powder, by the same *Barr*, provided her Father hath not given the £800 to the Poor, will be worth	2000
3.	A Vintner's Widdow, who formerly lived against *St Dunstan's* Church, by reason of her non-Reputation	500
4.	Three Sisters in *Shier Lane* very brisk, but 2nd hand, and go for Maids, each	800
5.	An old Maiden-Sempstress in Fleet Street.	500
6.	A Booksellers only Daughter in *St Paul's* Church Yard, if her Fathers Debts be all paid, value.	1600
7.	A rich Widdow, Humptback, and crooked Legs, who has buried 2 Husb.	1900
8.	A Country Farmer's Daughter, lately come to town, and lodges in *Essex Street*, a good face, but an ugly gate.	1100
9.	A famous Conventicler's Daughter, near *Covent Garden*, provided he has a good gathering this year, will give her	1500
10.	A Councellor's Daughter in the *Temple*, very well accomplished, only loves Brandy	2300
11.	An *Irish* Lady, very tall, aged 16.	2700
12.	A Soliciters Daughter, not streight but a good Face.	4000

13. Two Sisters, tall handsome Women, lodging by   £
     Shooe Lane, each   1000

14. A Plummers Daughter, in *Fleet Street*, brisk and
     airy, not to be bought under a Coach and 6.   1200

15. A Taylor's Daughter in the same Court, with a
     Flaxen Tow'r to cover her Carret head, worth   800

16. A Fat Widdow of *St Brides* Parish, she is but a
     little foolish, a Lumping Penny worth,   200

17. An Ale house keepers Daughter in *Bell-yard*, worth   0000
     (To advance a Cravat String of 18ᵈ each bidding)

18. A Barbers Wife near *St Dunstans* Church, lately
     divorced from her Husband, a pretty Woman,
     and fit for service.   What you please

19. The Widdow of the Famous *Dr S——fold*, late
     Student in Physick Astrology and Poetry, besides
     her Talent in a Napkin.   200 per. Ann.

20. A young Orphan, Right Honourable by the Fathers
     side, and Right by the Mothers   3000

     [12.]   One a Licence had got
           For to begg, God wot,
    And of a poor Scholar begg'd a Doller ;
         Thou hast Lice I do fear,
         But no sence, I swear,
    For to begg of a very poor Scholar.

[18.] An Author's House being on fire whilst he was poring on his Books, he called to his Wife and bad her look to it. *You know*, says he, *I don't concern myself with the household.*

[17.] One parting a Fray, was cut into the Scul : says the Surgeon, Sir, one may see your brains: Nay then I'l be hang'd, says he, for if I had had any brains, I had never come there.

[17.] A Gentleman losing his way galloping furiously over the plow'd Lands towards *Tame*, and meeting one, said, Friend is this the way to *Tame?* Yes Sir, says he, your Horse, if he be as wild as the Devil.

THE VIRGIN RACE
Or, York-shires Glory.

Being an Account of a Race lately Run at *Temple-Newnham-Green;* None being admitted to run, but such as were supposed Virgins. The first that came to the two Miles-Race end, was to have a Silver Spoon, the second, a silver bodkin, the third a Silver Thimble, and the fourth Nothing at all.

Tune is, *a New Game at Cards.*

[60.] You that do desire to hear,
Of a Virgin Race run in *York-Shire,*
Come and Listen, I'le declare,
Such News before, you never did hear ;
    For I think since the World begun
    But seldom Virgins Races run.

Four Virgins that supposed were
A Race did run I now declare,
Sure such a Race was never seen,
As this at *Temple Newnham Green.*
    In half-shirts & Drawers these Maids did run
    But Bonny *Nan* the Race has won

A Silver Spoon this *Nan* obtain'd
The next a Silver Bodkin gain'd
The third that was not quite so nimble,
Was to have a Silver Thimble ;
    And she that was the last of all.
    Nothing unto her share did fall.

In Drawers Red *Ann Clayton* run,
And she it was the Race that won ;
Pegg Hall as I may tell to you,
Did run in Drawers that were Blew ;
    Honest *Alice Hall* that was the third,
    Her Drawers were white upon my word.

A concourse great of People were
For to behold these Virgins there,
Who so well acted the Mans part,
And love a Man with all their heart ;
    But what means this, for well we know
    Maids through the Nation all do so.

Now let us come to Bonny *Nan*,
Who won a Race once of a man,
In *Bassing Hall Street* he did dwell
His name was *Luke*, 'tis known full well ;
    And let me now declare to you,
    At something else she'l beat him too.

Let none the *York-shire* Girls despise
Who are so Active now a days,
So brisk and nimble they do grow,
That few can match them, I do know :
    Then let us stand up for *York shire*,
    Those Country Girls I love most dear.

A *York shire* Girl who can outvie,
No City Girls can them come nigh,
They've Rosey Blushes in their Cheeks,
While City Girls are Green as Leeks,
This with my fancy will agree
A *York shire* Girl shall be for me.

Then here's a Health to a *York shire* Girl,
For in my eye she is a Pearl
Whose Beauty doth so charm mine eye,
That for her I would freely dye.
Her virtues do her face adorn,
And makes her look fresh as the Morn.

Now to conclude unto my friend
These Lines I freely recommend;
Advising him above the rest,
To love a *Yorkshire* Girl the best;
But let him use his skill for I
Will love a *Yorkshire* Girl until I dye

FINIS

Printed for J Wright, J Clark, W Thackeray, and T. Passinger—

[61.] There were two good fellows of ancient society (who had not seen one another in a great space of tyme) that one morning very luckily met each other in *Budge Row*, and after some signes of gladnesse to meet so happily, they agreed upon a mornings draught, which lasted almost till noon, in which time they were both sufficiently liquor'd. But their bellies being fuller than their brains, they did resolve to bring up the rear of that morning's action with a Cup of Canary; away they went to the Swan Tavern at *Dowgate*, where for three hours longer they sat pecking at one another, like two Game Cocks at the end of a battaile, untill both their Eyes were in a very glimmering Condition. In the mean time, whilst they were thus toaping, there fell an exceeding violent and continuing glut of Rain, so that it flowed up to the threshold of the Tavern door, and no passenger could get over: By this time my good fellows having call'd, and paid the reckoning, they both came reeling to the door, and seeing so broad a water tumbled down *Dowgate*, one of them swore it was the Thames, and began to call a Sculler; the other being unwilling to engage further, said he would take his leave, which he did with so low a bending Complement, that his britch touching a little too hard against the stump of a post which was behind him, that it made him rebound into the middle of the stream with his head forward. The unfortunate fellow was no sooner in, but he began to stretch forth his Armes and Leggs to swim; the other which stood upon the shore, cryed out lamentably for the danger of his friend, and deploring the loss of so good a fellow, and what loss his Wife and Children would suffer in his death. But in conclusion (as the last word of Comfort) he calls out to him in these words. Dost thou hear Friend! Friend! if thou canst but Gaine *Temple Staire's* thou wilt be safe, I warrant thee, unto which the swimming man made reply. A pox of Gaine, I do not think of Gaine, if I can but save myself, I care not.

Quidam erat.

[5.] A preaching fryar there was, who thus began,
The Scripture saith there was a certaine man :
A certaine man? but I do read no where,
Of any certaine woman[1] mention'd there :
A certaine man, a phrase in Scripture common,
But no place shewes there was a Certaine Woman :
And fit it is, that we should ground our faith
On nothing more than what the Scripture saith.

[12.]   A fellow once said
He would ne're keep his Bed,
Though sick, I heard him to tell it,
And his Reason was,
Nay I know the Cause,
For he still had a mind to Sell it.

---

[1] This is hardly warranted by fact. See Mark xii. 42 ; Luke xi. 27 ; Luke xxiv. 22.

[26.] A great *German* Prince, that was much addicted to Drinking, had drank so much one day, that the next he was very sick ; then his Fool came in to him and askt him, why he was so melancholly ? he told him his Sickness was occasion'd by drinking yesterday : Why then, says the Fool, if that be all, I'll be your Physician ; that is, if you are ill with drinking one day, take a Hare of the same Dog. Well, says the Prince, and what the second day ? The Fool told him the same again : And what the third day ? the same too. And what at the fourth ? Why the same. We'll come to the purpose, says he, and what the fifth day ? Why Faith, says he, then you'll be as arrant a Fool as I am.

Mercurius Matrimonialis

or

Chapmen for the Ladies lately
Offered to Sale by Way of Auction.

(procured by one of their own Sex)

[62.] 1. A Country Gentleman, who has a very delicate Seat between 20 and 30 Miles off *London*, and a very considerable Estate, a very Proper Comely Person, but not very Witty.

2. A Linnen Draper near the Stocks *Market*, a very handsome Genteel Man.

3. A Milliner on the *Royal Exchange*, much admired for his Handsomness and Gentility.

4. A Clergyman near *Exeter*, but now in Town, a pretty Black Man, a very good Scholar, proposes for a Joynture £200 per Ann. in Free-land.

5. A Bookseller near the *Exchange* a very Sober Man, a Man of a Good Trade, besides some Estate.

6. A Linnen Drapers Son in *Cornhill*, a very pretty genteel Man, his Father a Man of a very good Estate.

7. A Goldsmith behind the *Exchange*—so, so.—

8. A Miliner in *Cheapside*, near the end of *Bread Street*, very genteel but no conjurer.

9. For the Brewers Daughter, a Lace Man in *Pater Noster Row*, who loves the smell of Malt and good Ale, of good heighth and Stature, and Stomach answerable.

10. A Coffee Man, well lin'd with Broad Pieces of Gold, and has a good Trade, a Widdower, wants a Bar keeper.

11. A lusty, stout proportion'd Man, had a good Estate before the Fire,[1] and is still fit for Woman's Service.

12. A Bookseller's Son in *Paul's Church yard*, an extream Genteel man, and of the same kidney as the Mercer in *Covent Garden*.

13. A Commission Officer, full of Courage, brim full of Honour, a well proportion'd Man, and very beautiful and yet wants Money.

14. An Apothecary near *Bread Street Hill*, a very genteel Man, a Widdower.

15. A Young Gentleman now learning to Dance, wants a Wife to guide him, his Estate £150 per Ann.

16. A Haberdasher's Son in *Cheapside*, makes a great Figure in the World, his Education good, only wants a Wife, or Place.

17. A diminutive Bookseller, very difficult in his Choice, £5000 proves a Temptation to him.

18. A Mercer upon *Ludgate Hill*, Kin to a good Estate, his Trade indifferent:

19. A young Merchant, whose Estate lyes on the *Carriby Islands*, if his Cargo misses the *French Fleet*, he makes a good Joynture.

20. An Ancient Gentleman now purchasing an Estate, wants a rich Wife to stand by him.

21. A Goldsmith near the *Royal Exchange*, a Widdower, of a very considerable Estate, besides a great Trade, will make a good Joynture, and perhaps keep a Coach, he's a very brisk Man.

---

[1] Although this "squib" is not dated, this allusion makes it probable it was written in Charles II.'s time.

[51.]   One Climbing of a Tree, by hap,
        Fell downe and brake his arme,
        And did complaine unto a friend,
        Of his unluckie harme.
        Would I had counsel'd you before,
        (quoth he to whom he spake)
        I know a tricke for Climbers, that
        They never hurt shall take.
        Neighbour (sayd he) I have a Sonne,
        And he doth use to climbe,
        Pray let me know the same for him
        Against another time?
        Why thus, (quoth he) let any man
        That lives, climbe nere so hie,
        And make no more haste downe, than up,
        No harme can come thereby.

[61.] A Gentleman who had constantly beene a good fellow, meeting with some of his friends at a mornings draught, told his Companions that, God forgive him, *he went to bed like a beast* last night. Why? quoth they, were you so *drunk?* No, quoth he, *I was so sober.*

SELDOME CLEANELY [1]

or

A merry new Ditty, wherein you may see,
The tricke of a Huswife, in every degree.
Then lend your attention while I doe unfold
As pleasant a story as you have heard told.

    To the Tune of *Upon a Summers time.*

[63.]   Draw neere you Countrey Girles
        and lissen unto me,
      Ile tell you here a new conceit
        concerning Huswifery,
        concerning Huswifery.

      [1] For tune, see Appendix.

Three Aunts I had of late,
　　good Huswifes all were they,
But cruell death hath taken
　　the best of them away,
　　O the best &c—

O this was one of my Aunts,
　　the best of all the three,
And surely though I say it myselfe
　　a cleanly woman was she,
　　a cleanly &c.

My Uncle carelesse was
　　in wasting of his store,
Which made my Aunt to have a care
　　to looke about the more,
　　to looke &c—

When Winter time drew on
　　neere to All hollow day :

My Aunt did cast her wits about
　　to save her Straw and Hay.
　　to save &c—

And like a provident woman,
　　as plainely did apeare,
She starv'd her Bullockes to save her Hay,
　　untill another yeare.
O this was one of my Aunts,
　　the best of all the three
And surely, though I say't myselfe
　　a provident woman was shee.

But as she went to see
　　her cattell in the fields :
When she comes home, two pound of durt
　　hang dragling at her heeles.
O this &c

And there she let it hang
　　from Candlemas to May,
And then shee tooke a hatchet in hand,
　　and chopt it cleane away.
O this &c

In making of a cheese
　　my Aunt shewed her cunning,
Such perfit skill shee had at will,
　　shee never used running.[1]
O this &c

For having strain'd her milke
　　in turning once about,
Shee had the best Curd that ever you saw
　　by the sent [2] of the strayning clout.
O this &c

---

[1] Rennet.　　　　　[2] Scent.

M

Shee was the choysest Nurse
　　that lived in all the West;
Her face was white as the charcoal flower
　　so was her neck and brest.
O this was one of my Aunts,
　　the best of all the three,
And surely, though I say't myselfe,
　　a cleanly good Nurse was shee.

The garments which she did weare
　　did shine like the brazen Crock,
And where she went, she bore such a sent
　　that the flyes blew in her frock.
O this &c ·

My Aunt so curious was,
　　as I to you may tell,
She used to make fat puddings
　　in markets for to sell.
O this &c

The smallest Candle end
　　my Aunt would never lose
It would helpe to make her puddings fat
　　with the droppings of her nose.
O this &c
　　　　·

Another trick she had
　　as I shall now declare,
Shee never swept the house,
　　about foure times a yeare.
O this &c

And when she swept the Hall,
　　the Parler or the Spence,
The dust was worth to her at least.
　　a shilling or 14 pence.
O this &c

One day my Aunt was set
   by the fier side a spinning,
As she knew well what was to do
   to wollen or to linnen.
O this &c

A change came in her minde,
   her worke being in great hast,
She burn'd her Tow, her Wheele and all
   because she would make no wast.
O this &c

My Aunt so patient was
   of this I dare be bold,
That with her Neighbours shee
   was never knowne to scolde.
O this &c

Her lips with lothsome words
   she seldome would defile,
But sometimes she would whisper so loud
   you might heare her half a mile
O this &c

Yet one condition more
   unto you I will show,
Shee washt her dishes once a moneth,
   and set them on a row.
O this &c

If other wise she had
   but of a dish clout faile,
She would set them to the Dog to lick
   and wipe them with his tayle.
O this &c

But to conclude in hast,
   I hold it not amisse,
I love a cleanly huswife well
   as may appeare by this.

O this was one of my Aunts
the best of all the three,
And surely, though I say't myselfe,
a cleanely woman was she.   L. P [1]

FINIS.

London.   Printed for John Wright *junior*,[2] dwelling at the
upper end of the Old Baily.

Astrology (in the middle of the seventeenth century) was
beginning to fall into disrepute, and Butler, in *Hudibras*, as

well as Ben Jonson in *The Alchemist*, satirised unmercifully
both the science and its professors.   The accompanying
engraving "The Astrologer's Bugg Beare" refers to an eclipse
of the sun, an event, which even at that time was considered of
dire portent.   Take the title of one tract as a sample.   [3]"The
Shepherds Prognostication, Foretelling the sad and strange
Eclipse of the Sun, which will happen on the 29 of March

---

[1] ? Laurence Price.   ·   [2] He published from 1641 to 1683.
[3] Brit. Mus. Cat. $\frac{E. 1351.}{1}$

this present year 1652. which Eclipse will begin about eight of the Clock in the fore noon, and so continue till past the hour of eleven, which will be the dismallest day that ever was known since the year 33, when our Savior Christ suffered on the Crosse for the sins of Mankind, at which time the Seas did roare, the earth did quake, the graves did open, the temple rent from the top to the bottom, *Luke* 23. 45. And there was a darknesse over all the Land. This Prediction also foretells of many strange Presages and Passages which will follow after that horrible Eclipse of the Sun, and what will insue. With a perfect way whereby to avoid the insuing danger. By L. P." (? Laurence Price.) And the contents of the tract fully bears out its title.

But "L. P.," whoever he was, entered thoroughly into the joke of the thing, and, when it was all over, wrote a book, teeming with quiet satire, which was published on 9th April 1652, called—

The Astrologer's Bugg Beare.

[64.] In his little tract he chaffs the people most un-mercifully, yet very quietly, at times so much so that one might almost think it written in earnest. For instance : "A Usurer that was to receive money of a country man that was his debter on that day, durst not to venter fourth of his house; by which meanes the man rid forth out of London and paid not in his moneyes, for which cause the Usurer was about to cut his own throat, and had don it, if he had not bin prevented by some of his Neighboures.

Some other Christians were so fearefull of what would befall, that they sent their maids two dayes before Black monday for to fetch in faire water in a redynesse to wash, fearing that the ayre would infect the water.

Some tooke Medicines, Pils, and Antidotes, which was administred unto them by a supposed out landish doctor, which he had set bils for in severall places, caling his Medicines, an Antidote against the tirrible Eclipes of the Sun, so he got money, and they went away as wise as wood-cockes."

Ben Jonson, in "The Alchemist" gives a very vivid and amusing picture of an astrologer and his gull. Act 1, Scene 3. Subtle (the astrologer), Face (his agent), Drugger (a tobacconist).

[65.] *Subtle.* What is your name, say you, *Abel Drugger ?*
Drugger.   Yes Sir,
Sub.   A Seller of *Tobacco ?*
Dru.   Yes, Sir
Sub.   'Umh,
     Free of the Grocers ?[1]
Dru.   I, and't please you.
Sub.   Well,
     Your business *Abel ?*
Dru.   This, and't please your Worship,
     I am a yong beginner, and am building
     Of a new shop, and't like your worship, just
     At Corner of a Street : (Here's the plot on't.)
     And I would know, by art, Sir, of your Worship,
     Which way I should make my dore, by *Necromancie.*
     And where my Shelves. And which should be for Boxes,
     And which for Potts. I would be glad to thrive, Sir,
     And, I was wish'd to your Worship by a Gentleman,
     One Captaine *Face,* that say's you know mens *Planets,*
     And their good *Angels,* and their bad.
Sub.   I doe
     If I do see 'hem.[2]
Face.   What ! my honest *Abel ?*
     Thou art well met here.
Dru.   Troth, Sir, I was speaking
     Just as your Worship came here, of your Worship.
     I pray you, speake for me to Mr Doctor.
Face. He shall doe anything. Doctor, doe you heare ?
     This is my friend, *Abel,* 'an honest fellow.

     .   .   .   .   .

Sub. H'is a fortunate fellow, that I am sure on.

     [1] Company.
     [2] A play upon the word. Subtle meaning the gold coin called an Angel, value 10s.

Face. Already, Sir, ha' you found it? Lo' the *Abel*!

Sub. And in right way to'ward riches.

Face.   Sir!

Sub.   This Summer
He will be of the Clothing[1] of his Company.
And, next spring, call'd to the Scarlet.[2] Spend what
    he can.

Face. What, and so little Beard?

Sub.   Sir, you must thinke,
He may have a receipt to make hayre come.
But he'll be wise, preserve his youth, and fine[3] for't.
His fortune lookes for him, another way.

Face. 'Slid, Doctor, how canst thou know this so soone?
I am amus'd at that!

Sub.   By a rule, Captayne
In *Metaposcopie* which I doe worke by,
A certaine Starre i' the forehead, which you see not.
Your Chest-nut, or your Olive colourd face
Do's never fayle; and your long Eare doth promise.
I knew't, by certaine spotts too, in his teeth,
And on the nayle of his *Mercurial* finger.

Face. Which finger's that?

Sub.   His little finger, Looke.
Yo' were borne upon a Wensday.

Drug.   Yes, indeed, Sir.

Sub. The Thumbe, in *Chiromantie*, we give *Venus*;
The Fore-finger to *Iove*; the Midst, to *Saturne*;
The Ring to *Sol*, the Least to Mercurie,
Who was the Lord, Sir, of his *Horoscope*,
His *House of Life* being *Libra*. Which foreshew'd
He should be a Marchant, and should trade with
    Ballance.

Face. Why, this is strange! Is't not, honest *Nab*?

Sub. There is a Ship now, comming from Ormu's,
That shall yeeld him such a Commoditie
Of Drugs. This is the West, and this the South?

Drug. Yes Sir.

---

[1] *i.e.* be made a liveryman.   [2] Made sheriff.
[3] Pay the penalty instead of serving.

Sub.   And those are your two sides !
Drug.   I, Sir.
Sub. Make me your Dore, then, South ; your broad side,
      West ;
      And, on the East-side of your shop, aloft,
      Write *Mathlaj*, *Tarmiel*, and *Baraborat*
      Upon the North-part *Rael*, *Velel*, *Thiel*,
      These are the names of those *Mercurian* Spirits,
      That doe fright flyes from boxes.
Drug.   Yes Sir,
Sub.   And
      Beneath your threshold, bury me a Loade stone
      To draw in Gallants that weare spurres ; The rest
      Theyll seeme to follow."

In this play, too, Alchemy is scarified, as is also the Puritanism of the age.

[12.]   A very drunken Sot
             The Hickock had got,
      Cause he drank *Rosa Solis* and *Aqua Vitæ* ;
            Such Latine drink that he
            Declines *Hic*, *Hoc*, very free,
      But such English words as wou'd frignt ye.

[52.] A poore man travelling from door to coor a begging, being lately come from *Paris*, a City in *France* being invited by hunger to a good simple Country Swain's doore, to aske his almes ; his wife asked him what he was, and from whence he came ? Quoth the fellow, from *Paris*. From *Paradise* (quoth she) then thou knowest my old *John* there (meaning her former husband) I, quoth the fellow, that I doe. I pray thee (quoth she) how doth he doe ? Faith (quoth the fellow) poore, he hath meat and drinke enough, but vants cloathes and mony. Alas, quoth she, I am sory for i, I pray thee stay a little ; and, running up into her Chamber, fetcht downe her husbands new sute of cloathes, and five shilings in mony, and gave it to the fellow, saying, I pray thee renember me to my poore *John*, and give him this sute of clothes, and five shillings from me, and wrapt them up in a Fardle,[1] which the fellow took, and away he went. Presently her husband came home, and found her very pleasant and merry, singing up and downe the house, which she seldome used to doe, and he asked her the cause, Oh, husband, quoth she, I have heard from my old *John* to-day, he is in Paradise, and is very well, but wants clothes and mony, but I have sent him thy best sute, and five shillings in mony. Her husband seeing she was cozened, enquired of her which way the fellow went that had them. Yonder way, quoth she: he presently took his best horse, Hob, and rode after him for the clothes. The fellow seeing one ride so fast after him, threw the clothes into a ditch, and went softly forward; her husband overtaking the fellow, said, Didst not see one go this way with a little fardle of clothes at his back? Yes, quoth the fellow, he is newly gone into yonder little Wood. Oh, hold my horse, quoth he, whilst I runne in and finde him out. I will, quoth the fellow, who presently, as soon as he was gone into the wood, took up his fardell, leapt on horseback, and away he went: The Man returning for his horse, his horse was gone; then going home to his wife, she asked him if he overtook the fellow. I, sweet heart, quoth he, and I have lent him my best horse to ride on, for it is a great long way to Paradise. Truly, husband, quoth she, and I shall love thee the better so long as I live, for making so much of my old *John*. Which caused much good laughter to all that heard it.

[5.]   Tom vow'd to beat his boy against the wall,
    And as he strucke, he forth-with caught a fall:
    The boy deriding said, I doe averre,
    Y'have done a thing, you cannot stand to, Sir.

[32.] What is that goeth about the wood and cannot get in?
Solution. It is the bark of a tree, for never is the bark within the tree, but alwayes without.

              [1] A bundle.

The country-mans lamentation for the death of his *cow*.

A Country Swain, of little wit, one day,
Did kill his Cow, because she went astray :
What's that to I or You, she was his own,
But now the Ass for his Cow doth moan :
Most piteously methink he cries in vain,
For now his Cow's free from hunger and pain :
What ails the fool to make so great a stir,
She cannot come to him, he may to her.

To a pleasant Country Tune, called *Colly my Cow.*

[66.]   Little *Tom Dogget*
          what dost thou mean,
        To kill thy poor Colly,
          now she's so lean :
        Sing Oh poor Colly,
          Colly my Cow,
        For Colly will give me
          no more milk now.

Pruh high, pruh hoe,
Pruh high, pruh, hoe,
Pruh, Pruh, pruh, pruh, pruh, pruh, pruh,
Tal lal daw.

I had better have kept her,
   till fatter she had been,
For now I confess,
   she's a little too lean :
Sing Oh &c—

First in comes the Tanner,
   with his Sword by his side,
And he bids me five Shillings,
   for my Cow's Hide :
Sing Oh &c

Then in comes the Tallow Chandler,
   whose brains were but shallow,
And he bids me two and Six-pence,
   for my Cows Tallow :
Sing Oh &c

Then in comes the Huntsman
   so early in the Morn,
He bid me a Penny
   for my Cow's horn :
Sing Oh &c

Then in comes the Tripe-Woman
   so fine and so neat,
She bid me three halfpence
   for my Cow's feet ;
Sing Oh &c—

Then in comes the Butcher
   that nimble tongu'd Youth
Who said she was Carrion,
   but he spoke not the truth :
Sing Oh &c

This Cow had a Skin
    was as soft as the silk,
And three times a day
    my poor Cow would give Milk :
Sing Oh &c—

She every year
    a fine Calf me did bring,
Which fetcht me a pound,
    for it came in the spring :
Sing Oh &c

But now I have kill'd her,
    I can't her recall,
I will sell my poor Colly,
    hide, horns and all :
Sing Oh &c

The Butcher shall have her,
    though he gives but a pound ;
And he knows in his heart
    that my Colly was sound ;
Sing Oh &c

And when he has bought her,
    let him sell all together,
The flesh for to eat,
    and the hide for leather :
Sing Oh &c—

FINIS.

Printed for C. Passinger, at the seven stars in the
New Buildings on London-bridge—

[17.] A Miser having a sheep stolen from him, by a poor man, would needs send him to Prison, saying there was not so damn'd a Rogue in the World ; Pray, Sir, said he, *remember yourself, and be good to me—*

[12.]   A Glass, when a G
        Is took away, I.C.
    Is a Lass, I mean of the Game,
        Put L too away,
        What is't then, I pray,
    Why, an Ass, and you are the same.

[4.] A Nobleman having a mind to be merry, sent for his Chaplain, and told him, That, unless he could resolve him these three Questions, he should be discarded, and turn'd out of his Service; but if he cou'd, he shou'd have Thirty Guinneys, and the best Horse in his Stable; So he propos'd the Questions to him, which were these; *First, what compass the World was about? Secondly, How deep the Sea was? And Thirdly, What he thought?* The Poor Chaplain was in a peck of Troubles, and did not know how to answer them, or what to say, thinking them very unreasonable Questions; so that all he could do was to desire a little time to consider upon them, which the Earl granted. So he going along the Fields one day very melancholy, a Cobler of the Town, a Merry Fellow (who was very like the Chaplain, both in Physiognomy and Stature) met him, and ask'd him the reason of his sadness; which with some Reluctancy he told him: O Sir, says the Cobler, don't be dejected, chear up; I've thought of a device to save your Place, and get you the Money and Horse too; but you shall give me Ten Guinneys for my pains. So he agreed to't; and it was thus: Says he, I'll put on your Cloaths, and go to My Lord, and answer his Questions. Accordingly he went, and when he came before him, he answer'd him thus: To the first Question, *What Compass the World was about?* He answered, *It was four and twenty hours Journey; and if a man could keep pace with the Sun, he could easily go it in that time.* To the Second, *How deep the Sea was?* He answer'd *Only a stone's throw; for cast it into the deepest place of it, and in time it will come to the bottom.* To the third (which I fancy your Lordship thinks the most difficult to be resolv'd, but is indeed the easiest) which is; *What your Lordship thinks?* I answer, *That you think I am your Chaplain, when as indeed I am but the Cobler of Gloucester.* The Nobleman was so pleas'd with his witty Answers, that he perform'd his Promise to his Chaplain, and gave the Cobler Ten Guinneys for his Ingenuity.

[51.] An aged Gentleman sore sick did lie,
　　　Expecting life, that could not chuse but die :
　　　His Foole came to him, and intreated thus.
　　　Good Maister, ere you goe away from us,
　　　Bestowe on *Jacke* (that oft hath made you laffe)
　　　Against he waxeth old, your Walking-Staffe,—
　　　I will, (quoth he) goe take it, there it is :
　　　But on condition, *Jacke*, which shall be this,
　　　If thou doe meete with any while thou live,
　　　More foole than thou, the Staffe thou shalt him give.
　　　Maister, (sayd he) upon my life I will ;
　　　But I doe hope that I shall keepe it still.
　　　When Death drew neere, and faintness did proceed,
　　　His Maister called for a Devine with speed,
　　　For to prepare him unto Heaven's way.
　　　The Foole starts up, and hastily did say,
　　　Oh Maister, Maister, take your Staffe againe,
　　　That proove your selfe the most Foole of us twaine ;
　　　Have you now liv'd some foure-score yeares and odd,
　　　And all this time, are unprepared for God :
　　　What greater Foole can any meete withall,
　　　Than one that's ready in the Grave to fall,
　　　And is to seeke about his soules estate,
　　　When Death is op'ning of the Prison Gate ?
　　　Beare Witnesse friends, that I discharge me plaine ;
　　　Heere Maister, heere, receive your Staffe againe :
　　　Upon the same condition I did take it,
　　　According as you will'd me, I forsake it :
　　　And over and above, I will bestow,
　　　This Epitaph, which shall your folly show.
　　　　　Heere lyes a man, at death did Heaven clayme,
　　　　　But in his life, he never sought the same.

[26.] A Lady in this Kingdom hearing that a Lady, that was a Person of Quality, did much long for Oysters, she then sent a Foot-man of hers, that was an *Irish* Man, to the said Lady with a Barrel of Oysters, and as he was going, he met an Arch Wag by the way, who askt him whither he was going?   Then he told him : "O. *Donniel,* says he, you must gut them before you go, or else they will Poyson the Lady ; I Predde,[1] says he, show me how to do it.   So the Fellow took them and opened them, and took out all the Oysters and put them into a Wooden Dish that was by, and then put all the Shells again into the Barrell : *Now,* says he, *you may carry them, for they are all gutted: E. Fait,*[2] said *Donniel, for this kindness, I'll give thee a pint of Wine out of the Vails that I shall have of my Lady :* but I know not how they were accepted.

[12.]　　　A man found his Wife
　　　　　To be idle all her Life,
　　　Then he beat her very sore ;
　　　　　I did nothing, says she,
　　　　　I know it, says he,
　　Which makes me to beat you therefore.

[32.] What is that no man would have, and yet when he hath it, will not forgoe it ?
Solution. It is a broken head, or such like, for no man would gladly have a broken head, and yet when he hath it, he would be loth to loose his head, though it be broken.

[5.]　　To be indebted is a shame men say
　　　Then 'tis confessing of a shame to pay.

On a certaine present sent from an Archbishop to his friend.

[67.] Mittitur in Disco, mihi Piscis ab Archiepisco
Po non ponetur, quia potum non mihi detur.

Englished thus.

There was in a dish, sent me a fish, from an Arch bish
Hop I will not put heere, because hee sent me noe beere.

[1] Ay, prithee.　　　　　　　　　[2] I'faith.

NEWES FROM *MORE-LANE.*

or

A mad, knavish, and uncivil Frolick of a Tapster
dwelling there, who buying a fat Coult for Eighteen
pence, the Mare being dead and he not knowing how
to bring the Coult up by hand, killed it, and had it
baked in a Pastie, and invited many of his Neighbours
to the Feast and telling of them what it was: the
Conceit thereof made them all Sick, as by the following
ditty you shall hear.

> The Tapster fil'd the Cup up to the brim,
> And all to make the little Coult to swim ;
> But all that heares it sayes that for his gaine,
> He is no better than a Wagg in graine.

The Tune is, *A Health to the best of Men.*

[68.] There is a Tapster in *More lane*
   that did a Pasty make,
 All People doe of him complaine,
   now for his grosse mistake :
 Hee instead of Venson fine
   a good fat Coult did kill,
 And put in store of Clarret Wine,
   his humour to fullfill.

 A Peck of Flower at the least,
   with six pound of Butter,
 Hee made his Nighbours such a Feast
   and bid them all to supper :
 A curious fine fat Colt it was,
   and handled daintily :

The Tapster prov'd himself an Asse,
    for this his knavery.

Likewise there was a Baker too,
    that lived in that place,
And he was a pertaker too,
    I speak in his disgrace :
For he found Flower to make it,
    I speak not in his praise,
And afterwards did bake it,
    his knavery for to raise.

Likewise there was a Carman too
    and he found Butter for it,
But when the Knavery Neighbours knew
    they could not but abhor it ;
And then there was a Cooke, Sir,
    at *More gate* doth he dwell,
And he then under tooke, Sir,
    to make the Pasty well.

Some say it eate as mellow then
    as any little chick,
But I tell thee, good-fellow ; then
    it made the Neighbours sick :

N

The Tapster had his humour,
    but the Neighbours had the worst,
Yet I doe hear they had good Beere
    and dainty Pastry crust.

Then every joviall Blade, Sir,
    that lived in that place,
Their Money freely paid, Sir,
    they scorned to be bace :
They cal'd for Beere, likewise for Ale
    because the Coult should swim,
And of the Cup they would not faile,
    but fil'd it to the brim.

The Car-mans Wife cry'd out and said
    troath 'tis good Meat indeed,
So likewise said the Chamber-maid,
    when she on it did feed.
The Tapster bid them welcome then,
    and Wea-Hae did he cry
You are all welcome, Gentlemen,
    you'r welcome hartily.

The Glover's Wife was in a heat,
    and did both pout and mump,
Because they would not let her eat
    the Buttock and the Rump.
As for the merry Weaver's Wife,
    I will give her her due,
She spent her Coyne to end the strife
    among that joviall Crew.

This Colt was not so wholsome though
    as was a good fat Hogg,
Yet one came in and told the crew
    it was a mangie Dogg !
But he that told them was to blame,
    and was but a silly Dolt,
The Tapster bid him peace for Shame
    for 'twas a good fat Colt.

The Colt he cost me eighteen pence,
   the Tapster he did say,
I hope good Folks 'ere you goe hence,
   you for your Meate will pay.
Pox take you for a Rogue quoth one,
   another, he fel'd oaks,
Another said he was undone !
   'twas worse than Harty Choaks.

The Porter he did give nine pence
   to have it in a Pye,
The People ere they went from thence
   did feed most hartily :
It was the joviall Baker,
   and knavish Tapster too,
The Car-man was pertaker
   was not this a Joviall crew.

The Potecary he was there,
   Farr and the Sexton too,
The Tapster put them in great fear,
   he made them for to spue.
Now was not this a knave ingrain,
   to use his Neighbours so,
When knaves are scarce, hee'l go for twain,
   good People, what think you.

The Tapster he came in at last,
   and gave the People vomits,
I hope, (quoth he,) the worst is past,
   I have eased your foule Stomacks :
Wea-hea cry'd the Tapster then,
   how doe you like my sport,
The Women said, so did the Men,
   the Devill take you for't.

At *Brainford* as I heard some say
   a mangie Dog was eate :
This was not halfe so bad as that,
   and yet the fault was great :

Men of good fashon then was there
that went both fine and brave
Now all do say, that this doth heare,
the Tapster is a knave.

FINIS.

London, Printed for *William Gammon*, and to be sould in *Smithfield*.

[61.] There fell a great dispute betwixt *Jockey* a *Scotchman*, and *Jenkin* a *Welch man*, and the subject of it was about the fruitfullnesse of their Countries, and thus *Jockey* began. There was not a braver, fruitfuller Country in the world than *Leith* in *Scotland*: The *Welch man* answered him again, Picot, that was false, for there was no place so full of all sorts of fruite, as was in Wales. *Jockey* replyed again, that he knew a piece of ground in *Scotland* where the grass grew up so suddenly that if you throw a Staff in it over night, in that time the pasture would so over grow it, that you could not see it again the next morning. But *Jenkin* hearing this, with a great Scorne made him this answer, Py *Saint Taffe* that the throwing so small a thing as a Staff was nothing, for (quoth *Shinkin*) we have divers pieces of Cround in our Contry, that if you turn your Horse into them, you shall not see him next Morning.

[12.]   Why do Men not agree
With their Wives now we see
Men now are more Learn'd, and do brawl;
Tis false Concord we see
For the Masculine to agree
With the Feminine Gender at all.

[26.] Says a Fellow that had lost one of his Ears at *Newcastle*, for no goodness 'tis thought; when one told him a Story, 'Tis in at one ear and out at t'other. By my truth, says the other, then there's a great deal of wonder in the travel of these Tales, for thy two Ears be two hundred Miles asunder.

[52.] A Certaine Gentleman in Lincolneshire, being also a Justice of Peace, had an old servant many yeares called *Adam Milford*, who upon a time came unto his Master, and desired him, in regard that he had been his servant so many yeares, hee would now give him somthing to help him in his old age. Thou sayest true, quoth his Master, and I will tell thee what I will doe. Now shortly am I to ride up to London ; if thou wilt pay my costs & charges by the way, I will give thee, ere long, such a thing as shall be worth to thee an hundred pounds. I am content, quoth *Adam*, and so payed for all their reckoning by the way. Being come to London, hee put his Master in mind of his former promise that he had made to him. What did I promise thee anything ? Yes, quoth *Adam*, that you did ; for you said you would give me that which should be worth to me an hundred pounds, for bearing your Charges to London. Let me see your writing, quoth his Master. I have none, quoth *Adam*. Then thou art like to have nothing, quoth his Master ; And learne this of me, that when thou makest a bargain with any man, looke thou take a Writing, and beware how thou makest a Writing to any man. This hath availed me an hundred pounds in my dayes. When *Adam* saw there was no remedy, he was content ; but when they should depart *Adam* stayed behind his Master to reckon with his Hostis, and on his Master's Scarlet cloake borrowed so much mony, as came to all their charges he had laid out by the way. His Master had not ridden past two miles, but it began to raine apace : wherefore he called for his cloake. His other men made answer that *Adam* was behinde, and had it with him. So they shrowded them under a tree, till *Adam* came. When he came, his Master said all angerly, Thou knave, come give me my cloak : hast thou not served me well, to let me be thus wet ? Truely, Sir, (quoth *Adam*) I have laid it to pawne for all your charges by the way. Why, knave, quoth he, didst thou not promise me to beare my charges to London ? Did I ? quoth *Adam ;* I, quoth his Master, that thou didst. Let's see, shew me your writing of it, quoth Adam. Whereupon, his Master perceiving he was over-reacht by his man, was fain to send for his cloak againe, and pay the money.

There was a singular mania in this century for chronograms, or making up dates out of words, which will be best explained in the annexed example. Jas. Hilton, Esq., has by dint of vast trouble and research, been enabled to collect a large quantity of these, and his book[1] (of which only a very limited number were printed) will well repay the perusal of the curious.

Chronogramma.   Anno 1628.   obiit

*Georg*IV*s* DVX *B*VC*k*I*ngha*MI*æ*

[67.] Malignant characters that did portend
Duke-murthering Fate & his untimely end,
Constrain'd to die, that would have liv'd & fought
Xantippus like, but that fell Felton brought
Vncertaine quick[2] to a certaine end.
Vaine are designes, where one doth of his freind
Vsurpe too much, him you doe countermine
In breife the world applaudes this last designe.
It was his death, but now hee's dead & gone
Ill having heard of many, *felt* but *one.*

The date 1628 can be easily made by adding the Roman numerals, which are represented by the capital letters.

[5.]   All things have savour, though some very small,
Nay, a box on the eare hath no smell at all.

[17.] One having a scoulding Wife, swore he would drown himself. She followed him desiring him to forbear, or at least to let her speak with him. Speak quickly then, says he: Pray Husband, if you will needs drown your self, take my counsel to goe into a deep place; for it would grieve my heart to see you long a dying; with that the Fellow came back again and went to the Indies.

[52.] *Coomes* of *Stapforth* hearing that his wife was drowned comming from market went with certaine of his friends to see if they could finde her in the River; he, contrary to all

---

[1] Brit. Mus. Catalogue, 11905, a. a. 8.   Hilton, Jas., Chronograms; Lond., 1882, 8vo.   [2] Life.

the rest, sought his wife against the streame : which, they perceiving, said, He lookt the wrong way. And why so? (quoth he) Because (quoth they) you should look down the streame, and not against it. Nay (quoth he) I shall never finde her that way : for she did all things so Contrary in her lifetime, that now she is dead, I am sure she will goe against the streame.

[12.]   I've known many men
         Know each other now and then
Yet never the knowledge could get
         Of any Man before
         Though known many a score,
That ever knew himself yet.

[4.] Doctor *Fuller* overtook one M*r* *Woodcock* upon the Road, falling into Discourse in a facetious manner, ask'd him what difference there was between a Woodcock and an Owl, (supposing Mr *Woodcock* had not known him). He wittily replied, *That an Owl was Fuller in the Head, Fuller in the Face, Fuller in the Eyes, Fuller in the Neck, and Fuller all over.*

On Anne Angel marrying a Lawyer.

[67.]   Anne is an Angel, but what if she bee.
         What is an Angel, but a Lawyer's fee.

[67.]   A Welchman walking in ye darke for feare
         Some wall might hitte his face a box o' th' eare,
         Strecht out his armes, y^t if such danger Came,
         His hands might from his face avert ye same.
         At last betwixt his armes there came a post,
         Which hitte his nose, and stroke him downe almost ;
         Pluter of nayles, quoth he, I did not know
         My nose was longer than my armes till now.

The accompanying illustration is taken for its quaintness and as an example of caricature, the tract itself hardly repaying perusal.

[69.]   No-Body—*Why do'st thou father all thy Lies*
On Me? heaping Indignities
On one that never injur'd the?
Some-Body—*My Words and Acts hurt No-Body:*
No-Body—Som-Body *hath belied me much,*
No-Body *sure hath cause to grutch.*

[52.] A certain rich Farmer having lain long sick in Norfolk,
at last sent for a Physitian from the next Marke Towne : who
when he came, he felt his pulses, and viewed his water, &
then told them,   That he could by no means, nor physick
escape, the disease had so much power in his body, and so
went his way.   Within a while after, by God's good help (who
is the only giver of all health) the man escaped and was well
againe, and walking abroad, being still very weak and feeble,
he met with his Physitian, who, being very sore afraid to see
him, asks him, if he were not such a Farme ; Yes, truely
(quoth he) I am : Art thou alive or dead? (quoth he) Dead
(quoth he) I am ; and because I have experience of many
things, God hath sent me to take up all Physitans I can get :
which made the Physitian quiver and quake, and looke as

pale as ashes for feare. Nay feare not quoth the Farmer,
though I named all the Physitians, yet I meant thee for none:
for I am sure a verier dunce lives not this day, than thou art:
and then I should be a foole to take thee for one, that art
more fit to give dogges physicke than men, and so he left
him: but the Physitian never left quaking till he was out of
his Patients Sight.

To my Booke-seller.

[70.]   Thou that mak'st gaine thy end, and wisely well,
      Call'st a booke good, or bad, as it doth sell,
Use mine so, too; I give thee leave. But crave
      For the luck's sake, it this much favour have.
To lye upon thy stall, till it be sought;
      Not offer'd, as it made sute to be bought;
Nor have my title-leafe on posts, or walls,
      Or in cleft-sticks, advanced to make calls
For termers,[1] or some clarke-like serving-man,
      Who scarse can spell th' hard names; whose knight
        lesse can.
If, without these vile arts, it will not sell,
      Send it to *Bucklers-bury*,[2] there 'twill, well.

[61.] Two gentlemen met upon the Road, betwixt *Ware*
and *London*, the one was a wild young Gallant who had more
means than Manners, the other a very grave discreet and
temperate Citizen of *London;* who considering his own yeares,
conceived that the younger man would give him the way, and
by continuing his speed resolved to trye the young Gallants
manners, until their Horses heads met. But the young fellow
crost expectation, and uncivilly demanded his way of the

---

[1] Nares defines thus, "TERMER, a person, whether male or female,
who resorted to London in term time only, for the sake of tricks to be
practised or intrigues to be carried on at that period;" as in *Decker's Belman*,
"Some of these boothalers are called *termers*, and they ply Westminster
Hall; Michaelmas term is their harvest, and they sweat in it harder than
reapers doe at their works in the heat of summer."
[2] To wrap up spices or drugs. We should now say, "Send it to the
butterman."

elder; who replyed, Sir, since you will dispute it, I must tell
you, according to the rules of Civility, the Elder in our
Country have alwayes the way of their Younger : But the bold
Upstart answered him again, that his Horse would not give
way to a Foole. To which the old man replyed, But my
Horse will, and so resigned the way to my gallant.

> [12.]   A Man in a Hall,
>   His Dogg Cuckold did call;
>   Says a Woman stood by, 'tis a shame
>   To calle a Dogg so,
>   For I'de have you to know
>   'Tis a Christian bodies name.

[17.] A Lady was bragging that she had overthrown her
Enemy in Law : One of her Servants standing by, said, He
took a wrong Sow by the ear, when he meddled with your
Ladyship.

[17.] In a great Corporation in *England*, the Serjeants [1]
desired the Mayor they might have Gowns as formerly, for
which they had a president : [2] Gowns, says the Mayor, and
why not Coats? So calling for a pair [3] of Cards, said he
could cut off that Custom by a president also : he shewed
them the four Kings and four Queens in Gowns, but the four
Knaves all in short Coats.

> [5.]   Who woes a wife, thinks wedded men do know
>   The onely true content, I thinke not so ;
>   If Woe in wooers bee, that women court,
>   As the word Woe in wooers doth import ;
>   And Woe in woemen too, that Courted be,
>   As the word Woe in women we doe see.

[1] These must not be confounded with that awful being, now legally
extinct, a "Serjeant learned in the Law ;" but meant tipstaves, or
serjeants of the mace.   [2] Precedent.   [3] A pack.

A Merry Dialogue between
Thomas and *John*.

in the praise and dispraise of Women and Wine.

Thomas against the Women doth contend,
But John most stoutly doth their cause defend ;
Young and old read these lines that ensue,
You'l all confess that what I write is true,
I know no reason but that without dispute
This may as well be printed as sung to a Lute.

To a galllant delightful new Tune, well known among Musitioners, and in
Play-houses : Called *Women and Wine.*

Thomas

[71.] Some Women are like to the Wine,
    like the Sea, and like the Rocks,
But they that proves them soon may find 'em
    like the Wine and Weathercocks.
But if you'l believe me,
    i'le tell you true
What light Women are likeunto,
Wine, Women and Wine,
    thus you may compare them too.

John

Women most Constant Men doth find,
    not like the Sea, but like the Rocks,
They are evermore loving and kind,
    not like the Wine and Weather Cocks
But if &c

Thomas

Women have hooks, and women have crooks,
  so hath the Wine, so hath the Wine,
Which draws great Lawyers from their books
  more than the Wine, more than the Wine.
But if &c

John

Women have beauty and fair looks,
  So hath the Wine, so hath the Wine,
Far surpassing the Lawyers books
  more than the Wine, more than the Wine.

But if you'l believe me
* i'le tell you true*
What good Women are like unto,
Wine Wine, Women and Wine,
* thus may you compare them too.*

Thomas

Women are Witches when they may
  so is the Wine, so is the Wine,
Which causeth men from their Wives to stray,
  so will the Wine, so will the Wine.

But if you'l believe me
  i'le tell you true
What light Women are like unto,
Wine, Wine, Women and Wine,
  thus may you compare them too.

John

Women are witty when they may,
  so is not Wine, so is not Wine,
And causeth Men at home to stay,
  so doth not Wine, so doth not Wine.
But if &c

Thomas

Women have arms for to imbrace,
  more than the Wine, more than the Wine,
Which brings brave Gallants to disgrace,
  so doth the Wine, so doth the Wine.
But if &c

John

Women most sweetly do imbrace
  more than the Wine, more than the Wine,
And save their Husbands from disgrace,
  so doth not Wine, so doth not Wine.
But if &c

Thomas

Women's tongues are like sharp swords,
  so is the Wine, so is the Wine,
Which urgeth men to swear damn'd Oaths,
  so doth the Wine, so doth the Wine.
But if &c

John

Women's tongues do speak sweet Words,
  so doth not Wine, so doth not Wine ;
They can persuade from damned Oaths,
  so will not Wine, so will not Wine.
But if &c

Thomas

Women they do use to change,
    so doth the Wine, so doth the Wine,
And often times abroad will range
    when Sun doth shine, when Sun doth shine.
But if &c

John

Good Women they will never change,
    so will the Wine, so will the Wine,
For profit they abroad will range,
    Hail, Rain or Shine, Hail Rain or Shine.
But if &c

Thomas

Women they will fight and brawl,
    fill'd with Wine, fill'd with Wine,
Their Husbands they will Cuckolds call,
    inflam'd with Wine, inflam'd with Wine.
But if &c

John

Good Women they will comfort all,
    like the best Wine, like the best Wine,
Whatever Sorrow doth befall,
    so will good Wine, so will good Wine.
But if you'l believe me,
    i'le tell you true,
What good Women are like unto,
Wine, Wine, Women and Wine,
    thus you may compare them to.

Printed for J. Williamson,[1] at the Sun and Bible in Cannon Street
near London Stone.

[17.] A Welch man in heat of blood, challenged an Englishman at Sword and Buckler ; but the Englishman giving him a lusty blow on the leg which vext him, he threw down his Weapon, swearing *Splut, was not her Buckler brocd enough, but her must hit her on the leg ?*

[1] Published in 1665.

[52.] A *Bulkin*[1] well knowne in divers places for his mad conceits, and his couzenage, upon a time came into Kent to Sittingborne; and in divers Villages there-about set up bills that all sorts of people, young and old, that would come to Sittingborne, on such a day, they should find a man there, that would give a remedy for all kinds of diseases; and also would tell them what would happen unto any of them in five or Six yeares after: and he would desire but two pence a piece of any of them. Whereupon came people of all sorts and from all places: so that he gathered of the people that came to the value of twenty pounds: and he had provided a Stage, and set it up, and placed a chaire where he would sit: and so, they being all come in, and every one set in order, he comes to the gate, and takes the money from them that gathered it, and bids them looke that good rule be kept, and so they did: also hee bid them by and by sound the drumme, and then he would begin his Orations. He, when they were gone, with all haste gets him to the backe-side, and there having his Gelding, gets upon his backe, and away towards *Rochester* rides he, as fast as ever he could gallop. Now they, thinking he had beene preparing of things in a readinesse, sounded the drumme. The Audience looked still when he would come, and staying one, two, or three houres, nay more, thought sure they were cozened. Whereupon one of the Company seeing a paper in the chaire on the Stage, tooke it, wherein was written.

Now you have heard the sound of the drumme,
You may all depart like fooles as you come.

Whereupon the men falling to cursing and swearing, the women to scolding, scratching, and biting, were faine to depart like fooles indeed.

[12.] A Man being cold
In's Boots, was so bold.
To stand near the fire for remedy;

[1] Or bulchin, is a little bull, or bull calf.

You'l burn your Spurs, says *Jane*,
My Boots sure you mean ;
No, Sir, they are burnt already.

[26.] A Scholar coming home from *Cambridge* to his Father, his Father askt him what he had learnt ? Why Father, says he, I'll prove that this Capon is better than the blessing of God. How Zon, says he, come, let's hear it ; Why thus, Father, says he, nothing you know is better than the blessing of God, and this Leg of the Capon is better than Nothing : Ergo.

[52.] In London dwelt a mad conceited fellow, which with his wit lived with Gallants and domineered with good fellowes. Not very long agoe, in Hay-harvest, he gets a Pitchforke on his neck, went forth towards Islington in the morning, and meets with two loads of Hay, comming towards the City to be sold : for the which hee bargained with them that owned the same, for thirty shillings. But whither shall wee bring them ? quoth they. To the Swanne by Smithfield, said hee. And so went his way, and left them : then to the Swan he went, to the good man of the house, and asked if he would buy two loades of Hay ? Yes, quoth the Inne keeper, where be they ? Here they come, quoth he. What shall I pay, quoth the In-keeper ? Foure Nobles[1] a load, quoth the Make-shift. But at the last they agreed for twenty shillings. When they were come, he bad them unload the Hay. So while they were unloading of it, hee came to the Inne-holder, and said, I pray you let me have my money : for while my men unload, I will buy some stuffe to have home with me. The Inne-holder was content, and gave him money, and so hee went away. When the men had unloaded their Hay they came and demanded their money. I have paid your Master (quoth the Inne holder). What Master ? quoth they. Marry, quoth hee, he that bad you bring the Hay hither. Wee know him not quoth they. Nor I neither, quoth hee, but with him I bargained, and him have I paid ; with you I meddled not, and therefore go seeke him if you will. And so the poore men were cozened.

---

[1] A noble was 6s. 8d.

[72.]

A BOVLSTER LECTVRE.

Dum loquor ista, tacet

Surdo canis

This wife a wondrovs racket meanes to keepe,
While th'Husband seemes to sleepe but dies not sleepe:
But she might full as well her Lecture smother,
For ent'ring one Eare, it goes out at t'other.

The accompanying quaint illustration shows the antiquity of "Mrs. Caudle's Curtain Lectures."[1]

[1] At p. 107 the very phrase is mentioned, "These need not feare to have their shoulders besprinkled with *Zantippee's* livery; or to have their breakfast chang'd into a Morning *Curtaine Lecture*."

[5.] A friend of *Durus* comming on a day
To visite him, finding the doores say nay ;
Being lock'd fast up, first knocks, and then doth pause,
As Lord have mercy on's [1] had bin the cause ;
But missing it, he ask't a neighbour by
When the rich *Durus'* (doors) were lock'd and why !
He said it was a Custome growne of late
At diner time to lock your great man's gate,
Durus' his poor friend admir'd & thought the door
Was not for State lock'd up, but 'gainst the poore,
And thence departing empty of good cheere,
Said, Lord have mercy on us is not there.

[72.] A Man there was, who liv'd a merry life,
Till in the end he tooke him to a Wife ;
One that no image was (for shee could speake)
And now and then her husbands costrell [2] breake :
So fierce she was and furious, as in summe,
She was an arrant Devill of her tongue.
This drove the poore man to a discontent,
And oft, and many times did he repent
That e're hee chang'd his former quiet state,
But 'las, repentance then did come too late.
No cure he finde to cure this maladie,
But makes a vertue of necessitie,
The common cure for care to every man,
" A potte of nappy Ale :" where he began
To fortifie his braine 'gainst all should come,
'Mongst which the clamour of his wives loud tongie
This habit graffed [3] in him grew so strong,
That when he was from Ale, an houre seem'd long,
So well hee lik'd th' profession : on a Time
Having staid long at pot (for rule nor line
Limits no drunkard) even from Morne to Night,
He hasted home apace, by the Moone-light :
Where as he went, what phantasies were bred,

---

[1] Houses visited by the plague were marked by a cross chalk'd on the door, and also the words, "Lord have mercy on us."

[2] Head.   [3] Grafted.

I doe not know, in his distempered head,
But a strange Ghost appear'd, and forc'd him stay,
With which perplext, hee thus began to say :
" Good Spirit, if thou be, I need no charme,
For well I know, thou wilt not doe mee harme ;
And if the Devill ; sure mee thou shoulds't not hurt,
I wed't thy *Sister*, and am plagued for't.
The Spirit, well approving what he said,
Dissolv'd to ayre, and quickly vanished.

[17.] A Taylor sent his bill to a Lawyer for money ; the
Lawyer bid the Boy tell his Master, that he was not running
away (being very busie at that time). The Boy comes again,
and tells him he must needs have his money. Did'st tell him,
I was not running away? Yes Sir, but he bid me tell you,
that *though you were not running away, yet he was.*

[17.] A Schollar was lock'd out of *Wadham* Colledge, and
about ten a Clock he came and knockt ; the Porter came to
the Gate, and told him the Warden had took up the keys with
him : Pray, says he to the Porter, go to the Warden, and tell
him I am here : Truly, Sir, says he, the Warden is angry with
me already, I dare not do it : but if you'll go your self, it may
be he'll give you the keys.

[5.] He's rich that hath great in-comes by the year ;
Then that great belly'd man is rich, Ile swear :
For sure, his belly ne'r so big had bin,
Had he not daily had great comings in.

[26.] One meeting a mad Fellow that was drunk, ask't him
whither he was going? says he, I am going to the Tavern :
No, says t'other, that you are not ; for Drunkenness is the way
to Hell, and thither you are going. Puh, says the Drunkard,
you are therein much mistaken ; and I ne'r fear that, for I am
so drunk, that my Legs are not able to carry me so far ; and
what need I go thither agen, for I came from the Devil[1]
(*Tavern*) but now.

[1] In Fleet Street, close by where Temple Bar stood, now Messrs.
Childs' Bank.

PORTSMOUTH'S Lamentation

OR

A Dialogue between Two Amorous Ladies, E.G.[1] *and* D.P.[2]

Dame *Portsmouth* was design'd for *France,*
But therein was prevented ;
Who mourns at this Unhappy Chance,
and sadly doth lament it.

To the Tune of, Tom the Taylor, Or, Titus Oats.

[73.] I prithee *Portsmouth* tell me plain,
  without dissimulation,
When dost thou home return again,
  and leave this English Nation ?
Your youthful days are past and gone,
  you plainly may perceive it
Winter of age is coming on,
  'tis true, you may believe it.

[1] Eleanor, or Nell, Gwynne.
[2] Louise de Querouaille, Duchess of Portsmouth, a mistress of Charles II. from whom are descended the Dukes of Richmond, died November 1734, aged 88. This ballad was evidently written soon after the king's death in 1685.

And, *Nelly*, is't not so with thee,
   why dost thou seem to flout me,
I am in clos'd with misery,
   and sorrows round about me :
O, 'twas a sad and fatal hour,
   as ere could come to me,
When Death did all my joys devour,
   on purpose to undoe me.

Thy loss was much, I must confess,
   and much to be lamented,
Now thou art almost pittiless,
   thy design it is prevented :
To *France* 'twas thy intent to go,
   but therein did'st miscarry,
And trouble 'tis to thee I know,
   that thou art forc'd to tarry.

Fye *Nell*, this news is worse and worse,
   and doth increase my trouble,
That I must now unstring my purse,
   doth make my sorrow double :
From hence I thought for to convey
   what in this land I gained,
But I am here confin'd to stay,
   and now my credits stain'd.

Pish, lightly come, and lightly go,
   ne'er let this matter grieve thee,
Tho' fortune seems to be thy foe,
   and for a while to leave thee :
Yet shee again on thee may smile,
   then be not broken hearted,
Tho' from this little *Brittish* Isle,
   thou must not yet be parted.

With care and grief I am opprest,
   and I am discontented,
Sorrow is lodged in my Breast,
   my Youthful life lamented :

How did I vainly spend my time,
  tho' Riches still increased,
And played the Wanton in my prime,
  but now my comfort's ceased.

Well, thou hast laid up Riches store,
  to serve thee when afflicted,
And yet doth carp and crave for more,
  thou cans't not contradict it :
But let enough thy mind suffice
  since Fortune frowns upon thee,
Now shew thyself discreet and wise,
  or else what will come on thee ?

Could I but safely get to *France*,
  with all my Gold and Treasure,
Then would I briskly sing and dance,
  and Riot beyond measure ;
But I am crost in my design,
  which greatly doth torment me,
And 'tis in vain for to repine,
  what Plagues hath Heaven sent me.

Madam I fear it will grow worse,
  with patience strive to bear it,
And since you must unstring your purse,
  for it now be prepared :
Your debts in England must be paid
  believe me what I tell ye,
And thereat be not dismaied,
  but be advised by *Nelly*.

FINIS.

Printed for C. Dennisson [1] at the Stationer's Arms, within Aldgate.

It will be seen by the foregoing supposed portraits of Nell Gwynne and the Duchess of Portsmouth (which, by the way, do plenty of duty in other ballads) that the *patching* of this

[1] He published from 1685 to 1689.

age among women was in somewhat fantastic form, such a
patch as a coach and four not being unknown ; but few know
that the mercers (or linen-drapers, as we now call them)
patched themselves in order to show the effect to their fair
customers. The annexed example shows one who holds a
lady's vizard, or mask, for they did not then wear veils, which
are quite a modern invention, together with a feather-fan and
some ribands, or, as the frontispiece of the book records,
divulging the secrets of the toilet.

[74.]   Here's black Bags, Ribons, Copper Laces,
        Paintings, and beauty spots for faces?
        Masques, and Fans you here may have
        Taffity Gownes and Scarfes most brave
        Curled haire, and crisped Locks.
        Aprons white, and Holland Smocks:
        All sort of powders here are sold
        To please all People young and old.

> Then come my Customers touch and try,
> Behold and see, draw forth and buy.

Unfortunately this little penny book is generally too broad in its humour to be reprinted; but one extract, which may be reproduced, will suffice to show its quality:—"Cone who buys my new Fashion'd Periwigs, if there be any manner of Single man, Widdower, or Batchelor that thinks his owne naturall Haire not good enough for him, here is *Jack n a box*, that will fit him to a haire, with all sorts of Periwigs and all sorts of colours and fashions, both long Haire, or short Haire, Flaxen haire, or yellow haire, black, blew, red, tawny, browne, or Abraham [1] Colour, thats halfe Nits, and half Lice; or if any bauld pated fellow among you that have lost his hair off from his head, I have a Periwig for him of goodly long Haire, that will hang downe and cover all his shoulders, and that may serve to cover all his knavery: or, if any younger Brothers that desires to have their naturall Haire that growes upon their heads Dyed of another Colour? here are all sorts of powders, of several colours and Fashions, that will doe the trick gallantly."

To one that desired me not to name him.

[70.] Be safe, nor feare thy selfe so good a fame,
That, any way, my booke should speake thy name:
For, if thou shame, ranck'd with my friends, to goe,
I am more asham'd to have thee thought my foe

[4.] A Scholar meeting a Countreyman upon the Road rid up very briskly to him; but the Countreyman, out of respect to him was turning off his Horse to give him the Road, when the Scholar, laying his Hand upon his Sword, said, *'Tis well you gave me the Way, or I'd*—— *What wou'd you have done?* said the Countreyman, holding up his Club at him—— *Given it to you, Sir*, says he, pulling off his Hat to him.

---

[1] Nares thinks that *Abram*-coloured hair is a corruption for *auburn*, but it is just possible that, being a patriarch, very gray or white hair is meant.

[17.] One wondred there was so many Pick pockets about *London*, seeing there's a Watch at every corner : *Pah*, says another, *they'd as willingly meet with a watch as any thing else.*

[5.]   *More dew* the Mercer, with a kinde salute,
        Would needs intreate my custome for a suit :
        Here Sir, quoth he, for Sattins, Velvets call,
        What e're you please, I'le take your word for all.
        I thank'd, took, gave my word ; say then,
        Am I at all indebted to this man ?

[61.] A mad young Gallant, having rid as he feared, out of his way, overtook a blunt Country fellow, and asked him, which was the way to *Salesbury ?*   The Country man, intending not only to set him right : but withall to know whether or no he had committed any error in his way thither, asked him as the manner is, from whence he came, to which the surly Gallant answered, *Why what is that to you, from whence I came ?   You say true Master*, quoth the Bumkin, *It is nothing to me from whence you come, nor whether you goe.*   So he walkt away with his hands coupled behind him, and left the gentle fool to study out his way to *Salesbury.*

To review, or even to largely quote from the dramatists of the seventeenth century is not within the scope of this work, but I cannot refrain (because they are so scarce) from giving a sample of one of the " Drolls," as they were called— short plays performed in booths at the fairs, and very often abbreviated versions of the legitimate drama, as " Bottom the Weaver," from *A Midsummer's Night's Dream ;* "The Humours of the Gravemakers," from *Hamlet.*   In fact, as the preface to the book [75.], whence the accompanying Droll is taken, states, " The most part of these Pieces were written by such Penmen as were known to be the ablest Artists that ever this Nation produced, by Name, *Shake-spear*, *Fletcher*, *Johnson*, *Shirley*, and others ; and these Collections are the very Souls of their writings, if the witty part thereof may be so termed : And the other small Pieces composed by several other Authors, are such as have been of great fame in this last Age, when the publique Theatres were shut up, and the Actors forbidden to present us with any of their Tragedies, because we had enough of that in earnest, and Comedies, because the Vices of the Age were too lively and smartly represented; then all that we could divert our selves with, were these humours and pieces of Plays, which passing under the Name of a merry Conceited Fellow, called *Bottom the Weaver, Simpleton the Smith, John Swabber*, or some such Title, were only allowed us, and that by stealth too, and under pretence of Rope-dancing, or the like; and these being all that was permitted us, great was the confluence of the Auditors; and these small things were as profitable, and as great get-pennies to the Actors[1] as any of our late famed Plays. I have seen the *Red Bull*[2] Playhouse, which was a large one, so full that as many went back for want of room as had entred; and as meanly as you may now think of these Drols, they were then acted by the best Comedians then and now in being; and I may say, by some that then exceeded all now Living; by Name, the incomparable *Robert Cox* who was not only the principal Actor, but also the Contriver and Author of most of these Farces. How have I heard him cryed up for his *John Swabber*, and *Simpleton the Smith?* In which he being to appear with a large piece of Bread and Butter, I have frequently known several of the Female Spectators and Auditors to long for some of it: and once that well known Natural, *Jack Adams* of *Clarkenwel*, seeing him with Bread and Butter on the Stage, and knowing him, cryed out, Cuz, Cuz, give me some, give me some; to the great pleasure of the Audience. And so Naturally did he Act the Smith's part, that being at a Fair in a Countrey Town, and that Farce being presented, the only Master Smith of the Town came to him, saying, well,

---

[1] It is a curious fact that both Nares and Halliwell, in their glossaries, describe Drolls as being *puppet* shows, when, as is shown, they were acted by living people.

[2] This theatre was in Clerkenwell, at the corner of what is now Woodbridge Street, and here acted (in October 1617, if not again) Edward Alleyn, the founder of Dulwich College. It is frequently mentioned in contemporary books, notably by Prynne in his *Histrio Martix*, and by Pepys in his Diary, 4th August 1660, and 23d March and 26th May 1662.

although your Father speaks so ill of you, yet when the Fair is done, if you will come and work with me, I will give you twelve pence a week more than I give any other Journey-Man. Thus was he taken for a Smith bred, that was indeed as much of any Trade.

. . . Thus were these Compositions liked and approved by all, and they were the fittest for the Actors to represent, there being little Cost in Cloaths, which often were in great danger to be seized by the then Souldiers, who, as the Poet sayes, *Enter the Red Coat, Exit Hat and Cloak*, was very true, not only in the Audience, but the Actors too, were commonly, not only strip'd, but many times imprisoned, till they paid such Ransom as the Souldiers would impose upon them ; so that it was hazardous to Act any thing that required any good Cloaths, instead of which painted Cloath many times served the turn to represent Rich Habits . . . and this painting puts me in mind of a piece I once saw in a Country Inn, where was, with the best skill of the Workman represented King *Pharaoh* with *Moses* and *Aaron*, and some others, to explain which figures, was added this piece of Poetry

> Here *Pharaoh* with his Goggle Eyes does stare on
> The High Priest *Moses*, with the Prophet *Aaron*.
> Why, what a Rascal
> Was he that would not let the People go to eat the
>   Phascal.

The Painting was in every wayes as defective and lame as the Poetry, for I believe he who pictured King *Pharaoh*, had never seen a King in his life, for all the Majesty he was represented with was goggle Eyes, that his Picture might be answerable to the Verse."

We see by the above extract that much was not expected in a Droll ; and, verily, few could have been disappointed. To modern taste the humour of the majority is too coarse ; and, therefore, I have been obliged to take, as an exemplar, the most innocent of its class.

The Humour of Bumpkin.

Argument needless, It being a Thorow Farce
very well known—

[75.]   *Actors Names.*

Acteon, three Huntsmen, Bumpkin, three Country Wenches.

Enter first Huntsman, and Bumkin.

1. *Hunt.* Why, what's the matter?

Bump. Nay, I know not; but every day my great Guts, and my small Guts make such a Combustion in my belly, as passes, and my Puddings, (like Lances) run a-tilt at my heart, and make me queasie-stomacht.

1 *Hunt.* Canst thou not guess the reason of this trouble?

Bump. Yes, I think I can, and I'le be judged by thee, if my case be not desperate. I have a horrible mind to be in love.

1 *Hunt.* With whom?

Bump. With any body; but I cannot find out the way how to be in Love.

1. *Hunt.* Why? I'le instruct thee: Cans't thou be melancholly?

Bump. Yes, as a Dog, or a Hog-louse; I could even find it in my heert to cry presently.

1. *Hunt.* Canst thou sleep well?

Bump. I cannot tell, I never saw myself sleep.

1 *Hunt.* Is't possible that thou so long been an attendant upon my Lord Acteon, shoulds't be to learn the way to be in love.

Bump. I would it were not possible, on the condition thou wert hang'd and quartered.

1 *Hunt.* I thank you, Sir. But *Bumpkin* list to me; This day thou knows't the Maids and Young men meet to sport, and revel it about the May pole: Present thy self there, tell thy cause of grief, and I dare warrant thee a Sweet-heart presently.

Bump. If thou cans't do that, Ile marry her first and learn to love her afterwards.

1 *Hunt.* Hast hither, *Bumpkin* I'le go on before   (*Exit*)

Bump. And I will follow thee a dog trot.   Is it not a pitty: that a man of Authority as I am, having been chief Dog-Keeper to my Lord Acteon this five years, being a man so comely of person, and having such a pure complexion, that all fair Ladies may be ashamed to look on me, and that I should be distressed for a Sweet-heart? Maypole I come.

And if the Wenches there encrease my pains
And scorn to love, i'le beat out all their brains.

(Exit)

Enter Huntsmen with three Country Wenches.

2. *Co. Wench.* Is it possible would *Bumpkin* be in love?

1 *Hunt.* Yes, if he knew but how, and for that sickness I have undertaken to become his Doctor: For at the May Pole meeting 'tis decreed, a Sweet-heart must be purchast, come what will on't.

3. *Co. Wench.* Nay, if he be distressed, twenty to one he may find charitable persons there.   Come, strike up a *Farewel to Misfortune.*   (*Exit*)

Enter Bumpkin.

Bump. That is a Dance that I could never hit of: pray desist a woile, and hear my doleful Tale.

1. *Co. Wench.* He'l make us cry sure.

Bump. Be it known unto all men by these presents——

2. *Co. Wench.* An Obligation, we will be no witnesses.

Bump. Why then I'le hang my self

3. *Co. Wench.* We will be witness then.

Bump. What, to my hanging? O' my Conscience, if I should woo my heart out, I should never be the fatter for it.— Where's your promise now?

1. *Hunt.* You have not yet exprest yourself; be plain, tell them your grief; a remedy will follow.

Bump. If that be all, 'tis an easy matter, pray take notice that I am in love—with somebody.

2. *Co. Wench.* Would I were she.

Bump. Why, so you are, if you have a mind to it.

2 *Co. Wench.* Why then, you are my own.

3. *Co. Wench.* Pardon me, Sister, I bespake him yesterday.

(*They all hang about him*)

Bump. Yes, marry did she   (Goes to her).

1. *Co. Wench.* But I was she that won him at the May pole.

2 *Co. Wench.* Was that the Cause you strove so for the Garland.

Bump. What's that to you?   (*Goes to her.*)
Would I had any of them in quietness.

3. *Co. Wench.* But yet I must have share.

1. *Co. Wench.* So must I too.   (*All pull him*)

2. *Co. Wench.* I will not part without the better half.

Bump. Then who shall have me whole? what—are you mad?

3. *Co. Wench.* Theres reason for a madness in this Case.

1. *Co. Wench.* I will not loose my right. Let go, I say.

2. *Co. Wench.* He shall be mine, or else he shall be nothing.

Bump. Away you burrs, why do you stick so on me? Now by this hand, if nothing can perswade you, I'le drown myself for spight, that you may perish.   (*Horn*)

1. *Hunt.* Hark, hark, my Lord *Acteons* warning piece; That Horn gives us intelligence he doth intend to Spend this day in hunting: *Bumpkin* why stay you? the hounds will quarrel with you: we'l come after.

1. *Co. Wench.* Will you not stay, my Love?

Bump. I'le see you hang'd first, and by this hand, ere I will be in love again, I will feed my hounds with my own proper Carcase.   (*Exit*)

2. *Co. Wench.* Now he is gone, our dancing may go forward.

2. *Hunt.* My Lord Acteon stays, be quick, I pray.

3. *Co. Wench.* Quick as you will; the doing of it quick, makes it shew the better.   (*A Country Dance.   Then Exeunt.*)

Enter Acteon and Bumpkin.

Acteon. Be nimble, Sirrah.

Bump. Nimble? yes, as a bear that hath been lug'd to purpose: if Love be such a troublesome Companion I will entreat him to keep out of my Company.

Acteon. We consume the day.

Bump. They have saved me a labour.

Acteon. Fie, what mean you? The glory of the day calls us
to action.

1 *Hunt.* Sir, you may please to know, that yesternight I lodged
a boar within the neighbouring Forest.

Bump. Yes, Sir, and I lodged a Fox at a house hard by.

A pleasant new Ballad to sing both
Even and Morne,
Of the bloody murther of Sir *John*
Barley *corne.*

To the tune of, *Shall I lye beyond thee.*[1]

[76.]   As I went through the North Countrey
      I heard a merry greeting :
    A pleasant toy, and full of joy,
      two noble men were meeting.

And as they walked for to sport,
      upon a Sommers day,
Then with another nobleman
      they went to make a fray.

Whose name was sir John Barley Corne,
      he dwelt downe in a dale ;
Who had a kinsman dwelt him nigh,
      they cal'd him Thomas Goodale.

Another named Richard Beere,
      was ready at that time
Another worthy knight was there
      call'd sir William White Wine.

[1] For tune, see Appendix.

Some of them fought in a blacke Jacke
    some of them in a Can,
But the chiefest in a black pot,
    like a worthy noble man.

Sir John Barley-corne fought in a Boule,
    who wonne the victorie ;
And made them all to fume and sweare
    that Barley-corne should die.

Some said kill him, some said drowne,
    others wisht to hang him hie,
For as many as follow Barley-corne,
    shall surely beggers die

Then with a plough they plowed him up
    and thus they did devise,
To burie him quicke within the earth,
    and swore he should not rise.

With horrowes strong they combed him,
    and burst clods on his head ;
A joyfull banquet then was made
    when Barly-Corne was dead.

He rested still within the earth,
    till raine from skies did fall,
Then he grew up in branches greene,
    which sore amaz'd them all.

And so grew up till Mid-sommer,
    which made them all afeard,
For he was sprouted up on hie,
    and got a goodly beard.

Then he grew till S. *James* tide,
    his countenance was wan,
For he was growne unto his strength,
    and thus became a man.

With hookes and sickles keene
    into the field they hide [1]
They Cut his legs off by the knees
    and made him wounds full wide.

Thus bloodily they cut him downe
    from place where he did stand,
And like a thiefe for treachery,
    they bound him in a band.

So then they tooke him up againe
    according to his kind ;
And packt him up in severall sackes,
    to wither with the wind.

And with a pitch forke that was sharpe
    they rent him to the heart,
And like a thiefe for treason vile,
    they bound him in a cart.

[1] Hied.

P

And tending him with weapons strong
  unto the towne they hye,
And straight they mowed him in a mow
  and there they let him lie.

Then he lay groning by the wals,
  till all his wounds were sore,
At length they tooke him up againe,
  and cast him on the floore.

They hyred two with holly clubs,
  to beat on him at once,
They thwacked so on Barly-corne,
  that flesh fell from the bones.

And then they tooke him up againe,
  to fulfill womens minde,
They dusted him, and they sifted him,
  till he was almost blind.

And then they knit him in a sacke,
  which grieved him full sore,
They steeped him in a Fat,[1] God wot,
  for three days space and more.

And then they took him up againe,
  and laid him for to drie,
They cast him on a chamber floore,
  and swore that he should die.

They rubbed him and they stirred him,
  and still they did him turne,
The malt man swore that he should die,
  his body he would burne.

They spightfully tooke him up againe,
  and threw him on a kill [2]
So dried him there with fire hot
  and thus they wraught their will.

[1] Vat.   [2] Kiln.

Then they brought him to the mill,
    and there they burst his bones,
The Miller swore to murther him,
    betwixt a pair of stones.

Then they tooke him up againe,
    and serv'd him worse than that,
For with hot scalding liquor store
    they washt him in a Fat

But not content with this, God wot,
    that did him mickle harme ;
With threatening words they promised
    to beat him into barme.

And lying in this danger deep,
    for feare that he should quarrell,
They tooke him straight out of the fat,
    and tunn'd him in a barrell.

And then they set a tap to him,
    even thus his death begun ;
They drew out every drain of blood,
    Whilst any drop would run.

Some brought jacks [1] upon their backs.
    some brought bill and bow,
And every man his weapon had,
    Barly-Corne to overthrow.

When sir John Goodale heard of this
    he came with mickle might,
And there he took their tongues away,
    their legs or else their sight.

And thus sir John in each respect
    so paid them all their hire,
That some lay sleeping by the way,
    some tumbling in the mire.

[1] A thick leather coat ; here used in another sense as a "black jack" or leather can.

Some lay groning by the wals,
  some in the streets downeright,
The best of them did scarcely know
  what they had done ore night.

All you good wives that brew good ale
  God turn from you all teene,[1]
But if you put too much water in
  the devill put out your eyne.

FINIS.

London, Printed for *John Wright*,[2] and are to be sold at his shop
in *Guilt spurre* Street at the signe of the Bible.

A very slight comparison with Robert Burns' poem on this
subject will show how much he was indebted to this version, having
plagiarised, almost verbally, in many parts.

How Tarlton *tooke Tobacco at the first comming up of it.*

[77.] *Tarlton*, (as other Gentlemen used) at the first comming
up of Tabacco, did take it more for fashion's sake than otherwise, & being in a roome, set between two Men overcome with
Wine, and they never seeing the like, wondred at it ; and seeing
the vapour come out of *Tarlton's* nose, cryed out Fire, fire,
and then threw a Cup of Wine in *Tarlton's* face.   Make no
more stirre, quoth Tarlton, the fire is quenched : if the Sheriffes
come, it will turne to a fine, as the Custome is.   And drinking
that againe, Fie, sayes. the other, what a stinke it makes, I am
almost poisoned.   If it offend, saies *Tarlton*, let's every one
take a little of the smell, and so the savour will quickly goe :
but Tobacco whiffes made them leave him to pay all.

[5.] *Dick* had but two words to maintain him ever,
  And that was, Stand ; and, after, stand—Deliver.
  But *Dick's* in Newgate, and he fears shall never
  Be blest again with that sweet word, Deliver.

---

[1] Sorrow.
[2] A John Wright at the Bible, near Newgate, published between 1624
and 1627; but a J. Wright in Giltspur Street published from 1670 to 1690.
In the Roxburghe Ballads are three editions of this ballad, catalogued (?)
1650, 1690, 1730.

[12.] A tall Man void of wit,
We may compare him fit
To a House six Stories high at least ;
Where commonly we see
That the upper Rooms be
Worst furnish'd than any of the rest.

[78.] One hearing a Usurer say he had been on the pike of *Teneriff* (which is supposed to be one of the highest hils in the worlde) asked him why he had not stay'd there, for he was perswaded hee would never come so neere heaven againe.

[32.] I consume my mother that bare me, I eat my nurse that fed me, then I dye leaving all blind that saw me.
Solution. Meant of the flame of a Candle, which having consumed both wax and weeke, goeth out leaving them in the dark that saw by it.

The following shows the extent to which political satire can be carried, and its wit and rarity must be my apology for introducing it :—

The PARLIAMENTS X *Commandements*

[79.] 1. Thou shalt have no other Gods but the LORDS and COMMONS assembled at Westminster.

2. Thou shalt not make any Addresses to the King, nor yeeld obedience to any of his Commands ; neither shalt thou weare any Image either of him or his Posterity ; thou shalt not bow down unto him, nor Worship him, for Wee are jealous Gods, and will visite such sinnes unto the third and fourth Generation of them that hate us, and will not observe our Votes, Orders, and Ordinances.

3. Thou shalt not take the Names of Us, your GODS in vaine, for we cannot hold you guiltlesse that take our Names in vaine.

4. Remember that thou keep holy the Fast Day, for that is Our Sabbath ; in it thou shalt doe no manner of Work, for we have blessed that Day, and hallowed it.

5 Thou shalt neither yeeld Honor nor Obedience to the King (thy Countries Father) or thy Naturall Father or Mother, so Wee will make thy dayes long in the lands which we shall take from the ungodly and wicked ones, to bestow upon thee.

6. Thou shalt Remove the Wicked One from his Throne, and his Posterity from off the face of the Earth.

7. Thou shalt edify the Sisters, and abundantly increase and multiply the Saints.

8. Thou shalt get all thou canst; part from nothing; doe no right, take no rong, neither pay any Debts.

9. Thou shalt be a Witness for us, against whomsoever we judge to be Wicked, that so We may cut them off, that the Saints may enjoy abundance of all things.

10. Thou shalt enjoy thy Neighbours House, his Wife, his Servant, his Maid, his Oxe, or his Asse, or any thing that belongs unto him ; Provided he first be Voted (by US) to be a wicked or ungodly Person.

> All these Commandements Wee require you, and every of you with all diligence to observe; and We your LORDS and GODS will incline your hearts to keepe the Same.

The Parliaments PATER NOSTER.

Our Fathers, which think your Houses of Parliament to be heaven; you would be honoured as GODS, because CHARLES his Kingdome is come unto you; your wills must be done on earth, as unto the God of heaven; you have gotten the day, and dispose of our daily bread; you will not forgive any, neither must you look to be forgiven; you lead us into rebellion and all other mischiefs, but cannot deliver us from evil. Yours is the Kingdom, the power and glory, Parliament everlasting. *Amen.*

The ARTICLES of the FAITH.

I Beleeve in CROMWELL, the Father of all Schisme, Sedition, Heresy and Rebellion, and in his onely Son *Ireton*, our Saviour, begotten by the Spirit in a hole, borne of a winching Mare, suffered under a house of Office at *Brainford*, he deserves to be drawn, hang'd and quartered, and to remain unburied : for he descended into *Hull*, the third day he rose up in Rebellion against his KING, and now sitteth at the right hand of the gods at Westminster.   He beleeves there is no Holy Ghost, nor Catholique Church, nor forgiveness of sins, but the Communion of the Sisters, the resurrection of his Members, and Parliament everlasting.   AMEN.

> *Ordered.*—That these new Commandements, Pater Noster, and Creed be read in all Parish Churches and Congregations, throughout England and Wales.

> [12.]   One told a Principal
>   That some Rogues of his Hall
> Had abus'd him late in his Stall ;
>   I desire some redress
>   And you can do no less,
> 'Cause of 'em you are the Principal.

The Miser mump'd of his Gold.

or

The merry Frolick of a Lady of Pleasure in *Bartholomew* Fair ; shewing how she fed the
Usurer with Pig, but made him pay
for the Sawce.

To the Tune of *Let Cæsar live long.*   *Licensed according to order.*

> [80.] A Lady of Pleasure in Bartholomew Fair.
> Was powder'd and painted, nay drest in her Hair ;
> In such rich Apparel she then did appear,
> As if her Estate was ten thousand a Year :
> *Of each huffing*[1] *Gallant she would make an Ass,*
> *She fed them with Pig, but they paid for the Sawce.*

[1] Swaggering.

Among all the rest I will mention but one,
A Miser, who is in fair London well known ;
Yet I will forbear now to mention his Name,
Because I am willing to keep free from blame :
   Of this wretched Miser she made a meer Ass
   She fed him with Pig, but he paid for the Sawce.

Tis known this old Miser he seldom did eat
From Years-end to Years end a meal of good meat ;
Except it was given him freely, and then
He would eat as much as five labouring Men :
   He hapn'd to meet with this beautiful Lass
   Who fed him with Pig, but he paid for the Sawce

It hapn'd this Miser went over the Rounds[1]
And under his Arm he had seven score Pounds :
The which he was going that Morning to lend :
This Lady she met him, and said My dear Friend
   Your former good Nature lays claim to a Glass :
   She found Wine and Pig, but he paid for the Sawce.

The Miser he told here he dare not drink Wine
Nor any such liquors until he had Din'd :
Quoth she, since we here did so luckily meet,
I now am resolved to give thee a treat :
   Away to her chamber they straightways did pass,
   She fed him with pig, but he paid for the Sawce.
      [1] Had been collecting money.

A Dinner she straightways provided with speed,
The Miser he like an old Farmer did feed;
Concluding that he should have nothing to pay,
But to eat and drink, aye, and so go his way;
 The Lady supply'd him with Glass after Glass,
 She found him with Pig, but he paid for the Sawce.

This Lady supply'd him with Liquor good store,
Till he was not able to drink any more;
Full bowls of Canary he had drank so deep,
That all of a sudden he fell fast asleep:
 Thus of this Old Miser she made a meer Ass,
 She fed him with Pig, but he paid for the Sawce.

She shook him, and finding that he would not wake,
The Sevenscore Pound she did presently take;
Then locking the Miser up in an old Chest,
This brings me, in short, to the Cream of the Jest:
 Thus her waggish purpose was soon brought to pass,
 She fed him with Pig, but he paid for the Sawce.

Now he having told her before where he dwelt,
In this subtle manner she cunningly dealt;
Straight calling a Porter to finish this strife,
The Miser she sent in a Chest to his Wife:
 Without e're a Penny in Silver, alas!
 Thus she fed him with Pig, but he paid for the Sawce.

This Lady she gave him two Shillings at first,
And bade him be sure he was true to his Trust;
Now for to deliver his Burthen with Care,
For why, I must tell you it is Merchant's Ware:
 And thus the poor Miser was made a meer Ass,
 She fed him with Pig, but he paid for the Sawce.

Now just as the Porter came to his own Door,
The Miser awak'd, and loudly did roar;
The honest poor Porter was frighten'd, alack!
Supposing that he had Old Nick at his back:
 But it was the wretched Old Miser, alas!
 Who was fed with Pig, but he paid for the Sawce.

The Wife she was frighten'd this Wretch to behold,
The Miser stark-mad for his Silver and Gold ;
But all was in vain, tho' he search'd *Smithfield* round,
The Lady of Pleasure was not to be found :
> *Thus of an Old Miser she made a meer Ass,*
> *She gave him roast Pig, but he paid for his Sawce.*

[77.] In the Country where the Queenes Plaiers were accepted into a Gentleman's house, the waggon unloading of the apparell, the Wagoner comes to *Tarlton* & doth desire him to speake to the Steward for his horses. I will saies he : & comming to the Steward, Sir, saies *Tarlton*, where shall our horses spend the time ? The Gentleman looking at *Tarlton* at that question, suddenly answered, If it please you, or them, let them walke a turne or two, or there is a faire garden, let them play a game or two at bowles in the Alley : and departs thence about his other businesse. *Tarlton* commending the sudden wit of the Steward, saith little. But my Steward, not quiet, tels to the Gentlewomen above, how he had driven *Tarlton* to a *non plus* with a jest, whereat they all did laugh heartily : which a Serving man loving *Tarlton* well, ranne and told him as much. *Tarlton*, to adde fuell to the fire, and loth to rest thus put off with a jest, goes away and gets two of the horses into the Garden, & turnes them into the bowling Alley, who with their heeles made havocke : being the Gentleman's only pastime. The Ladies above from a window, seeing horses in the Garden Alley call the Knight, who cries out to *Tarlton*, Fellow, what meanest thou ? Nothing, Sir, saies he, but two of my horses are at seven up, for a peck of Provender ; a foolish match that I made. Now they being in play at bowles, run, run, your Steward may come after and cry rub. rub : at which, though they smiled, yet the Steward had no thankes for his labour, to set the horses to such an exercise, & they could not blame *Tarlton*, who did but as he was bidden. But by this Jest, oates and hay, stable room and all, was plenty.

[81.] Fast bind, fast find : my Bible was well bound ;
A Thiefe came fast, and loose my Bible found :
Was't bound and loose at once ? how can that be ?
'Twas loose for him, although 'twas bound for me.

[78.] One sayd a prodigall was like a brush that spent it self to make others goe handsome in their Cloathes.

[61.] A little crooked Gentleman had lately taken a very fair house to dwell in, and having nobly furnished it, he invites a friend of his who was a very merry man to see it, and to judge of his bargaine : the Gentleman asked him what rent he paid ? The Crooked man answered him, that he gave an hundred pounds for a fine, and fifty pounds a year. Quoth his friend, I do not like your bargain. No ! quoth the crooked Man, I am told that it is a very good penny worth. I am not of their mind, replyed his friend, for would any man be so mad to give fifty pounds a year for a house, that he cannot stand upright in. So they both laught, and went to dinner.

[5.]   Mistris *Marina* 'mongst some gossips sate,
Where faces were the Subject of their Chat ;
Some look'd too pale, some seem'd too fiery red,
Some brown, some black, and some ill fashioned.
Good Lord (quoth she) you all are much to blame,
Let's alone, and praise the maker of the same :
Her Chamber maid, who heard her, standing by,
Said, then love me, for that you know was I.

[82.] Myselfe caried an old fellow by water, that had wealth enough to be Deputy of the Ward, and wit sufficient for a Scavenger ; the water being somewhat rough, hee was much afraid, and (in stead of saying his prayers) he threatened me, that if I did drowne him, hee would spend a hundred pound, but hee would see me hanged for it ; I desired him to be quiet and feare nothing, and so in little space I landed him at the Beares Colledge on the Bank-side,[1] (alias Paris Garden.) Well (said he) I am glad I am off the water, for if the Boat had miscarried, I could have swum no more than a Goose.

---

[1] Paris Garden, Southwark, was a famous place for bear-baiting and other sports.

[12.]   One Goodman *Strong*
             Said his Wife did long,
        And what was it for but Mackrill?
             But he told him no,
             It must not be so,
        She's well now, and that will make her ill.

[17.] There were three Brothers named *Buck*, and having venison, made three Pasties; and one of those who were invited was nam'd *Cooke*, and thinking to play upon the Brothers, said, Here is *Buck, Buck, Buck.* True, says one of the Brothers, Buck is good meat, but what says the Proverb; *God sends meat, and the Devil sends Cooks.*

[4.] A Fool being very sick, and like to dye, one that went to see him, went to comfort him, bidding him Chear up. *For if you dye,* says he, *four proper Fellows shall carry you to Church: Ay but,* quoth he, *I had rather by half go thither myself.*

THE WELSHMAN'S PRAISE OF WALES.

[83.]   I's not come here to tauke of *Prute*,
         From whence the *Welse* does take her Root;
         Nor tell long Pedigree of Prince *Camber*,
         Whose Linage would fill full a Shamber;
         Nor sing the Deeds of old Saint *Davy*,
         The Ursip of which would fill a Navy;
         But hark ye now for a liddel Tales   .
         Sal make great deal to the Credit of *Wales*:
              For hur will tudge your Ears,
              With the Praise of hur Thirteen Seeres,
              And make you as Clad and Merry,
              As Fourteen Pot of Perry.

         'Tis true was wear him *Shirkin Frieze*,
         But what is that? we have store of Sheize;

And Got is plenty of Coates Milk,
That sell him well, will buy him silk
Enough to make him fine to Quarrel,
At *Hereford Sizes* in new *Apparel.*
And get him as much Melmet perhap
Sall give it a Face to his *Monmouth Cap.*

But then the Ore of *Lemster,*
By Cot is Uver a Sempster ;
That when he is Spun or Did
Yet match him with her Thrid.

And this the Backs now, let us tell ye
Of some Provisions for the Belly ;
As *Cid* and *Gote* and great *Gote's Mother,*
And *Runt* and *Cow* and great *Cow's Uther:*

And once but taste on the *Welse Mutton*,
Your *Engliss Seeps* not worth a Button ;
Then for your *Fisse*, shall shoose it your Dish,
Look but about, and there's a *Trout*,
   A Salmon, Cor or Chevin,
   Will feed you Six or Seven,
   As taull Men as e'er Swagger
   With *Welse Club* and long *Dagger*.

But all this while was never think
A word in praise of our *Welse* Drink ;
Yet for aull that, is a Cup of *Bragat*,
Aull *England* Seer may cast his Cap at ;
And what you say to *Ale* of *Webley*,
Toudge him as well, you'll praise him Trebley.
As well as *Metheglin*, or *Sider*, or *Meath*
Sall sake it your Dagger quite out o' the Seath.
   And *Oate Cake* of *Guarthenion*,
   With a goodly Leek or Onion,
   To give as sweet a rellis,
   As e'er did Harper *Ellis*.

And yet is nothing now all this,
If of our Musicks we do miss ;
With *Harp* and *Pipes* too and the *Croud*
Must aull come in and tauk aloud.
As loud as *Bangu*, *Davy's* Bell,
Of which is no doubt you have hear tell,
As well as our louder *Wrexam* Organ,
Or rumbling Rocks in the Seer of *Glamorgan*,
   Where look you but in the Ground here,
   And you sall see a Sound there,
   That put her all togedder,
   Is sweet as Measure Pedder.

[52.] In Barnet was a young woman, that when her husband lay a dying, sorrowed out of measure, for feare that shee should lose him. Her father came to her, desiring her to be contented : for he had provided her another husband, a far more handsome man. But she did not onely continue in her sorrow, but was also greatly displeased, that her father made any motion to her of any other husband. As soone as her other husband was buried and the Sermon was done, and they were at supper, between sobbing and weeping, shee rounded her father in the eare, and said, Father, where is the young man that you told me should bee my husband? for very shortly I purpose to be maried. At which her father suddenly fell a laughing.

[82.] A Gallant in his youth was much addicted to dicing, and many times when he had lost all his money, then hee would pawne his cloake, and so goe home without either cloak or coyne, which grieved the Lady his Mother very much : for remedy whereof, she caused all his doublets (of what stuffe so ever) to be made with canvasse painted backes, whereon were fashioned two fooles, which caused the Gentleman ever after to keepe his cloake on his backe, for feare two of the three should be discovered.

[12.]
I was took by a fly,
Says a Fish ; but I deny
That, for had he not took the fly
At first in his mouth,
He had not, in truth,
Then have been tost up so high.

[52.] There was an unthrift in London, that had received of a Merchant certain Wares, which came to fifty pounds, to pay at three moneths ; and at three moneths. But when he had it he consumed and spent it all : so that at the six moneths end there was not any left to pay the Merchant : Wherefore the Merchant arrested him. When he saw there was no other remedy, but either to pay the debt, or go to prison, he sent to a subtill Lawyer, and asked his Counsell how he might clear himself of that debt. What wilt thou give me, (quoth he) if I do? Five marks (quoth the other) and here it is : and as soon as you have done, you shall have it. Well, said the Lawyer, but thou must be ruled by my counsell, and do thus : When thou commest before the Judge, whatsoever he saith unto thee, answer thou nothing, but cry Bea, still, and let me alone with the rest. So when he came before the Judge, he said to the Debter, Dost thou owe this Merchant so much money? Bea (quoth he). What, beast? (quoth he) answer to that I aske thee. Bea (quoth he again.) Why, how now? quoth the Judge, I think this fellow hath gotten a sheeps tongue in his head : for he answereth in the sheeps language. Why, Sir, quoth the Lawyer, do you think this Merchant that is so wise a man, would be so foolish, as to trust this Ideot with fifty pounds worth of ware, that can speak never a word? No, Sir, I warrant you— And he persuaded the Judge to cast the Merchant in his own suit. And so the Judge departed, and the Court brake up. Then the Lawyer came to his Client, and asked him his Money, since his promise was performed, and his debt discharged. Bea (quoth he.) Why, thou needs't not cry Bea any longer, but pay me my money. Bea, (quoth he again). Why thou wilt not serve me so, I hope, (quoth the Lawyer) now I have used thee so kindly? But nothing but Bea could Master Lawyer get for his paines, and so was faine to depart with a flea in his eare.

[5.]   *Dolens* doth shew his purse, and tels you this,
  It is more horrid than a Pest-house is ;
  For in a Pest-house many mortals enter,
  But in his purse, one angell dares not venture.

[61.] An old merry Parson that lived in the old merry dayes, being a little purblined by being a very good fellow that would alwayes pay his Clubb,[1] having sat up late on the Satterday night, was a little unfitted in his eyes to read right the next morning ; turned to a Chapter in *Exodus*, the beginning of the Chapter began thus, *And God told Moses* &c, but, his eyes failing him, like a true Clubber he read thus, *And the Lord told Noses*[2] &c—

[78.] Two Gentlemen talking in latin, in the presence of a woman, she grew jealous that they spake of her, and desired

---

[1] *i.e.* His share of the liquor consumed.
[2] Counted heads, so that all should pay their due proportion.

them to speake english that she might answer them, for she said she was perswaded when men spake latin, although they spake but two words, that still one of them was naught: where upon one of the Gentlemen sayd presently, *Bona mulier,*[1] she replyed, I know *bona* is good, but I'le warrant ye the other word meanes something that's nought.

The

Young-Man & Maidens Forecast;

shewing how

They Reckon'd their *Chickens* before they were Hatcht.

To the Tune of, *The Country Farmer,* Or *The Devonshire Damosels.*
This may be Printed R.P.

[84.] I'll tell you a Jest of a Provident Lass,
　　　 Whose Providence prov'd her a Provident Ass;
　　　 She laid forth her store in such brittle Ware,
　　　 That very small profit did fall to her share;
　　　 Thirteen to the Dozen of Eggs she would buy,
　　　 And set a Hen over them carefully;
　　　 As long as she went her footing she watch'd,
　　　 She counted her Chickens before they were Hatch'd.

　　　 Said she, if these Chickens five Capons do prove,
　　　 Capons be Meat which Gentlemen love;
　　　 Those Chickens she would sell to buy a Sow-Pig,
　　　 That it might have young ones e're it was big;
　　　 Then with her Pigs she would have an Ewe,
　　　 It may have Lambs not kill'd with the Dew;
　　　 And, as she was thinking to buy her a Calf,
　　　 Her Heels they flew from her a Yard and a half.

　　　 Her Heels kiss'd the ground, and up flew her Leggs,
　　　 Down came her Basket, and broke all her Eggs;
　　　 There lay her Pigs, her Chickens, her Lambs,
　　　 She could not have young ones unless she had Dams;

---

[1] *Good woman.*

Q

Thus Fortune did frown by a fall that she catcht,
Her Chickens prov'd Addle, before they were Hatcht:
Attend but a while, and I'le briefly declare,
Bad fortune did likewise fall to the Man's share.

And now the Man to the Market will go,
To see what Dame Nature on him will bestow;
He bought him five Eggs, thinking to Thrive,
And thus did the business finely contrive;
Said he, if these Eggs five Cocks they will frame,
And most of them prove to be Cocks of the Game,
So soon as their Spurs are long enough grown,
Then I may ingross a Cock Pit of my own.

Then may I have Gallants of every sort,
Both Lords, Knights and Squires, and all to see sport,
If they Fight bravely these Gallants to please,
I may come to get Means by the rearing of these:
And when I have done, I'll get me a rich Wife,
That I may live happy all days of my Life;
And in the Church we will be loving matcht,
But count not your Chickens before they are Hatcht.

And when he came home he set his Eggs by,
He could not get up, the Roost was so high;

But fetching a Ladder, that unhappy time,
It was his hard luck with his Eggs for to Climb ;
These Ladders prove fatal to many a Man,
And are undone by them now and then ;
So was this poor Man undone by a Fall,
Down comes the Basket, Man, Eggs and all.

There lay the poor Man with a fall almost Lame,
His Cock-Pits and Gallants, and Cocks of the Game ;
The loosing of this grieved him to the Life,
Yet the grief it was more in the loss of his Wife ;
All you young Men live vertuous Lives,
And think to get Portions now by your Wives ;
Take warning by me before you are Matcht,
Pray count not your Chickens before they be Hatcht.

FINIS.

Printed for *P. Brooksby* at the *Golden Ball* in *Pye Corner*
near *West Smithfield.*

[17.] In *Ireland,* a Bag-piper coming for *England* with his
Snapsack on his shoulder, as he sate at dinner in a wood,
three Wolves began to accost him ; then he threw one bread,
and another meat, and still they crept nearer to him ; Upon
which, being afraid, he took his bagpipes and began to play,
at which noise the Wolves all ran away : A pox take you,
says he, If I had known you had loved Musick so well, you
should have had it before dinner.

[26.] A man was condemned the last Sessions to be
hang'd for a Robbery ; but before and after he was condemned, his careful, dear, and loving wife bid him take no
care ; for she had took care that he should not die ; which
made the man live more dissolutely than he would have done,
but for his wife's confidence ; which Confidence she continued
to him till the night before he was to be hang'd ; and then
she came to him and told him, That all the great Promises
made to her were come to nothing ; for she could not procure
him a Pardon by any means whatever ; which put the poor

man into such a Grief and Trembling that he was scarce himself. Come, husband, says she, take Heart, for though I cannot get you a Pardon, yet I'll tell you what I'll do for you ; I will make you an excellent Cawdle tonight, which will make you sleep well, and another to morrow morning to comfort up your heart before you are hang'd : for truly I believe it troubles you as well as me, that I could not get your pardon ; therefore pass it by this once ; but if ever you come to be hang'd again, I'll warrant you, I'll get you pardon.

[12.]   Says a man nam'd *John*,
          In every place the Sun
     Does rise every Morning soon ;
          'Tis not so, in every place,
          For my Son t' his disgrace,
     Never rises till the Afternoon.

[52.] A Gentleman of Norfolk, as he was riding towards London in the Winter time, and sitting by the fire side with his Host, untill supper could be made ready, there happened a Rabbit to be at the fire a rosting, which the Gentleman perceived to bee very leane, as he thought. Quoth he unto his Host, We have Rabbits in our Country, that one will drip a pottle, and baste itselfe. The In-keeper wondred with himselfe, and did think it to be a lie, but would not say so, for manners sake, and because he was his guest : but, thinking to requite him, Now truely, quoth he, it is very strange : but I can tell you of as strange a thing as that : Which the Gentleman was desirous to heare. Quoth he, I had as fine a Grayhound as any was in England : and if I had happened to goe abroad to my grounds, the Grayhound would alway go with me. And sometime there would start out a Hare before me, which my Grayhound would quickly catch. It fortuned that my dogge died, and for very love that I bare to him, I made me a bottle of his skin, to carry drinke withall, So, one time in hay harvest, my folkes being making of hay in my grounds, and the weather being hot, I filled my bottle with Beere, to carry to them, lest they should lack drink. And as

I was going along, there starts a Hare out of a bush before me : and as it was my custome, I cryed, Now, now, now. My bottle leaping from my girdle, ran and catcht the Hare. What, (quoth the Gentleman) me thinks that should be a lie. Truly sir, said the In-keeper, so did I think yours was.   The Gentleman perceiving that he was requited for his kindnesse, held himselfe contented.

> [85.] *Jack* drink away
>   Thou hast lost a whole Minute,
>   Hang Wenches and Play ;
>   There's no pleasure in it.
>   Faith take t'other glass
>   Though the Nights old and grey,
>   We may all have a pass
>   To the Grave before day.
>   And in the cold forsaken Grave,
>   There's no drink, *Jack*, no drink,
>   No wine nor women, can we have :
>   No Company but Worms that stinck.
>   Then name thy own health and begin it.

[86.] The beginning of our late unnaturall broyles, was, among other causes imputed chiefly to the imposition of Ship-money, for which Mr *Hambden* was condemned in the Exchequer in a penall Sume by the consent of ten of the judges, who gave their opinion that that Taxe was legal, only Judge *Hutton*, and Judge *Crook* declared against it, so that a stop was put to the levying of it, whereupon a Countryman, no friend to the prerogative, said Wittily, The King may get Ship-money by *Hooke*, but not by *Crook ;* but since that time other taxes ten times heavyer have been taken from us by *Hook* and *Crook* together.

[17.] A Country Farmer being sick, he and his Wife came to a Doctor, who advised him to drink Asses Milk and Sugar every morning, but if you can get no Asses milk come to me and I'll help you to some : says his Wife to him, pray *do you think that the Doctor gives suck ?*

[61.] There was a Gentleman whose onely study and practice was Manhood, as football playing, Wrastling, Pitching the ball, throwing of Weights, Riding, and Fencing, in which active practises he was so perfect, that he over match'd all men that came neer him, insomuch, that he was the Glory of the *West of England*, and he was the Conqueror of all men that came to him, and grew froward that he could not find any man fit to match him, but it happened that one day after hunting, at a drinking Match in an Ale house, by chance he met a *North Countryman* who was highly extolling a great Gamester like himself in the *North*, who performed all exercises that were manly, and a person that was an over commer of all that durst engage him. The *Western* Gentleman desired his name and habitation, which was soon told him. But when he heard it, he was impatient of further delay, and therefore in order for a Journey to him he provided himself of all conveniences, and rid into the North, where with little enquiry he found the Gentleman's house, and knocking at the gate, he was informed by a Servant that his Master was in his Parke a mile off. The Traveller returned thanks, and with his Horse in his hand (guided by the Servants direction) he went to him, where he found him mending of a pale. Now take notice that this *North Country* Gentleman was a very stout man, but of very few words; and the *Western* Gentleman of as many, who thus began to accost him : Sir, I have intelligence that you are the stoutest man in all the *North*, and I am as highly reputed in the *West*, which hath provoked me to find you out, that we may trye both our strength and our skill, so far that fortune and time may Crown one of us, the only glorious man in *England*. The *North* Countryman was still at his worke : but heard distinctly all that he said : but returned no answer, onely when the other had ended speaking, and expected a reply the *North* Countryman comes fairly to him, puts his hand under his twist,[1] and pitcheth him over the Park pales ; the *West* Country man seeing him do that so easily, began to think there was no contending with him, and therefore very civilly, with his Hat in his hand, gave him a return in these words, I thank you, Sir, heartily. Pray throw my Horse over too.

[1] Cotgrave says "twist" answers to the French "fourchure," a fork, or division, *i.e.* he caught hold of him between his legs.

[5.]   Be not wroth *Cotta*, that I not salute thee,
        I us'd it whilst I worthy did repute thee ;
        Now thou art made a painted Saint, and I,
        Cotta, will not commit Idolatry.

[4.] A Lusty young Man in *Somersetshire*, after he had been Married about four Months, grew very Lean and Feeble, so that he cou'd hardly crawl a long ; He, one day, seeing a Butcher run over a Plough'd Field after a Mad Bull, ask'd him the reason of it. Why, says the Butcher it is to Tame him : O, says the Fellow, Let him be Married, let him be Married ; if that don't Tame him, I'll be hang'd.

The Scolding WIFE.

To a pleasant New Tune.

[87.]   There was a young man for lucre of gain
        he low'd a Widow well,
    His friends did tell him often and plain,
        in scolding she did excel.

    Why that is no matter, quoth he,
        so I may have her Bags of Gold,
    Let her not spare to Brawl and Scold,
        for I'll be as merry, as merry can be.

    This Woodcock wedded his hearts desire,
        a Widow with Money enough ;
    They was not so soon out of the Quire,
        ee'r she began to snuff.[1]

    Methink you be very fine,
        you can no quicker get you hence,
    Without such large and great expence,
        of Sugar'd Sops and Musick to dine.

        [1] To take umbrage.

They was not all at supper set,
   or at the board sate down,
E'er she began to brawl and scold,
   and call'd him a peaking Clown :

That nothing could he doe
   that was pleasing in her sight,
But still she scolded day and night,
   which made this merry man's heart full of woe.

If he had provided any good cheer,
   for him and her alone,
Then she wou'd a said, with words more hot,
   you might a done this of your own ;

If sparingly he will be,
   then she would have said, with words more hot,
I will not be pinch'd of what I brought,
   but of mine own I will be free.

That nothing he could doe,
    that was pleasing in his sight
But still she scolded day and night,
    which made this merry man's heart full of woe.

A hundred times he curst
    the Priest, the Clerk, the Sexton too.
And tongue that did the Widow wooe
    and legs that brought him first. ·

It fell out upon a day
    that with his friends he did devise
To break her of her scolding guise,
    and what they did they shall be wary ;

They got and tyed her Arms,
    she could not them undoe.
And many other pretty Charms
    they used her unto.

Her Petticoat was rent and torn,
    upon her Back they did put on,
They tore her smock sleeves all along,
    as if a Bedlam she had been born ;

Her hair about her head they shook,
    all with a Bramble bush.
They ring her Arms in every crook
    till out the blood did gush,

And with an Iron Chain
    fast by the leg he did her tye
There within an old dark House by ;
    so soon he went away again ;

And with a countenance so sad
    he did his Neighbours call.
Quoth he my Wife is Mad,
    she doth so rave and brawl ;

Help Neighbours all therefore,
to see if that you can reclaim,
My Wife into her Wits again
for she is troubled wondrous sore,

FINIS.

Printed for B. Brooksby at the Golden Ball in Pye Corner.

[82.] A Cardinall of Rome had a goodly faire house new built, but the broken brickes, tiles, sand, lime, stones, and such rubbish as are commonly the remnants of such buildings, lay confusedly in heapes and scattered here and there : The Cardinall demanded of his Survayor wherefore the rubbish was not conveyed away : The Survayor said that he proposed to hyre an hundred Carts for the purpose. The Cardinall replyed that the charge of Carts might be saved, for a pitt might bee digged in the ground and bury it. My Lord, said the Survayor, I pray you what shall wee doe with the earth which we digge out of the said pit? Why, thou Coxcombe, said the Cardinall, canst thou not dig the pit deepe enough, and bury all together?

[77.] At *Salisbury*, *Tarlton* & his fellowes were to play before the Maior & his brethren : but one of his company (a yong man) was so drunke, that he could not ; whereat *Tarlton*, as mad angry, as he was mad drunke, claps me on his legs a huge pair of bolts.[1] The fellow dead asleepe, felt nothing. When all was done, they convayed him to the Jayle on a Man's back, and intreated the Jailer to doe God good service, and let him lye there til he waked. While they were about their sport, the felow waked, & finding himselfe in durance, & the Jaile hung round with bolts and shackles, he began to blesse himselfe, & thought sure in his drunkennesse hee had done some mischiefe. With this hee called to know, but none came to him ; then hee thought verily his fault was capitall, and that hee was close prisoner. By and by comes

---

[1] Shackles or fetters.

the Keeper, and mooved him, that one so yong should come to so shamefull a death as hanging. Anon, another comes, and another with the like, which further put him in a puzzle. But at last comes *Tarlton* and others, intreating the Keeper, yet if it might bee, that they might see their fellow ere they went. But hee very hardly was intreated. But at length the poore drunken Signior cald out for them. In they come. Oh *Tom*, saies *Tarlton*, hard was thy hap, in drunkennes to murder this honest man, and our hard hap too, to have it reported, any of our company is hang'd for it. O God, O God saies the fellow, is my fault so great? then commend me to all my friends. Well, short tale to make, the fellow forswore drunkennes, if hee could escape, and by as cunning a wile (to his thinking) they got him out of prison by an escape, and sent him to London before, who was not a little glad to be gone. But see how this iest wrought : by little and little the fellow left his excessive drinking, and in time altered his desire of drunkennes.

[12.]   A Barber left handed
          Trim'd so well, that he bandy'd [1]
With all the Barbers in the *Strand*,
For he trims dextrously ; [2]
          But that I deny,
'Cause he does it with his left hand.

[17.] *John* came to *Thomas* his house to speak with him : but *Thomas* came to the door, and bid his Maid say he was not at home, which *John* overheard ; Two or three days after, *Thomas* came to speak with *John*, and *John* looks out a window, and told him he was not at home : Why do you say so? do I not see you at home? Hey day, says *John*, I believed your Maid you were not at home and you will not believe me my own self.

---

[1] Was at feud. *Minsheu* gives its meaning "to join in a faction" and its equivalent in French as "bander," "mutiner." *Fleming* translates "bander" "to rise—to band against one."

[2] Dexter, *Lat.*, right hand.

[78.] One said a tooth drawer was a kind of unconscionable trade because his trade was nothing else but to take away those things whereby every man gets his living.

[61.] There was a Gentleman who had been very smartly drinking at the Feathers Tavern in *Cheapside*, where there is a very long entry from the street door to the Bar, and a drinking roome by the way where were many civill persons with their wives at supper, but their door was only shut to and not latched ; and this Gentleman staggering thorough, reeld against this door, and fell head long into the Room, to the sudden astonishment of the Company, who rise up and demanded the reason of that rudenesse ; the poor Gentleman with very much adoe got up, and staggering with his hat in his hand he made hard shift to cry them all mercy in these words, Gentlemen and Ladyes, I pray excuse my boldnesse, and consider I am not the first that have fallen into ill Company.

The following throws much light on the habits of people in the reign of Charles II., and is valuable as it shows a phase of life not often depicted.

[85.]   *A Lampoon on the* Greenwich *Strowlers.*

Oh ! assist me you Powers, who have Rhimes at command,
For I faith I've a weighty business in hand.
Of the late *Greenwich* Strowlers I'me now going to sing,
But all things in order—first, God save the King.

Hem ; hem ; now put we off to the matter,
On *Easter* Sunday, the Raskals took water ;
Where landing at *Greenwich*, they agreed that a share
Should be settled o' th' Sculler, instead of his fare.

Then up they march'd to the sign of the Bull,
Where asking for Lodging, quoth the folks we are ful.
But we'el see for some for you, and so with that wheadle,
Ud's lid, exit's the Landlord, and enter the Beadle.

With that their Chief Actor begins for to bristle,
Quoth he, p'shaw waw, let the Beadle go whistle,
For I can ; and he did, too, produce straight a Pattent,
That had the King's Hand and Seal, and all that in't.

Well this rub of fortune is over ; but stay,
They call for a Reckning, theres six Pence to pay.
Now mark how damn'd fortune these Strowlers do's cozen,
They pawn all their stock to pay the half dozen.

But promising th' Host that he should Tricket free,
See their Plays every day, and his whole family.
He releases 'em straight, and now all the rabble
Marcht up to go lye in their Play house,—a Stable.

.   .   .   .   .   .

.   .   .   .   .

I confess they had never a Scene at all,
They wanted no copy, they had th' original.
For the Windowes being down, and most part of the roof,
How could they want Scenes when they had prospect enough.

Now we will suppose that *Munday* is come,
And the Play is proclaymed by beat of a Drum.
Faith, now you're supposing, let it be *Tuesday* morn,
For of *Monday*, I know no more than the child unborn.

It's said that they Acted not upon *Monday*,
Something was wanting, and so they lost one day.
They send unto *London*, what's lacking is gotten,
And so on the next day, w'ye all things did cotten.

The Prizes they took, were a Londoners groat,
A Gentleman's size,[1] but his skipkennel's [2] pot.
The Townsmen they let in for drink and good chear,
The School boys for peace, and the Seamen for fear.

---

[1] Sixpence—the 6 on dice being called "size."
[2] Footman or footboy.

On *Tuesday* at three a clock I was we'e 'em,
I kist their doorkeeper, and went in to see 'em.
Being enter'd an Actor[1] straight brought me a stool,
Hee'd a held my cloak too, but I wa'nt such a fool.

The first that appear'd, when I was come in,
With her train to her ankles, was who but the Queen.
She civilly made me a curtsy and straight,
Retired to sit on her Fagots of state.

Then in came the King with a Murtherous mind,
Gainst his new married Queen, which when I did find,
I call'd him a side, and whispering in's Ear,
Desired him to fetch me a Flagon of Bear.

There's twelve pence, said I, take the rest for your pains,
Your Servant said he, Sir, sweet Mr *Haines.*
His Majesty, faith, I must needs say was civil,
For he took up his Heels, and ran for't like a Devil.

Meantime I addrest myself to his Bride,
And took her unto the tireing House side;
A hay loft it was which at a dead lift,
Instead of a better serv'd then for a shift.

But mark the Fate of her Civility,
The Players did rant both at her and me:
And therefore because for fear she'd be lack'd
I ordred the Drummer to beat a long Act.

He beat and he beat, but no Queen appear'd,
He beat till at length the house was all clear'd:
By my Troath a sad loss, but to make 'em amends.
I threw 'em a Crown, and we were all Friends:
And so this Renowned History ends.

---

[1] This is an allusion to the custom of the gallants sitting on stools on the stage, so frequently spoken of by the dramatists of the sixteenth century. Indeed Queen Anne found it necessary to issue two proclamations forbidding people other than actors to go on the stage.

[52.] A Gentleman upon a time having a man that could write and read well, rebuked him one day for idlenesse, saying, If I had nothing to do, like thee, I would to recreate my wit, set down all the fooles I knew. The fellow, making little answer, tooke his pen and inke, and as his Master had wished him, fell to setting down a Catalogue of the fooles that he was well acquainted with: among whom, and first of all, he set down his Master, who, reading his name, would needs know the nature of his folly; Marry, quoth he, In lending your Cozen twenty pound this other day: for I think he will never pay you. Yea but (quoth his Master) what if he do pay me? Then (quoth his man) I will put out your name, and put down his for a foole.

[20.] A Gentleman in *North Wales* was standing in a Sunshiny day, upon a high rock near the Sea-Side in those parts ; and as he was looking about, he saw an Island some Four miles from the shore or there abouts, upon which Island he spy'd two Hares playing one with another : Well, says he, are you got over there now; for I am sure I cours'd you both yesterday with my two Greyhounds, and then you shew'd me a trick, but now I'll shew you one. So he went immediately home, and fetch't his two Greyhounds, and a great Morter piece which he had of a Thousand pound weight, which he fastened between the two Dogs Necks; but he was forced to fasten a Cord to it also, lest the Dogs might run away with it ; and when they had carry'd it to the Rock aforesaid, he charg'd the Morter piece, and presently the two Greyhounds slipt into it (for it seems they had been used to it) which two Greyhounds he ram'd in very well, and then discharg'd the Morter piece with no hurt at all to the Greyhounds (for you must know he shot with white Powder) and it so happened that says he, I protest t'ye Gentlemen (upon my honest word and Credit 'tis true) that the two Greyhounds each lighted upon a Hare as they were playing, and then kill'd 'em and immediately left the Island, and swam through the Sea with the Hares in their mouths, which were one boil'd and t'other roasted for my dinner. One ask't him what colour his Greyhounds were? He swore they were both black before, but the White Powder did so Change their Colour, that they were both turn'd grey ; and so from them all of their kind were called Grey hounds, for their sakes to this day. They told him they thought this probable enough to be improbable. O Gentlemen, says he far be it from me to tell you a lie, for if you won't believe me, pray ask my Dogs.

Upon Thorough-good, an unthrift.

[5.] Thy Sirname *Thorough-good* befitteth thee,
Thou *Thorough-good*, and good goes thorough thee,
Nor thou in good, nor good in thee doth stay,
Both of you thorough goe, and pass away.

[77.] *Tarlton* having been domineering[1] very late one night, with two of his friends, and comming homewards along Cheapeside, the Watch being then set, Master Constable asked, Who goes there? Three merry men, quoth *Tarlton*. That is not sufficient, What are you? quod M. Constable. Why, saies *Tarlton*, one of us is an eye maker, and the other a light maker. What saiest thou, knave, doest mocke me? the one is an eye maker, the other a light maker, which two properties belong unto God onely : commit these blasphemers, quoth the Constable. Nay, I pray you, good M. Constable, be good in your Office, I will approve what I have said to be true, qd *Tarlton*. If thou canst, saies the Constable, you shall passe, otherwise you shall be all three punished. Why (qd. *Tarlton*) this fellow is an eye maker, because a Spectacle maker, and this other a maker of light, because a Chandler, that makes your darkest night as light as your Lanthorn. The Constable, seeing them so pleasant, was well contented. The rest of the Watchmen laughed : & Tarlton with his two Companions went home quietly.

[78.] One perswaded his friend to marry a little woman because of evils the least was to be chosen.

[26.] A crafty Fellow being extremely in debt, and being

---

[1] Roystering.

threatened by his Creditors, that they would have him, if he was above ground, got himself into a Cellar, and there lay with the Tapster; and being reproved for so doing, he told them there's no fear of catching him there, because 'twas underground, and they durst not break their Oaths, because they swore they would have him above Ground.

THE

UNFORTUNATE FENCER;[1]

or

The Couragious Farmer of Gloucester-shire

shewing

How this huffing Spark went down into those Parts, Challenging any one at all sorts of Weapons; and at length (was) shamefully Conquer'd by a Country Farmer.

To the Tune of *The Spinning Wheel.*   Licensed according to Order.

[88.]   You that delight in merriment,
            be pleased attend a while,
        I hope to give you all content,
            this very Song will make you smile;
        'Tis of a Fencer brave and bold,
            adorn'd with rich embroider'd Gold.

        This Spark in pomp, and rich array,
            from *London* rid with right good will,
        That he young Lords might learn to play
            all sorts of Weapons by his skill;
        And whereso e'er this Fencer came,
            the drum, and trumpet blaz'd his fame.

            [1] For tune, see Appendix.

R

This huffing Fencer, fierce and Stout,
  to *Gloucester* City did repair,
And for a Sign he then hung out
  a Sword of grand Defiance there;
The which a Farmer did espy,
  as he by Chance was passing by.

The jolly Farmer brisk and bold,
  as soon as he the Sword beheld,
He cry'd what is there to be sold?
  what! is your Room with Rapiers fill'd?
The Valiant Fencer did reply
  I come my Valour here to try.

With that he did his Rapier shake,
  and said let who will here arrive,
I do a noble Challenge make,
  to fight the stoutest man alive:
The Farmer said I'll answer thee,
  if that you dare to Cope with me.

The Fencer cry'd, you sorry knave,
  here by this Rapier in my hand,
I'll send the to thy silent Grave,
  against my force no Clown can stand;
It shall be try'd the Farmer cry'd,
  I value not your huffing Pride.

Next Morning they a Stage prepare,
  the drums did beat and trumpets sound,

Right joyfull tydings to declare,
  this Gallant trac'd the City round,
Dress'd in his Shirt of Holland fine,
  with Sword that did like Silver shine.

The Stage he mounted brisk and gay,
  and eke the Farmer straight likewise ;
To whom the Huffing Spark did say,
  of you I'll make a Sacrifice ;
This work in short I will compleat,
  you should have brought a Winding Sheet.

No more of that, but let's fall to,
  I hope to make my Party good ;
And e'er this World I bid adieux,
  who knows but I may let you blood ;
With that he cut him o'er the Face,
  and thus began the Spark's Disgrace.

But when they came to Quarter Staff,
  the Farmer bang'd the Spark about ;
Which made all the Spectators laugh,
  and with Huzzas they all did shout ;
He made his Head and Shoulders sore,
  he ne'er had been so thrash'd before.

Thus fairly did he win the day,
  which put the Fencer in a Rage,
Who through the Crowd did sneak away,
  while the stout Farmer kept the Stage ;
Huzzas of joy did echo round,
  while he with Victory was Crown'd.

FINIS.

Printed for P. Brooksby,[1] J. Deacon,[2] J. Blare,[3] J. Back.[4]

[1] Philip Brooksby had two shops,—one, the Golden Ball, near Bear Tavern, in West Smithfield ; the other, Harp and Ball, also Golden Ball, in Pye Corner.

[2] J. Deacon lived at the Rainbow, near David's Inn, or St. Andrew's Church, Holborn.

[3] Josiah Blare's shop was the Looking Glass, on London Bridge.

[4] John Back also lived on London Bridge, at the sign of the Black Boy.

[86.] King *James* with some of his Nobles having lost their way in a *Forest* in the persuit of a Deer, came at last a hungry to the side of the same *Forest* where they espied a little House ; thither hyed the King, and demanded first what victuals in the House, then with some comfortable leysure the way ; the good wife sets before the King a good piece of powdered [1] Beefe and a bag pudding, the King and his Followers fell to eat heartily, & having contented his *hostess* rid away : by the road side at some distance, a boy presents himself scraping with his legs, bare headed, whereon was a thick scald : Sirrah, said the Lords, cover your head, have you never a Cap ? where do you dwell ? In yonder Cottage an't please you (pointing to the place where the King dined) I had a Cap yesterday, but to day my mother made use of it for a pudding bag ; Quoth the King, it did me no harme in the eating, it shall do me lesse in thinking of it ; come, put on, and let us jog it down ; but it stirred the stomacks of his Traine.

[17.] One *Pace* a bitter Jester in Queen *Elizabeth's* daies, came to Court : Come says the Ladies, *Pace*, we shall now hear of our faults : No, says he, I don't use to talk of that which all the Towne talks of.

[12.]   One saw an Old Woman,
          Which indeed is Common,
     With her nose to meet with her chin ;
          'Tis strange, says he, me-thinks,
          For when that she drinks
     The De'el a drop can she get in.

          He was then told the cause,
          And what the reason was
     That her teeth were fell out, and her chin
          And Nose, like loving Neighbours,
          Think well of their Labours,
     To reconcile 'em agen.

[1] Salted.

[52.] A Worshipfull Gentleman in London, having on a time invited divers of his friends to supper to his house, and being at supper, the second course comming in, the first was one of the Gentleman's own men, bringing a Capon; and by chance, stumbling at the portall door, the Capon flew out of the platter and ranne along the board to the upper end of the table where the Master of the house sate, who making a jest of it, said, By my faith it is well, the Capon is come first, my man will come anon too, I hope. By and by came his man, and takes up the Capon, and layes it in the platter, and sets it on the board. I thank you Sir, quoth his Master, I could have done so my self. I, quoth his man, it is an easie matter, sir, for one to do a thing when he sees it done before his face.

[17.] Some Tylers working on the top of the house, one by chance dropt down through the rafters; Says one, I like such a Fellow dearly, for he is one that goes through his work.

[26.] Another swore, that he in his Travels round about the World, which he had encompast Three times and half in Seven years time, but could not finish the other half, because he fell very Sick, and so was forc't to return back agen; and in his return, he came to a King's Court, but I cannot for my life remember the place, because I have been in so many; and there, says he, I saw a Lute of a very great bigness, and Thirty Ells long, bating only three inches, and Three broad; and swore that the least string upon it was bigger than his Thumb. Then they askt him how it possibly could be plaid on? He told them that a Man and his Wife that were Gyants (of which there's abundance in that Country) had Two large Iron Bows, made each with Eight Feet like Gridirons, with which he, and his dear Consort (which I think is the best name for her now, in regard of that Musick) scrat ore the strings; that is, she on the Treble part, and He on the Bass, whilst Eight great Mastiff Dogs ran up and down the Frets of the Lute, with their bare feet, and stopt directly in Tune as they plaid; (but you must conceive that these dogs were bred up to't, or else 'twere a thing impossible) to the admiration of all strangers

that were there; and the Case of that Lute served for a
kennel for the Eight Dogs to lie in : but it seems 'tis common
with them there, for they made nothing of it; and this he
made good by whole Volleys of thundering Oaths.

[5.] A fat house keeper makes leane Executors.   The
Devill is not alwaies at one doore.   He puls with a long rope,
that waights for anothers death.

Come buy this new Ballad, before you doe goe ;
If you raile at the Author, I know what I know.

To the Tune of, *Ile tell you but so.*

[89.]   It is an old saying
   that few words are best,
And he that sayes little,
   shall live most at rest :
And I by experience
   doe finde it right so,
Therefore Ile spare speech,
   but I know what I know.

Yet shall you perceive well,
 though little I say,
That many enormities
 I will display :
You may guesse my meaning
 by that which I show,
I will not tell all
 but I know &c.

There be some great climbers
 compos'd of ambition,
To whom better-born men
 doe bend with submission :
Proud Lucifer climbing
 was cast very low,
Ile not stay these men.
 but I know &c.

There be many Foxes
 that goe on two legges,
They steale greater matters
 than Cocks, Hens and Egges ;
To catch many Guls
 in Sheepes cloathing they goe
They might be destroy'd
 but I know &c.

There be many men
 that Devotion pretend,
And make us beleeve
 that true Faith theyle defend :
Three times in one day
 to Church they will goe,
They cozen the world,
 but I know &c.

There be many rich men
 both Yeomen and Gentry,
That for their owne private gaine
 hurt a whole Countrey :

By closing free Commons,
   yet they'le make as though
Twere for common good,
   but I know &c.

There be divers Papists
   that to save their Fine,
Come to Church once a moneth
   to heare Service Divine:
The Pope gives them power,
   as they say, to doe so
They save money by't too
   but I know &c.

There be many Upstarts
   that spring from the Cart,
Who gotten to th' Court
   play the Gentleman's part:
Their fathers were plaine men,
   they scorne to be so,
They think themselves brave
   but I know &c.

There be many Officers
   men of great place,
To whom, if one sue
   for their favour and grace,
He must bribe their servants
   while they make as though
They know no such thing,
   but I know &c.

There be many Women
   that seem very pure,
A kisse from a stranger
   they'le hardly endure:
They are like Lucretia,
   modest in show.
I will accuse none,
   but I know &c.

Likewise there be many
    dissembling men,
That seeme to hate Drinking
    and Women, yet when
They meet with a Wench
    to the Taverne they'le goe,
They are civill all day
    but I know &c.

There be many Batchelors
    that to beguile
Beleeving kind Lasses,
    use many a wile,
They all sweare that they love,
    when they meane nothing so,
And boast of these tricks
    but I know &c.

There's many an Usurer,
    that like a Drone,
Doth idly live
    upon his moneys Lone :
From Tens unto Hundreds
    his money doth grow,
He sayes he doth good,
    but I know &c.

There be many Gallants
    that goe in gay Rayment,
For which the Taylor
    did never receive payment;
They ruffle it out
    with a gorgeous show,
Some take them for Knights,
    but I know &c.

There be many Rorers
    that swagger and rore,

As though they in the warres had been,
 seven yeeres or more :
And yet they never lookt
 in the face of a Foe ;
They seeme gallant Sparkes
 but I know &c.

There's many both Women
 and Men that appeare
With beautifull Outsides
 the Worlds eyes to bleare :
But all is not Gold
 that doth glister in show,
They are fine with a Pox,
 but I know &c.

There's many rich Trades-men
 who live by Deceit,
And in Weight and Measure
 the poore they doe cheat,
They'le not sweare an Oath
 but indeed, I, and No,
They truly protest.
 but I know &c.

There be many people
 so given to strife,
That they'le goe to Law
 for a two-penny Knife,
The Lawyers ne're aske them
 why they doe so,
He gets by their hate,
 but I know &c.

I know there be many
 will carpe at this Ballet,
Because it is like
 sowre Sawce to their Pallet ;

But he, shee, or they,
   let me tell ere I goe,
If they speak against this Song
   I know what I know.

Printed by the Assignes of Thomas Symcocke.[1]

[82.] A Proper Gentlewoman went to speak with a rich
Mizer that had more Gowt than good manners, at her taking
leave hee requested her to tast a Cup of Canara : Shee
(contrary to his expectation) tooke him at his word and
thanked him. Hée commanded *Jeffrey Starveling* his man,
to wash a glasse, and fill it to the Gentlewoman. Honest
Jeffrey fill'd a great glasse about the bignesse of two Taylors
thimbles, and gave it to his master, who kist it to save cost,
and gave it to the Gentlewoman, saying that it was good
Canara of six yeeres old at the least, to whom shee answered
(seeing the quantity so small,) Sir, as you requested me, I
have tasted your wine, but I wonder that it should be so
little, being of such a great age.

[61.] There were two notable boon Companions which
when they were met were alwayes so indeared to each others
Company that very seldom an earlier houre than midnight
could part them, but when they were drunk they had two
troublesome infirmities, *Jack* could not goe nor *Will* could
not speak ; therefore one night before they fell to drinking,
they made Articles of Agreement that when they were drunke
Will should carry *Jack*, and *Jack* should speak for *Will*, and
after this agreement to drinking they went pell-mell, untill the
one was drunk, and the other lame : So after they had paid
the Reckoning, *Will* takes up *Jack* a pick-pack and carries
him to *Ludgate*, and being very weary sets him down in the
dark close by the prison. The Constable and Watch who
were within the Gate hearing a bustle, called out, saying, Who

---

[1] Published in 1620, and assigned his patent the same year. He is
also heard again of in 1642, when his patent was petitioned against, but
unsuccessfully.

goes there? Come before the Constable. *Will* could goe well enough, but could not speak, so he went over to the Constable, who examined him whence he came, and why he was out so late, and where he lived; to which *Will* could answer nothing, but make mouths: but *Jack* having his tongue at liberty, as he was sitting in the blind hole, cryes to the Constable, Sir, he cannot speak. Upon that the Constable asked who was that which spake, and commanded him to come before him; to which *Jack* made answer, Sir, I can't goe, at which the Constable and Watch laught; *Will* took up his load again and away they marcht.

To his Quill.

[5.] Thou hast been wanton, therefore it is meet,
    Thou shouldst do penance—do it in a sheet.

[128.] Caricature of different religious sects.   1646.

Adamite   *Seeker*

Arminian

Diuorcer

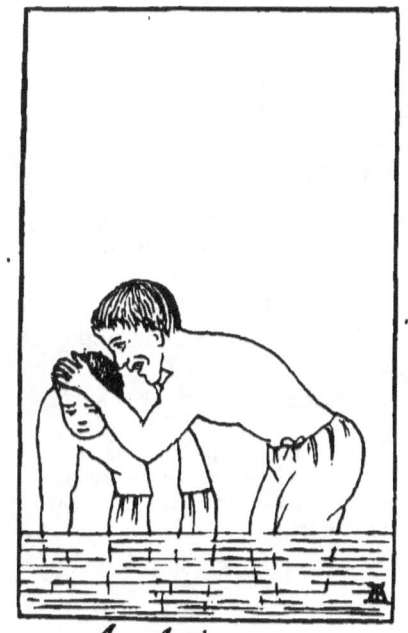

Anabaptist

Iesuit

[78.] One said Physitians had the best of it, for, if they did well, the world did proclaime it, if ill, the earth did cover it.

[77.] Upon a time, as *Tarlton* and his Wife (as passengers) came sailing from Southampton towards London, a mighty storme arose, and endangered the Ship, whereupon, the Captaine thereof charged every man to throw into the Sea the heaviest thing he could best spare, to the end to lighten somewhat the Ship. *Tarlton*, that had his Wife there, offered to throw her over-boord : but the company rescued her ; and being asked wherefore he meant so to doe? he answerd, She is the heaviest thing I have, and I can best spare her.

[4.] A *Welshman* that was condemned to be hanged, had the benefit [1] of Clergy granted to him, and so was burnt in the Hand ; which when it was doing, they bid him say. God bless the King. Nay, says he, God bless hur Father and Mother ; for if they had not taught hur to read, hur might have been hanged for all the King.

[4.] One asking a certain Person how his friend came off at the Sessions House? he told him he was to be Burnt in the Hand ; Pish, says the other, that's a small matter ; for, for a little Fee, the'll Burn him in the Hand with a cold Iron.

[5.]   Marriage as old men note, hath likened bin
       Unto a publique feast, or common route,
       Where those that are without, would fain get in,
       And those that are within would faine get out.

[26.] A Gentleman that had a great Wit, and well belov'd among the great ones, and therefore invited often amongst them ; but it seems had a very sore Leg ; he, being at a Noble mans Table, greedily cat'd at a Goblet of Wine. Says my Lord to him, Prithee *Jack* drink it not, for 'twill hurt thy Leg. O my Lord, says he, take no care for my Leg, for I have care enough of that, for I always drink o' the t' other side.

---

[1] This plea was put in for mitigation of punishment, the person presumably being a clerk or learned person, exemplified by his being able to read, the punishment then being commuted to burning on the hand. In later days it became a farce, as a bribe would have the effect of being apparently branded with only a warm or cold iron.

𝕮𝖍𝖊 𝕮𝖗𝖚𝖊𝖑𝖑 𝕾𝖍𝖗𝖔𝖜:¹

or

The Patient Mans Woe

Declaring the misery, and the great paine
By his unquiet wife he doth dayly sustaine.

To the Tune of *Cuckolds all arowe.*

[90.]   Come Batchelors and Married Men,
        and listen to my Song;
    And I will shew you plainely then,
        the injury and wrong
    That constantly I doe sustaine,
        by the unhappy life,
    The which does put me to great paine,
        by my unquiet Wife.

¹ For tune, see Appendix.

Shee never linnes[1] her bauling,
  her tongue it so loud,
But alwaies shee'l be railing,
  and will not be contrould ;
For she the Briches still will weare,
  although it breedes my strife,
If I were now a Batchelor,
  I'de never have a Wife.

Sometime I goe i' th' morning
  about my dayly worke,
My wife she will be snorting,
  and in her bed she'le lurke ;
Untill the Chimes doe goe at Eight,
  then she'le begin to wake,
Her mornings draught well spiced straight,
  to cleare her eyes she'le take.

As soon as shee is out of bed,
  her Looking Glass she takes,
So vainely is she dayly led,
  her mornings worke she makes ;
In putting on her brave atyre,
  that fine and costly be,
Whilst I worke hard in durt and mire,
  alacke what remedy.

Then she goes forth a Gossiping,
  amongst her own Comrades,
And then she falls a bowsing[2]
  with her merry blades :
When I come from my labour hard,
  then shee'le begin to scould,
And calls me Rogue without regard,
  which makes my heart full cold.

When I for quietnesse sake desire,
  my wife for to be still ;
She will not grant what I require,
  but sweares shee'le have her will ;

---

 [1] Ceases, or leaves off.   [2] Drinking.

Then if I chance to heave my hand,
    straightway she'le murder cry;
Then judge all Men that here do stand
    in what a Case am I.

And if a Friend by chance me call,
    to drinke a pot of Beere;
Then she'le begin to curse and brall,
    and fight and scratch and teare:
And sweares unto my worke she'le send
    me straight without delay,
Or else with the same Cudgels end,
    shee will me soundly pay.

And if I chance to sit at meate
    upon some holy day,
She is so sullen she will not eate,
    but vexe me ever and aye:
She'le pout, and loure, and curse and bann,
    this is the weary life,
That I do leade, poore harmlesse man,
    with my most dogged wife.

Then is not this a pitteous Cause,
    let all men now it trie,
And give their verdits by the Lawes,
    betweene my wife and I:
And judge the Cause who is to blame,
    Ile to their Judgement stand,
And be contented with the same
    and put thereto my hand.

If I abroad goe any where,
    my businesse for to doe,
Then will my Wife anone be there,
    for to encrease my woe;
Straightway she such a noise will make,
    with her most wicked tongue,
That all her Mates her part to take,
    about me soon will thronge.

8

Thus am I now tormented still,
  with my most wicked Wife,
All through her wicked tongue so ill
  I am weary of my life :
I know not truely what to doe,
  nor how myselfe to mend :
This lingring life doth breede my woe,
  I would 'twere at an ende.

O that some harmlesse honest man,
  whom Death did so befriend,
To take his Wife from of his hand,
  his sorrowes for to end :
Would change with me to rid my care,
  and take my Wife alive,
For his dead Wife unto his share,
  then I would hope to thrive.

But so it likely will not be,
  that is the worst of all,
For to encrease my dayly woe
  and for to breed my fall :
My wife is still most froward bent,
  such is my lucklesse fate,
There is no man will be content,
  with my unhappy state.

Thus to conclude and made an ende
  of these my Verses rude,   .
I pray all wives for to amende,
  and with peace to be endude :
Take warning all men by the life
  that I sustained long,
Be carefull how you chuse a Wife,
  and so Ile ende my Song.

FINIS.

Arthur Halliarg.[1]

London.   Printed by *M. P.* for *Henry Gosson*[2] on London Bridge
neere the Gate.

[1] This ballad is supposed to be unique, and is the only known work
of Halliarg, who is not mentioned by Hazlitt.

[2] The date of this ballad in the Museum Catalogue is 1610 (?).

[91.] A Bishop on a time examining one that sought to be admitted into the ministery, asked him how many Sacraments there were; to which question, he, after long pause, answered there were 9; Nine, quoth he, how prove you that? Why, quoth hee, there are 7 beyond sea, and two in *England;* at which the B. laughing at his ignorance, yet grieved for his folly, sent him away as worthily frustrate of his expectation.

[4.] A Man being ask'd whether his friend *Tom*, that was lately dead, had left him any Legacy? No, faith, says he, Not a Tester to drink his health.

[26.] In the Wars in *Germany*, between the *Swedes* and them, there was so great a Frost one Winter, that Two Men desiring to talk with one another, and one was on one side of the River, and t'other on the other, and as they spoke one to another, the Frost was so great, that it froze[1] up their words, which was not audible then, nor indeed (upon my reputation) could not be heard till Nine days after, when it chanc'd to thaw: which one of the company hearing said 'twas a brave Country to speak Treason in; for whatsoever a Man said, a Man could not be heard; Nay, the very lowings of the Bulls and Cows were froz'n up also, that the owners had much ado to find them to fodder them, for want of hearing them as formerly. Nay, by your favour, says another, there is another Country, which had as great a Conveniency to speak Treason in as that had, from 1648 to 1660, and there one might speak any sort of Treason, and was never call'd to an account for it: Nay, the more Treason they spoke, they were the better esteem'd; so that there was no need of a frost at that time in *England*.

[52.] There was a notable drunkard of Rochester, whom his wife perswaded as much as in her lay, to leave that Sinne; but the more she spake the worse he was, and because she controuled him, he would all to beat her, So she let him alone; and because his use was still to stay out till almost

---

[1] A somewhat similar story may be found previously, in *Rabelais*, and some sixty years subsequently, in *Baron Munchausen*.

midnight, she went to bed, and bad her Maid tary up for him, and make a good fire : and the maid did as her Mistresse commanded.   One night when he came home the Maid let him in, and he stood by the fire and warmed himself; but his head being too heavy for his body, down he fell into the fire along.   The Maid ranne crying, Oh Mistresse, Mistresse, my Master is falne into the fire.   No Matter, Maid (quoth she) let him take his pleasure in his owne house, where he will himselfe.

[4.]   A Gentleman not richest in discretion,
Was alwayes sending for his own phisition.
And on a time he needs would of him know,
What was the cause his pulse did go so slow ?
Why (quoth the Doctor) thus it comes to passe,
Must needs go slow, which goes upon an asse.

[82.]   An unhappy boy that kept his father's sheepe in the country, did use to carry a paire [1] of Cards in his pocket, and meeting with boyes as good as himselfe would fall to Cards at the Cambrian game of whip-her-ginny,[2] or English one and thirty ; at which sport, hee would some dayes lose a sheepe or two : for which if his father corrected him, hee (in revenge)

[1] A pack.
[2] The same author mentions this game again in "Taylors Motto," as also many other games then in vogue, the names of which are curious—

" The Prodigall's estate, like to a flux,
The Mercer, Draper, and the Silk man sucks ;
The Taylor, Millainer, Dogs, Drabs and Dice,
Trey trip or Passage, or the Most at thrice ;
At Irish, Tick tacke, Doublets, Draughts or Chesse,
He flings his money free with carelessnesse :
At Novum, Mumchance, mischance (chuse ye which)
At One and Thirty, or at Poore and rich,
Ruffe, flam, Trump, noddy, whisk, hole, Sant, New Cut,
Unto the keeping of foure Knaves he'l put
His whole estate at Loadum, or at Gleeke,
At Tickle me quickly, he's a merry Greeke,
At Primefisto, Post and payre, Primero,
Maw, Whip-her-ginny, he's a lib'rall *Hero;*
At My-sow-pigg'd : and (Reader never doubt ye,
He's skill'd in all games except) Looke about ye.
Bowles, shove-groate, tennis, no game comes amiss,
His purse a purse for any body is."

would drive the sheepe home at night over a narrow bridge, where some of them falling besides the bridge, were drowned in the swift brooke. The old man being wearied with his ungracious dealing, complained to a Justice, thinking to affright him from doing any more the like. In briefe, before the Justice the youth was brought, where (using small reverence, and lesse manners) the Justice said to him, Sirrah, you are a notable villaine, you play at Cards, and lose your father's sheepe at one and thirty. The Boy replied that it was a lye. A lye, quoth the Justice, you saucy knave, dost thou give me the lye? No, qd the boy, I gave thee not the lye, but you told me the lye, for I never lost sheepe at one and thirty; for when my game was one and thirty I alwayes wonne. Indeed, said the Justice thou saist true, but I have another accusation against thee, which is, that you drive your fathers sheepe over a narrow bridge where some of them are oftentimes drowned: That's a lye too, quoth the boy, for those that go over the bridge are well enough, it is onely those that fall beside which are drowned: Whereto the Justice said to the boys father, Old man, thou hast brought in two false accusations against thy sonne for he never lost sheepe at one and thirty, nor were there ever any drowned that went over the bridge.

The

Unfortunate WELCH MAN

or

The Untimely Death of *Scotch* JOCKEY.

If her will Fight, her cause to right,
as daring to presume
To Kill and Slay, then well her may
take this to be her Doom.

To the Tune of *The Country Farmer.*   This may be Printed *R. P.*

[92.] Stout *Shonny-ap-Morgan* to *London* would ride,
    To seek Cousen *Taffie* whatever betide ;
    Her own Sisters Son, whom her loved so dear,
    Her had not beheld him this many long year :

Betimes in the morning stout *Shonny* arose,
And then on the Journey with Courage her goes,
A *Cossit*[1] of Gray was the best of her Close,
Her Boots they were out at the heels and the toes.

A Sword by her side, and with *Bob* the Gray Mare,
Her rid on the Road like a Champion so rare ;
At last how it happened to her hard Lot,
To meet with young *Jockey*, a bonny brisk Scot ;
Then *Jockey* was jolly, and thus he did say,
Let's gang to the Tavern, drink wine by my fay,
Then *Shonny* consented, and made no delay,
But *Jockey* left *Shonny* the Reckoning to pay.

While *Morgan* was merry, and thinking no ill,
The *Scotchman* he used the best of his skill ;
Considering how he might scamper away,
For why Sir, he never intended to pay :
But like a false Loon he slipt out of door,
And never intended to come there no more,
Poor Shonny-ap-Morgan, was left for the Score,
Cotzo her was never so served before.

Her paying the Shot, then away her went,
The *Welch* blood was up, and her mind was bent,
For speedy pursuing he then did prepare,
Then Morgan did mount upon *Bob* the Gray Mare :
Then Whip and Spur stout *Shonny* did ride,
And overtook *Jockey* near to a Wood side,

[1] ? Corset.

And pull'd out her Sword in the height of her Pride,
And wounded poor *Jockey* who presently dy'd.

Then *Shonny* was taken and hurry'd to Jail,
Where her till the Sessions did weep and bewail ;
And then at the last, by the Laws of the Land,
Was brought to the Bar to hold up her Hand ;
O good her Lord Shudge poor *Shonny* did cry,
Now Whip her, and send her to Wales her Country ;
Or cut off a Leg, or an Arm, or an Eye,
For her is undone, if Condemned to dye.

But this would not do, poor *Shonny* was cast,
And likewise received her sentence at last ;
A Gentleman Robber just at the same time,
Received just Sentence then due for his Crime ;
Then *Shonny-ap-Morgan* her shed many tears,
Her heart was possessed with sorrow and fears,
The Gentleman Thief likewise hung down his ears,
For then he expected his antient Arrears.

The day being come, they must both bid adieu,
Forsaking the world and the rest of their Crew ;
The Spark was attir'd so gallant and gay,
But *Shonny* was poor, and in ragged array :
And when they came both to the Gibbet Tree,
The Gentleman gave to the Hangman a Fee,
And said, let this *Welch man* Hang farther from me,
So vile and so ragged a Rascal is he.

The Welch-man he heard him, and was in a rage,
That nothing almost, could his anger asswage ;
But fretting and chaffing, he thus did begin,
Her will make her to know that her came of good kin ;
Besides her will tell her her hearty belief,
That her is no more than a Gentleman Thief,
That robbed on the Roads, and the Plain and the Heath,
Her now will Hang by her in spight of her teeth.

FINIS.

Printed for *J. Deacon* at the *Angel* in Guiltspur Street.

[82.] A Country fellow (that had not walked much in streets that were paved) came to *London*, where a dog came suddenly out of a house, and furiously ran at him : the fellow stooped to take up a stone to cast at the Dog, and finding them all fast rammed, or paved in the ground ; quoth hee, what strange Country am I in? where the people tye up the stones, and let the dogs loose.

[93.] *George (Peele)*, with others of his Associates, being mery together at the Taverne, having more store of Coyne than usually they did possesse ; although they were regardlesse of their silver, yet they intended for a season to be good husbands, if they knew how to be sparing of that their pockets were then furnished withall : Five pounds they had amongst them, and a plot must be cast how they might bee merrie with extraordinarie cheere three or foure dayes, and keepe their five pounds whole in stocke : *George Peele* was the man must doe it, or none, and generally they coniured him by their loves, his owne credit, and the reputation that went on him, that he would but in this shew his wit : and, withall, hee should have all the furtherance that in them lay.   *George* as easie, as they earnest, to be wonne to such an exploit, consented and gathered their money together, and gave it all to *George*, who should be their purse bearer, and the other foure should seeme as servants to *George Peele* and the better to colour it, they should goe change their cloakes, the one like the other, so neere as they could possible : the which, at *Beelzebub's* brother, the Broker's, they might quickly doe : This was soone accomplished, and *George* was furnished with his blacke Sattin suit, and a paire of bootes, which were as familiar to his legges, as the pillory to a Bakers or Colliers [1] necke, and hee sufficiently possest his friends with the whole scope of his intent, as, gentle Reader, the sequell will shew.   Instantly they tooke a paire of Oares, whose armes were to make a false gallop no further than Brainford, where their faire was paid to them so liberally, that each of them the next tide to London, purchased two new wastcoates, yet should these good benefactors come to their usuall places of trade, and if they spie a better fare than their

[1] Now termed coal merchants.

owne, that happily the Gentleman hath more minde to goe
withall, they will not onely fall out with him that is of their
owne sweet transporters, as they are, but abuse the fare
they carrie with foule speeches, as, a Pox, or the Devill go
with you: as their Godfather *Caron* the Ferry-man of Hell
hath taught them. I speake not this of all, but of some that
are brought up in the East, some in the West, some in the
North, but most part in the South: but for the rest they are honest compleat men, leaving them to come to my honest *George;*
who is now merry at the three Pigeons[1] in Braineford, with
Sacke and Sugar, not any wine wanting, the Musicians playing,
my host drinking, my hostis dauncing with the worshipfull
Justice, for so then he was tearmed, and his Mansion house in
Kent, who came thither of purpose to be merry with his men;
because he could not so conveniently neere home, by reason
of a shrewish wife he had: my gentle hostis gave him all the
entertainment the house could afford, for M. *Peele* had paid
royally; for all his five pounds was come to ten groats. Now
George Peele's wit labors to bring in that five pounds there was
spent, which was soone begotten. Being sot at dinner, My
host, quoth *George,* how fals the Tyde out for London; not
till the evening, quoth mine Hoste, have you any businesse,
Sir? Yes, marry, quoth *George,* I intend not to goe home
this two dayes: Therefore, my Hoste, saddle my man a horse
for London, if you be so well furnished, for I must send him
for one bag more, quoth *George,* ten pounds hath seen no
Sunne this six moneths. I am ill furnished if I cannot furnish
you with that, quoth my Hoste, and presently sadled him a

---

[1] This sign, which exists at Brentford now, was that of a famous house
at that time. It is noticed in the old comedy of "The Roaring Girl, or
the Catchpole," thus—

> "Thou art admirably suited for the Three Pigeons
> At Brentford; I swear I know thee not."

And Ben Jonson in his "Alchemist" makes *Subtle* say to *Doll Common,*
"We will turn our course to Brainford, westward, if thou saist the word
. . . My fine flitter-mouse[1] my bird o' the night, wee'll tickle it at the
pigeons." It has been suggested, with some show of probability, that this
sign took its origin from the three doves which Noah sent out from the
ark.

---

[1] A bat.

good Nag, and away rides one of *George's* men to London,
attending the good house of his Master *Peele* in London ; In
the meane time *George* bespeakes great cheare to Supper,
saying he expected some of his friends from London.   Now
you must imagine there was not a peny owing in the house,
for he had paid as liberall as *Cæsar*, as far as *Cæsar's* wealth
went.   For indeed most of the money was one Cæsar's an
honest man yet living in London : but to the Catastrophe.
All the day before, had one of the other men of *George Peele*
been a great soliciter to my Hostis, she would beg leave of his
Master he might go see a Maid, a sweet heart of his, so farre
as Kingstone, and before his Master went to bed, he would
returne againe ; saying he was sure shee might command it at
his Masters hands.   My kinde Hostis willing to pleasure the
yong fellow, knowing in her time what belonged to such
matters, went to Master *Peele*, and moved him in it : which he
angerly refused.   But she was so earnest in it, that shee swore
hee should not deny her, protesting he went but to see an
uncle of his some five miles off.   Marry, I thanke you, quoth
George, my good Hostis, would you so discredit me, or hath
the knave no more wit, than at this time to goe, knowing I
have no horse here, and would he, base cullian, go afoot ?
Nay, good Sir, quoth mine Hostis, be not angry, it is not his
intent to goe afoot ; for hee shall have my Mare, and I will
assure you, Sir, upon my word, he shall be here againe, to
have you to bed.   Wel, quoth *George*, Hostis Ile take you at
your word, let him goe, his negligence shall light upon you.
So be it, quoth mine Hostis : so down goeth she, and sends
away civill *Thomas*, for so she cal'd him, to his sweet heart
backt upon her Mare : which *Thomas* instead of riding to
Kingstone, tooke London in his way, where, meeting with my
other horseman, attended the arrivall of *George Peele*, which
was not long after.   They are at London, *George* in his
Chamber at Brainford, accompanied with none but one
Anthony Nit, a Barber, who Din'd and Sup't with him continually, of whom he had borowed a Lute to passe away the
melancholy afternoone, of which he could play as well as
Banke's[1] his horse.   The Barber very modestly takes his leave ;

[1] See footnote, p. 125.

George obsequiously bids him to supper, who (God willing) would not faile. *George* being left alone with his two supposed men, gave them the meane how to escape, and, walking in the Court, *George* found fault with the weather, saying it was rawish, and cold : which words mine Hostis hearing, my kinde Hostis fetched her Husbands holiday Gowne; which George thankfully put about him, and withall called for a cup of Sacke, after which he would walke into the Meddowes, and practise upon his Lute. 'Tis good for your worship to do so, quoth mine Hostis : which walk *George* took directly to Sion,[1] where, having the advantage of a paire of Oares at hand, made this Journey to London, his two Associates behind, had the plot in their heads by *Georges* instruction for their escape : for they knew he was gone; my Hostis, she was in the Market buying of provision for Supper : mine Hoste he was at Tables,[2] and my two masterlesse men desired the maids to excuse them if their Master came, for, quoth they, we will goe drinke two pots with my Smug Smithes wife at old Brainford. I warrant you, quoth the Maides. So away went my men to the Smith's at old Brainford; from thence to London, where they all met, and sold the Horse and the Mare, the Gowne and the Lute, which money was as badly spent, as it was lewdly got. How my Hoste and my Hostis lookt when they saw the event of this; goe but to the three Pigeons at Brainford, you shall know.

[94.] Two being in a Tavern, the one swore the other should pledge him : why then, quoth the other, I will; who went presently down the stairs, and left him as a pledge for the Reckoning

[91.] First my mother brought me forth, when shortly after, I, the Daughter, bring forth my mother againe.

Resolution. Of water is first made ice, which afterwards melts, and brings forth water againe, and so the daughter brings forth the mother, as the mother first the daughter.

---

[1] Sion House, now the seat of the Duke of Northumberland, is oppo-site the western end of Kew Gardens.

[2] Backgammon, or any other games played on the same board.

Times Alteration

or

The Old Mans rehearsall, what brave dayes he knew
A great while agone, when his old Cap was new.

To the Tune of *Ile nere be drunke againe.*

[94*.]　When this Old Cap was new,
　　　　tis since two hundred yeere,
　　　No malice then we knew,
　　　　but all things plentie were :
　　　All friendship now decayes,
　　　　(beleeve me this is true)
　　　Which was not in those dayes,
　　　　when this old Cap was new.

　　　The Nobles of our Land
　　　　were much delighted then,
　　　To have at their command
　　　　a Crue of lustie Men :

Which by their Coates were knowne
   of Tawnie, Red or Blue,
With Crests on their sleeves showne
   when this old Cap was new.

Now Pride hath banisht all,
   unto our Lands reproach,
Then he whose meanes is small,
   maintaines both Horse and Coach.
Instead of an hundred Men,
   the Coach allows but two ;
This was not thought of then,
   when this old Cap was new.

Good Hospitalitie
   was cherisht then of many,
Now poore men starve and die,
   and are not helpt by any
For Charitie waxeth cold,
   and Love is found in few ;
This was not in time of old,
   when this old Cap was new.

Where ever you travel'd then,
   you might meet on the way
Brave Knights and Gentlemen,
   clad in their Country Gray ;
That courteous would appear,
   and kindly welcome you,
No Puritans then were,
   when this old Cap was new.

Our Ladies in those dayes
   in civill Habit went,
Broad-cloth was then worth prayse,
   and gave the best content ;
French Fashions then were scorn'd,
   fond Fangles then none knew,
Then Modestie Women adorn'd,
   when this old Cap was new.

A Man might then behold,
  at Christmas, in each Hall,
Good Fires, to curbe the Cold,
  and Meat for great and small.
The Neighbours were friendly bidden,
  and all had welcome true,
The poor from the Gates were not chidden,
  when this old Cap was new.

Black Jackes to every man
  were fill'd with Wine and Beere,
No Pewter Pot nor Kanne
  in those dayes did appeare :
Good cheare in a Noble-mans house
  was counted a seemly shew,
We wanted no Brawne nor Sowse
  when this old Cap was new.

We tooke not such delight
  in Cups of Silver fine,
None under the degree of a Knight,
  in Plate drunk Beere or Wine.
Now each Mechanicall man,
  hath a Cup-board of Plate for a shew,
Which was a rare thing then,
  when this old Cap was new.

Then Briberie was unborne,
  no Simonie men did use,
Christians did Usurie scorne,
  devis'd among the Jewes.
Then Lawyers to be Feed, `
  at that time hardly knew,
For man with man agreed,
  when this old Cap was new.

No Captaine then carowst
  nor spent poore Souldiers Pay,
They were not so abus'd
  as they are at this day.

Of seven dayes they make eight,
　　to keepe from them their due,
Poore Souldiers had their right
　　when this old Cap was new.

Which made them forward still
　　to goe, although not prest,
And going with good will,
　　their fortunes were the best.
Our English then in fight
　　did forraine Foes subdue,
And forst them all to flight,
　　when this old Cap was new.

God save our gracious King,
　　and send him long to live,
Lord, mischiefe on them bring,
　　that will not their almes give.
But seeke to rob the Poore,
　　of that which is their due ;
This was not in time of yore,
　　when this old Cap was new.

　　　　　　　　　　　　　　M. P.[1]

FINIS.

Printed for the Assignes of Thomas Symcocke.

[77.] In the Country *Tarlton* told his Hostesse he was a Conjurer. O, Sir (sayes she) I had pewter stolne off my shelf the other day, help me to it, and I will forgive you all the pots of Ale you owe mee, which is sixteene dozen. Sayes *Tarlton,* To morrow morning the Divell shall help you to it, or I will trounce him. Morning came, and the Hostesse and he met in a roome by themselves. *Tarlton,* to passe the time with exercise of his wit with circles and tricks, fals to coniure, having no more skill than a dogge. But see the iest, how contrarily it fell out : as he was calling out, *mons, pons, simul* & *fons,* and such like, a Cat (unexpected) leapt

　　　　　　[1] ? Martin Parker.

from the gutter window, which sight so amazed *Tarlton*, that he skipt thence, & threw his Hostesse downe, so that he departed with his fellowes, and left her hip out of joynt, being then in the Surgeons hands, & not daring to tell how it came.

[4.] One ask'd a Fellow if he would go into the Water with him : No, says he, I'll never go into the Water till I have learnt to Swim.

[26.] A Woman accidentally coming into the room where they were, and hearing them speak of that Frost[1] in *Germany*, told some such stories ; but when she saw the Company began to scruple at the truth of it (which I wonder they did, if they consider but her following discourse) then she up and told them That her dear and loving Husband, peace be with him, was in that great Frost, out late one night, which, truly, Gentlemen, I believe was the occasion of his death ; though he lingred Fourteen or Fifteen years after it ; he, I say, riding that night, came to a Common, where were great store of very good Cole-pits, insomuch that he fell down to the bottom in one of them, and his Horse fell directly upon him ; that it was impossible at that time of night, and in such weather, to be relieved in that great distress ; and, having lain so for a long time, and no hopes to be relieved at all, he presently bethought himself, and immediately rose, and went to the next Village, and there borrowed a Pickaxe and a Spade, and then came back with 'em to the Pit, and first digged out himself, and then his Horse, and so about Five a Clock in the Morning came home ; but so weary and so cold, that he could not unbutton his Doublet : Nay, says she, after I had hope (*sic*) him off with all his Cloaths : he was so benumb'd, that I was forc'd to take a Warming Pan of hot Coles, and so went all over his body, yet was he so cold, that he scarcely felt, though the Warming Pan sometimes stood a pretty while together in one place ; which truly, Gentlemen, I was fain to do for my Dear Husband : which confirmed them in the belief of it, that it was as true as any of the rest, and gave her

---

[1] See ante, p. 259.

thanks for it also, and so she made them half a dozen reverend Courchys and bid 'em good by.

On a Cobler.

[5.] Death at a Coblers doore oft made a stand,
And alwaies found him on the mending hand;
At last came death in very foule weather,
And ript the soale from the upper leather:
Death put a trick upon him, and what was't?
The Cobler call'd for's awle, death brought his Laste.

[82.] There was a Scottish Gentleman that had sore eyes, who was counselled by his Physitians to forbeare drinking of wine: but hee said hee neither could nor would forbeare it, maintaining it for the lesser evill, to shut up the windowes of his body, than to suffer the house to fall downe, through want of repair.

[52.] In Gloucestershire dwelt one that cured frantick men in this manner; when the fit was on them he would put them in a gutter of water, some to the knees, some to the middle, and some to the neck, as the disease was on them. So one that was well amended, standing at the gate, by chance a Gentleman came riding by with his Hawks and his Hounds. The mad fellow called him, and said, Gentleman, whether go you? On hunting (quoth the Gentleman.) What do you with all those Kites and Dogs? They be Hawks and Hounds, quoth the Gentleman. Wherefore keep you them? (quoth the other). Why, (quoth he) for my pleasure. What do they cost you a yeare to keepe them? Forty pounds (quoth the Gentleman) And what do they profit you? (quoth he) Some ten pounds (quoth the Gentleman) Get thee quickly hence, quoth the fellow, for if my Master finde thee here, he will put thee into the gutter up to the throat.

The next illustration is a scathing satire on the treatment of the army in Ireland. Perhaps the tersest notice of the history of this time is in *The Chronological Historian*, by W. Toone. "16 Feb. 1646. The Parliament sent a Committee to form the Army for Ireland.—The Commissioners found the Army not inclined to obey them."

T

The humble Petition of us the Parliaments poore
Souldiers in the Army of Ireland, whereof
many are starved already, and many dead
for want of Chirurgions.

[95.] That we the poor distressed Souldiery under the
Parliaments Service in Ireland, having heretofore served the
Parliament under the Lord Generall Essex, Valiant Massey,
and noble Sir William Waller, and the rest, &c, did in all
faithfulnesse, hardship and desperate service as ever any,
hazzard our lives and fortunes, and did according to order obey

and disband, then not so much as doubting of all our Arreares, and now have almost served you two years in all integrity and faithfulnesse both Winter and Summer, wet and dry, frost and Snow, having no other bedding than the bare ground for our beds, and the skies for their covering, and when dry in the day and night, no other signe to drink at but the Sun and Moone, and nothing but water, having no plenty, but cold backs, hungrie bellies, and puddle water, and when sore wounded, not a Surgeon to dresse us, or if a Surgeon, no chest, nor salve, nor oyntments ; and for bread many times not a loafe of two pence under sixpence, and rotten Cheese sent, not fit for a dog, and for butter, it went from London to Dover, and mistook Dublin and went to Dunkirk, and for our new Cloathes all made of the French fashion, and being too little for any of us, were carried to France to cloath them, hardly hats to our heads but what our haire growes through, and neither hose or shooes, doublet or breeches, tearing our Snapsacks to patch a hole to hide our naked and starved flesh, and our swords naked for want of scabberds : Thus with our backs without cloaths and our bellies without food, and not a penny to buy anything, and the kernes having burnt all the corne and destroyed all fit for succour, we forced to march bare legged and bare footed, having neither fire nor food, we perish in misery, and our Commanders being in a manner in the same case, having nothing but good words to pay us with, shewing us often your Orders upon Orders for our pay, plenti-fully promising but not performing, and thus wee dropping downe dead daily in our marching, and so feeble and so weak, being not able to fight or do any more service without some supply, but all like to starve and die in misery, when all meanes is anticipated, and the Tax of 60000l. wholly ingrossed by your Army from us, and your Souldiery quartered in Kings houses, and clad Gentile like, and fed in Free-quarter to the full, and lie in good beds, and take their pleasure and ease in rest and peace.

We humbly desire our hungry bellies may once be filled, and our naked backs be cloathed, and our legs and feet be hosed and shooed, and our Surgeons once more fitted, and all recruited with food to supply us once more, that we may go out again to finish that work we have begun, and not to lie like Drones to eat up others meat, and we do not doubt, but with Gods blessing to give you a happy account of the Conquest of the whole Land, and shall ever pray for a happy Parliament.

DUBLIN : Printed by *W. B. 1648* (*Feb. 18. 1647*).

GOOD ALE FOR MY MONEY[1]

The Good-fellowes resolution of strong Ale,
That cures his nose from looking pale.

To the Tune of The Countrey Lass.

[96.]   Be merry my friends, and list a while
            unto a merry jest,
        It may from you produce a smile,
            when you heare it exprest :
        Of a young man lately married,
            which was a boone good fellow ;
        This song in 's head he alwaies carried,
            when drinke had made him mellow.
        I cannot go home, nor I will not go home,
            it's 'long of the oyle of Barly,
        I'le tarry all night for my delight,
            and go home in the morning early.

        No Tapster stout, or Vintner fine,
            quoth he shall ever get
        One groat out of this purse of mine
            to pay his masters debt :
        Why should I deal with sharking Rookes,
            that seeke poore guls to cozen,
        To give twelve pence for a quart of wine,
            of ale 'twill buy a dozen.
        'Twill make me sing, I cannot go home &c

[1] For tune, see Appendix.   *The Country Lass* is identical with *Stingo.*

The old renowned Ipocrist[1]
and Raspie[2] doth excell,
But never any wine could yet
my honour please to swell :

The Rhenish wine or Muscadine,
sweet Malmsie is too fulsome,
No, give me a cup of Barlie broth
for that is very wholesome.
'Twill make me sing &c—

Hot Waters are to me as death,
and soon the head oreturneth,

[1] Hippocras, a compound of wine, sugar, and spice mixed and strained through a cloth.
[2] Or raspis—raspberry wine.

And Nectar hath so strong a breath
   Canary when it burneth.
It cures no paine but breakes the braine,
   and raps out oathes and curses,
And makes men part with heavie heart,
   but light it makes their purses.
I cannot go home &c

Some say Metheglin[1] beares the name,
   with Perry and sweet Sider,
'Twill bring the body out of frame,
   and reach the belly wider :
Which to prevent I am content
   with Ale that's good and nappie,
And when thereof I have enough,
   I thinke myselfe most happy.
I cannot go home &c

All sorts of men when they do meet,
   both trade and occupation,
With curtesie each other greet,
   and kinde humiliation :
A good coale fire is their desire,
   whereby to sit and parly,
They'le drinke their ale and tell a tale
   and go home in the morning early.
I cannot go home &c

Your domineering swaggering blades,
   and Cavaliers that flashes,
That throw the Jugs against the walls,
   and break in peeces glasses.
When Bacchus round cannot be found,
   they will in merriment
Drink ale and beere and cast of care,
   and sing with one consent.
I cannot go home &c

              Lawrence Price.

Printed at London.

[1] A mixture of honey and water, boiled and fermented.

[52.] A notable yong Rogue, having plaid some notable knavish pranke, was for the offence to be whipt, and as hee was ready to be tied to the Cart, hee said to the Beadle that should whip him; Here is ten Shillings for thee, I pray thee use mee kindly, and deale not too cruelly with me : to whom the Beadle promised great curtesie ; but being tied fast to the Cart, hee whipt him very severely. The fellow called unto him, and bad him remember his promise : What knave (quoth the Beadle) do'st prate and talke, and knowest not the Law. Afterward being released he bethought himselfe how he might be revenged on the Beadle, and seeing him stand in the Market, pickes a pocket, and puts the purse into the Beadles pocket, and goes to the fellow, from whom he had stolne the purse, saying, Friend, do you misse nothing ? who presently cryed out, saying He had lost his purse. Yonder Beadle hath it (quoth hee) and you shall finde it in his pocket, I saw him take it. The man that had lost his purse goes unto the Beadle, and apprehended him, for his purse, who utterly denied he had it, neither knew of any such matter. But being found about him, he was condemned to die for it. The pick-pocket being imprisoned againe for some small fault desired he might be hangman that day, and it being granted : When the Beadle came to be hanged, Sirrah (quoth the pick pocket) do you remember how you whipt me the other day when I gave you ten shillings ? I. (quoth the Beadle) I pray thee forgive me, I am now ready to dye. I. sirrah (quoth hee) thank me for it, for I pickt the purse and put it in your pocket. With that the Beadle began to cry aloud, saying, Hold, hold. What, knave, (quoth the pick pocket) do'st talke and prate, and knowest not the Law. And so he turned him beside the ladder.

[17.] A fat man riding upon a lean horse, was ask'd, Why he was so fat, and the horse so lean ? said : Because I look to myself, and my man to my horse.

[4.] A Blind Minister coming to speak with a Gentleman, the Gentleman's man came running to him, and told him that the blind Minister was come *to see him.*

The very rare book from which the accompanying illustration is taken is not of interest to the general reader. It is a dialogue between the miller and those who bring their wives, etc., to be ground young again; but the woodcut itself is very curious as a caricature.

[97.]

[26.] Another Fellow said that he had heard all their stories, and did think at first that some of them had been untruths, but now, says he, I am better satisfied; and I will tell you what I know upon my own knowledge. I was once in some company where I heard one of them say that to his knowledge a Raven would live a hundred years: so the next day I went and bought me one purposely to make a Tryal, and put him into a Cage and taught him to sing; and I think in my Conscience no Bird but a Raven could sing like him. Well, says he, I kept this Bird above a hundred years; nay, if I should say two hundred, I should not lie, (and fed him all the time myself.) At last being very tame I turn'd him out of the Cage and put him into a Room, where I had only a Goose, but never a Gander for her: I know not how it happened, but the Raven and the Goose fell in league together (for you must know 'twas a Cock Raven,) and she brought ten young ones, all coloured half black, and half white; and those Five which were black towards the head cry'd just like a Raven, and those that were white towards the head, cry'd like Geese, and I eat one of the former, that was black towards the head; and, if you'll believe me, I have had ever since such a strange croaking in my Stomach, especially if I see any Carrion, that 'tis a great disturbance to me: Nay, one of my Neighbours upon some occasion call'd my Wife *Carrion;* and though I did not love her before; yet ever since I have had a great kindness for her. Then they told him that the strangness of this story made it true, and the Proverb makes it good, that is *'Tis not so strange as true.*

The following caricature of *Shrovetide,* which has more artistic merit than most similar productions, has a companion in *Lent,* which, however, not being able to procure the original, I do not give.

[98.] Fatte *Shrovetyde* mounted on a good fatt *Oxe,*
Suppos'd that *Lent* was mad, or caught a *Foxe,*[1]
Armd *Cap a pea* from head unto the heele,
A Spit, his long sword, somewhat worse than steele,
(Sheathed in a fatt Pigge, and a Peece of Porke)
His bottles fil'd with Wine, well stopt with Corke.
The two plump Capons fluttering at his Crupper,
And's shoulders lac'd with Sawsages for Supper;
The Gridir'n (like a well strung Instrument)
Hung at his backe, and for the Turnament
His Helmet is a Brasse Pott, and his Flagge
A Cookes foule Apron, which the wind doth wagg,
Fixd to a Broome, thus bravely he did ride,
And boldly to his foe, he thus replyde.
   What art thou, thou leane jawde Annatamie
All spirit (for I no flesh upon thee spie)
Thou bragging peece of ayre and smoake that prat'st,
And all good fellowship and friendship hat'st.
You'le turne our feasts to fasts, when, can you tell
Against your spight, we are provided well.

[1] *I.e.* foxed or drunk.

Thou sayst thou'lt ease the Cookes, the Cooks could wish
Thee boyld, or broyld with all thy froathy fish,
For one fish dinner takes more paines and cost
Than three of flesh, bak'd, roast or boyld, almost.

SHROVETIDE

Jou that have Fofting Dearth, and flaving Livers,   SHROVE Behold your Champion Shrovetyde in this fray
Spits bright hang'd up, and teeth and Platers Cleaves   TYDE. Would murder Lent, and every fafting day

Youle take away our playes, our sports and pleasure,
And give the Butchers time for ease and leasure.
Alasse poor scabbe, how barren are thy hopes
The Fencers, Beares, and Dauncers on the Ropes,

Is manly sport, or lawlesse recreation
Which all thy sev'n weeks time, are still in fashion,
The truth is, thou aswagest few mens hunger,
And hast no faithfull friend but the Fishmonger.
There's little danger to attend on me,
When men are drownd at Sea to furnish thee.
Pease pottage, and dryde beanes, by proofe we find,
Offends and fills men with unwholsome wind,
And ere I'le be a slave and pinch my maw
I'le breake all Proclamation, rule and Law,
Wee'le fill our Tubs with powdred flesh, beside
By licenc't Butchers we will be supplyde
With fresh meat; so hungry *Lent* adieu,
We are resolv'd to feed in spight of you

FINIS

LONDON

Printed by M. S. for *Thomas Jenner*, and are to be sold at his Shop at the South Entrance of the Royal Exchange 1660.

[93.] *George* (*Peele*) was not so merry at London with his Capons and Claret, as poore *Anthony* the Barber was sorrowfull at Brainford for the losse of his Lute, & therefore determined to come to London to seeke out *George Peele*, which by the meanes of a Kinsman that *Anthony Nit* had in London, his name was *Cuts or Feats*, a Fellow that had good skill in tricks on the Cards, and he was well acquainted with the place where *George's* common abode was, and for kindred sake he directed the Barber where he should have him, which was at a blinde Ale house in Sea-cole Lane.[1] There he found *George* in a greene Jerkin, a Spanish platter fashioned Hat, all alone with a Pecke of Oysters. The Barber's heart danc'd within him for joy he had so happily found him; he gave him the time of the day. *George* not a little abashed at the sight of the Barber, yet went not to discover it openly; he that at all times had a quicke invention, was not now behind hand to entertaine my Barber, who knew for what his comming was.

---

[1] This lane was between Snow Hill and Fleet Lane.

George thus saluted him, My honest Barber, quoth *George*,
welcome to London, I partly know your businesse, you come
for your Lute, doe you not? Indeed Sir, quoth the Barber,
for that is my comming. And beleeve me, quoth *George*, you
shall not lose your labour, I pray you stand to, and eat an
oyster, and I'le go with you presently : For a Gentleman in
the Citie of great worship, borrowed it of me for the use of
his Daughter, that plays exceeding well, and had a great
desire to have the Lute ; but, Sir, if you will goe along with
me to the Gentlemans house, you shall have your Lute with
great satisfaction, for had you not come, I assure you I had
sent to you ; for you must understand that all that was done
at Brainford among us mad Gentlemen, was but a jest, and no
otherwise. Sir, I think not any otherwise, quoth the Barber,
but I would desire your worship, that as you had it of me in
lone, so in kindnesse you would helpe me to it againe. What
else, quoth *George*, Ile goe with thee presently, even as I am,
for I came from hunting this morning, and should I go up to
the certain Gentlemen above, I should hardly get away. I
thank you Sir, quoth the Barber, so on goes *George* with him
in his greene Jerkin, a wand in his hand very pretty, till he
came almost to the Alderman's House, where, making a
sodaine stay, Afore God, quoth George, I must crave thy
pardon at this instant, for I have bethought myselfe, should
I go as I am, it would be imagined I had had some of my
Lords hounds out this morning, therefore I'le take my leave
of thee, and meet thee where thou wilt about one of the Clock.
Nay good Sir, quoth the Barber, goe with me now, for I
purpose, God willing, to be at Brainford tonight. Saist thou
so, quoth George, why then I'le tell thee what thou shalt doe,
thou art here a stranger, and altogether unknowne, lend me
thy Cloake and thy Hat, and doe thou put on my greene
Jerken, and I'le goe with thee directly along. The Barber,
unwilling to leave him untill he had his Lute, yeelded to the
change. So when they came to the Gentleman's porch he
put on *George's* greene Jerken and his Spanish Hat : and he
the Barbers Cloake, and his Hat ; either of them being thus
fitted, *George* knocks at the doore, to whom the Porter bids
heartily welcome, for *George* was well knowne, who at that

time had all the oversight of the Pageants, he desires the Porter to bid his friend welcome, for he is a good fellow and a keeper, Master Porter, one that at his pleasure can bestow a haunch of Venison on you : Marry that can I, quoth the Barber. I thank you Sir, answered the Porter, Master *Peele*, my Master is in the Hall, pleaseth it you to walke in ? With all my heart, quoth *George*, in the meane time let my friend beare you company. That he shall, Master *Peele*, quoth the Porter, and if it please him he shall take a simple dinner with me. The Barber gives him harty thankes, nothing doubting Master *Peele* any way, seeing him knowne, and himselfe so welcome, fell in Chat with the Porter. *George Peele* goes directly to the Alderman, who now is come into the Court in the eye of the Barber, where *George* after many complaints, drawes a black paper out of his bosome, & making action to the Barber, reads to the Alderman as followeth, I humbly desire your worship to stand my friend in a sleight matter ; yonder hard favoured knave, that sits by your Worship's Porter, hath dog'd me to arrest me, and I had no other meanes but to take your Worship's house for shelter ; the occasion is but triviall, onely for stealing of a piece of flesh, myselfe consorted with three or foure gentlemen of good fashion, that would not willingly have our names come in question. Therefore this is my boone, that your Worship would let one of your servants let me out at the Garden doore, and I shall think myselfe much indebted to your Worship. The kind Gentleman, little dreaming of *George Peele's* deceit, took him into the Parlor, gave him a brace of Angels, & caused one of his servants to let *George* out at the Garden doore, which was no sooner opened, but *George* made way for the Barber seeing him any more, and all the way he went, could not choose but laugh at his knavish conceit ; how he had guld the simple Barber, who sat all this while with the Porter, blowing of his nayles ; to whom came this fellow that let *George* out. You whorson Keeperly Rascall, quoth the fellow, dare you come any honest Gentleman in my Masters house ? Not I, so God helpe me, quoth the Barber, I pray Sir where is the Gentleman Master *Peele* that came along with me ? Farre enough, quoth the Fellow, for your comming neere him, he is gone out at the Garden doore. Garden doore? quoth the Barber, Sir, I am no Keeper, I am quite undone: I am a Barber dwelling at Brainford, and, with weeping teares, up and told him how *George* had used him. The servant goes in & tels his Master; which when he heard, he could not but laugh at the first: yet in pitty of the poore Barber, he gave him twenty shillings towards his losse. The Barber, sighing, tooke it, and towards Brainford home he goes, and whereas hee came from thence in a new Cloake and a faire Hat, hee went home weeping in an old Hat, and a greene Jerken.

The accompanying illustration is taken from a tract, in itself of no literary merit or humour, but the picture is amusing, representing a "Brown[1] Dozen of Drunkards, ali-ass Drink-haros, Jocoseriously descanted to our wine drunk, wrath drunk, and zeale drunk staggering times."

[99.]

[94.] A drunken fellow returning home towards evening, found his wife hard at her spinning; she reproving him for his ill husbandry, and commending herself for her good huswifery,

---

[1] Most probably meant for a *round* dozen, or baker's dozen, as there are thirteen depicted and thirteen characters in the tract.

he told her that she had no great cause to chide, for as she had been spinning, he came home all the way reeling.

[91.]   There was a man bespake a thing,
        Which when the owner home did bring,
        He that made it did refuse it,
        And he that bought it would not use it,
        And he that hath it doth not know,
        Whether he hath it, I, or no.

Resolution   A Coffin bought by another for a dead man.

[86.] One affirmed that he had been in a certain Country, where their Bees were as big as our Sheep. This impudent lye one began to examine, and therefore said, sure then the Bee-hives must be of a huge bignesse; No, saith the other, they are no bigger than ours; How then can they get in? said one. This bogled[1] the lyar like a Mouse in pitch; at last he answered, let them whom it concerns look to that.

A Health to all Good-Fellowes:

or

The good Companions Arithmaticke.

To the Tune of, *To drive the cold Winter away.*

Be merry my hearts, and call for your quarts,
    and let no liquor be lacking,
We have gold in store, we purpose to roare,
    untill we set care a packing.
Then Hostis make haste, and let no time waste,
    let every man have his due,
To save shooes and trouble, bring in the pots double,
    for he that made one made two.

I'le drink up my drinke, and speak what I thinke,
    strong drinke will make us speake truely,

---
[1] Puzzled, bothered.

We cannot be termed all drunkards confirmed,
  so long as we are not unruly.
Wee'le drinke and be civill, intending no evill,
  if none be offended at me,
As I did before, so I'le adde one more,
  and he that made two made three.

The greedy Curmudgin sits all the day snudging[1]
  at home with browne bread and small beare,
To Coffer up wealth, he starveth himselfe,
  scarce eats a good meale in a yeare.

But I'le not do so, how ere the world go
  so long as I have money in store
I scorne for to faile, go fil us more Ale,
  for he that made three made four.

Why sit you thus sadly, because I call madly,
  I meane not to leave in the lurch,
My reckoning Ile pay ere I go away,
  else hang me as high as a Church.
Perhaps you will say, this is not the way,
  they must pine that in this world will thrive,
No matter for that, wee'le laugh and be fat,
  for he that made foure made five.

        [1] Being mean, miserly.

To those my good friends my love so extends,
    I cannot truely expresse it ;
When with you I meet, your words are so sweet,
    I am unwilling to misse it.
I hate all base slaves that their money saves,
    and all those that use base tricks,
For with joviall blades, I'm merry as the Maids,
    for he that made five made six.

Then drink about round till sorrow be dround,
    and let us sing hey downe a derry,
I cannot endure, to sit thus demure,
    for hither I came to be merry.
Then plucke up a good heart before we depart,
    with my Hostesse we will make it even,
For I am set a madding, and still will be adding,
    for he that made six made seven.

Sad mellancholly will bring us to folly,
    and this is deaths principall magent, (*sic*)
But this course I will take, it never shall make
    me looke otherwise than an agent.
And in more content my time shall be spent,
    and I'le pay every man his right,
Then hostesse go fill, and stand not so still,
    for he that made seven made eight.

At home I confesse, with my wife honest *Besse*,
    I practise good husbandry well,
I follow my calling, to keep me from falling ;
    my neighbours about me that dwell
Wil praise me at large for maintaining my charge,
    but when I to drinking incline
I scorne for to shrinke, go fetch us more drinke,
    for he that made eight made nine.

Then while we are here, wee'le drinke Ale & Beer,
    and freely our money wee'le spend,
Let no man take care, for paying his share,
    if need be I'le pay for my friend.

U

Then·Hostesse make haste, and let no time waste,
　you're welcome all, kind Gentlemen,
Never fear to Carowse, while there is beere in the house,
　for he that made nine made ten.

Then Hostesse be quicker, and bring us more liquor,
　and let no attendance be missing,
I cannot content me, to see the pot empty,
　a full cup is well worth the kissing.
Then Hostesse go fetch us some, for till you do come,
　we are of all joyes bereaven,
You know what I mean, make haste, come again,
　for he that made ten, made eleven.

With merry solaces, quite voyd of all malice,
　with honest good fellowes thats here,
No cursing nor swearing, no staring nor tearing,
　amongst us do seeme to appeare.
When we have spent, all to labour we fall,
　for a living wee'le dig, or wee'le delve,
Determin'd to be both bounteous and free,
　he that made eleven, made twelve.

Now I think it is fit and most requisit,
　to drinke a health to our wives,
The which being done, wee'le pay and be gone,
　strong drinke all our wits now deprives.
Then, Hostesse, let's know the summe that we owe,
　twelve pence there is for certain
Then fill t'other pot, and here's money for't
　for he that made twelve made thirteene.

FINIS.

London, Printed for *Henry Gossen.*

[52.] An untravelled Irish man intended to see England,
and arriving at London, chanced to light on a Barbers shoppe,
supposing by his cluster of Basons hanging at the door, it must
of necessity be some penny-pottage Ordinary : and, wanting

the language, entred the shop, and pointed to his mouth, meaning some victuals to stay his hunger. The Barber gathered by this signe, that the poore fellow had pain in his teeth, and desired to have one pluckt out; willed him to sit downe in his Chaire, and approached with his dismall instruments towards the fellows chaps. The Irishman began to wonder at this strange kinde of feeding, giving the Barber to understand (so well as he could) he was never brought up to that kinde of feeding, and with an unmannerly thrust bad him, Avant.[1] The Barber, half discontented, tumbled the Irish man with his Chair upside down, who, sprawling on the ground began to seeke after the doore, and made as much haste to his lodging as he could : where, meeting with one of his Countrymen, hee prayed him, of all loves, to depart this Country of England, and returne to that worthy Ireland. For, (quoth he) they be ill divels here, and no honest men, since when a poore stranger makes shew of hunger, the knavish Inhabitants will break out men's teeth like dogs, and so send us to our Country again with never a tooth in our heads : which caused much good mirth to all that heard it.

[17.] A great Lord being in the Tower was visited by some other Lords; and being merry, one began the Kings health, which he refused to pledge. They told him 'twould be ill taken : Why truly, my Lords, saies he, I'll pray for the Kings health, but drink for my own.

[4.] A gentleman ordr'd a Crane for Supper ; but his Cook, having a Sweetheart in a longing condition, cut off a Leg and sent her; so the one Legg'd Crane was set on the Table, which the Gentleman seeing, was enrag'd at his Cook ; but he, being an arch Wag, readily told the Gentleman that Cranes had but one Leg, and avowed it with that Confidence, that he gain'd upon his wise Masters belief; but he, resolving to observe it as he was walking in the Fields one Frosty Morning, he saw a flock of Cranes, and, sending for his Cook, they held up one of their Legs under their Wings, as is

---

[1] Avaunt, begone.

the Custom of those birds in the cool weather. So, says his
Cook, I hope your Worship is satisfied that they have but one
Leg; but the Gentleman going pretty near to them, cries
Cush, and frighted them up. Whereupon both Legs appear'd.
Look, says the Gentleman, they have now two Legs. Oh,
says the Cook, if you had cried *Cush* to that in the Dish, it
wou'd have had two Legs too.

[26.] A Gentleman that had bred up a Young Colt, and
had taught him many pretty pieces of Activity, but one among
the rest, that of leaping so well, that no Ditch or Hedg,
though never so broad or deep but he whipt over: nay, an
ordinary House was nothing with him, or small Country
Church also, but yet could never leap over the Steeple. It
fortun'd that the Gentleman having occasion to ride abroad
on him, came to a River that was about Twenty yards wide,
which you'll say was very broad; yet this poor beast leapt
with him to the very brink of the River on the other side, and
there by chance lighted upon a stump of a Tree which ran
into his Belly; which the Master seeing, alighted, and so left
the poor Beast in that condition, yet would not kill him, and
so went away. About six months after, this Gentleman was
riding that way with his Man, and as they rode, says his
Master, Don't you see something move yonder? Yes, says
he, I think I see a Tree go; and coming near to it, they put
aside all the Boughs, and there spied his late Horse, which he
thought had died there: so they cut off all the Boughs, which
were so many as to load almost three Carts, and then he took
the poor Beast home, and cur'd him of all but the stump of
the Tree which was in his Belly; and, indeed he need not do
it, for he receiv'd a great advantage by it every year; that is,
at least two or three load of Wood, which serv'd him to burn
in his Chamber; for he would never burn any other than
that, out of the love he bore to that poor beast of his. But
some that heard him tell it, thought it savour'd too much
of the Legend: Why, if you won't believe me, ask my Man,
who knows it as well as I, and shall swear it too, if you
please.

[18.]   Here at last doth she lie in quiet,
Who whilst she lived was ever unquiet.
Her Husband prays, if by her Grave you walk,
You'd gently tread, for if waked, she'll talk.

The following was written in 1646, and is a satire on the
then feeling of the army.

𝕲𝖍𝖊
𝕸𝖊𝖗𝖈𝖊𝖓𝖆𝖗𝖕

𝕾𝖔𝖚𝖑𝖉𝖎𝖊𝖗

I.

[100.]   No money yet, why then let's pawn our swords,
And drinke an health to their confusion
Who doe instead of money send us words,
Lets not be subject to the vain delusion
    Of those would have us fight without our pay,
    While money chinks, my Captain i'le obey.

II.

I'le not be slave to any servile Groom,
Let's to the Sutlers and there drink and sing
My Captain for a while shall have my room,
Come hither *Tom*, of Ale two douzen bring,
 Plac'd Ranke and File, Tobacco bring us store,
 And as the Pots doe empty, fill us more.

III.

Let the Drum cease, and never murmure more,
Untill it beat, warning us to repair
Each man for to receive of Cash good store,
Let not the Trumpet shril, ere rend the ayre,
 Untill it cites us to the place where we
 May heaps of silver for our payment see.

IV.

I come not forth to doe my Countrey good,
I come to rob, and take my fill of pleasure,
Let fools repel their foes with angry mood,
Let those doe service while I share the treasure :
 I doe not mean my body ere shall swing
 Between a pare of crutches, tottering.

V.

Let thousands fall, it nee'r shall trouble me,
Those puling fools deserve no better fate,
They mirth's Apposers were, and still would be,
Did they survive, let me participate,
 Of pleasures, gifts, while here I live, and I
 Care not, although I mourne eternally.

VI.

I laugh to think how many times I have
Whiles others fighting were against the foe,
Within some Thicket croucht myself to save,
Yet taken for a valiant Souldier tho,
 When I amongst them come, for I with words,
 Can terrifie, as others can with swords.

VII.

Damme you Rogue if thou provoke my wroth
[1] I'le carve thee up, and spit thee, joynt by joynt
There's none that tasted of my fury hath,
But fear and tremble lest I should appoint
    A second penance from them, when my brow
    Is bent, marke how the rascalls to me bow.

[1] Canes qui multum latrant, raro mordent.

VIII.

Thus menacing I'm taken for to be
A man indeed, when I should fear to fight
With coward *Thersites*, and if that he
Were my Antagonist, but I delight
    To fight and pash dame *Ceres* treasure [2]
    To quaff *Lyen's* bloud [3] I take great pleasure.

[2] All manner of victuals.
[3] Wine.

IX.

Proceed yee brethren, doe each other hate,
And fight it to the last, *I wish the Wars*
May ever untill doomsday prosperate,
And time nee'r see a period of the jars :
    For I before like to a slave did live,
    Now like unto a *Lurdain* [4] doe I thrive.

X.

Fill us more Ale, me thinks thy lazie gate
Is slower than the Tortoise, make more speed,
An tha'st a Female of an easie rate
Lets see her, for my flesh doth tumults breed :
    Run on, thoul't wish when that day comes thou must
    Give an account, that thou hadst been more just.

[4] An ignominious name given the *Danes* by *English* men, for their slothfull and lasieliving.

[86.] A Country honest fellow upon the first coming out of the Parliament coyne, taking it in his hand, and turning it backward and forward ; when he had read the circumscription of it, said, Here are Crosses enough, I trow me, but how long they shall last I know not, for I see here *the Commonwealth of England*, and *God with Us* are not of one side.

[93.] *George* (*Peele*) on a time being happily furnished both
of horse and money, though the horse he hired, and the money
he borrowed : but no matter how he was possest of them, and
towards Oxford he rides to make merry with his friends and
fellow students : and in his way he tooke Wickham, where he
sojourned that night : Being at supper accompanied with his
Hostis, among other table-talke, they fell into discourse of
Chirurgerie, of which my Hostis was a simple professor.
George Peele observing the humour of my she Chirurgion,
upheld her in all the strange cures she talked of, and praised
her womanly endevour; telling her, he loved her so much the
better, because it was a thing that he professed, both Physicke
and Chirurgirie; and *George* had a Dictionary of Physicall
words, that it might set a better glosse upon that which he
seemingly profest : and told his good Hostis, at his returne he
would teach her something that should doe her no hurt; for
(quoth he) at this instant I am going about a great Cure as
farre as Warwick-shire to a Gentleman of great living, and one
that hath beene in a Consumption this half yeare, and I hope
to doe him good. O God (quoth the Hostis) there is a
Gentleman not a quarter of a Mile off, that hath beene a
long time sicke of the same disease : Beleeve me, Sir, (quoth
the Hostis) would it please your Worship e're your departure
in the morning, but to visit the Gentleman, and but spend
your opinion of him, and I make no question but the Gentlewoman will bee very thankfull to you. I' faith (quoth *George*)
happely at my returne I may, but at this time my haste is such
that I cannot : and so good night, mine Hostis. So away
went *George* to bed ; and my giddy Hostis, right of the nature
of most women, thought that night as long as tenne, till shee
was delivered of that burthen of newes which she had received
from my new Doctor : (for so hee termed himselfe). Morning
being come, at breake of the day, mine Hostis trudges to this
Gentlemans house, acquainteth his wife what an excellent man
she had at her house : protesting he was the best seene in
Physicke, and had done the most strangest cures that ever she
heard of; saying that if shee would but send for him, no
question he would doe him good. The Gentlewoman glad to
heare of any thing that might procure the health of her Hus-

band, presently sent one of her men, to desire the Doctor to come and visit her Husband. Which message when *George* heard, hee wondred ; for hee had no more skill in Physicke than in Musicke, and they were as distant both from him, as heaven from hell. But, to conclude, *George* set a bold face on it, and away he went to the sicke Gentleman ; where, when hee came, after some complement to the Gentlewoman, hee was brought to the Chamber, where the ancient Gentleman lay wonderfull sicke : for all Physicke had given him over : George beginnes to feele his Pulses and his temples, saying, hee was very farre spent; yet, quoth hee, under God I will doe him some good, if Nature bee not quite extinct. Where-upon hee demanded whether they had ever a Garden ? That I have, quoth the Gentlewoman. I pray you direct me thither, quoth *George.* Where, when hee came, hee cut a handfull of every Flowre, Herbe and Blossome, or whatsoever else in the Garden, and brought them in the lapid [1] of his Cloake, boyled them in Ale, strained them, boyled them againe, and when he had all the juyce out of them, of which he made some pottle [2] of drinke, he caused the sicke Gentle-man to drinke off a maudlin [3] Cup full, and willed his wife to give him of that same at morninge, noone, and night : pro-testing, if any thing in this world did him good, it must bee that : giving great charge to the Gentlewoman to keepe him wonderfull warme : and at my returne, quoth *George,* some tenne dayes hence, I will returne and see how hee fares : For, quoth he, by that time something will be done ; and so I will take my leave. Not so, quoth the Gentlewoman, your Wor-shippe must needes stay and take a simple dinner with mee to day. Indeede, quoth *George,* I cannot now stay, my haste is such, I must presently to Horse. You may suppose *George* was in haste untill he was out of the Gentleman's house : for hee knew not whether he had poysoned the Gentleman or not, which made him so eager to bee gone out of the Gentleman's house. The Gentlewoman seeing shee could by no meanes stay him, gave him two brace of Angels, which never shined long in his purse, and desired him at his returne to know her house : which *George* promised, and with seeming nicenesse

---

[1] Lappet.　　[2] A measure of two quarts.　　[3] Query, *middling*-sized.

took the gold, and towards Oxford went he, fortie shillings heavier than he was, where hee bravely domineered while his Physicall money lasted.   But to see the strangenesse of this : Whether it was the vertue of some herbe which hee gathered, or the conceit the Gentleman had of *George Peele*, but it so pleased God the Gentleman recovered, and in eight dayes walked abroad ; and that fortunate potion which *George* made at randome, did him more good than many pounds that he had spent in halfe a yeere before in Physicke.   *George* his money being spent, he made his returne towards London ; and when he came within a mile of the Gentlemans house, hee enquired of a Countrey fellow how such a Gentleman did. The Fellow told him, God be praised, his good Landlord was well recovered by a vertuous Gentleman that came this way by chance.   Art thou sure of it ? quoth *George*.   Yes, beleeve me, quoth the fellow, I saw him in the Fields but this morning. This was no simple newes to *George*.   He presently set spurres to his Horse, and whereas hee thought to shunne the Towne, hee went directly to his Inne : at whose arrivall, the Hostis clapt her hands, the Oastler laught, the Tapster leapt, the Chamberlaine ran to the Gentlemans house, and told him the Doctor was come.   How joyfull the Gentleman was, let them imagine that have any after-healths.   *George Peele* was sent for, and after a Million of thankes from the Gentleman and his friends, *George Peele* had 20 pounds delivered him : which money, how long it was a spending, let the Tavernes in London witnesse.

[14.] A Man of *Wales* between *S* *David's* day and *Easter*,
    Was on's host score for cheese great store, a tester.
    His host did chalk it up behind the doore,
    And said, For cheese, good Sir, come pay your score.
    I wonder then, quoth he, what meaneth these ?
    Dost think her Country knows not chalk from Cheese ?

THE

𝔐𝔢𝔯𝔯𝔶 𝔊𝔬𝔰𝔰𝔦𝔭'𝔰 𝔙𝔦𝔫𝔡𝔦𝔠𝔞𝔱𝔦𝔬𝔫,

To the Groats worth of good Councel Declaration.

Some Women can drink, and be drunk night and day,
For all the fault is laid most on the Men, they do say,
For if a Man do intend for to thrive,
Then he must be sure to ask leave of his Wife.

To the Tune of *Digbies Farewel.*

A Company of Gossips that love strong bub,[1]
   that met at an Alehouse, and there they did club,
They called for the short Pot, and likewise for the long.
   come Tapster, be quick, for we soon must begon.
They cupt it about, and they made such great hast,
   till their nose and their face were all of a blaze.
A Man he may work all the days of his life,
   but he must ask his Wife's leave if he intends for to thrive.

What is't for a Man to marry a Wife,
   if she proves a drunkard, hee'l be weary of his Life,

   ¹ Drink.

As there is in *London* and *England* all or'e
　they'l take it so sweetly till they lye on the floor.
When a knot of merry Gossips are gotten together,
　they then take no care for fare or foul weather.
There's many a Husband takes pains and do's thrive,
　but he must ask his Wife's leave if he intend for to thrive.

When the Ale and the Brandy doth work in their head,
　they care not a pin how their Children are fed,
Then one saies here Sister i'le drink unto thee
　our Husbands are bound to maintain us truly.
I have a shilling saies one, I have two saies another,
　we will let it fly now we are together.
And thus you may see although a Man strive
　he must ask his Wifes leave if he intend for to thrive.

When their Bellies are full they are bound to give o're,
　they have drunken so much they can drink no more,
Then they'l hast to go home when they hardly can stand,
　you laugh for to see them then go hand in hand.
A Man he is mad that hath got such a Wife,
　he may work and may toyl all the days of his Life.
　　　There's many a Husband &c

They tottor and wattor and fall in the Dirt,
　then the Boys they will shout, and them will make sport,
Sometimes they cry a Hare and sometimes cry a ——
　to see them so drunk then they cry out the more ;
Its a inconvenience for a Woman (to) do so
　to take so much drink that she can hardly go.
　　　There's many a Husband &c—

There is some that is known that will drink all the day,
　& within night come home drunk, & not a word they
　　can say,
I'le promise you true there so heavy i' th' head,
　they lye on the Stairs and they cannot go (to) Bed :
It needs now must be a great shame unto those.
　for a Woman so drunk she cannot put of her Cloaths.
　　　There's many a Husband &c

Some Women will set there Husband o' th' Skore,
  more than they are able to pay to be sure,
When they are absent and taking of Pains,
  thus they lye at the Alehouse, and consume all their gains ;
Which makes many a Man to fret all his life,
  because he is so tide to such a careless Wife.
      There's many a Husband &c

But for civil good Women I have nothing to say,
  they deserve a great praise though all these go astray,
They are a great shame to the rest of their Sex,
  and many a good Woman to see them is vext :
For a Woman to bring herself in such a Snare,
  and of Husband and Children have no better care.
      There's many a Husband &c

It is good for a Woman (to) live in a good way,
  & keep at home with her Family, that nothing goes astray,
Then her Husband will love her the better sure,
  and let her want nothing that he can procure :
For a Woman that's given to wast and consume,
  makes many a honest man be not for home.
      There's many a Husband &c

What is't for a Woman to drink and to swill,
  and never be satisfied till her Belly be full,
And then there, one husband they straight will abuse,
  with all the base names that they ever can use :
And then, if her Husband but strike her a blow,
  she ready crys Murther, all this we may know.
      There's many a Husband &c

And now all good Women that heareth this Song,
  I pray you forgive me if I have done you any wrong,
I will not condemn all for half a Skore,
  I dare say in our Parish, wee have a great many more :
Besides other places ; God send them to mend,
  and then I do hope they take me for their friend.
      There's many a Husband &c

And now to conclude, there is no more to be said,
　I wish that this Song it often be read
Amongst the good Women that love for to club,
　and spendeth their money in Brandy and Bub :
And then you shall see what brave days they will spend,
　your Housekeeping will be better at every Day's end.
　　　　　There's many a Husband &c

Printed for P. Brooksby at the Golden Ball in Pye Corner.

[52.] A Gentleman of Franckford in Germany, had borowed of a Jew (of the same town) a thousand Duckets,[1] and missing his day of payment, he sought from time to time to absent himself from his Creditor.　Not long after, the Jew espied him going into a Barbers shop, and ran presently and fetcht a couple of Sergeants to arrest the debter, now at the Barbers a trimming.　Which done the Jew came and found the Gentleman halfe shaved, and demanded whether hee would instantly discharge his debt, or accept the arrest.　The Gentleman being driven to a non plus, caught sudden hold of his sword and asked the Jew if hee would not attend till his beard was all shaved?　The Jew answered, Yea, with all his heart.　Why then, (quoth the Gentleman) Barber and Serjeants beare witnesse what the Jew hath promised.　Contented (quoth the Jew.)　Well, Barber, then I will not have my beard shaven this twelve moneth.　The Jew began to stamp, curse, and ban, and finally procured the Sergeants to carry him before a Governor, who, well considering the matter, dismissed both the gentleman and the Jew, as both free men, without farther challenge of debt, untill the Gentlemans beard was all shaven, which till his dying day he never suffered.　And the Jew lost his money.

[17.] A new Mayors Wife of a Town in the West, came to Church the first *Sunday* after her husband was chosen ; and just as she came into the Church, the people began to stand up at the Creed ; which the poor heart mistook, and took it

---

[1] A coin struck by dukes : a ducat was worth in silver about 4s. 6d., in gold about 9s. 6d.

to be an honour done purposely to her; An't please God, says she, I'll requite you all before my Husband goes out of his Office.

[4.] A certain King being sick, one pray'd that he might reign as long as the Sun and Moon should endure, and the Prince his Son after him.

[4.] Some Scholars having a spight against their Master, because of his Harshness to them, resolved to play him some trick; so knowing him to be a very Curious neat Man, they daubed the Railes of the Stairs with some Tar. Now the Master coming down in the Dark, laid his Hands in it, which set him into a terrible feu'd; so he call'd all his Schollars, and took them into strict Examination; but, suspecting one above the rest, he was very sharp upon him, urging him to confess it, telling him he did it. The Boy utterly denied it; but the Master was the more pressing upon him. Indeed, said the Lad, with all the Asseverations imaginable, I did it not, but if you please, I'll tell you who had a hand in it: Hereupon the Master thought to have found out thë Truth, and so very eagerly asked him who? Your Worship, Sir, says he: Whereupon he was dismissed, with the applause of all his Fellows, for his Ingenuity.

[26.] In a discourse at Table, wherein they chiefly treated of strange things, and one among them said, that he had a piece of the Hawthorn Tree in a Box, which always bloom'd on Christmass day for many years together, and at last was robb'd of it by some of the Parliament Forces, and could never get it again. Why, says one, how could it live and bloom as you say without some earth, or the Sun's influence? Why, says he, d'ye think if it have that vertue to bloom on Christmass-day, that it had not the vertue also to bloom without the help of the Sun or earth? and so let out some Oaths to confirm it.

But another being by, to fit him in his Story; and to make it appear to be truth (as you know it was) began to confirm what t'other had said, with some Oaths too. For, says he, I

my self have seen that Haw thorn Tree bloom a hundred
Christmas-day, and if I were to say a Hundred more, I should
not lie; and I went once thither, when they were come to
the Berries, which were red, large and hard; and so took
some of them, and button'd me a Suit and Coat with it, as
the fashion is now (for you know our fashion in England for
Cloaths never alters) and when I and some others were at
Church together upon Christmass day in the morning, little
thinking of it, about Ten of the Clock precisely (he swore)
that the branches sprung out so fast and so thick, that he was
covered all over with them; insomuch that he lookt as if he
had been in a Wood, and so heavy they were upon him, that
he could not stir till one went out of the Church and fetcht
an Axe, and cut away all the Boughs, that he might see his
way out; and when they had done, he went home in this
posture to his lodging; and swore also, that there was as much
Wood cut off, as serv'd him all that Winter for fewel to his
Chamber; but however, says he, I had rather be at the charge
of the Wood than to be served so agen.   But Gentlemen I
tell you this to confirm what that worthy Gentleman told you
before : whereas you were in doubt for a great while whether
it was truth or no : but I hope there's no doubt now : and so
swore it agen.

[78.] One demanded of a wild yong Gentleman the reason
why he would sel his land? who answered because he hoped
to go to heven, which he could not possibly do til he forsook
earth.

[91.]   Learning hath fed me, yet I know no letter,
        I have liv'd among books, yet am never the better :
        I have eaten up the Muses, yet I know not a verse,
        What student is this, I pray you rehearse?
    Resolution, A Worme bred in a booke.

[18.] A Preacher, whose Sermons no body cared to hear,
intreated a Friend of his to come to hear him.   But he
begged his Excuse, saying, that he was loth to disturb him
in his Solitude.   Another who had not the luck to please his

Auditors; He did better last Year, said one.   How can that be? said another, for he did not preach at all.   In that very Thing he did better, reply'd the first.

[17.] One told a Bakers Son, that his Father was a Knave: Truly, says he, *Though I say it, that should not say it,* my Father is as honest a man as ever lived by bread.

complaint of M, Tenter-hooke the *Proiector,* and Sir *Thomas* Dodger the *Patentee.* [1]

If any aske, what things these Monsters *be,*
Tis a Projector *and a* Patentee:
Such, as like Vermine o're this Land did crawle,
And grew so rich, they gaind the Devill and all.

[101.]   Loe I, that lately was a *Man* of fashion
      The *Bug-beare* and the *Scarcrow* of this Nation

[1] " On a broadside, entitled as above, is a woodcut, which represents a ' Projector ' who has a pig's (? fox's) face, a fox's ears, screws for legs, and fish hooks for fingers, bears a measure of coal, and a barrel of wine on

Th' admired mighty *Mountee banke* of *Fame*,
The Juggling *Hocus Pocus* of good name,
The Bull-begger, who did affright and feare,
And rake, and pull, teare, pill, pole, shave, and sheare,
Now *Time* hath pluck'd the *Vizard* from my face,
I am the onely Image of disgrace.
My ugly shape I hid so cunningly
(Close cover'd with the cloake of honesty)
That from the *East* to *West* from *South* to *North*,
I was a man esteem'd of ex'lent worth.
And (Sweet Sir *Thomas Dodger*) for your sake,
My studious time I spent, my sleepes I brake,
My braines I tost with many a strange vagary,
And (like a Spaniell) did both fetch and carry,
To you, such *Projects*, as I could invent,
Not thinking there would come a Parliament.
I was the great *Projector*, and from me,
Your Worship learn'd to be a *Patentee*,
I had the Art to cheat the Common-weale,
And you had tricks and slights to passe the Seale.
I tooke the paines, I travell'd, search'd, and sought
Which, (by your power) were into Patents wrought.
What was I but your journey man, I pray,
To bring youre worke to you, both night and day :
I found *Stuffe*, and you brought it so about
You (like a skilfull *Taylor*) cut it out,
And fashion'd it, but now (to our displeasure)
You fail'd exceedingly in taking measure.
My legs were Screws, to raise thee high or low,
According as your power did *Ebbe* or *Flow* :
And at your will I was Screwd up too high

his legs respectively, tobacco pipes, dice, roll tobacco, playing cards, and a bundle of hay slung to his body, papers of pins on his right arm, and a measure for spirits on his left arm, a barrel (? for soap or butter) and a dredger, (? for starch) on the skirts of his coat.

"The introduction of screws here may be illustrated by the speech of Alderman Chambers, who was prosecuted in the Star Chamber for saying that merchants were more screwed up and wronged in England than in Turkey; he was fined £2000."—*Catalogue of Prints and Drawings in the British Museum*, No. 263.

That tott'ring, I have broke my necke thereby.
For you, I made my *Fingers fish-hookes* still
To catch at all *Trades*, either good or ill,
I car'd not much who lost, so we might get,
For all was *Fish* that came into the Net.
For you, (as in my Picture plaine appeares)
I put a *Swines face* on, an *Asses eares*,
The one to listen unto all I heard
Wherein your Worships profit was prefer'd,
The other to tast all things, good or bad.
(As Hogs will doe) where profit may be had.
Soape, *Starch*, *Tobacco*, *Pipes*, *Pins*, *Butter*, *Haye*,
Wine, *Coales*, *Cards*, *Dice*, and all came in my way,
I brought your worship, every day and houre,
And hope to be defended by your power.

Sir *Thomas Dodgers Answer.*

Alas good *Tenter hooke*, I tell thee plaine,
To seeke for helpe of me tis but in vaine :
My *Patent* which I stood upon of late,
Is like an *Almanacke* that's out of *Date*.
T'had force and vertue once, strange things to doe,
But now it wants both force and vertue too.
This was the turne of whirling *Fortune's* wheele,
When we least dream'd we should her changing feele.
Then *Time*, and fortune, both with joynt consent
Brought us to ruine by a Parliament :
I doe confesse thou broughtst me sweet conceits
Which now I find were but alluring baits,
And I, (too much an Asse) did lend mine eare,
To credit all thou saydst, as well as heare.
Thou in the *Project* of the *Soape* didst toyle,
But 'twas so slippery, and too full of oyle,
That people wondred how we held it fast
But now it is quite slipp'd from us at last.
The *Project* for the *Starch* thy wit found out,
Twas stiffe a while, now limber as a Clout,
The Pagan weed (*Tobacco*) was our hope
In *Leafe*, *Pricke*, *Role*, *Ball*, *Pudding*, *Pipe*, or *Rope*.

Brasseele, Varina, Meavis, Trinidado,
Saint *Christophers, Virginia,* or *Barvado ;*
Bermudas, Providentia, Shallowcongo,
And the most part of all the rest (*Mundungo*[1]).
That Patent, with a whiffe is spent and broke,
And all our hopes (in fumo) turn'd to smoake.
Thou framdst the *Butter* Patent in thy braines,
(A Rope and Butter take thee for thy paines.)
I had forgot *Tobacco Pipes,* which are
Now like to thou and I, but brittle ware.
Dice run against us, we at *Cards* are crost,
We both are turn'd up *Noddies,*[2] and all's lost.
Thus from *Sice-sinke,*[3] we'r sunke below *Dewce-ace,*[4]
And both of us are Impes of blacke disgrace.
Pins pricke us, and *Wine* frets our very hearts.
That we have rais'd the price of *Pints* and *Quarts.*
Thou (in mine eares) thy lyes and tales didst foyst.
And madst me up the price of *Sea-coales* hoyst.
Corne, Leather, Partrich, Pheasant, Rags, Gold twist,
Thou brought'st all to my *Mill,* what was't we mist ?
Weights, Bon lace,[5] *Mowstraps,* new, new, *Corporation,*
Rattles, Seadans,[6] of rare invented fashion,
Silke, Tallow, Hobby-horses, Wood, red herring,
Law, Conscience, Justice, swearing, and *For-swearing.*
All these thou broughtst to me, and still I thought
That every thing was good that profit brought,
But now all's found to be ill gotten pelfe,
I'le shift for one, doe thou shift for thyselfe.　　Finis.

John Taylor[7]

London.　　Printed by *E. P.* for *Francis Coles,* dwelling
in the Old Baily.　1641.

[1] Trashy tobacco—from the Spanish *Mondôngo,* paunch, tripes, black pudding.

[2] Fools ; but there was also a game at cards called noddy, supposed to have been the same as cribbage.

[3] Corrupt French terms used for the numbers on dice—six-five.

[4] Two-one.　　　[5] Bone-lace.

[6] Sedan chairs, which are said to have been introduced into England in 1581, and first used in London in 1623.　Sir Sanders Duncombe obtained a patent, or privilege, for them in 1634.　　[7] The water poet.

[82.] A *Mayor* that was on hunting (by chance) one asked him how hee liked the *Cry:* a pox take the *Dogs*, saith he, they make such a bawling, that I cannot heare the *Cry*.

[82.] An old Justice was fast asleepe on the Bench when a poore Malefactor was judged to bee hanged; at which word the Justice suddenly awaked, and said to the Thiefe, My friend, I pray let this bee a warning to you, looke you doe so no more, for wee doe not show every man the like favour.

[94.] One seeing another wear a Threadbare Cloak, asked him whether his Cloak was not sleepy, or no? Why do you ask? said the other. Because, saith he, I think it hath not had a Nap this seven years.

[102.]   *Monsieur Domingo* is a skilfull man,
For much experience he hath lately got,
Proving more Physick in an alehouse can,
Than may be found in any Vintner's Pot;
Beere he protests is sodden and refin'd,
But this he speakes, being single penny lin'd,

For when his purse is swolne but sixpence bigge,
Why then he sweares; now by the Lord I thinke
All Beere in Europe is not worth a figge:
A cup of Claret is the onely drinke,
And thus his praise from Beere to Wine doth goe
Even as his Purse in pence doth ebbe and flowe.

[93.] *George* (*Peele*) was invited one night by certaine of his friends to supper, at the White Horse in Friday Street: and in the evening as he was going, hee met with an old friend of his, who was so ill at the stomacke, hearing *George* tell him of the good cheere he went to, himselfe being unprovided both of meate and money, that he swore he had rather have gone a mile about, than have met him at that instant. And beleeve me, quoth George, I am heartily sorry that I cannot take thee along with mee, myselfe being but an invited guest; besides, thou art out of Cloathes, unfitting for such a company.   Mary, this I'le doe, if thou wilt follow my advice, I'le help thee to thy supper.   Any way, quoth hee to *George* doe thou but devise the meanes, and I'le execute it. *George* presently told him what hee should doe; so they parted.   *George* (was) well entertained, with extraordinary welcome, and seated at the upper end of the Table; Supper being brought up, H.M. watched his time below; and when he saw that the meate was carried up, up hee followes, (as *George* had directed him) who when *George* saw, You whorson Rascall (quoth *George*) what make you heere?   Sir, quoth he, I am come from the partie you wot of.   You Rogue, quoth *George*, have I not forewarned you of this?   I pray you, Sir, quoth hee, heare my Errand.   Doe you prate, you Slave? quoth *George*, and with that, tooke a Rabbet out of the Dish, and threw it at him.   Quoth hee, you use me very hardly. You Dunghill, quoth *George*, doe you out face me? and with that took the other Rabbet, and threw it at his head; after that a Loafe; then drawing his dagger, making an offer to throw it, the Gentleman staid him : meane while HM. got the Loafe and the two Rabbets, and away he went : which when *George* saw he was gone, after a little fretting, he sate quietly. So by that honest shift, hee helped his friend to his supper, and was never suspected for it of the Company.

[17.] Two Clerks belonging to one Church, and having both of them sate up most part of the night, were both asleep when Sermon was done : a man jogg'd one of them, and bid him sing a Psalm, for Sermon was done.   Sing, *All People*, saies he : The other then awak'd, and hearing him say so said, *Hang all people*, sing me the *hundred Psalm*.

[4.] One boasting of his Credit, said, He knew a Scrivener that would lend him Fifty Pounds at any time, on his own Bond, without either Scrip or Scrowl.

[26.] One told a Story that a Miller had a Horse for many years together, whose name was *Roan*, and being tired with working all day, poor Jade, slept soundly at night; which a thievish fellow espying, flay'd off his Skin, whilest he slept, and went away with it: But Old *Roan* when he awak't (though 'twas a bitter cold night) yet, poor thing, he came home to the Mill door and neighed very loud, which the honest Miller, hearing, awak't his Wife, and askt her whether that was not the neighing of old *Roan?* Truly, Husband, says she, it is, let us rise and see what's the matter with him; and when they came out, they wondred to see him in such a pickle: Well Husband, says she, since 'tis as 'tis, I'd have you kill Five or Six of your Sheep (and tomorrow being Market Day, we can sell their Flesh there) and take all the Skins and clap 'em hot upon poor Roan; which he presently did, with his dear Wife's help, and clapt them hot upon the Horse's flay'd Back; which with the Cold night were presently froz'd on, and the Horse as well or rather better in health than ever he was in his life, and I am sure you'll say warmer: And this Horse, said he, they kept for many years after, and every year it brought him Thirty Tod[1] of Wool: And I hope you will believe it; but if you dont believe it, I pray take notice, that I am not bound to find you stories and belief too. Then they all concluded it was true—lie so.

[91.] What is that which produceth teares without sorrow, takes his journey to heaven, but dies by the way, is begot by another, yet that other is not begot without it? *Resolution.* Smoake.

[103.] A Clipper[2] being Sentenc'd to Death, when he came to *Tyburn*, the Parson was very busie in preparing him for another World, amongst other things he told the Criminal, that it was no small Happiness to have had so much time to Repent, that he might have died suddenly, and by many Accidents, and so have been snatch'd away in a Moment, and gone Headlong down to Hell; but that now he was almost sure he shou'd go to Heaven, and lie in *Abraham's* Bosom; Say you so, Sir, says the poor Patient, 'tis very good News, but if you please you shall have my Place, for I had rather stay here a little longer.

---

[1] A tod of wool weighs 28 lbs.   [2] Of coin, a capital offence.

[17.] A Witch being at the stake to be burnt, she saw her Son there ; and being very dry, desir'd him to give her some drink : No, Mother, says the Sweet conditioned Son, 'twill do you wrong, for the dryer you be, you'll burn all the better.

[4.] A foolish young Esquire, being newly come to his Estate (taking after the old Miser his Father, grew covetous.) He hearing his Steward say, he had killed him a Bullock against Christmas. What, said he, do you mean to undo me by such extravagant Expenses ? I will have but half a one killed at a time.

A Song in Praise of the Leather Bottel.[1]

Shewing how Glasses, and Pots are laid aside,
And Flaggons and Noggins they cannot abide ;
And let all Wives do what they can,
'Tis for the Praise and Use of Man ;
And this you may very well be sure,
The Leather Bottel will longest endure ;
And I wish in Heaven his Soul may dwell
That first devised the Leather Bottel

To the Tune of *The Bottle Maker's Delight*, &c.

[104.]   God above that made all things,
      The Heavens, the Earth, and all therein,
      The Ships that on the Sea do Swim,
      To keep Enemies out that none comes in ;
      And let them do all what they can,
      'Tis for the Use and Praise of Man.
        And I wish in Heaven his Soul may dwell
        That first devised the Leather Bottel.

      Then what do you say to these Cans of Wood ?
      In faith they are, and can, not be good ;
      For when a Man he doth them send
      To be filled with Ale, as he doth intend ;
      The Bearer falleth down by the way.
      And on the ground the Liquor doth lay ;

[1] For tune, see Appendix.

And then the Bearer begins to ban,
And swears it is long of the Wooden Can.
But had it been the Leather Bottel,
Although he had fallen, yet all had been well
 Then I Wish &c.

Then what do you say to these Glasses fine?
Yes, they shall have no Praise of mine;
For when a Company they are set
For to be merry, as we are met;
Then if you chance to touch the Brim,
Down falls the Liquor and all therein,

If your Table Cloath be never so fine,
There lies your Beer, Ale, or Wine:
It may be for a small Abuse,
A young Man may his Service lose;
But had it been a Leather Bottel,
And the Stopple in, then all had been well.
 And I wish &c

Then what do you say these black Pots three?
True, they shall have no praise of me,
For when a Man and his Wife falls at Strife,
As many have done, I know, in their Life;
They lay their Hands on the Pot both,
And loth they are to lose their Broath;

The one doth tug, the other doth hill,
Betwixt them both the Liquor doth spill ;
But they shall answer another Day, ¡
For casting their liquor so vainly away ;
But had it been in the Leather Bottel,
They might have tugg'd till their Hearts did ake,
And yet their Liquor no harm could take ;
They might have tugg'd till their Hearts did ake.
    Then I wish &c

Then what do you say to the Silver Flaggons fine?
True, they shall have no Praise of mine ;
For when a Lord he doth them send
To be filled with Wine as he doth intend ;
The Man with the Flaggon he doth run away,
Because it is Silver most gallant and gay :
O then the Lord he begins to ban,
And swears he hath lost both Flaggon and Man ;
There's never a Lord's Serving-man or Groom,
But with his Leather Bottel may come ;
    Then I wish &c

A Leather Bottel we know is good,
Far better than Glasses or Cans of Wood,
For when a Man is at work in the Field,
Your Glasses and Pots no Comfort will yield ;
Then a Leather Bottle standing him by,
He may drink always when he is a dry ;
It will revive the Spirits, and comfort the Brain,
Wherefore let none this Bottle refrain ;
    For I wish &c

Also the honest Sith-man[1] too,
He knew not very well what to do,
But for his Bottle standing him near,
That is filled with good Household beer ;
At Dinner he sits him down to eat,
With his good hard Cheese and Bread or Meat ;
Then this Bottle he takes up amain,

[1] Mower.

And drinks, and sets him down again ;
Saying, Good Bottle, stand my Friend,
And hold out till this day doth end ;
    For I wish &c

And likewise the Haymakers they,
When as they are turning and making their Hay ;
In Summer-weather, when as it is warm,
A good Bottel full then will do them no harm ;
And at Noon time they sit them down,
And drink in their Bottels of Ale Nut Brown ;
Then the Lads and the Lasses begin to tattle,
What should we do but for this Bottle ?
They could not work if this Bottle were done,
For the Day's so hot with heat of Sun.
    Then I wish &c

Also the Leader, Lader, and the Pitcher,
The Reaper, Hedger and the Ditcher,
The Binder, and the Raker and all
About the Bottels ears do fall ;
And if his Liquor be almost gone,
His Bottel will he part with to none,
But says, my Bottel is but small
One Drop I will not part withal :
You must go drink at some Spring or Well,
For I will keep my Leather Bottel.
    Then I wish &c

Thus you may hear of a Leather Bottel,
When as it is filled with Liquor full well,
Though the Substance of it be but small,
Yet the Name of the thing is all.
There's never a Lord, an Earl or Knight,
But in a Bottel doth take Delight :
For when he is hunting of the Deer,
He often doth wish for a Bottel of Beer :
Likewise the Man that works at the Wood,
A Bottel of Beer doth oft do him good
    Then I wish &c

Then when this Bottel doth grow old,
And will good Liquor no longer hold,
Out of the Side you may take a Clout,
Will mend your Shooes when they'r worn out ;
Else take it and hang it upon a Pin,
It will serve to put many odd Trifles in,
As Hinges, Awls, and Candle-ends,
For young Beginners must have such things ;
Then I wish in Heaven his Soul may dwell,
That first devised the Leather Bottel.

London : Printed by and for *W. O.* and sold by the Booksellers
of *Pye Corner,* and *London Bridge.*

[105.] When *Scogin* had broght to Oxford such things as he
had in London, hee lacked furres for his gownes, and Miniver
furres for his hood.   Whereupon hee went to an Alderman in
Oxford, which was a Skinner, and said unto him, It is so that
I must proceed Master of Arts, at the next Act, and I have
bestowed my money at London, and now I have need of furres
(as you know) wherefore if I shall have of you as much as
shall serve me, I will content you with thankes.   Then said
the Alderman, make your gownes and your hood, and send
them to me, and they shall be furred as other Masters be.
Then said *Scogin,* you shall have them within these two days,
and then I pray you make me a bill what I shall pay for every
thing.   It shall be done, said the Alderman.   When as the
gownes and hood were furred, he went to fetch them home,
and said to the Alderman, I pray you let me see my charge :
the bill was brought forth, and the sum did rise to sixe pound
and odde money.   The Alderman said, When shall I have my
money ?   Scogin answered, within these seven weeks, or else
the next time that you and I doe meet after the said terme
set.[1]   The terme of time passed over, and the Alderman sent
for his money.   Scogin said to the messenger, have me com-
mended to Master Alderman, and tell him when he and I doe
meet, I will content him according to my promise ; so, on a
time, *Scogin* went to Korfax,[2] and he espied the Alderman,

---

[1] Commences.
[2] Carfax, a place in Oxford, where four streets meet ; supposed to be
a corruption of *quatre voies.*

and then he returned backe. The Alderman made good footing after him to overtake him and said unto him, Sir, you said that you would pay me my money within seven weekes, or else any time after that we did meet together. It is true, said *Scogin*, my day is expired, but my promise is not broken ; No, said the Alderman, so that you pay me my money now. Now, said *Scogin*, nay not so, wee meet not together yet, for now you did but overtake me, and when we doe meet, you shall have your money; but if I can, said *Scogin*, I will not meet you this seven Yeares, if I can go backward. Wherefore a plaine bargain is best, and in bargaines making, fast bind, fast find.

[103.] A Gentleman having left a Bag of Money in a Hackney Coach, besides an Advertisement in the *Gazet*, he put up a paper at the *Exchange*, that he would give a sixth part (*viz* £20) to the Coachman, if he would bring him his Money ; the Fellow, hearing of the offer, went to the *Exchange* and writ on the Paper, *Then shall I be the Loser*, which was all the Gentleman had for his Coin.

[26.] One swore most plentifully, That he saw a Lobster kill a Hare upon *Salisbury Plain ;* then they all began to think indeed that was a lie, till he very discreetly told them how it was; for the Lobsters that are taken at *Weymouth, Southampton,* and upon the Sea-Coasts thereabouts, are presently convey'd in Panniers into the Midland Country, and by the way on *Salisbury Plain* did drop a very good Lobster, and a Hare a little after, came close to the Lobster : which the Lobster feeling, with his Claw presently catcht him fast by the foot, and so kill'd him ; and swore also that they put it into a Pie, and both bak't together (but I don't mean with the skin and the shell on) then you'd think't a lie indeed ; and so sent up to *London*, and eaten there.

[102.] Alas, *Delfridus* keepes his bed, God knowes,
Which is a sign his worship's very ill :
His griefe beyond the grounds of Phisike goes ;
No Doctor that comes neere it with his skill,

Yet doth he eat, drink, talke, and sleepe profound,
Seeming to all men's judgements healthful found.

Then gesse the cause he thus to bed is drawne
What? think you so? may such a hap procure it?
Well; faith, 'tis true, his Hose is out at pawne,
A breechlesse chance is come, he must indure it :
His Hose to Brokers Jayle committed are,
His Singular, and only Velvet paire.

[17.] A man on his death bed bequeathed all that he had
to his three Sons; to the first he gave all his Land, for he
said he had been very dutiful, but he said he hoped his Father
would live to enjoy it all himself: To the second, he gave all
his money and goods, for he had been dutiful also, and he
wisht his father might live and enjoy it all himself: And to
the third, he said, Thou hast been a Villain, a Rogue, and a
Vagabond; I first give to thee the benefit of the Stocks, to
keep both thy legs warm; and next *Bridwell*, where thou
shalt dine upon freecost with Mr *Lashington* every day; and
then I bestow the Gallows upon thee at last: Truly Father,
says he, I thank you, and *I hope you'll live to enjoy them* all,
yourself.

[94.] One asked the reason why Lawyers Clerks writ such
wide lines : Another answered, It was done to keep the peace ;
for if the Plaintiff should be in one line, and the Defendant in
the next, the lines being too near together, they might perhaps
fall together by the Ears.

[4.] Mr *Noy*[1] the Attorney General, making a Venison
Feast in a Tavern where *Ben Johnson* and some of his Com-

[1] "Noy, when Whitlocke came to him about the Bill, advised with
him about the King's Patent concerning an association between England
and Scotland for fishing. Noy loved a little drollery, and gave White-
locke eleven groats out of his little purse. Here, said Noy, take these
single pence ; and I give you more than an attorney's fee, because you will
be a better man than an Attorney-General ; and this you will find to be
true. This was in 1629."—*Lives of Eminent Sergeants at Law, by H. W.
Woolrych, Lond. 1869.*

panions were Drinking, and he having a mind to some of the Venison, wrote these Verses, and sent them to Mr *Noy*

> When all the World was drown'd,
> No Venison could be found ;
> For then there was no Park :
> Lo here we sit,
> Without e're a bit,
> *Noy* has it all in his Ark.

For the ingenuity of which, Mr *Noy* sent him a good corner of a Pasty, and half a Dozen Bottles of Sack to wash it down.

At another time, *Ben Johnson* intending to go through the Half Moone Tavern in *Aldersgate Street*, was denied entrance, the Door being shut : upon which he made these Verses.

> Since the *Half-Moon* is so unkind,
> to make me go about,
> The *Sun* my Money now shall take,
> the *Moon* shall go without.

And so he went to the *Sun Tavern* at *Long Lane* end, forsaking the *Half-Moon* for this affront.

[91.] When I lived, I fed the living, now I am dead, I bear the living, and with swift speed walke over the living. *Resolution.* A Ship made of an Oake, growing, fed Hogs with Acorns, now beares men, swims over fishes.

The English Irish Souldier

With his new Discipline, new Armes, old Stomacke, and new taken pillage, who had rather Eate than Fight.

[106.]   If any Souldate
>   think I do appeare,
>   In this strange Armes
>   and posture, as a Jeere,
>   Let him advance up to me
>   he shall see,
>   Ile stop his mouth
>   and we wil both agree.

Our Skirmish ended
  our Enemies fled or slaine
Pillage wee cry then,
  for the Souldiers gaine,

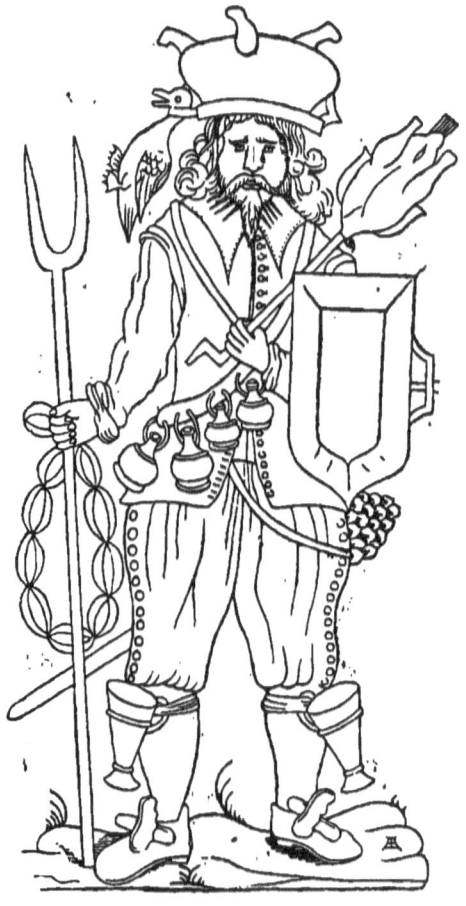

And this compleat Artillery
  I have got,
The best of Souldiers,
  I think, hateth not.

My Martiall Armes
　　dealt I amongst my foes
With this I charged stand
　　'gainst hungers blowes';
This is Munition
　　if a Souldier lacke,
He fights like *Iohn a dreams* [1]
　　or Lent's thin *Jacke.* [2]

All safe and cleare,
　　my true Arms rest awhile,
And welcome pillage
　　you have foes to soile.
This Pot, my Helmet,
　　must not be forsaken,
For loe I seiz'd it
　　full of Hens and Bacon.

Rebels for Rebels drest it
　　but our hot rost
Made them to flye
　　and now they kisse the post.
And better that to kisse
　　than stay for Pullets
And have their bellies
　　cram'd with leaden bullets.

This fowle my Feather is,
　　who wins most fame,
To weare a pretty Duck
　　he need not shame ;
This Spit my well chargd
　　Musket with a Goose,

[1] *i.e.* a stupid, semi-idiot, as—

　　" A Dull and Muddy Mettled rascal, peak,
　　Like *John a dreams,* impregnant of my cause,
　　And can say nothing."—*Hamlet,* Act ii. Scene 2.

[2] " A Jack a Lent" was a straw-stuffed image which was shot at,
beaten, thrown at, and otherwise ill-treated during Lent.　It was supposed
to represent Judas Iscariot.

Now cryes come eate me,
  let your stomacks loose.

This Dripping Pan's my
  target, and this Hartichoke
My Basket-hilted blade
  can make 'em smoake,
And make them slash and cut
  who most Home puts,
Ile most my fury
  sheath into his guts

This Forke my Rest is,
  and my Bandaleers
Canary Bottles,
  that can quell base feares,
And make us quaffe downe
  danger, if this not doe,
What is it then? can raise
  a spiritt into fearfull men.

This Match are linkes
  to light down to my belly
Wherein are darksome chinks
  as I may tell yee,
Or Sassages, or Puddings,
  choose you which,
An excellent Needle,
  Hungers wounds to stitch.

These my Supporters,
  garter'd with black pots,
Can steele the nose
  & purg the brain of plots ;
These tosts my shooestrings,
  steept in this strong fog,
Is able of themselves
  to foxe a Dog.

These Armes being vanisht,
  once againe appeare

A true and faithful Souldier
  As you were ;
But if this wants,
  and that we have no biting
In our best Armours
  we make sorry fighting

FINIS

Printed at *London* for *R. Wood* and *A. Coe* 1642.

[93.] There was a Gentleman that dwelt in the West Countrey, and had staid here in London a Tearme longer than hee intended, by reason of a Booke that *George* (*Peele*) had to translate out of Greeke into English : and when he wanted money, George had it of the Gentleman, but the more he supplyed him of Coine, the further off he was from his Booke, and could get no end of it, neither by faire meanes, entreatie, or double payment : for *George* was of the Poeticall disposition, never to write so long as his money lasted ; some quarter of the Booke being done, and lying in his hands at randome.

The Gentleman had plotted a meanes to take such an order with *George* next time he came, that he would have his Booke finished. It was not long before he had his Company ; his arrival was for more money ; the Gentleman bids him welcome ; causeth him to stay dinner, where falling into discourse about his Booke, found it was as neere ended, as he left it two moneths ago. The Gentleman, meaning to be gul'd no longer, caused two of his men to binde *George* hand and foot in a Chayre : a folly it was for him to aske what they meant by it : the Gentleman sent for a Barber, and George had a beard of an indifferent size, and well growne : he made the Barber shave him beard and head, left him as bare of haire, as he was of money : the Barber he was well contented for his paines, who left *George* like an old woman in mans apparell : and his voyce became it well, for it was more woman than man. *George* quoth the Gentleman, I have always used you like a friend, my purse hath beene open to you : that you have of mine to translate, you know it is a thing I highly esteeme : therefore I have used you in this fashion, that I might have an end of my Booke, which shall be as much for your profit as my pleasure. So forthwith he commanded his men to unbinde him, and putting his hand into his pocket, gave him two brace of Angels; quoth hee, Master *Peele*, drinke this, and by that time you have finished my booke, your beard will be growne, untill which time, I know you will be ashamed to walke abroad. *George* patiently tooke the gold, said little, and when it was darke night, took his leave of the Gentleman, and went directly home: who, when his wife saw, I omit the wonder shee made, but imagine those that shall behold their husbands in such a case. To bed went *George*, and ere morning hee had plotted sufficiently how to cry *quid pro quo* with his politick Gentleman.

George had a Daughter of the age of tenne yeeres, a Girle of a pretty forme, but of an excellent wit: and she had *George* so tutored all night, that although himselfe was the Author of it, yet had hee beene transformed into his Daughters shape, he could not have done it with more conceit. *George* at that time dwelt at the Banke Side from whence this she-sinnow,[1] early in the morning, with her haire dichevalled, wringing her hands, and making such pittifull moane with shrikes and teares, and beating of her brest, that made the people in a maze: some stood wondring at the Childe; others plucked her to know the occasion; but none could stay her by any meanes, but on shee kept her journey, crying, O, her Father, her good Father, her deare Father, over the Bridge, thorow Cheapside, and so to the Old Bailey, where the Gentleman sojourned, there sitting her selfe downe, a hundred people gaping upon her, there she begins to cry out, Woe to that place, that her Father ever saw it: she was a Cast-away, her Mother was un-done: till with the noise, one of the Gentlemans men comming downe, looked on her, and knew her to be *George Peeles* Daughter: hee presently runnes up, and tels his Master, who commanded his man to bring her up. The Gentleman was in a cold sweat, fearing that George had, for the wrong that he did him the day before, some way undone himselfe. When

---

[1] A woman very finely dressed. "Whereas she wont in her feathered youthfulnesse to looke with amiable eye on her gray breast, and her speckled side sayles, all *sinnowed* with silver guilles."—*Pierce Penilesse his Supplication to the Divell, by Thos. Nash.* 1592.

the Girle came up, he demanded the cause why she so lamented, and called upon her Father ? *George* his flesh and blood, after a million of sighs, cried out upon him, he had made her Father, her good Father, drowne himselfe. Which words once uttered, she fell into a Counterfeit swoone, whom the Gentleman soon recovered. This newes went to his heart, and he, being a man of a very milde condition, cheered up the Girle, made his men to go buy her new cloathes from top to toe, said he would be a Father to her, gave her five pounds, bid her go home and carry it to her mother, and in the evening he would visit her. At this, by little and little she began to be quiet : desiring him to come and see her Mother. He tels her, he will not faile, bids her goe home quietly. So downe stayres goes she peartly,[1] and the wondring people that staid at doore, to heare the manner of her griefe, had of her nought but knavish answers, and home went she directly. The Gentleman was so crossed in mind, and disturbed in thought at this unhappy accident, that his soule could not be in quiet, till he had beene with this wofull widdow, as hee thought, and presently went to Blacke Fryers, tooke a payre of Oares, and went directly to *George Peeles* house, where hee found his wife plucking of Larkes, my crying Crocadile turning of the Spit, and *George* pinn'd up in a blanket, at his translation. The Gentleman, more glad at the unlookt for life of *George*, than the losse of his money, tooke part in the good cheere *George* had to dinner, wondred at the cunning of the Wench, and within some few daies after had an end of his Booke.

[77.] There was a great huge man 3 yards in the Waste, at *S. Edmondsbury* in *Suffolk*, that died but of late daies, (one *M. Blague* by name) & a good kinde Justice too, carefull for the poore ; this Justice met with *Tarlton* in Norwich : *Tarlton*, said he, give me thy hand ; But you, Sir, being richer, may give me a greater gift, give me your body ! and imbracing him could not halfe compasse him : being merry in talke, said the Justice ; *Tarlton* tell me one thing, what is the difference betwixt a Flea and a Louse ? Marry, Sir, said *Tarlton*, as much and like difference, as twixt you and me ; I like a Flea

---

[1] Briskly, lively.

(see else) can skip nimbly : But you, like a fat Louse creepe
slowly, and you can go no faster, were a Butcher's axe over
you, ready to knock you on the head.   Thou art a knave,
quoth the Justice.   I, Sir, I knew that ere I came hither, else
had I not been here now, for ever one knave (making a stop)
seekes out another : the Justice understanding him, laughed
heartily.

[17.] A Gentleman had a desire to hire two resolute Ruffians
to do some exploit upon one that had abused him : A little
after his man brings him two whose faces were slasht and cut :
No, says he, I'll have none of you, but if you can bring me
those men that gave you those wounds, they are for my turn.

[4.] A Sea Captain was invited to a Hunting Match, who
when he came home related what sport he had after this
manner : Our Horses, says he, being well Rigg'd, we man'd
them ; and the Wind being at West South West, (Fifteen of us
in Company) away we stood over the Downs ; in the time of
half a Watch, we spied a Hare under full Sail, we Tackt, and
stood after her, coming up close, she Tacks, and we Tackt,
upon which Tack I had like to run aground ; but getting clear
off, I stood after her again ; but as the Devil would have it,
just as I was going to lay her aboard, bearing too much Wind,
I and my Horse overset and came Heel [1] upwards.

A *Leicester-shire* Frolick ;

Or, The Valiant Cook-Maid.

Being a merry composed Jest of Five Taylors that had been
at work till their Wages came to 5 pounds, likewise a merry
conceited Cook-maid that lived in the house, went to her
Master, and desired him to lend her a horse, and she would
venture her skill to take the 5 pounds from these five Taylors,
without either Sword or Pistol, in a jesting way, to make her
Master some sport and to show her valour : her Master loving

[1] ? Keel.

mirth more than sadness, agreed to it; so a Horse was sadled, and other things to disguise herself, because she might not be known: away she went (it being in the Evening) and met them before they got home, with nothing in her hand but a black pudding, the faint hearted Taylors delivered her their Money very quietly, for fear they should a been shot through with a Black Pudding, and what followed after is expressed in the following Ditty.

Tune is Ragged & Torn.   With Allowance.

[107.]   I'le tell you a pretty fine jest,
      if that you do please it to hear,
For the truth on't I do protest,
      I'm sure that you need not to fear:
It is of a valiant Cook-maid,
      that lived at a Nobleman's place
And five Taylors that once was afraid
      when as they lookt her in the face.
O this was a valiant Cook-maid,
      without either Pistol or Gun,
But with a Black Pudding did fright,
      five Taylors and put them to th' run.

¹ This engraving is from another version, $\frac{C. 22 f. 2}{101}$

This Noble-man upon a time,
  had great store of work for to do,
But to bring every thing into rhyme,
  'twill study my brains you must know ;
Five Taylors that lived hard by,
  that worked for fourpence a day,
For Beef and for Pudding at night,
  they'd better do so than to play.
    O this &c

These Taylors a great while did work,
  two Masters, and their three men,
They laboured as hard as a Turk,
  with Stitching both too and agen ;
And when that their work it was done,
  their money unto them was told,
Full five good pounds it is known,
  Of Silver, but not of red Gold.
    O this &c

And when as their money they'd got,
  then who was so jocond as they,
Each Man of the best drank his pot,
  and homewards they straight took their way ;
A Cook-Maid there was in the house,
  that us'd full merry to be,
Who went to her Master in haste,
  and these words unto him did say.
    O this &c

Master, if that you please,
  some pastime I for you will make
But to lend me a horse then (quoth she)
  and this money I from them will take ;
Her Master, then hearing the jest,
  would try what this Cook-maid could do,
Some mirth he did think it the best,
  as Gentlemen will do, you know.
    O this &c

A horse then was sadled with speed,
   and boots and Spurs she put on,
And other materials most fit,
   because she would not be known ;
A horse-back she straight got astride,
   with a Hogs-Pudding in her hand,
And meeting these Taylors in haste,
   she presently bid them to stand.
        O this &c

Deliver your Money (quoth she)
   or else your manhoods now try,
Or by this same thing in my hand,
   every man of you shall dye ;
Then out her Black-Pudding she pull'd,
   which sore did the Taylors affright,
They thought it had been a Pistol well charg'd,
   because 'twas late in the night.
        O this &c

They beg'd their lives she might save,
   we are but poor Taylors (quoth they)
And truly no money we have,
   for we work but for four pence a day ;
You lye, like all Rogues (quoth she)
   and do not my patience provoke,
For 5 pounds you have tane for your work,
   so presant that word did them choak.
        O this &c.

That money deliver with speed,
   if that you think well on your lives,
Or by this same thing you shall bleed,
   the which will go farther than knives ;
Then out of their pockets their money they took,
   with many a sorrowful tear,
And gave it into her hand,
   here's all on't each Taylor did swear.
        O this &c—

And when she their money had got,
  she set Spurs and away she did run,
The Devil go with you (quoth they)
  for i'me sure that we are undone ;
But when that this Cook-maid came home,
  strait unto her Master she told,
And show'd him his money again,
  how passages went she did unfold.
    O this &c.

The poor Taylor making his complaint to the Esquire

But here comes the cream of the jest,
  those Taylors which was such Men,
After they'd stood pausing awhile,
  then back they returned again ;
They came with a pittiful tone,
  their hair stood like men bewitcht,
To th' Gentleman they made their moan,
  for their mony their fingers it itcht.
    O this &c

The Gentleman laugh'd in conceit,
  how many was there said he,
Sure you were all men sufficient
  to a beaten above two or three ;
Truly we saw but one man,
  the which took our Money away,
But we feared he had partakers in store,
  or else he should never a carried the day.
      O this &c

He was well mounted upon a good steed,
  and a Pistol that put us to studying,
You lye like all fools (quoth she)
  it was but a black Hogs-Pudding ;
Thus they the poor Taylors did jeer,
  and the Cook-maid laugh'd in conceit,
That with nothing but a black Pudding,
  and that five Taylors did beat.
      O this &c.

Then straightway the Gentleman spoke,
  what will you give then (said he)
To have all your money again,
  and the face on't once more to see :
Quoth the Taylors we'l give the ton half,
  and that's very fair you do know,
Altho' that we were such fools,
  to part with our good silver so.
      O this &c

Then straitways he call'd for the Cook,
  then the Taylors did laugh in their sleeve,
And set her to conjuring strait,
  which made the poor Taylors believe ;
That she by her art had it found,
  and show'd them the place where it lay,
Which made the poor Taylors to smile,
  so merry and jocand was they.
      O this &c.

Here take half the money said they,
    the which we did promise to you,
And for you we ever will pray,
    for such Cook-Maids there is but a few ;
I'le have none of your money she said,
    as sure as i'me here alive,
One may know what Cowards you are,
    to let a Hogs-Pudding to fright you all 5.
      O this &c.

And thus the old Proverb is true,
    nine Taylors do make but one man,
And now it doth plainly appear,
    let them all do what they can ;
For had they been stout hearted Lads,
    they need not called for aid,
Nor afraid to tast of a Pudding,
    nor yet be'n out-brav'd by a Maid.
      O this &c

FINIS.

Printed for P. Brooksby, at the Golden-Ball, at Pye-Corner, near West Smithfield.

How Jacke *by playing of the Whiting got his dinner.*

[105.] When the sicknesse was at Oxford, on a time *Scogin* went out of Oxford, and did lye at S. Bartholemewes by Oxford, and hee had a poore scholler to dresse his meat : On a Friday he said to his scholler, *Jacke*, here is twopence, goe to the market and buy me three whitings, the which his scholler did ; & when hee was come home, *Scogin* said, *Jacke*, goe seeth me a whiting to my dinner : *Jacke* heard him say so, and deferred the time, thinking hee should fare ill when that his master had but a whiting to dinner. At last *Scogin* said, doth the fish play ? *Jacke* said, would you have one play without a fellow ? *Scogin* said, *Jacke* thou saist truth, put another whiting into the pan. Then *Jacke* prepared his fish to seeth them : then *Scogin* said, *Jacke* doth the fish play now ? *Jacke* said, I trow they be mad or else wood,[1] for one doth fight with the other, that I have much adoe to keepe them in the pan.   Then said *Scogin*, put the other whiting betwixt them to break the strife.   *Jacke* was then glad, thinking he should get somewhat to dinner, and sod[2] the fish and had his part.

[26.] One swore pretty largely too, That he knew a Hare, that after he was taken and garbaged,[3] did give the Dogs a chase for five or six miles together; then they cry'd out all 'twas a loud lie.   No, says he, it can't be a loud lie, for it seems you don't allow it.   Yes, says they, we do allow it for a lie.   But, says he, I do avow it for truth, and thus it was, for the Hare being tied to a Huntsman's Saddle in a string, it happened that the string slips, and the Hare in the string hung down between the Horses Legs upon the Ground, and the Horse being mettlesome, gallopt away with the Hare at his heels, and the Dogs marcht after; but the truth was, the Man could not hold the Horse in : Nay then, say they, this may be impossibly possible.

Another very sober Man told a story; That once he went a coursing alone with a Grey hound Bitch, that was great with Whelp; and, having started a Hare, it hapned the Hare went through a Muse[4] is a Hedg where a Carpenter had hid his Axe, lying it seems with the edge upwards : and so the Hare being with young, in going through that Muse, cut her belly with the edge of the Axe; and then out started 8 young Hares, and began to run immediately; but the Grey hound Bitch suddenly following the Hare through the very same Muse, by Chance Cut her belly also, and out came Eight Whelps; which eight Whelps ran after the eight young Hares, and the Bitch after the Old Hare and Kill'd em all.   Now, says he to them, Some nice people may take this for a lie,

---

[1] Or *wode*, mad or furious.   [2] Or *sodden*, boiled.
[3] Disembowelled.
[1] Or *muset*, a hole in a hedge through which game passes.   *Ed. Topsell* in his "*Histore of* foure footed beasts," Lond. 1607, says, "But the good and aproved hounds, on the contrary, when they have found the hare, make shew thereof to the hunter, by running more speedily, and with gesture of head, eyes, ears, and taile winding to the hares *muse*," etc.

but I think 'tis as probable as any of the rest, because the wonder is greater : that there should be but just the number of Eight Whelps, and Eight young Hares, and if true *Probatum est.*

[82.] Seigneur *Valdrino* (paymaster to the Campe of *Alphonsus* King of *Aragon*) a man exquisite in Courtship and complement; as two or three were at strife laying Wagers what Countryman he was; a blunt bold Captaine asked what was the matter : why Captaine, said one, we are laying a wager what Countriman my Lord Treasurer *Valdrino* is : Oh, said the Captaine, I can tell you that, I am sure he was borne in the land of *Promise*, for I have served the King in his wars, these seven yeers without pay, and ever when I petition to my Lord, he payes me with no coyne but promises, which makes me half assured that hee is that Countryman.

Epitaph on a Scholler.

[5.]   Forbeare, friend, t' unclaspe this booke
Onely in the fore front looke,
For in it have errours bin,
Which made th' authour call it in :
    Yet know this 't shall have more worth,
    At the second comming forth.

[17.] A Gardener being to be hang'd, his Wife came to give him his last kiss at the Gallows : Out, you Baggage, says he, we are like to thrive well at the years end ; there can't be a meeting in all the Country but you'll be sure to make one— Go home and weed, home and weed.

[91.]   There is a body without a heart,
That hath a tongue, and yet no head,
Buried it was, e're it was made ;
And loude doth speake, and yet is dead.
Resolution.   A Bell, which when it is cast, is founded in the ground.

And thus you hear how cruelly
    my wife doth still abuse me,
At bed, at board, at noon and night
    she always did misuse me :
But if I were a lusty Man
    and able for to baste her,
Then would I surely use some means,
    that she should not be my Master.
       But if ever &c

You Batchelors that sweet-hearts have,
    when as you are a Wooing,
Be sure you look before you leap,
    for fear of your undoing :
The after wit is not the best,
    and he that weds in hast sir,
May like to me, bewail his case,
    if his wife do prove his Master.
       But if ever &.

You Married Men that have good wives,
    I wish you deal well by them,
For they more precious are than Gold,
    if once you come to try them :
A good wife makes a husband glad,
    then let him not distast her,
But a Scold will make a man run mad,
    if once she proves his Master.
       But if ever &c

Printed for *F. Coles, T. Vere,*[1] *J. Wright, J. Clarke, W. Thackeray,*
and T. Passinger.

[93.] There was some halfe dozen of Citizens, that had
oftentimes beene solliciters to *George* (*Peele*), he being a Master
of Art at the Universitie of Oxford, that hee would ride with
them to the Commencement, it being at Midsomer. *George,*
willing to pleasure the Gentlemen his friends, rode along with
them. When they had rode the better part of the way, they

      [1] Published from 1648 to 1680.

baited at a village called Stoken, five miles from Wickham ;
good cheere was bespoken for dinner, and frolicke was the
company, all but *George*, who could not be in that pleasant
vaine that did ordinarilie possess him, by reason he was without mony : but he had not fetcht fortie turnes about the
Chamber, before his noddle had entertained a conceit how
to money himself with credit, and yet glean it from some one
of the Company. There was among them one excellent Asse,
a fellow that did nothing but friske up and down the Chamber,
that his money might bee heard chide in his pocket : this
fellow had *George* observed, and secretly convay'd his gilt
Rapier and Dagger into another Chamber, and there closely
hid it : that done, he called up the Tapster, and upon his
cloake borrowes 5 shillings for an houre or so, till his man
came, (as he could fashion it well enough :) so much money he
had, and then who more merry than *George!* Meate was
brought up, they set themselves to dinner, all full of mirth,
especially my little foole, who dranke not of the conclusion
of their feast : dinner ended, much prattle past, every man
begins to buckle to his furniture : among whom this Hich-
cock missed his Rapier : at which all the Company were in a
maze ; he, besides his wits, for he had borrowed it of a speciall
friend of his, and swore he had rather spend twenty Nobles.
This is strange, quoth *George*, it should be gone in this fashion,
none beeing heere but our selves, and the fellowes of the house,
who were examined, but no Rapier could be heard of : but
George in a pittifull chafe, swore it should cost him fortie
shillings, but hee would know what was become of it, if Art
could do it ; and with that he caused the Oastler to saddle
his Nag, for *George* would ride to a Scholler, a friend of his,
that had skill in such matters. O, good M. *Peele*, quoth the
fellow, want no money, heere is forty shillings, see what you
can doe, and, if you please, I'le ride along with you. Not so,
quoth *George*, taking his fortie shillings, I'le ride alone, and
be you as merry as you can till my returne. So *George* left
them, and rode directly to Oxford ; there he acquaints a friend
of his with all the circumstances, who presently tooke Horse,
and rode along with him to laugh at the Jest. When they
came backe, *George* tels them he has brought one of the

rarest men in England : whom they with much complement bid welcome. He, after a distracted countenance, and strange words, takes this Bulfinch by the wrist, and carried him into the privy, and there willed him to put in his head, but while he had written his name and told forty : which he willingly did : that done, the Scholler asked him what he saw ? By my faith, sir, I smelt a villainous sent, but I saw nothing. Then I have, quoth he, and with that directed him where his Rapier was : saying, it is just North East, inclosed in Wood, neere the earth : for which they all made diligent search, till *George* who had hid it under a settle, found it, to the comfort of the fellow, the joy of the Company, and the eternall credit of his friend, who was entertained with Wine and Sugar ; and *George* redeemed his Cloake, rode merrily to Oxford, having Coine in his pocket, where this Loach spares not for any expence, for the good fortune he had in the happy finding of his Rapier.

[94.] One said the Midwifes Trade, of all Trades, was most commendable, because they lived not by the hurts of other men as Surgeons do ; nor by the falling out of friends, as Lawyers do ; but by the agreement betwixt party and party.

[105.] On a time Scogin did send Jacke to Oxford to market, to buy a penny worth of fresh herring. Scogin said, bring foure herrings for a penny, or else bring none. Jack could not get foure herrings but three for his penny ; and when he came home, Scogin said, how many herrings hast thou brought? and Jacke said, three herrings, for I could not get foure for a penny. Scogin said he would none of them : Sir, said Jacke, then will I, and here is your penny againe. When dinner time was come then Jack did set bread and butter before his Master, and rosted his herrings, and sate downe at the lower end of the table and did eate the herrings. Scogin said, let mee have one of thy herrings, and thou shalt have another of mee another time. Jacke said, if you will have one herring, it shall cost you a penny. What, said Scogin, thou will not take it on thy Conscience : Jacke said, my conscience is such, that you get not a morsell here, except I have my penny again.

Thus contending together, Jacke had made an end of his herrings : A Master of Arts of Oxford, one of Scogins fellowes, did come to see Scogin, and when Scogin had espied him, hee said to Jacke, set up the bones of the herrings before me : sir, said Jacke, they shall cost you a penny. Then said Scogin, what, wilt thou shame me? No, sir, said Jacke, give me my penny again, and you shal have up the bones, or else I will tell all. Scogin then cast down a penny to Jacke, and Jacke brought up to Scogin the herring bones : and by this time the Master of Arts did come in to Scogin, and Scogin bad him welcome, saying, if you had come sooner you should have had fresh herrings to dinner.

[26.] A confident bold Fellow at a *Nisi prius* in the Country, having a Trial then in Law, and fearing that the Trial would go against him, said to the Judge, My Lord, I do not desire your Sentence now, but only your Opinion at the present ; and I will wait upon your Lordship for Judgment at some other time. Well, says the Judge, if you'd only have my Opinion now, why then my Opinion is, That if you had had Judgment to be hang'd seven years ago, the Country would have been more quiet than it is now. Well, my Lord, says he, if this be your Opinion, then your Judgement and mine doth not suit at all, so that I'le have nothing to do with you, but go to another Judge.

Poor *Robin's* Prophesie,

or

The merry Conceited Fortune-Teller.

Although the Poet makes no large Apology,
Some insight he may have into Ass-trology,
Then buy this Song, and give your Judgment of it,
And then perhaps you'l say he's a Small Prophet
For he can tell when things will come to pass,
That you will say is strange as ever was.

Tune of, *The Delights of the Bottle* &c.[1]
With Allowance.   Ro. L'Estrange.[2]

[109.] All you that delight to hear a new song,
Or to see the world turn'd topsie turvy e're long,
Come give good attention unto these my Rhimes,
And never complain of the hardness of times,
For all will be mended, by this you may find,
And Golden days come, when the Devil is blind.

And first for the Shopkeeper, this I can tell,
That after long trusting, all things will be well,
The Gallant will pay him, what ever's his due
And make him rejoyce when he finds it is true :
False weights, & false measures, he then will not mind,
But honest will prove, when the Devil is blind.

The Country Client that comes up to Term,
Likewise from this subject, good news he may learn,
A benefit which he shall never more leese
For Lawyers hereafter will plead without Fees :
You shall have Law freely, if you be inclin'd,
Without any charge, when the Devil is blind.

The Usurer open his Coffers will throw,
And break all his Locks both above and below,
He'l burn all his Parchments, and cancel his Bands,

---

[1] For tune, see Appendix, same as *The Leather Bottel.*
[2] Licensed from 1663 to 1685.

And freely return all his Morgaged Lands ;
Young heirs will be glad for to see them so kind,
But that will not be till the Devil is blind.

The Learned Phisitian who valued his wealth,
Will now be more chary of all peoples health,
And make it his business howe're he doth thrive,
To pussle his brains for to keep men alive :
Nor Mountebank Bills in the Streets you shall find,
For they'l keep in their lies, when the Devil is Blind.

Your Lady of pleasure that us'd for to rant,
And Coach it about with her lusty Gallant,
Will then become modest, and find a new way
To live like a Nun in a Cloyster all day :
Her Pride, and her painting she never will mind,
But seem like a Saint when the Devil is blind.

Yea the Bullies themselves that did use for to rore,
And spent great estates in good wine and a w——
Shall leave off their gameing, and fairly take up,
And scarcely will tast of the Grape half a Cup,
But leave good Canary, and Claret behind,
Small Tipple to Drink, when the Devil is blind.

The Hecks [1] and the Padders [2] who used to prey,
And venture abroad for no purchase, no pay,
Shall work for their livings, and find a new trade,
And never more travel like Knights of the Blade ;
Let Newgate stand empty, and then you will find
All this will prove true, when the Devil is blind.

All Trades men will strive for to help one another,
And friendly will be, like to Brother and Brother,
And keep up their prices that money may flow,
Their charge to maintain and to pay what they owe :
Then two of a trade shall agree, if you mind,
And all will be well when the Devil is blind.

The Tapsters no more shall their Ticklers froth,
No Coffee men blind us with their Ninny broth,
Full measures of liquor shall pass through the Land,
And men without money the same shall command ;
You'l say 'tis a wonder when this you do find,
And that you will sure when the Devil is blind.

Not onely the City shall find this welfare,
But throughout the Country the same they shall share,
No cheating and couzening tricks shall be us'd,
For by such deceit we have all been abus'd ;
Those men who of late with *Duke Humphrey* have din'd
With plenty shall flow, when the Devil is blind.

[1] Probably a contraction for *hector* or bully.　　[2] Footpad.

Then let us be merry and frolick amain,
Since the golden world is returning again,
We shall be all Gallants, as sure as a Gun,
When this work is finisht that's hardly begun ;
Then Poets in both pockets Guinneys[1] shall find,
And purchase estates when the Devil is blind.

FINIS.

Printed for *F. Coles, T. Vere, J. Wright* and *J. Clarke.*

[110.] Evermore when Maister *Hobson*[1] had any busines abroad, his prentices wold ether bee at the taverne, filling there heads with wine, or at the dagger in cheapeside, cramming their bellies with minced pyes, but above al other times, it was their common custome (as London prentises use) to follow their maisters upon Sundays to the Church dore, and then to leave them and hie unto the taverne, which Maister *Hobson* on a time perceving one of his men to doe, demanded at his comming home what the Preachers text was : Sir (quoth the fellow) I was not at the beginning ; what was in the middle (quoth Maister *Hobson*) Sir, (qd the fellow) then was I asleepe : said Maister *Hobson* againe, what then was the conclusion ?

[1] Guineas were made from the gold from the West Coast of Africa, and were first coined in 1663, the African company having by charter the right of stamping an elephant on the coin.

[2] He must not be confounded with the Cambridge carrier, whose famous dictum has passed into a proverb, " Hobson's choice, that or none," that is, his inflexible rule was for his customer to take the horse he apportioned to him or go without. Our Hobson may be best described in the words of his editor :—" In the beginning of Queene *Elizabeths* most happy raigne, our late deceased Soveraigne, under whose peaceful government long flourished this our Country of *England ;* There lived in the Citty of London, a merry Citizen named old *Hobson,* a haberdasher of small wares, dwelling at the lower end of *cheapside,* in the *Poultry :* as well known through this part of *England,* as a Sergeant knows the Counter-gate, he was a homely plaine man, most commonly wearing a button'd cap close to his eares, a short gowne girt hard about his middle, and a paire of slippers upon his feete of an ancient fashion ; as for his wealth it was answerable to the better sort of our Cittizens, but of so mery a disposition, that his equal therein is hardly to be found ; hereat let the pleasant disposed people laugh, and the more graver in Carriage take no exceptions, for here are merriments without hurt, and humorous jests savoring upon wisdome ; read willingly, but scoffe not spitefully, for old *Hobson* spent his dayes merrily."

then Replyed his servant, I was come, Sir, away before the end; by which meanes he knew well he was not there, but rather in some tippling house offending Gods majesty, and the lawes of the land. Therefore the next Sunday morning after, Maister *Hobson* called all his servants together, and in the sight of many of his neighbors and their prentises, tooke a peece of chaulke, & chaulkd them all the way along to the Church derectly, which proved a great shame to his owne servants, but a good example to all others of like condition; after this was never the like mesdemenour used amongst them.

[17.] One affirmed that he had seen a Cabbage so big, that Five hundred men on hors back might stand under its shade; and I for my part, says another, have seen a Caldron so wide, That Three hundred men wrought therein, each distant from the other twenty yards: Then the Cabbage-lyer ask'd him, For what use was that Caldron? Says he, To boil your Cabbage in.

[67.] A man excused ye beating of his wife, because she was his owne flesh, saying, may I not beat mine owne flesh? and she upon that excused ye scratching of him, saying, May I not scratch mine own head?

[102.]   An honest Vicker, and a kind consort,
That to the Alehouse friendly would resort,
To have a game at Tables now and than,
Or drinke his pot, as soone as any man:
As faire a gamster, and as free from brawl,
As ever man should need to play withall:
Because his Hostesse pledg'd him not carouse,
Rashly in choller did forsweare her house.
Taking the glasse, this was the oath he swore,
Now by this drinke, I'le nere come hither more.
But mightily his Hostesse did repent,
For al her guests to the next Ale house went,
Following their Vickars steps in everie thing:
He led the Parish even by a string.
At length his ancient Hostesse did complaine

She was undone unlesse he came againe.
Desiring certain friends of hers and his,
To use a pollicie, which should be this :
Because with cunning he should not forsweare him,
To save his oath, they on their backs might bear him.
Of this good course the Vicker well did thinke,
And so they alwayes carried him to drinke.

[4.] The Lord *Bacon* going the Northern Circuit, a Fellow that was try'd for Robbing, was very importunate with the Judge to be favourable to him, telling him he was a kin to his Lordship : Why, how so? said the Judge. Why answered the Fellow, An't please your Lordship, your Name is *Bacon*, and my name is *Hog*, and those two are alike. 'Tis true, said the Judge ; but you and I can't be kindred till you are Hang'd, for *Hog* is never good *Bacon* till 'tis Hang'd.

[26.] Another Story was, That he being in a Low room, with some Gentlemen a drinking a bottle of Ale ; he saw the Man of the House open a Bottle, and the Cork flew up with such a Violence, that it strook his Hat off his Head, and after that went through the Cieling of that Room and another Room above that, which was two pair of Stairs high, and kill'd a Man and his Wife as they lay in Bed, and from thence flew up into the Garret, and they could not get it out with a Hammer and Mallet.

Sir, says another, to make good your Story, which I saw with my own Eyes, that being with some others in an upper Room, one was then opening a Bottle of Ale, and the Cork then flew up with such a violence thorow the Top of the House, that it broke the Cieling and Tiles also, and kill'd a Kite as he was flying just then over the House ; and the hole was so big which the Cork had made, that down fell the Kite thorow the hole, and they, opening the Kite to see where she was wounded, found two great Chickens in her Belly, which they sold to pay for their Drink, and after that, would never drink in any other Room in that House : but I don't know that it ever hapned so agen ; for these things, though there be truth in 'em, don't happen every day so.

[103.] A Woman very much addicted to Tipling, and having a Cup of a large size, out of which she usually drank, and in which she never left a drop, her Husband chid her for it, and said, It was not decent for a Woman to drink so great a quantity: She told him, that the Virgin *Mary* being at the bottom of the Cup, she could not but admire her beautiful Face: upon which he broke that Cup, and bought her another something less, with the Devil painted at the bottom of it; however, She always swallowed up all the Liquor in it; and being repremanded again by her Husband for her excessive Drinking: Oh, says she, I do it because the foul Fiend should not have one drop of it.

𝔑𝔬 𝔐𝔬𝔫𝔢𝔶, 𝔫𝔬 𝔉𝔯𝔦𝔢𝔫𝔡.

The Spendthrift he, when 'tis too late,
Laments his sad and Wretched state:
And all good Men he doth advise,
That they would Merry be and wise.

The Tune is $\begin{cases} \textit{All you that do desire to play} \\ \textit{At Cards, to pass the time away.} \end{cases}$

[111.] All you that freely spend your Coyn,
Come learn by this advice of mine;
That you no more so play the Fool,
Nor Tipple in the Fuddling-School:
For when that you have spent your store,
Your Host will turn you out o' th door.

This by experience I do know,
Who too too lately found it so:
Five hundred pound was left to me,
Which I consum'd immediately:
And when my Money was all gone,
I like an Ass was lookt upon.

While I had Gold and Silver store,
I thought the world did me adore:

For then each false dissembling Curr,
Would cry, your humble servant, Sir :
But now my Money is all spent,
Too late, poor Fool, I do lament.

When I was in Prosperity,
Each Tap-lach [1] that I passed by :
Would cringe and bow, and swear to be
My Servant to Eternity :
But now alas, my Money's gone,
And Servants I have never a one.

But now if to their house I go,
E're drink they draw, they'l surely know

[1] Used as a term of contempt for a publican, *taplash* being very small beer, or the refuse of the casks.

If that my Pocket it will speak,
Which is enough my heart to break :
If not, then he who was my friend,
Out of the door soon will me send.

Oh, what a dreadful thing is this,
That I of all my Servants miss ;
And those who did me oft invite,
To drink with them now do me slight :
But if again I Money get,
I surely then shall have more wit.

Yet is not spending all the Crime,
For idly then I spent my time,
And rather than Companions lack,
I'de pick up every Idle Jack :
And he that would me Master call,
Should me command, my Purse and all.

The Hostis she would flatter then,
And say I was a pretty Man :
And this so tickled then mine ear,
That I my praise so oft did hear :
Come hang't said I, giv's t'other Pot,
And thus I feasted every Sot.

At last I had no Money left,
And then was I of joys bereft ;
My Host and Hostis they did frown,
And said I was a Drunken Clown :
So then was I dispis'd by all,
That me before did Master call.

From street to street as I did pass,
Folks cry'd, there goes a Drunken Ass,
Who not long since had Money store,
But now no Creature is more poor :
For Pots and Pipes made him so low,
That like a Beggar he doth go.

Then who would pitty such a one,
Who could not keep himself alone,
If Wife and Children he had had,
The case had then been far more sad :
But he no pitty doth deserve,
If for a bit of Bread he starve.

This is the pitty I do find,
That when I had it was so kind,
To him that said he was my friend,
I'de give him Wine and Money lend ;
But now myself I have undone,
My Company all men do shun.

Let this my case a warning be,
That none may play the Fool like me :
A greater plague there cannot be,
Than falling from Prosperitie
Into a state so deadly low,
Your nearest friends will not you know.

Account your Money as your friend,
So shall you flourish to the end,
But when you come of friends to borrow,
It will but aggravate your sorrow :
To see how they will slight you then,
And say you are the worst of men.

Your Pot Companions will you slight,
In whom they once did take delight,
And while your Money it doth last
With Oaths they'l tye their friendship fast :
But when that you have wasted all,
Then from you will your Servants fall.

Such servants you may have good store,
Who help to eat you out of door,
And by their drinking in Excess,
Will help to make you Money less :
Then Young-men warning take by me,
That of my Money was too free.

This doth my Passion much provoke,
To think when I am like to Choake,
Those that I heretofore did feast,
They will not mind me in the least:
Nor make me drink, who once were proud,
To drink with me to be allow'd.

My Kindred and Relations near,
Who once did vow they lov'd me dear;
Will know me not, but me despise,
As loathsom to their scornful eyes:
For without Money there's no Friend,
And thus my Song in Woe doth End.

FINIS.

Printed for *F. Coles, T. Vere, J. Wright, J. Clarke, W. Thackeray,*
and *T. Passinger.*

[105.] *Scogin* on a time had two eggs to his breakefast, and *Jacke* his scholler should rost them, and as they were rosting, *Scogin* went to the fire to warme him, and as the eggs were rosting *Jacke* said, Sir, I can by sophistry prove that here be three Eggs. Let me see that, said *Scogin*. I shall tell you, sir, said Jacke: Is not here one? Yes, said *Scogin*. And is not here two, said *Jacke?* Yea, said *Scogin*, of that I am sure. Then *Jacke* did tell the first egge againe, saying, is not this the third? O said *Scogin, Jacke* thou art a good sophister. Wel, said *Scogin*, these two eggs shal serve me for my break fast, and take thou the third for thy labour, and for the herring that thou didst give mee the last day. So one goode turne doth aske another, and to deceive him that goeth about to deceive, is no deceit.

[94.] A Gentleman Hawk'd in another mans ground, to which the surly owner shew'd himself angry; at which the Gentleman spet in his face. What is your reason for that? said the Farmer. I cry you mercy, said the Gentleman, I gave you warning, for I hawked before I spet.

[67.] A Scholar traveyling, and having noe money, call'd at an Alehouse, and ask'd for a penny loafe, then gave his hostesse it againe, for a pot of ale ; and having drunke it of, was going away. The woman demanded a penny of him. For what ? saies he. Shee answers, for ye ale. Quoth hee, I gave you ye loafe for it. Then, said she, pay for ye loafe. Quoth hee, had you it not againe ? which put ye woman to a *non plus*, that ye scholar went free away.

[93.] *George* (*Peele*) lying at an old Widdowes house, and had gone on so farre on the Score, that his credit would stretch no further : for she had made a vow not to depart with drinke or victuals without ready money. Which *George* seeing the fury of his froward Hostis, in griefe kept his Chamber ; called to his Hostis and told her, she should understand that he was not without money, how poorely soever he appeared to her, and that my diet shall testifie : in the meane time, good Hostis, quoth he, send for such a friend of mine. Shee did : so his friend came : to whom *George* imparted his mind ; the effect whereof was this, to pawne his Cloake, Hose and Doublet, unknowne to his Hostis : for, quoth *George* this seven nights doe I intend to keepe my bed. (Truly hee spake, for his intent was that the bed should not keepe him any longer). Away goes he to pawne his apparell ; *George* bespeakes good cheere to supper, which was no shamble butcher stuffe, but according to the place ; for, his Chamber being remote from the house, at the end of the Garden, his apparell being gone, it appeared to him as the Counter ; therefore to comfort himselfe he dealt in Poultrie. His friend brought the money, supped with him : his Hostis hee very liberally payed, but cavelled with her at her unkindnesse : vowing that while he lay there, none should attend him but his friend. The Hostis reply'd, A God's name, she was well contented with it : so was *George* too : for none knew better than himselfe what he intended ; but in briefe thus he used his kinde Hostis. After his Apparell and Money was gone, hee made bolde with the feather bed hee lay on, which his friend-ship convey'd away, having as villanous a Wolfe in his belly as *George*, though not altogether so wise ;

for that feather bed they devoured in two daies, feathers and all, which was no sooner digested, but away went the Coverlet, Sheetes and the Blancket; and at the last dinner, when *George's* good friend perceiving nothing left but the bed-cords, as the Devill would have it, straight came into his mind the fashion of a halter; the foolish kind knave would needs fetch a quart of sacke for his friend *George;* which Sacke to this day never saw Vintners Cellar; and so he left *George* in a cold chamber, a thin shirt, a ravished bed, no comfort left him, but the bare bones of deceased Capons. In this distresse, George bethought him what he might doe; nothing was left him; and as his eye wandred up and downe the empty Chamber, by chance he spied out an old Armour; at which sight George was the joyfullest man in Christendome; for the Armour of Achilles, that Ulysses and Ajax strove for, was not more precious to them, than this to him: for hee presently claps it upon his backe, the Halbert in his hand, the Moryon on his head, and so gets out the backe way, marches from Shorditch to Clarkenwell, to the no small wonder of those spectators that beheld him. Being arrived to the wished haven he would be, an old acquaintance of his furnished him with an old Sute and an old Cloake for his old Armour.

[102.]   A Lawier being sicke and extreame ill,
Was mooved by his friends to make his will,
For they with one consent resolved all;
He never more would see Westminster Hall.
Hee feeling in himselfe his end was neere,
Unto their counsell did encline his eare;
And absolute gave all the wealth he had
To franticke persons, lunaticke and mad,
To no man else he would a pennie give,
But only such as doe in *Bedlem* live.
This caused his friends most strangely to admire,
And some of them his reason did require?
Quoth he, my reason to you I'le reveale:
That you may see with equitie I deale.
From mad mens hands I did my wealth receave,
Therefore that wealth to madmens hands I leave.

[110.] Not farre from maister *Hobsons* house, there dwelled one of those cunning men, otherwise called fortune tellers, such cossoning[1] companions, as at this day, (by their Crafts) make simple women beleeve how they can tell what husbands they shall have, how many children, how many sweetharts, and such like : if goods bee stole, who hath them, with promise to helpe them to their losses againe ; with many other like deceiptfull elusions.   To this wise man (as some termes him) goes maister *Hobson*, not to reap any benefit by his crafty cunning, but to make a Jest, and tryall of his experience, so, causing one of his servants to lead a masty[2] dog after him, staying at the Cuning mans doore with the dog in his hand, up goes master Hobson to ye wise man, requesting his skil, for he had lost ten pound lately taken from him by theeves, but when and how he knew not well.   The cunning man knowing maister *Hobson* to be one of his neighbors, and a man of a good reputation, fell (as he made showe) to conjuring and casting of figures, and after a few words of incantation, as his common use was, hee tooke a very large faire looking glasse, and bad Maister *Hobson* to looke in the same, but not to cast his eyes backward in any Case ; the which hee did, and therein saw the picture of a huge and large oxe with two broad hornes on his head, the which was no otherwise, but as hee had often deceitfully shewd to others, a cossoning fellow like the cunning man himselfe, clothed in an oxe hide, which fellow he maintained as his servant, to blinde the peoples eyes withall, and to make them beleeve hee could shew them the Divill at his pleasure in a glasse : this vision maister *Hobson* perceving, & gessing at the knavery thereof, gave a whistle for his dog, which then stayed below at the doore, in his man's keeping, which whistle being no sooner hard but the dog ran up the stayers to his maister, as hee had beene mad, and presently fastned upon the poor fellow in the oxe hide, and so tore him as it was pittifull to see.   The Cunning man cried for the passion of God take off your dog.   No, (quoth Maister *Hobson*) let the Divill and the Dogge fight, venture thou thy divill, and I will venture my dog.   To conclude, the oxe hide was torne from the fellows backe, and so their knaveryes were discovered, and their cunning shifts layd open to the world.

---

[1] Cozening, cheating.   [2] Mastiff.

[94.] A Country fellow going down *Ludgate Hill*, his heels by chance slipping from him, fell upon his Breech : one standing by, told him that *London* Streets were stout and scornful : It may be so, quoth he, yet I made them to kisse my Breech, as stout as they were.

The London Ladies Vindication

of

Top - Knots :

With the many Reasons that She shows for the Continuation of the same :

As also proving Men to be as Proud as themselves.

To the Tune of, *Here I love, There I love :* Or, *The two English Travellers.*

Licensed according to Order.

[112.] Young Women and Damsels that love to go fine,
Come listen a while to this Ditty of mine,
In spight of all Poets, brave Girls, we will wear
Our Towers and Top Knots, with Powdered Hair.

I am a young Woman, 'tis very well known,
And I am resolv'd to make use of my own,
In spight of all Poets, brave Girls, we will wear
A Tower and Top Knot, with Powdered Hair.

They talk of a Calf which was seen in our dress,
But let us take Courage, Girls, nevertheless.
In spight of those Rumours, we'll constantly wear
A Tower and Top Knot, and Powdered Hair.

We are not such Fools to believe what they say,
'Tis fit that young Women should go fine and gay,
In spight of their Bugbears, brave Girls, let us wear,
Rich Towers and Top Knots, with Powdered Hair.

Were we to be Ruled by some sort of Men,
We should go like Women of Fourscore and Ten,
In spight of those Cox combs, brave Girls, we will wear
Rich Towers and Top Knots, with Powdered Hair.

Like Beautiful Angels we strive to appear,
The Hearts of our Husbands in order to cheer,
Then what is the Reason that we may not wear
Rich Towers and Top Knots, with Powdered Hair.

If we are the Pleasure and Joy of their Life,
Pray when can they take more delight in a Wife,
Then at the same time when rich Garments they wear,
With Towers and Top Knots, and Powdered Hair.

We see the young Misses and Jilts of the Town,
Have six Stories high, as they walk up and down,
Then pray tell me why should not honest Wives wear
Rich Towers and Top Knots, with Powdered Hair.

If we an't as Fine and as Gaudy as they,
Who knows but our Husbands might soon run astray,
Consider this, Women, and still let us wear
Our Towers and Topknots, with Powdered Hair.

It is but a Folly to tell us of Pride,
While we have these Arguments still on our side ;
As long as we live we will flourishing wear
Rich Towers and Top Knots, with Powdered Hair.

Nay further I'le tell ye the case it is thus,
That all is not sav'd which is put in the Purse ;
A Shopkeepers Lady she utters much Ware
When drest in her Top Knots, with Powdered Hair.

What Man would not have his Wife richly Array'd
When as he well knows it enlarges his Trade ;
Come, come, I must tell ye, 'tis fit we should wear
Rich Towers and Top Knots, with Powdered Hair.

Sometimes when our Husbands are out of the way,
Pray tell me what huffing young Gallants will stay,
If that a fine Delicate Wife were not there ?
Then Hey for the Top Knots, and Powdered Hair.

Some young-men may flout us, yet mark what I say,
There's no Woman living, now Prowder than they ;
Observe but the many knick-knacks which they wear.
More Costly than Top Knots, or Powdered Hair.

Their Wigg, Watch, and Rapiers we daily behold,
And Embroidered Wastcoats of Silver and Gold ;
Likewise, Turn up Stockings, they constantly wear
More Costly than Topknots, or Powdered Hair.

If Pride be a sin and a folly, why then
Han't we a far better Example from Men ?
If Gaudy Apparel those Gallants do wear,
We will have our Top Knots and Powdered Hair.

Printed for P. Brooksby, J. Deacon, J. Blare, J. Black

[103.] A Gentleman in a Town in *Hartfordshire*, being
much in Debt, was oblig'd to keep House close, a Bailiff who
had been promised a great reward to take that Gentleman,
having made several attempts in vain to snap him, at last

resolv'd upon one that he thought could not fail, so pretending himself in dispair, came by the Gentlemans Parlor Window, (which was next the Street, and where he sat Writing every Day) and pulling out of his Pocket a Halter, made a Nooze, and seemed as if he intended to Hang himself therewith ; a Grindstone was before the Door, upon which he got up, and threw the Rope over a good Bough of the Tree, and fastned it, and then put his Head in, concluding the Gentleman would whip out, and so he should arrest him ; but as the Devil would have it, the Grindstone which stood firm like a Rock for him to get up, tumbled down as soon as ever the Halter was about his Neck, the Innocent, Unwary Gentleman seeing what past, sallied out, to Cut the Rope, and save the Man ; but the Bailiff's Follower lying in Ambuscade, snap'd the Gentleman as soon as ever he peept out, and carried him off, and let his Master hang ; who carried the Jest too far, and when the Gentleman told the Bailiff's Follower that his Master would soon be Dead if he did not cut him down—Let him be D——— said he, I have got my Prize, and I shall have the Reward, and my Masters place too.

[26.] A Man being very much diseas'd and weak, was bemoaning himself to his only Son, whom he lov'd very well. For, *Jack*, says he, if I stand, my Legs ake, if I kneel my Knees ake, if I go, my Feet ake, if I lie then my Back akes, if I sit my Hips ake, if I lean, my Elbows ake. Why truly, Father, says he, (like a good dutiful Child) I advise you, Father, to hang yourself an hour or two, and if that does not do, then come to me again.

[67.] A Scholer being at a Parson's house, stole a Pig ; the Parson looking out at his window, spied him and said, Scholer, Scholer, I'le none of that. Noe more you shall, quoth ye Scholer, and ran away with it.

[82.] A Nobleman of France (as hee was riding) met with a yeoman of the Country, to whom he said, My friend, I should know thee, I doe remember I have often seene thee :

My good Lord, said the Countryman, I am one of your Honors poore tenants, and my name is T. I. I remember thee better now (said my Lord) there were two brothers of you, but one is dead, I pray which of you doth remaine alive.

The aforesaid Nobleman having had a Harper that was blinde playing to him after supper, somewhat late, at last hee arose, and commanded one of his servants to light the Harper downe the staires : to whom the Serving man sayd, my Lord, the Harper is blind; thou ignorant knave, quoth my Lord, he hath the more need of light.

[105.] When that *Scogin* had taught his scholler that hee with helpe might be Sub deacon, he said to him, thou shalt goe to take orders, and I will go with thee. And if thou dost stand in any doubt, take heed to my booke, and give an eare to me, and I will helpe thee as much as I can. When all they that should take orders, were come to oppositions, *Scogin* did come forth with his scholler. And the Ordinary did oppose him with a verse of the Psalter ; which was this, *Moab, Agareni, Gebal, Amon & Amalek, cum habitantibus Tirum. Scogins* scholler was blanke or amazed. Sir, said *Scogin* to the Ordinary, you shall understand that *Moab, Agareni, Gebal, Amon & Amalek, cum habitantibus Tirum,* were unhappy fellowes, for they did trouble the children of Israel, and if they trouble my scholler, it is no marvell : but now I doe tell thee, my scholler, be not afraid of *Moab, Agareni, Gebal, Amon & Amalek, cum habitantibus Tirum,* for I will stand beside to comfort thee, for *Moab, Agareni &c* can do thee no harm for they be dead. By reason that *Scogin* did so oft repeate these words, the scholler did reade this verse aforesaid : and through *Scogins* promise, the Ordinary was content that his scholler should take Orders, and be Sub deacon. After this when the orders were given againe, *Scogin* did speake to his schollers Father, to send in a letter three or foure peeces of gold. The Schollers Father was content so to doe ; so that his son might be Deacon. Then said *Scogin* to his scholler, thou shalt deliver this letter to the Ordinary, when he doth sit in oppositions, and as soone as he feeleth the letter, he will perceive that I have sent him some money, and he will say to thee

Quomodo valet magister tuus? that is to say, how doth thy Master? thou shalt say *Bene :* that is to say, well. Then will he say, *Quid petis?* What thing doest thou aske? Then thou shalt say, *Diaconatum*, to be a Deacon. Then the Ordinary will say, *Es tu literatus?* art thou learned? & thou shalt say *Aliqualiter*, somewhat. Now said *Scogin*, thou hast no more than three words to beare in mind in Latine, which is to say *Bene, Diaconatum*, and *Aliqualiter*. The father and the scholler were glad that by Scogins letters & the money he should be Deacon, & went to the oppositions, and delivered his letter with the money. The Ordinary perceiving money in the letter, said to the scholler. *Quid petis?* that is to say, what dost thou aske or desire? The scholler remembring *Scogins* words, that the first word was *Bene*, he said *Bene*, that is, well. When the Ordinary heard him say so, he said *Quomodo valet Magister tuus?* How doth thy Master? The scholler said, *Diaconatum* that is to say Deacon. The Ordinary did see he was a foole, & said, *Tu es stultus*, thou art a foole : the scholler said *Aliqualiter*, that is to say, somewhat. Nay, said the Ordinary not *Aliqualiter*, but *Totaliter*, a starke foole. Then the scholler was amazed, and said, sir, let me not goe home without mine Orders, and heere is another Angell of gold for you to drinke. Well, said the Ordinary, on that condition you will promise me to goe to your booke and learne, you shall bee Deacon at this time. Heere a man may see that money is better than learning.

[17.] In a wedding between a Gentleman of a great Family and no Wealth, and a Widdow of great Wealth; says one This is like a Black pudding; the one brought *blood*, and the other *Suet* and *Oatmeal.*

[110.] In the beginning of Queene Elizabeaths raigne, when the order of hanging out lanterne and Candlelight first of all was brought up; the bedell of the warde where Maister *Hobson* dwelt, in a darke evening crieing up and downe, hang out your lantornes; using no other words. Whereupon Maister *Hobson* tooke an empty lantorne, and according to the beadles call hung it out. This flout by the Lord Maior was taken in ill part, and for the same offence was sent to the counter; but being released, the next night following, the beadle thinking to amend his call, cried with a loud voice, hang out your lantorne and Candle.   Maister *Hobson* hereupon hung out a lantorne and candle unlighted, as the beadle againe commanded, whereupon he was sent againe to the counter.   But the next night the beadle being better advised, cryed, hang out your lantorne and candle light, hang out your lantorne and candle light, which maister *Hobson* at last did, to his great commendations, which cry of lanthorne and candle light is in right manner used to this day.

[94.] One observ'd it to be a good fashion that was worn now a days, because the Taylors had so contrivd it, that there was little or no Waste in a whole Suit.

The illustration to this satire on drunkenness (which is dated September 1652) is indebted for its point to the foxes, it being then a cant term when a man was drunk to say he was *foxed;* the geese denote the foolish behaviour of men when under the influence of drink.

BARNABIES SUMMONS:

or,

Paie your Groat in the Morning.

[113.] Intended for all Malaga Men, called Vintners, Sack drawers, White wine, Claret, Rhenish, Bastard Sherry, or Canary Blades, and Birds, together with all Ale Brewers, Beer Brewers (alias) Hogshead fillers, Barrellers, Tapsters, or Firkinners: As also for all Drawers, Tub Tapsters, Quaffers, Huffers, Puffers, Snuffers, Rufflers, Scufflers, and Shufflers, with Wine bibbers, Sack suckers, and Toast makers; not forgetting other depending Officers of a lower Rank, of our stumbling Fraternity, viz Bench whistlers, Lick-wimbles, Suck spigots, Hawkers, Spewterers, Maudliners, Fox catchers, including in the said Warrant as a Reserve, our true and trusty Friends for the speedier effecting our designe and purpose, All

Vulcans, Crispins, Tinkers, Pedlars, and of late our endeared friends, the Society of Upstart Printers, and Newes Mongers; and excluding by special command, all Three peny Ordinary Sharks, as Bakers, Weavers, Tailors, Usurers, Snip Eared Scriveners, Presbyters, either English, Scotch, or Dutch, (but stay there a little) for though the last of these be good for nothing else, yet they are stout Drinkers and Drunkards; and therefore if they please to tiple as formerly they have done, and must doe now, they shall have the benefit of this our Warrant, provided they neither drink all, nor too much; our

Warrant for the generall content of all Bonos Socios is set out in maner and forme following, that all whom it may concern (as it does too many) may, if they can stand, understand it.

The WARRANT.

Know all men by these presents, that we, Sir *Resolute Rednose*, of the Town of *Taplow*, in the County of Cumberland, with our dear and trusty Cosins Sir *Ferdinando Fiery Face*, Lord *Sigismund Ruby Nose*, together with our associates and fellow Commissioners, Sir *William Swill-boule*, Sir *Gregory Toss-pot*, Sir *Thomas Spend-all*, Sir *Alexander Dry lips*, Sir *Lewis Lick-Spiggot*, *Edward Barley*, *Thomas Maltster*, *Richard Brewer*, and *Geffery Tapster* Esquires &c. By vertue of a *Mandamus*, or a *fieri facias*, issued unto us from the great

Wine Cellar in *Bacchus* Prerogative Court, near to Stumbling Alley, from the Lord *James Fill-Pot*, and Signeur *Jeronymo Tap-lash*, do Enact, appoint, and ordaine, that any and every person, male or female, of what Countrey soever, being taken so drunk, that they are without wit, sence, or reason, shall forth-with pay to the under Officers herein named, viz, to John *Bottle nose*, *William Suck-all*, *Gerard Turn-Tub*, and *Jenkin ap Morgan* of *Ale-ton*, or to their Deputy, or Deputies, the full and just sum of 4^d without any resistance or delay upon the next Morning; but in case of any of the Delinquents in the Premises, shall be so ingenuous as to confesse their fault with-out distraining, that then this Penalty shall not exceed above 2$^{d.}$ But in case the parties are resolved to ride the old ridden Jade called *Cut*, or a Dog of the same Haire [1] next morning, without any remorse, and will presume to hunt the Fox againe, that then our said Bayliffs, and Deputies are forthwith either to joyne with them, or else to suspend the execution of this our said Warrant, till he or they may be sober, which is much feared will not quickly be effected ; and therefore, for the better and surer progresse herein, that Justice may be the sooner executed, we enjoyn all Constables of Burroughs and Parishes as well high as Petty, to be assisting to this our merry Warrant, and do desire them if they or any of their substitute Officers can find leasure from sleep, or their nodding benches, to examine the Premises and Persons, to shew due respects unto them, considering well that the case and cause not only hath been their own, but suddenly and shortly will be again, as soon as they can either meet with merry Company or good moneys.   Hereof they or any of them are not to faile at their utmost perils.

To all Constables, Head bor-oughs, and other petty Officers, and stout Drinkers, whom this specially concernes.

Given at our Mannour of *Flushing* in the *Full Moone Tavern* at Sun rising
            Anno 155432.
Upon the last day of the first of March.
            Ut Supra.

Sic in orig.

[26.] One told a Story (which he swore was of certain as you know all these things are,) For, says he, I was riding to Saint *Albans*, and riding through a Lane, that was of stiff Clay, as I was galloping, my Horses foot sticking in, pluckt off shoe and hooff too, and so I gallopt on for three or four Miles ; and my horse never complained, that I never saw a horse gallop so well on three legs in my life ; at length he began to limp, then I lighted to see what he ailed and found both shooe and hooff gone ; so, fearing to pay for the horse, got presently up agen, and gallopt as fast as I could drive ; and fortunately my Horse leg lighted agen in the same place, and pull'd up hooff, shoe and all, which was better fastened than when I came out ; and so I performed my journy, and got that night as far as I rid.

[91.]   One evening as Cold as Cold might be,
With frost and haile, and pinching weather,
Companions about three times three
Lay close all in a pound together.
Yet one after another they tooke a heate,
And died that night all in a sweat.
Resolution. A pound of Candles.

Dead and Alive.

. This DITTY out of *Gloucestershire* was sent,
To *London*, for to have it put in Print ;
Therefore draw near, and listen unto this,
It doth concern a Man that did Amiss ;
And so to shun the Anger of his WIFE,
He thought with Poyson for to end his Life,
But instead of Poyson he drank Sack,
For which his Wife did soundly pay's back—

To the Tune of *Old Flesh* &c.—

[114.]   There was a shaving Royster,
as I heard many tell,
In *Michal-Danes* fair forest,
in *Gloucestershire* did dwell ;

Some call'd him *William Wiseman*,
   but in that they were to blame,
Some call'd him *Leonard Lackwit*,
   but that was not his name ;
His name was *Simple Simon*,
   as it is well approv'd,

And among his Friends and Kinsfolks,
   he dearly was belov'd :
He capor'd and he vapour'd
   and he liv'd a merry life,
But yet, good Man, at all times,
   he could not rule his Wife.

His Wife she was a Woman,
   that lov'd a cup of Sack,
And she would tipple soundly,
   behind her Husband's back ;

A bottle she had gotten that
   would hold two quarts or more,
Well fill'd with wine she hang'd it
   behind her chamber door :
And she told unto her Husband
   that it was poyson strong,
And bad him not to touch it,
   for fear of doing wrong :
If thou drink but one drop on't,
   (quoth she) 'twill end thy life ;
Therefore in time take heed,
   and be ruled by thy Wife.

This Simon's wife had plenty
   of fatting hogs and pigs,
With geese, ducks, hens, and turkies,
   that laid great store of eggs :
Both Sheep and such like cattel,
   fine ews and pritty lambs,
Which up and down the forrest
   did feed, and suck their dams ;
She put trust to her Husband
   to look unto them all,
To keep them safe from danger ;
   now mark what did befal :
He did his best endeavour
   to shun all sorts of strife,
And yet through strange misfortune
   he could not please his Wife.

One morning she sent him
   to field to keep her sheep,
And charg'd him to be watchful,
   and take heed he did not sleep :
A piece of bread and butter
   she gave him in his hand,
Whereby she made him promise
   to do as she did command.
But see what happened to him,
   when he came to the field,

He fell asleep, while foxes
    three of his lambs had killed :
This bred a great dissention
    and rais'd a world of strife,
Till *Simon* for his fault
    had beg'd pardon of his Wife.

Another day she sent him
    her ducks and geese to tend,
And charg'd him on her blessing,
    he should no more offend :
Her goslins and her chickens
    with him she put in trust,
Who took a stick and told them,
    for they were twenty just :
But a woful chance befel to
    poor *Simon* before night,
For seven of his chickens
    were took prisoners by the kite :
This vexed him, and it made him
    half weary of his life,
For he knew not what answer
    to make unto his Wife.

Next morning when that *Simon*
    was sent to milk the cow,
Another strange mishap there was
    done to him by the sow ;
For whilst that he was driving
    the little pigs away,
The sow came into the dairy-house
    and swill'd up all the whey ;
The cheese out of the cheese fat
    she did both tear and hawl,
And so threw down the cream-pot,
    and made an end of all :
Wherewith she burst her belly,
    and so she lost her life,
And poor *Simon* knew not what answer
    to make unto his wife.

2 B

When's Wife came in the dairy-house,
   and saw what there was done,
A strong and fierce encounter
   she presently begun ;
She pull'd him by the ears,
   and she wrung him by the nose,
And she kickt him on the belly,
   while the tears ran down his hose.
And she vow'd to be revenged
   before the morrow day,
For all the brood of chickens,
   which the kite had carried away :
Poor *Simon* stood amazed,
   being weary of his life,
For he good Man was tired
   with his unruly Wife.

For when that he perceived
   his Wife in such a rage,
Nor knowing how, nor which way
   his fury to asswage :
He cunningly got from her,
   and to the chamber went,
Thinking himself to poyson,
   for that was his intent ;
So coming to the bottle,
   which I spoke of before,
He thought it to be poyson,
   which hung behind the door :
He vow'd to drink it all up,
   and end his wretched life,
Rather than live in thraldom,
   with such a cursed Wife.

So opening of a window, which
   stood towards the South,
He took the bottle of sack,
   and set it to his mouth :
Now will I drink this poyson,
   (quoth he) with all my heart ;

So that the first draught he drunk on't
   he swallowed near a quart:
The second time that he set
   the bottle to his snout,
He never left off swigging,
   till he had suckt all out:
Which done, he fell down backward
   like one bereft of life,
Crying out, I now am poysoned
   by means of my cursed Wife.

Quoth he, I feel the poyson
   now run through every vein,
It rumbles in my belly,
   and it tickles in my brain;
It wambles in my stomack,
   and it molifies my heart,
It pierceth through my members,
   and yet I feel no smart;
Would all that have curst wives,
   example take hereby,
For I dye as sweet a death sure,
   as ever man did dye:
'Tis better with such poyson,
   to end a wretched life,
Than to live, and be tormented
   with such a wicked Wife.

Now see what followed after,
   his Wife by chance did walk,
And coming by the window,
   she heard her *Simon* talk;
And thinking on her bottle,
   she up the stairs did run,
And came into the chamber,
   to see what he had done;
When as she saw her Husband,
   lying drunk upon his back,
And the bottle lying by him,
   but never a drop of sack:

I am poyson'd, I am poyson'd,
    quoth he, long of my Wife,
I hope I shall be at quiet
    now I have lost my life.

Pox take you, are you poyson'd,
    (quoth she) I now will strive,
And do my best endeavour
    to make you run alive :
With that a quill of powder
    she blew up in his nose,
Then like a man turn'd antick,
    he presently arose ;
So down the stairs he run straight,
    into the open street,
With hooping and hollowing,
    to all that he did meet ;
And with a loud voice cryed out,
    I am raised from death to life,
By virtue of a powder, that
    was given me by my Wife.

Some folks that did behold him,
    were in a grievous fear,
For seeing of a Madman,
    they durst not him come near :
He leaped and he skipped,
    thorow fair and thorow foul,
Whilst the people gaz'd upon him
    like pyce upon an owl :
His Wife she followed after,
    thorow thick, and thorow thin,
And with a basting cudgel
    she soundly bang'd his skin :
And thus poor *Simon* cryed out
    I'm raised from death to life,
By virtue of a powder, that
    was given me by my Wife.

At last a friend of *Simon's*
    which was to him some kin,

By fair and kind persuasions,
    open'd door and let him in ;
He sent for *Simon's* Wife, and
    so made them both good friends,
Who kindly kist each other,
    and so all discord ends ;
The Neighbours all rejoyced
    to see them thus agreed,
And like a loving couple
    to bed they went with speed.
No doubt but *Simple Simon*
    that night well pleas'd his wife,
For ever since that time, he
    hath lived a quiet life.

London : Printed by and for *W. Onley,*[1] and *A. Melbourn ;*[2] and sold by the Booksellers of *Pye Corner* and *London Bridge.*

[93.] *George* (*Peele*) was making merry with three or foure of his friends in Pye Corner ; where the Tapster of the house was much given to Poetrie : for he had ingrossed The Knight of the Sunne, Venus and Adonis, and other Pamphlets which the Stripling had collected together ; and knowing *George* to be a Poet, he tooke great delight in his company, and out of his bounty would bestow a brace of Cannes of him. *George* observing the humour of the Tapster, meant presently to worke upon him. What will you say, quoth *George* to his friends, if, out of this spirit of the Cellar, I fetch a good Angell, that shall bid us all to supper. We would gladly see that quoth his friends. Content your selfe, quoth *George.* The Tapster ascends with his two Cannes, delivers one to Master *Peele,* and the other to his friends : gives them kind welcome : but *George,* in stead of giving him thankes, bids him not to trouble him : and beginnes in these termes : I protest, Gentlemen, I wonder you will urge me so much ; I sweare I have it not about me. What is the matter ? quoth the Tapster. Hath any one

---

1 Published between 1650 and 1702.
2 Published between 1670 and 1697.

angered you ? No, faith, quoth *George*, Ile tell thee, it is this : There is a friend of ours in Newgate, for nothing but onely the command of the Justices, and he being now to be released, sends to me to bring him an Angell : now the man I love dearely well ; and if hee want tenne Angels he shall have them ; for I know him sure : but heere's the misery, either I must goe home, or I must be forced to pawne this ; and pluckes an old Harry-groat out of his pocket. The Tapster lookes upon it : Why, and it please you, Sir, quoth he, this is but a groat. No, Sir, quoth *George*, I know it is but a groat : but this groat will I not lose for forty pound : for this groat had I of my mother, as a testimony of a Lease of a House I am to possesse after her decease ; and if I should lose this groat, I were in a faire case : and either I must pawne this groat, or there the fellow must lye still. Quoth the Tapster, If it please you, I will lend you an Angell on it, and I will assure you it shall bee safe. Wilt thou ? quoth *George;* as thou art an honest man, locke it up in thy Chest, and let me have it whensoever I call for it. As I am an honest man, you shall, quoth the Tapster. *George* delivered him his groat ; the Tapster gave him ten shillings : to the Taverne goe they with the money, and there merrily spend it. It fell out, some time after, the Tapster, having many of these lurches,[1] fell to decay, and indeede was turned out of service, having no more coine in the world than this groat, and in this misery, hee met *George*, as poore as himselfe. O, Sir, quoth the Tapster, you are happily met ; I have your groat safe, though since I saw you last, I have bid great extremitie ; and I protest, save that groat, I have not any one penny in the world ; therefore I pray you, Sir, helpe me to my money, and take your pawne. Not for the World, quoth George : thou saist thou hast but that Groat in the world : my bargaine was, that thou shouldst keepe that groat, untill I did demand it of thee : I ask thee none. I will doe thee farre more good ; because thou art an honest fellow, keepe thou that groat still, till I call for it : and so doing, the proudest Jacke in England cannot justifie that thou art not worth a groat ; otherwise, they might : and so, honest Michael, farewell. So George leaves the poore Tapster picking of his fingers, his head

---

[1] Drains on his purse.

full of proclamations what he might doe : at last sighing, hee ends with this Proverbe

> For the price of a Barrel of Beere
> I have bought a groats worth of wit,
> Is not that deare ?

[67.] In a certaine towne there was a goose stolne, and it could not bee found, out who stole it; so ye minister a while after at service, bade all ye people kneele downe, who answered I. (aye)   Many did, but saith hee, he that stole ye goose doth not.   But I doe, quoth hee, and was taken.

[103.] An English Gentleman taking into his Service (in pure Compassion) an Irishman, who was forc'd to leave his Country upon his Conversion from the Romish (of which he was a Priest) to the English Church : Employed him in Errands, and sometimes let him follow him, to acquaint him with the Town ; and having staid at a Coffee House some time, in ,expectation of a Man with whom he had Business, who not coming, he left his Servant there, to tell him that he could stay no longer, but was gone to such a Tavern.   The Fellow immediately run after his Master, and ask'd him What he should say to the Gentleman if he should not come ?

[110.] A poore begger man, that was foule, blacke, and loathsome to behould, came on a time to Maister *Hobson* as he walked in Moore feelds, and asked something of him for an almes, to which Maister *Hobson* said, I prethee, good fellow, get thee from me, for thou lookst as thou camst lately out of hell.   The poore begger man, perceving hee would give him nothing, answered forsooth, Sir, you say true, for I came lately out of Hell indeed ; why didst not thou tarry there still ? quoth maister *Hobson ;* nay, Sir, quoth the begger, there is no Roome for such begerr men as I am, for all is kept for such gentlemen Cittizens as you be : this wity answere caused Maister *Hobson* to give the poore man a teaster.[1]

[82.] A Fellow having more drinke than wit, in a winter evening made a foolish vowe, to take the wall of as many as

---

[1] Sixpence.

hee met betwixt the Temple bar, and Charing Crosse; and comming neere the Savoy, where stood a Poste, a little distance from the wall, the Drunkard tooke it for a man, and would have the wall, beginning to quarrell and give the Poste foule words: at which a man came by, and asked the matter, and whom he spake to: hee answered hee would have the wall of that fellow that stood so stiffly there: my friend, said the other, that is a Poste, you must give him the way. Is it so, said the fellow, a pox upon him, why did he not blow his horn?

[26.] Two Baboons being to be seen at their first coming to *London*, abundance of Citizens and others did resort thither to take a view of them, and did heartily laugh at their ugliness, and the strange faces which they made; which a most motherly and very discreet woman being present, did sharply thus rebuke 'em. "D'ye think you do well to laugh at strangers, who understand not your Language, and if you were in their Country, you'd take it for a great abuse, I warrant you, if they should laugh at you."

[4.] King *James* Riding a Hunting in Essex, comes to a Gate which he must go through, and seeing a Country Clown at it, he says to him, Prethee, good Fellow, open the gate. But he, knowing who it was, answered, No, a'nt please your Grace, I am not worthy to be in that Office; but I'le run and fetch Mr *Johnson*, who is a Justice of the Peace, and lives a Mile off, and he shall open it for your Grace: so he ran away as fast as he could, and left the King to open it himself.

THE FRENCH DANCING-MASTER

AND THE

ENGLISH SOLDIER. .

Or, the Difference betwixt Fidling and Fighting

Displayed in a DIALOGUE betwixt an ENGLISHMAN

and a FRENCHMAN.

Englishman.

[115.] *Monsieur*, good morn, whither away so faste?
Some great importance sure doth cause this haste;
Your running looks do in effect thus say,
Monsieur is gone, 'cause Landlord asketh pay.

Frenchman.

Begar me no sush man, me scorn de shift
Me plus Affaires dat me from home do lift.

Englishman.

You scorn to shift, tis true I think you say,
Witness your *Shirt*, not washt this many a day.

Frenchman.

Par me foy de Rascall to degrase,
Ne autre man in de *varle* live in such case;
Begar though me no speak si bon English,
Me thrush Tord in de belly if de speak dis;
Begar me de born Gentil-man de *France*
Me can learn English *a le mode* de Dance:
Me play ode leetle l'idle, me can sing,
Par ma foy, no Poet *Orphus* sush Musick bring;
Begar, you no sush man in all de *England* have,
For de Fidle, and de Dancing brave.

Englishman.

But when you come to meet your Foe in face
The Fidler and the Fidler's out of case.

Frenchman.

Begar de art *Jack-napes* to a teetle,
Me be brave Fellow, me can feight a leetle ;
Me wear *Feader* in de Hat, me have *Tord* by side,
Me be de Gentil-man when me on de *Horse* ride ;
Englishman be a Clown, make Leg like a de Beare,
Frenchman be de Gentil-man, he fidle, and he dance rare.

Englishman.

'Tis true, in dancing you do us excel,
But can you, as the English, fight as well ?
When *Mars* unsheaths his Sword, and Canons roar,
And men lye welt'ring in their purple gore,
When Towns are burnt, and Cities are destroy'd,
To what use will your Dancing be employ'd ?

Frenchman.

Begar he de great Fool to speak sush ting,
Brava, brava, de Dance, de Fidele, Sing ;
No sush ting in de varle, to peepe, to dance,
To be dreass like de Madam, *a le Mode France.*

Englishman.

Brave Monsieur ! gallant Monsieur ! wondrous rare !
Fidling and fooling, none with thee compare !

Frenchman.

Begar, he be de Rogue, de Villain, de Carle,
To speak 'gainst de Dance, de brave ting in de varle ;
Begar me do love it out of all de Cry,
Par ma foy he speak 'gainst it, tell loud lye :
France-man is de Gentilman in de high Sphere,
Vat is de Clown vas dis skip de Angleterre
De French Monsieur skip and leap like de Spright,
He caper and kick, is not dat a rare Shite ?

Englishman.

A rare Shite 'tis indeed, I needs must say,
To see men skip like Puppets in a Play;
To act the Mimick, fidle, prate and Dance,
And cringe like Apes, is a le mode France:
But to be resolute, one to fight with ten,
And beat them, 's proper unto English men.

Frenchman.

Begar France man is couragio, feight like te Tiffell,
He kill, he slay, cutt men off de midle;
De brave Monsieurs, de *Oliver*, de *Rowland*,
Begar de feight as long as de could stand;
Amadis de Gaule, de *Roy Charlemain*,
De make blood run down like drops of de rain,
Begar, with new fashion so exc'lent! so rare!
No men in de varle wid de French make compare.

Englishman.

But *Monsieur*, have you never heard report
Of Poictiers, Cresey, and of Agen-court?
When *France* was drown'd with streams of Frenchmen's
   blood,
And English Valor could not be withstood?
Sixth HENRY in *Paris* Crown'd in State,
And *France* (submissive) did on *England* wait.
When only TALBOT's Name did bear such sway,
To make Ten thousand French men run away?
Is not *France*, and the Nation still the same,
Whom *England* did in all Encounters tame?
Have we not Hero's still who are endu'd
With Valor, (Stars of the first Magnitude?)
YORKS Duke, Brave ALBEMARLE, equal to those
Our Ancestors, who French men did oppose?
With other Worthies of deserved Fame,
Make Frenchmen tremble for to hear their Name.

Frenchman.

Begar dis true, de English-man speak right,
France leave to Dance, and now de learn to Fight.
Adieu Monsieur.

LONDON, Printed in the Year 1666.

[103.] A Nobleman often hunting, used to be always near
his Huntsman, who was an excellent old Servant, and one of
whom he priz'd, and was often familiar with ; but at coming to
a Hedge or Ditch, he wou'd call him, *Jack* do you leap first.
Not I by G——, my Lord, (reply's he) do you go first and break
your Neck, if you please, I value mine a little more.

[82.] A Countrey woman at an Assize was to take her oath
against a party ; the said party entreated the Judge that her
oath might not bee taken ; the Judge demanded why he
excepted against her : my Lord (quoth hee) shee is a Recusant or Romane Catholique, and they hold it in no matter
of Conscience to swear any thing against us.   Come hither,
woman, said the Judge, I doe not thinke thou art a Recusant,
I am perswaded that for fourty shillings thou wilt sweare the
Pope is a knave : Good, my Lord, said shee, the Pope is a
stranger to mee, but if I knew him as well as I know your
Lordship, I would sweare for half the mony.

[116.] The following satire is given merely as a type :

From Commonwealth Coblers, and zealous State Tinkers,
From Speeches and Expedients of Politick Blinkers,
From Rebellious Taps, and Tapsters, and Skinkers.

                                        Libera nos.

From Elephant Baptists, and their doughty free State,
From looking in *Newgate* through Reformation Grate,
And from their last sayings and Hempen-ruff Fate.

                                        Libera nos.

From Papists on one hand, and Phanatick o' th' t'other,
From Presbyter *Jack*, the Popes younger brother,
And Congregational Daughters far worse than their Mother.

                                        Libera nos.

l

From Religions that teach men to kill and to slay,
From faith that is coupled with the word Disobey,
And from Sectaries e'er having of another day.

> Libera nos.

From Members that constantly quarrel with the Head,
And subjects that for Sterling, pay their Sovereign with Lead,
And preserve Kings and Governments by wishing them dead.

> Libera nos.

From over short Parliaments, and over long,
From a selling our Birth rights for an old song,
And breaking *Mag. Charta* to make it more strong.

> Libera nos.

From taking away Juries by Parliament Votes,
And securing from Popery by cutting of throats,
From a Beam in our Eye, to cure them of Motes.

> Libera nos.

From "Vox"es, and factious saucy Addresses,
To repeal those good Laws of honest Qu. *Bess'es*
From Fanaticks rage, and the Popes God bless us.

> Libera nos.

From a Bill that to take away Ale and Cake voices,
Robs all the old Freeholders, at Elections, of Choices,
And enables Fanaticks to make greater Noises.

> Libera nos.

From the wisdom of *Bedlam*, and the anger of Fools,
From the whipping and learning of meeting house Schools
And the Exit of Traytors, and Commonwealth Tools.

> Libera nos.

Of the following satire only a portion is given, as the pamphlet (of ten pages) is too long to give *in extenso* :—

[117.] Received out of the Treasuries of the Excize, Customs and the Exchequer £430,000.

Disbursed as followeth

The ACCOMPT.

	L.	S.	D

Imprimis. For three and twenty long Cloaks, at Seven Pounds Ten Shillings, per Cloak, to cover the Committee[1] of Safety's Knavery. — 243. — —

Item. For Six Dozen of large fine Holland Handkerchiefs, with great French Buttons, for the Lord *Fleetwood*, to wipe away the Teares from his Excellencies Cheeks, at Twenty Shillings per Handkerchief. — 72. —. —

Item Paid his young Daughters Musick-Master, and Dancing Master, for fifteen Moneths Arrears, due at the Interruption of Parliament — 59. 5. —

Item For four rich Mantles for his Lady, two lac'd and two embroidered, and a brave New Gown, made to congratulate her Husband's new Honor. — 270. —. —

Item Bestowed by her Order, upon the Journey men Taylors, and given to him that brought home and tryed on the said Gown, seven pieces in gold. — 7. 14. —

Item For an innumerable company of Pectoral Rolls and Lozenges, to dry up his Excellencies Rheum, at two pence a piece — 30. 2. 2

Item For two Rolls of Spanish Tobacco for Colonel *Sydenham*, at twenty shillings per pound, according to the Protectors rate, and five black Pots to warm Ale in, at twelve pence a piece, together with ten Groce of glaz'd Pipes, at nine shillings the groce. — 45. 13. 4.

---

[1] A committee of 23, which was inaugurated on 26th October 1659 to take upon themselves the exercise of the Government, till another form of Government should be agreed upon, which they declared should never be in single hands again, as a Chief Magistrate, a King, or even the House of Lords.

	L.	S.	D
Item For two gilt Horn bookes for his great son, at two shillings, sixpence a piece	5.	—	
Item laid out for seven rich new Gowns, bespoke at *Paris* for the Lady *Lambert*, to be worn seven several dayes one after another, at her Husbands coming to the Crowne, every Gown valued at Sixty pound, one with the other	480.	—.	—
Item for Pins and Gloves for the said Lady	83.	9.	—
Item for vamping Colonel *Clarks* Riding boots, and for new Spur Leathers	10.	—.	—
&c &c &c &c—			

Parody was almost unknown, but the following will serve as an example :—

Song.

[118.] I must confess, upon a day,
When all my thoughts were Westward ha,
Near *Hampton Court* I saw a Face,
The Throne of Modesty and Grace ;
In whose each motion might be seen
Hadassa and the Southern Queen ;
Her Smiles were arguments to prove
The *Phœnix*, and the God of Love.
From these the Pencil learnt those Draughts
Of *Titan's* Beams, and *Cupid's* Shafts.
  Bless me, said I, since I must die,
My Heart a Sacrifice shall lie,
Burnt with the Lustre of her eye.

The Mock.

And I, being lately Eastward bound,
To take a merry Countrey Round,
There I beheld a Thing call'd Woman,
Save him that hath her, Match for no man !
In whose behaviour you may spell,
What *Job's* Wife was, and *Jezabel.*

Her looks make good the doubtful story
Of *Acharon* and Purgatory.
From these the Painter had advice
To limn the Toad and Cockatrice.
    This made me cry, since Friends must part,
E're this vile wretch shall have my heart,
I'le suffer.   Drive away the Cart.

[105.] There was an olde woman that had but one tooth in her head, & that did ake very sore, she went to Master *Scogin* for remedy. Come with me, mother, said *Scogin*, & you shall be healed by & by. He then got a packthreed, and went to the Smiths forge with the woman, and he said to the Smith, I pray you, heate me a Coulter in your Forge. I will, said the Smith. Then he went to the old woman, and said, Mother, let me see your tooth, and she did so : he took his packthreed and bound it fast about the tooth, & tyed the other end of the thred at the ring of the forge doore, whereat the Smith used to tie his horses & mares, and when the Coulter was glowing hot, *Scogin* tooke the Coulter and ran with it against the old woman, saying ; Why dost thou stand here like an old mare ? I will run thee through with this hot Coulter. The woman being afraid, gave a braid[1] with her head, and ran her way, & left her tooth behind her. *Scogin* ran after the woman, and she cryed out for helpe (for she was afraid that *Scogin* would have burnt her.) The Smith ran after *Scogin* for his Coulter, for he was afraid that *Scogin* would run away with it.

[94.] One perswaded a Scholar that was much given to rambling, and going abroad, to sell or put away his Cushion, and it would be a means to make him sit harder to his study.

[26.] A Scholar in *Oxford* was often sent to by a Citizen for Money, which he pretended was due to him, and finding his answer not according to expectation he took the boldness and went to him himself, and modestly said to him in private : Sir, There's some Money betwixt you and I. Say you so, says

---

[1] A start, a toss of the head.

the Scholar, I pray where is it? we'll divide it if you please. Sir, says he, I have taken your word for it hitherto. Truly, says he, so you are like to do till you are paid.

[4.] A young lad being chid by his Uncle, for lying a Bed so long in a Morning, telling him that such a one had found a Purse of Money by rising early in the Morning: I, says the Lad smartly, but he rose too early that lost it.

[110.] Maister *Hobson* on a time in company of one of his neighbors, roade from London towards Sturbridge faire, so the first night of there jorny they lodged at *Ware* in an Inne where great store of Company was, and in the morning when every man made him ready to ride, and some were on horsbacke setting forward, the Cittizen, his neighbour found him sitting at the Inne gate, booted and spurd, in a browne studdy, to whome hee saide, for shame, Maister *Hobson*, why sitte you heare, why doe you not make your selfe redy to horsebacke, that we may set forward with company? Maister Hobson replyed in this manner, I tarry (quoth he) for a good cause. For what cause? quoth his neighbour. Mary, quoth Maister *Hobson*, here be so many horses, that I cannot tell which is mine owne, and I know well, when every man is ridden and gone, the horse that remaneth behind, must needs be mine.

[17.] A Puritan coming to a Cheese mongers to buy Cheese, when he gave him a tast, he put his hat before his eyes, to say Grace; Nay, says he, I see instead of tasting my Cheese, you intend to make a meal of it.

The BEGGARS
CHORUS

IN THE JOVIAL CREW.

To an excellent New Tune.[1]

[119.]   There was a jovial Beggar,
      he had a wooden Leg,
Lame from his Cradle,
      and forced for to Beg;
And a Begging we will go, we'll go, we'll go,
And a Begging we will go.

A Bag for my Oatmeal,
      another for my Salt,
A little pair of Crutches,
      to see how I can halt;
And a Begging, &c

A Bag for my Bread,
      another for my Cheese,
A little Dog to follow me,
      to gather what I leese.
And a Begging &c

A Bag for my Wheat,
      another for my Rye,

[1] For tune, see Appendix.

A little Bottle by my side,
   to drink when I'm a dry.
And a Begging we will go, we'll go, we'll go,
And a Begging we will go.

To *Pimlico* we'll go,
   where merry we shall be,
With ev'ry Man, a Can in's hand,
   and a Wench upon his knee.
And a Begging &c

Seven years I served
   my old Master Wild,
Seven years I begged
   whilst I was but a Child
And a begging &c

I had the pretty knack
   for to wheedle and to cry,
By young and by old
   much pitied e'er was I.
And a begging &c

Fatherless and Motherless
   still was my Complaint,
And none that ever saw me
   but took me for a Saint.
And a begging &c

I begg'd for my Master,
   and got him store of Pelf,
But *Jove* now be praised,
   I now beg for myself.
And a begging &c

Within a hollow Tree
   I live, and pay no Rent,
Providence provides for me,
   and I am well content.
And a begging &c

Of all occupations
 a Beggar lives the best,
For when he is a weary,
 he'll lie him down and rest.
And a begging &c

I fear no Plots against me,
 but live in open Cell;
Why who woud be a King
 when a Beggar lives so well?
And a begging &c.

Printed for R. Brooksby *at the* Golden Ball *in* Pye-Corner.

[67.] A Company went to an Inne without money, when ye reckoning was to be pay'd, one called his hostesse, asking her what it was: she said two shillings. Then he askt her what one should pay for bloodshed: she answered ten groats. Then, said he, cut my finger and give me ye rest[1] againe.

[52.] One *Dromo*, a certaine Tiler, sitting upon a ridge of a House, laying on certaine roofe tiles, looking backe, and reaching somewhat too far for a little morter, that lay by him, fell backward and by good hap, fell upon a man that was sitting under the house, whom with his fall he bruised to death, but thereby saved his owne life. Not many dayes after, a sonne of the dead mans, caused this man to be apprehended for murther, and, having him before the Judge, cried unto the Judge for justice: who asking the prisoner what hee could say for himselfe, received this answer. Truly, Sir, I never thought the man any hurt, neither did I thinke to fall: but since it was my hap to hit upon him to save my life, if it please your Lordship, I am contented that he shall have justice; for my selfe, I had no malice to his father, though I see he hath a great deale to me: but let him doe his worst, I care not, I aske no favour: let him go up to the top of the house where I sate, and I will sit where his father sate; let him fall from the place as cunningly as hee can, and fall upon

---

[1] *i.e.* give me the change.

mee to save his life, I will bee contented. The Judge seeing the mans innocency, and how farre he was from intent of any evill to the man whom he had slaine, willed the complainant to take this course for his contentment : which he refusing, was dismissed the Court, and the Prisoner thus by his wity answer released.

[110.] There was a certaine farmer that lost forty pounds betwixt *Cambridge* and *London*, and being so great a summe, he made proclamation in all market Townes there abouts, that whosoever had found forty and five pounds, should have the five pounds for his labour for finding it, and therefore he put in the five pound more than was lost. It was Maister *Hobsons* fortune to find the same sum of forty pounds, and brought the same to the baylive of *Ware* & required the five pounds for his paines, as it was proclaymed. When the country farmer understood this, and that he must needs pay five pounds for the finding, he sayd that there was in the purse five and forty pounds, and so would hee have his owne mony and five pounds over. So long they strove, that the matter was brought before a Justice of the Peace, which was one Maister *Fleetwood*, who after was Recorder of London ; but when Maister *Fleetwood* understood by the bayleife that the proclamation was made for a purse of five and forty pound, he demanded where it was. Here, quoth the baylie, and gave it him. Is it just forty pound? said Maister *Fleetwood*. Yes truly, (quoth the bayleife) Here maister *Hobson*, sayd Ma. *Fleetwood*, take you this mony for it is your owne, and if you chance to find a purse of five and forty pound, bring it to this honest farmer. That is mine, quoth the farmer, for I lost just forty pound. You speake too late (quoth Maister *Fleetwood*). Thus the farmer lost the mony, and maister *Hobson* had it according to justice.

[67.] Mr. French the King's Fisher, beeing a Widower, married a young woman, and shortly died, on whom one made this distich.

> By fish hee liv'd, by fish hee thriv'd,
> He touched y[e] flesh, and so hee died.

[103.] An Alderman of *Norwich*, having a Maid servant Married from his House, went two or three Years after to see her, and ask'd (amongst other things) how many Children she had? Truly Sir, says she, none. O Lord, replys he, what should be the reason of that? I don't know, says the Woman. Alas! adds the Old Fellow, now I remember me, your Mother had none.

[105.] After a while *Scogin* came to London, hee married a young woman, taking her for a maid, as other men doe. At last he thought to prove his wife, and fained himselfe sicke. Oh good wife, saies he, I will shew you a thing, and if you will promise me to conceale it. She said, Sir, you may tell mee what you will, I were worse than accursed, if I should disclose your counsell: O wife, said *Scogin*, I had a great pang to day in my sicknesse, for I did parbrake,[1] and cast out a Crow. A Crow? said shee. Yea, said *Scogin*, God helpe me. Be of good comfort said she, you shall recover and doe well. Well wife, said *Scogin*, goe to Church and pray for me: shee went to the Church, and by & by one of her gossips met with her and asked how her husband did. I wis,[2] said she, a sore sick man he is, and like to die, for there is an evill signe and token in him. What is that, Gossip? said shee. Nay, by gisse,[3] I will not tell it to any man alive. What, said the woman, you may tell me, for I will never bewray your counsell. By gisse, said *Scogin's* wife, if I wist that you wold keep my counsel, I wold tel you. Then said the woman, whatsoever you doe tell, I will lay it dead under my feet. Oh, said *Scogins* wife, my husband parbraked two Crowes. Jesus, said the woman, I never heard of such a thing. This woman as she did meet with another gossip of hers, shewed that *Scogin* had parbraked three Crowes. So it went on from one gossip to another, that ere Mattens were finished, all the parish knew that *Scogin* had parbraked twenty Crowes. And when the Priest was ready to goe into the Pulpit, one came to request him and all the Parish to pray for *Scogin*, for he had parbraked twenty Crowes. The Priest blessed him and said

---

[1] Or parbreak, to vomit.   [2] Suppose or think.
[3] An oath, a corruption of *Jesus*.

to the Parishioners, I doe pray you pray for Scogin, for he is in perill of his life, and hath parbraked 21 Crowes. By and by one went to *Scogin*, and said, Sir, is it as it is spoken in the Church of you? What is that, said *Scogin.* The Priest said in the Pulpit that you parbraked 21 Crowes. Said *Scogin,* what a lie is this? By & by the bels were told for sacring, and *Scogin* hied him to Church, lustily and merry, and when the men and women did see him in the Church, they looked upon one another, and marvelled of this matter. After Masse, *Scogin* asked what were they that they should bring such a tale upon him. At last the matter was so boulted out, that the original of the cause began at Scogins wife.

[17.] A poor Countrey Boy came up to *London* to be an Apprentice to a Cobler, and seeing the Lord Mayors show, and hearing that Sir *Simon Eyre* who formerly was Lord Mayor, had been apprentice to a Shoemaker; one said to him, Is not this a brave show: I, says the Boy, *'tis this we must all come to.*

[4.] A silly old fellow meeting his God son, ask'd whither he was going? To School, said the Boy: That's well, said he, there's a Penny for you; Be a good Boy, and mind your Book, and I hope I shall live to hear thee Preach my Funeral Sermon.

[94.] It was said by one, that a Hangman had a contemplative Profession, because he was never at work, but he was put in minde of his own end.

[94.] Why do Ladies so affect slender wastes, said one? 'Tis (replied another) because their Expences may not be too great.

[67.] John Hall, beeing in a sheete (of printing, or writing) called, Knave, is said to have Carried it to ye Vice Ch. (ancellor) Dr Gouch to complaine, who beeing walking in his garden, and vexed that hee would trouble him wth such a

frivolous matter, tare yᵉ sheete & cast it abroad.   John gathers
up all ye pieces : yᵉ Dʳ demanded why ?   Hee answered, I
would bee loth to leave yᵉ Knave in your worship's garden.

[94.] One commending a Taylor for his dexterity in his
Profession ; another standing by, ratified his opinion, saying,
Taylors had their business at their fingers ends.

The Bad-Husbands Folly

or

Poverty made known.

A Man may waste and spend away his store,
But if misery comes he has no help therefore,
This man that brought himself into decay,
Shews other Good fellows that they go not astray.

To the Tune of *Come hither my own sweet Duck.*

[120.]   To all Good-Fellows now,
            I mean to sing a Song,
    I have wrought my own decay,
            and have done myself great wrong :
    In following the Ale-house,
            I have spent away my store,
    Bad Company did me undo.
        but i῀le do so no more.

    That man that haunts the Ale house,
            and likewise the Drunken Crew,
    Is in danger to dye a Beggar,
            without any more ado ;
    Would I might be an Example
            to all Good fellows sure ;
        Bad Company &c

    I had a fair Estate of Land,
            was worth forty pound a year,

I sold and Mortgaged all that,
    and spent it in strong Beer:
My wife and friends could not rule me,
    until I did wax poor.
        Bad Company &c

I came unto my Hostis,
    and called for Liquor apace,
She saw my money was plenty,
    and she smiled in my face:
If I said fill a Flaggon,
    they set two upon the score,
        Bad Company &c

I ranted night and day,
    and I let my Money flye,
While my wife was almost dead with grief
    to hear her Children cry:
For they were almost starv'd and pin'd
    they wanted food so sore.
        Bad Company &c

At two a Clock i' th' morn
    I would come Drunken home,
And if my wife spoke but a word,
    I'de kick her about the Room;

And domineer and swear,
 and call her—— and——.
  Bad Company &c

Then I fell sick upon the same,
 and lay three months and more,
But never an Alewife in the Town,
 would come within my door :
But my poor wife was my best friend,
 and stuck to me therefore.
  Bad Company &c

My wife she sold her Petticoat,
 and pawn'd her Wedding Ring,
To relieve me in my misery,
 in any kind of thing :
O was not I a woful man,
 to waste and spend my store,
*And let my wife & children want at home
 but I'le do so no more.*

When I began to mend a little,
 I walke to take the air,
And as I went along the Town,
 I came by my Hostises door :
I askt her for to trust me two-pence,
 she denyed me the more,
*The Money that I have .spent with her,
 but I'le do so no more.*

As soon as I get strength agen
 i'le fall to work apace,
To maintain my wife and children,
 for my Hostises are base :
I see who is a mans best friend,
 if he be sick or poor.
  Bad Company &c

And when I do get money agen,
 I'le learn for to be wise,

And not believe that Drunken Crew,
    that filled my ears with lyes :
And carry it home unto my wife
    and of my Children take more care.
        Bad Company &r

He runs a very long Race
    that never turns again ;
And brings himself unto disgrace,
    and has poverty for his pain ;
But now I will be careful sure,
    and forgo the Ale-house door.
        Bad Company &c

Now to conclude and make an end
    what I have put in Rhime,
That all Good-fellows they may se
    to mend their lives in time :
And learn for to be Thrifty,
    to save something by in store.
        Bad Company &c.

Printed for I. Deacon, at the Angel in Guilt Spur street,
without Newgate.

[110.] There dwelled not farre from Maister *Hobson*, two very ancient women, the youngest of them both was above three score yeares of age, and uppon a time sitting at the taverne together, they grew at varience which of them should be the youngest (as women, indeede, desier to be accompted younger than they be) in such manner that they layd a good supper, of the valew of twenty shillings, for the truth thereof, and Maister *Hobson* they agreed upon to be their Judge of the difference. So after Maister *Hobson* had knowledge thereof, the one came to him, and as a present gave him a very faire pidgion pye, worth some five shillings, desiering him to passe the vardet [1] of her side ; within a while after, the other came, and gave Maister *Hobson* a very faire grayhound, which kind of dogges he much delighted in : praying him likewise to be favorable on her side, wherefore hee gave judgment that the

        [1] Verdict.

woman that gave him the grayhound was the yonger, and so she wonn the supper of twenty shillings, Which she perceiving, came to him and sayd, Sir, I gave you a pidgion pie, and you promised the verdit should goe on my side. To whome Maister *Hobson* said, of a truth, good woman, there came a grayhound into my house, and eate up the pidgion pye, and so by that meanes I quite forgot thee.

[103.] A Soldier Quartering in Cambridge, often observ'd a Young Country Wench that Sold Piggs a Market Days, whereupon he went to her, and desir'd to see some of her Pigs, she having several, he said, he would have one alive, so she shewed him one that she had in a Bag. Well, Sweet heart, said he, I live hard by, I will go and shew the Pig to my Captain; if he like it, you shall have three shillings for it, but in the mean time I will leave the Money with you; thus having got the Pig tied up in the Bag, he went to his Lodging, and put in a Dog in the Bag instead of it, and returning quickly to the Damsel, said his Captain did not like the Pig, and therefore she took the Bag without looking into it, and gave him his Money again. Not long after came a French man in haste to buy a Pig, and he not liking those that were dead, would have a live One; Sir, said she, I have one of the same bigness alive, the Price of it is three Shillings, I will not sell it a Farthing Cheaper; well, said he, if you will not, here is your Money, but how shall I carry it? Why, for a Groat you shall have the Poke and all. Poke, what is dat? said Monsieur. 'Tis a Bag. Is dat de Poke? well here's a Groat. Thus away he goes with his Bargain home, but when he comes to look in the Poke, he see the Dog, O de diable, (said he) is dis de Pig? de Dible take me, if I do buy Pig in de Poke agen.

The Brewer.[1]

[121.]   Of all the trades that ever I see,
       Theres none to the Brewer compared may be;
       For so many several wayes works he,
          Which nobody can deny.

[1] A satire on Oliver Cromwell.

A Brewer may put on a noble face,
And come to the wars with such a grace,
That he may obtain a Captains place;
    Which nobody can deny.

A Brewer may speak so learnedly well,
And raise such stories for to tell,
That he may be come a Colonel;
    Which &c

A Brewer may be a Parliament man,
For so his knavery first began,
And work the most cunning plots he can;
    Which &c

A Brewer may be so bold a Hector,
That when he has drunk a cup of Nectar
He may become a Lord Protector;
    Which &c

A Brewer may do all these things, you see,
Without controul, nay he may be
Lord Chancellor of the University:
    Which &c

A Brewer may sit like a Fox in his cub,
And preach a Lecture out of a tub,
And give the world a wicked rub;
    Which &c

But here remains the strangest thing,
How he about his plots did bring,
That he should be Emperour above a King;
    Which no body can deny, deny;
    Which no body dares deny.

[17.] Two Gentlemen riding from *Shipton* to *Burford* together, and seeing the Miller of *Burford* riding softly before on his sacks, resolved to abuse him; so one went on one side of him, and t'other on the other, saying Miller, now tell us, which art thou, more Knave or Fool? Truly, says he, I know not which I am most but I think *I am between both.*

[105.] On a time as *Scogin* was riding to the Abbot of Bury, hee asked of a Cowheard how far it was to Bury. The Cowheard said twenty miles. May I, said *Scogin*, ride thither to night : yea, said the Cowheard, if you ride not too fast, and also if you ride not a good pace, you will be wet ere you come halfe waye there. As *Scogin* was riding on his way, he did see a cloud arise that was blacke, and being afraid to be wet, he spurred his horse and did ride a great pace, and riding so fast, his horse stumbled and strained his leg, and might not goe. *Scogin* revolving in his mind the Cowheards words, did set up his horse at a poore mans house, and returned to the Cowheard, supposing that he had beene a good Astronomer, because hee said, if you ride not too fast, you may be at Bury tonight, and alsoe if you doe not ride fast you shal be wet ere you come there. *Scogin* said to the Cowheard, what shall I give thee to tell mee, when I shall have raine or faire weather? There goeth a bargain, said the Cowheard : what wilt thou give me? *Scogin* said, Twenty shillings. Nay, said the Cowheard, for forty Shillings I will tell you and teach you, but I will be paid first. Hold the money, said *Scogin*. The Cowheard said, Sir, doe you see yonder Cow with the cut tail? Yea, said *Scogin*. Sir, said the Cowheard, when that she doth begin to set up her rumpe, and draw to a hedge or bush, within an houre after we shall have raine : therefore take the Cow with you, and keepe her as I doe, and you shall ever be sure to know when you shall have faire weather or foule. Nay, said *Scogin* keepe thy Cow still, and give me twenty shillings of my mony. That is of my gentlenes saith the Cowheard, howbeit you seeme to bee an honest man, there is twenty Shillings.

JOAN'S Ale is New;[1] OR:

A new merry Medley, shewing the power, the strength, the operation, and the vertue that remains in good Ale, which is accounted the Mother-drink of *England.*

All you that do this merry Ditty view,
Taste of *Joan's* Ale, for it is strong and new.

To a pleasant New Northern Tune.

[122.]   There was a jovial Tinker,
Which was a good Ale Drinker,
He never was a shrinker,
 believe me this is true.
And he came from the wild[2] of Kent,
When all his money was gone and spent,

[1] For tune, see Appendix.   [2] Weald.

Which made him like a Jack a Lent.
 And Jones Ale is new,
 And Jones Ale is new Boys,
 And Jones Ale is new.

The Tinker he did settle,
Most like a man of Mettle,
And vow'd to pawn his Kettle,
 now mark what did ensue.
His Neibors they flockt in apace,
To see Tom Tinker's comely face,
Where they drank soundly for a space,
 Whilst Jones Ale &c

The Cobler and the Broom-man,
Came next into the room man,
And said they would drink for boon man
 let each one take his due.
But when good liquor they found,
They cast their caps upon the ground
And to the Tinker they drank round ;
 Whilst Jones Ale &c

The Rag man he being weary,
With the bundle he did carry,
He swore he would be merry,
 and spend a shilling or two.
And he told his Hostis to her face,
The Chimney Corner was his place
And he began (to) drink apace.
 And Jones Ale &c

The Pedler he grew nigher,
For it was his desire,
To throw the Rags i'th' fire,
 and burn the bundle blew.
So whilst they drank whole flashes,
And threw about the Glasses,
The rags were burnt to ashes,
 And Jones Ale &c

And then came in a Hatter,
To see what was the matter,
He scorned to drink cold water,
   amongst that Jovial crew.
And like a man of courage stout,
He took the quart-pot by the snout,
And never left till all was out,
    O Jones Ale &c

The Taylor being nimble
With Bodkin, Shears, and Thimble,
He did no whit dessemble,
    I think his name was *True*
He said that he was like to choak,
And called so fast for lap and smoak,
Until he had pawned his Vinegar Cloake,
    For Jones Ale &c

Then came a pittiful Porter,
Which often did resort there,
Quoth he i'le shew some sport here,
    amongst this jovial crew.
The Porter he had very bad luck,
Before that it was ten o'clock,
The fool got drunk and lost his frock,
    For Jones Ale &c.

The bony brave Shoomaker,
A brave Tobacco taker,
He scorned to be a Quaker
   I think his name was *Hugh.*
He called for liquor in so fast,
Till he forgot his Awl and Last,
And up the reckonings he did cast,
    Whilst Jones Ale &c

And then came in the Weaver,
You never saw a braver,
With a Silk-man, and a Glover,
    Tom Tinker for to view

And so to welcome him to Town,
They every man spent half a crown,
And so the drink went merrily down,
    For Jones Ale &c

Then came a drunken *Dutchman*,
And he would have a touch, man,
But he soon took too much, man,
    which made them after rue.
He drank so long as I suppose,
'Till greasie drops fell from his nose,
And like a beast befoul'd his hose,
    Whilst Jones Ale &c

A Welshman he came next, Sir,
With joy and sorrow mixt Sir,
Who being partly vext Sir,
    he out his dagger drew.
Cuts-plutter-a-nails, quoth *Taffie* then,
A Welshman is a Shentleman
Come Hostis fill's the other Can,
    For Jones Ale &c.

Thus like to men of courage stout,
Courageously they drank about,
Till such time all the ale was out,
    as I may say to you.
And when the business was done,
They every man departed home,
And promised Jone again to come,
    when she had brew'd anew.

FINIS.

Printed for F. Coles. T. Vere. J. Wright, J. Clarke,
W. Thackeray and T. Passinger.

[17.] A Shoomaker thought to mock a Collier being black, saying, What news from Hell? how fares the Devil? Faith, says the Collier, he was just riding forth as I came thither, and wanted nothing *but a Shoomaker to pluck on his boots.*

[123.]

THE SCOTS HOLDING THEIR YOUNG KINGES NOSE TO Ye GRINSTONE

Come to the Grinstone Charles tis now to late
To Recolect, tis presbiterian fate

You Couinant pretenders must I bee
The subiect of your Tradgie Comedie.

Stoope Charles

Jockie

The date of this curious political caricature is 14th July 1651. It must be remembered that Charles II. was crowned at Scone on 1st January 1651, and this satire deals with the behaviour of the Scots towards their young monarch. It is too long to give *in extenso*, but the following will give a fair idea of its tenor. Above the illustration are printed these lines :—

> "I. Jockey turne the stone of all your plots,
Jockey.   For none turns faster than the turne-coat Scots

> We for our ends did make thee King, be sure
Presbytor.   Not to rule us, we will not that endure.

> You deep dissemblers, I know what you doe,
King.   And for revenges sake, I will dissemble too."

On either side of the print is a long poem, of which I will
only give the commencement :—

> "This Embleme needs no learned Exposition,
> The World knows well enough the sad condition
> Of Regall Power, and Prerogative
> Dead, and dethron'd in *England*, now alive
> In *Scotland*, where they seem to love the Lad,
> If hee'l be more obsequious than his Dad.
> And Act according to Kirk Principles,
> More subtile than were Delphick Oracles.
> For let him lye, dissemble, kill and slay,
> Hee's a good Prince that will the Kirk obey," etc. etc.

[110.] Upon a new yeares day Maister *Hobson* sitting at
dinner in a Poets Company, or one, as you may tearme him, a
writer of histories, there came a poore man and presented him
a cople of orringes, which hee kindly tooke as a new yeares
guift, and gave the poore man for the same, an angell of goold,
and there upon gave it to his wife to lay it up among his other
jewels, considering that it had likewise cost him an Angel, the
which she did.   The Poet sitting by, and marking the bounty
of Ma. *Hobson* for so small a matter, he went home, and
devised a booke contayning forty sheets of paper, which was
halfe a yeare in writing, and came and gave it to Maister
Hobson in dedication, and thought in his mind, that he, in
recompencing the poore man so much for an orringe, would
yeeld far more recompence for his booke, being so long in
studying.   Maister *Hobson* tooke the Poets booke thankfully,
and perseving he did it onely for his bounty shewed for the
orringe given him : willed his wife to fetch the said orringe,
which he gave to the Poet, being then almost rotten, saying,
here is a jewel which cost me a thousand times the worth in
gould, therefore I think thou art well satisfied for thy bookes
dedication : the poet seeing this, went his way all a shamed.

[26.] A deaf Man was selling Pears at the Towns end in
St Gileses, and a Gentleman riding out o' th' Town, askt him
what 'twas a Clock?   He said Ten a Penny, Master : Then

he askt him agen what 'twas a Clock? He told 'em indeed he could afford no more. You Rogue, says he, I'll kick you about the streets. Then says the man, *Sir, if you won't, another will.*

[4.] A woman coming to a Parson, desir'd him to preach a Funeral Sermon on her Son that was lately dead; the Parson promised her to do it; but she desiring to know the Price of his Sermon ; he told her it was Twenty Shillings. Twenty Shillings ! says she, An Ass spoke for an Angel, and won't you speak under Twenty Shillings? The Parson being a little netled at her, told her she was better fed than taught. Sir, says she, 'tis very true; for my Husband feeds me, and You teach me.

[93.] *George* (*Peele*) was at Bristow, and there staying somewhat longer than his coyne would last him, his Palfrey that should bee his Carrier to London, his head was growne so big, that he could not get him out of the stable ; it so fortuned at that instant, certaine Players came to the Towne, and lay at that Inne where *George Peele* was : to whom *George* was well knowne, being in that time an excellent Poet, and had acquaintance of most of the best Players in England ; from the triviall sort hee was but so so ; of which these were, only knew *George* by name, no otherwise. There was not past three of the Companie come with the Carriage, the rest were behinde, by reason of a long Journey they had ; so that night they could not enact ; which *George* hearing, had presently a Stratageme in his head, to get his Horse free out of the stable, and Money in his Purse to beare his charges up to London. And thus it was : Hee goes directly to the Maior, tels him he was a Scholler and a Gentleman, and that he had a certaine Historie of the Knight of the Rodes ; and withall, how Bristow was first founded, and by whom, and a briefe[1] of all those that before him had succeeded in Office in that worshipfull Citie : desiring the Maior, that he, with his presence, and the rest of his Brethren, would grace his labors. The Maior agreed to it, gave him leave, and withall appointed

---

[1] A list or catalogue.

him a place : but for himselfe, hee could not be there, being in
the evening : but bade him make the best benefit he could of
the Citie ; and very liberally gave him an Angell, which *George*
thankfully receives, and about his businesse he goes, got his
Stage made, his Historey cryed, and hyred the Players Apparell,
to furnish out his Shew, promising to pay them liberally ; and
withall desired them they would favour him so much, as to
gather him his money at the doore ; (for hee, thought it his
best course to imploy them, lest they should spie out his
knaverie ; for they have perillous heads.)   They willingly
yeeld to doe him any kindnes that lyes in them ; in briefe,
carry their apparell in the Hall, place themselves at the doore,
where *George* in the meane time, with the tenne shillings he
had of the Maior, delivered his Horse out of Purgatorie, and
carries him to the Townes end, and there placeth him, to be
ready at his comming.   By this time the Audience were
come, and some forty shillings gathered, which money *George*
put in his purse, and putting on one of the Players Silke
Robes, after the trumpet had sounded thrice, out he comes,
makes low obeysance, goes forward with his Prologue, which
was thus :

A trifling Toy, a Jest of no account, pardie.
The Knight, perhaps, you think for to bee I :
Think on so still ; for why, you know that thought is free,
Sit still a while, I'le send the Actors to ye.

Which being said, after some fire workes that hee had made of
purpose, threw out among them, and downe stayres goes he,
gets to his Horse, and so with fortie shillings to London ;
leaves the Players to answer it ; who when the Jest was
knowne, their innocence excused them, beeing as well gulled
as the Maior and the Audience.

[82.] There was a faire ship of two hundred tuns lying at
the Tower Wharfe at *London*, where a Countryman passing
by, most earnestly looked on the said ship, and demanded
how old shee was.   One made answer that she was a yeare
old.   Good Lord blesse me, said the Countryman, is shee so

big growne in one yeere, what a greatnesse will shee bee by the time she comes to my age?

[82.] Twelve Schollers riding together, one of them said, my masters, let us ride faster. Why? quoth another, methinks wee ride a good pace, I'le warrant it is foure mile an hour. Alas, said the first, what is foure mile an houre amongst us all?

[17.] A patient man coming home from work, but it seems did not bring home to his Shrewish Wife so much money as she expected; with that she flew about his ears, and did so jole him! Good wife, says he, be quiet, for I would willingly wear my bands without cuffs, if you please.

[105.] On a night *Scogin* and his chamber-fellow, and two or three of the Bishops servants being merrily disposed, consult how they might have good cheere and pay no money, and every one invented a way as they thought best. At last *Scogin* said, I have invented a cleanly shift. At the signe of the Crowne against Peter's Church, is a new Tapster, which ere this hath not seene any of us, and he is also purblind, so that if he see us hereafter, he cannot know us. Therefore wee will goe thither and make good cheere, and when we have a reckoning, we will contend who shall pay all; then will I say to avoid the contention, that the Tapster shall be blinded, and we wil run round about him, and whosoever he catcheth first, let him pay for all, and so we may escape away. Every man liked *Scogin's* device best, so in conclusion they came thither, and had good cheere, for they spared no cost: so that in the end their reckoning drew to ten Shillings. Then as *Scogin* had devised afore, they did. The Tapster was blinded, so they ran round about him, and first *Scogin* got out, and then another, so that at last they got all away, and left the tapster groping in every place about the house for him that should pay the shot. The master of the house being in a chamber next to the place where they were, and hearing the stamping that they made, came in to see what they did, whom the Tapster caught in his armes, saying, Sir, you must pay the reckoning. Marry, said his Master, so I thinke I must indeed, for here is no body else to pay it. Then the Tapster and his Master sought and enquired for *Scogin* and the rest, but they could neither find them, nor heare newes of them.

[94.] Hangmen practice their cunning for the most part upon good natur'd men, because they are ready to forgive, before the hurt be attempted.

[4.] A Parson who had not much Wit to spare, seeing his Son play roguish Tricks, Why, Sirrah, said he, did you ever see me do so, when I was a Boy, as you are?

[4.] A Precise Fellow hearing much swearing in a Bowling Green, said, For Shame Gentlemen, forbear, it is God's great mercy the Bowling Green doth not fall on your Heads.

Nick and Froth;

or

The Good-fellows Complaint for want of full Measure.

Discovering the Deceits, and Abuses of Victuallers, Tap-
sters, Ale Drapers ; and all the rest of the Society
of Drunkard Makers, by filling their drink in false
Flaggons, Pimping Tankerds, Cans call'd Ticklers ;
Rabbits, Jugs, and short Quarterns, To the Grand
Abuse of the Society of Good Fellowship.

*Good Fellows Drinks their Liquor without flinching ;
Then why should knavish Tapsters use such pinching.*

Tune of, We'l Drink this Old Ale no more, no more.

[124.]   All you y^t are Free-men of Ale-Drapers Hall,
And Tapsters wherever you be,
Be sure you be ready to come at my call,
And your Knavery here you shall see.

A Knot of Good-fellows we are here inclin'd,
To Challenge you out if you dare,
A very sharp Tryal you're like to find,
Although it be at your own Bar.

Your Cheats and Abuses we long did abide,
But times are so wondrous hard,
That Loosers may speak, it cannot be deny'd,
Of our Measure we have been debar'd.

But now we'l show you a trick (you knaves)
And lay you open to view,
It's all for your Froth and your Nick (you slaves)
And tell you no more than is true.

If in a cold Morning we chance to come,
And bid a Good Morrow, my Host,
And call for some Ale, you will bring us black Pots
Yet scarce will afford us a Toast.

For those y^t drink Beer, 'tis true as i'me here,
Your Counterfeit Flaggons you have,
Which holds not a Quart, scarce by a third part,
And y^t makes my Hostis go brave.

But now Pimping Tankerds are all in use,
Which drains a Man's Pocket in brief,
For he that sits close, and takes off his Dose,
Will find that the Tankerd's a Thief.

Bee't Tankerd or Flaggon, which of them you brag on,
We'l trust you to Nick and to Froth,
Before we can Drink, be sure it will shrink,
Far worser than *North* Country Cloth.

When Summer is coming, then hey, brave boys,
The tickling Cans they run round,
Pray tak't in good part, for a *Winchester* Quart [1]
Will fill six, I dare lay you a Pound.

Your Rabbits and Jugs, and Coffee House Mugs,
Are ready whene're you do call,
A P— take his Trade, such Measure that's made,
I wish that old Nick had them all.

When we have a Fancy our Noses to Steel,
And call for some *Nance* [2] of the best,
Be sure the short Pot must fall to our lot,
For now they are all in request.

Scarce one house in twenty, where measure is plenty,
But still they are all for the Pinch ;
Thus, every day they drive Custom away,
And force us good-Fellows to flinch,

Sometimes a Man may leave something to pay,
Though seldom he did it before ;
With *Marlborough* Cholke you his patience provoke,
Whenever he clears off his score.

The women likewise which are not precise,
But will take a Cup of the best,
Tho they drink for pleasure, they'l have their measure
Or else you shall have little rest.

There's *Billings-gate* Nan, all her whole gang,
Complaining for want of their due ;
True Topers they are, as e're scor'd at Bar,
For they'l drink till their Noses look blew.

---

[1] A Winchester quart holds nearly half a gallon.
[2] Nantz brandy.

A Pot and a Toast will make them to boast,
Of things that are out of their reach ;
So long as a Groat remains in the Coat,
They over good Liquor will preach.

In *Shoo Makers Row* there's true hearts you know,
But give them their Measure and weight,
They'l scorn for to stir but stick like a Bur,
And Tope it from Morning till Night.

Then there's honest *Smug* y^t with a full jug
Will set all his Brains in a float ;
But you are such Sots as to fill him small Pots,
Will scarce quench y^t spark in his Throat.

With many such Blades, of several Trades,
Which freely their Money will spend ;
But fill them good drink, they value not chink
Wherever they meet with a friend.

Most Trades in ye Nation gives their approbation,
How that you are much for to blame ;
Then make no excuses, but cease your abuses,
And fill up your Measure for shame.

FINIS.

A Preachment on Malt.

[26.] Certain Townsmen of *Prisal*, returning from a merry
Meeting at a certain Ale-House, met in the fields a Preacher,
who had lately made a bitter sermon against Drunkards, and
among other opprobrious words, called them Malt worms.
Wherefore they agreed to take him, and by violence compel
him to preach a Sermon, and his text should be MALT. The
Preacher, thinking it better to yield, than contend with them
in their cause, began his Sermon as followeth.

There is no preaching without Division, and this Text
cannot well be divided into many parts, because it is but one
word, nor into many Syllables, because it is but one Syllable.
It must therefore be divided into Letters, and they are found

to be four, *viz* M. A. L. T.   These letters represent four inter-
pretations, which Divines commonly do use thus.   M. Moral,
A. Allegorical, L. Literal, T. Tropological.

The Moral Interpretation is well put first, and first to teach
you boysterious Men some good manners, at least, in procur-
ing your attention to the Sermon; Therefore M. Masters. A.
All. L. Listen T. To the Text.

An Allegory is when one thing is spoken of and another
thing meant; The thing spoken of is Malt, the thing meant
is the Oyle of Malt, commonly call'd Ale, which to you Drunkards is so precious, that you account it to be M. Meat. A.
Ale. L. Liberty. T. Treasure.

The Literal sense is as it hath been often heard of heretofore, so it is true according to the letters.   M. Much.   A. Ale.
L. Little.   T. Thrift.

The Tropological sence applyeth that which is now to
somewhat following, either in this world, or in the world to
come; the thing that now is, is the effect which Oyl of Malt
produceth and worketh in some of you, *viz* M. Murther; in
others A. Adultery; in all L. Loose living : in many T. Treason,
and that which hereafter followeth in this world, and in the
world to come is M. Misery.   A. Anguish.   L. Lamentation.
T. Trouble.

I shall now come to a Conclusion, and withal, to perswade
you boysterious men to amend, that so you may escape the
danger whereinto many of you are like to fall, but I have no
hopes to prevail, because I plainly see, and my Text as plainly
telleth me, it is M. to A. that is a Thousand Pound to a Pot
of Ale you will never mend; because all Drunkards are L.
Lewd.   T. Thieves; but yet for discharging my Conscience
and Duty, First towards God, and Secondly towards you my
Neighbours, I say once again, concluding with my Text, M.
Mend A. All; and L. Leave, T. Tippling : otherwise M.
Masters, A. All, L. Look for T. Terrour and Torment.

By this time the Ale wrought in the Townsmens Brains
that then were between Hawk and Buzzard,[1] nearer sleeping
than waking, which the Preacher perceiving, stole away, leaving them to take their nap.

[1] In a *doubtful* condition.

[82.] An Apprentice in the market, did aske the price of an hundred Oysters; his friend perswaded him not to buy them, for they were too small. Too small, reply'd the Prentice, there is not much losse in that, for I shall have the more to the hundred.

[110.] Maister *Hobson* being still very good to poore and most bountyfull to aged people, there came to him usually twice or thrice a weeke, a silly poore ould blinde man to sing under his window, for the which he continually gave him twelve pence a time. Maister *Hobson* having one of his servants so chorlish and withall so covitous that he would suffer the blind man to come no more, unles he shared halfe his benefit: the which the blind singing man was forst to give, rather than loose all: after twice or thrice parting shares, Maister *Hobson* had thereof intelligence, who consulting with the blind man, served his servant in this maner; still he looked for halfe whatsoever he got, so this at last was Maister *Hobsons* guift, who gave commaundement that the blind man should have for his singing three score Jeerkes with a good whippe, and so to be equally parted as the other guifts were, the which were presently given: the blinde mans were but easie, but Master *Hobsons* mans were very sound ones, so that every Jerke drewe blood; after this he never sought to deminish his masters bounty.

[4.] Some Gentlemen coming into a Tavern, whose Sign was the *Moon*, (where for a Fancy they sold nothing but Claret, for which they were very noted, and had great Custom) called for a bottle of Sack; whereupon the Drawer told them they had none: At which, they, not a little admiring,[1] as not knowing the Humour, asked the Drawer the reason, who told them, *The Man in the Moon drinks Claret.*[2] The Fancy of which

---

[1] Wondering.

[2] There was a roystering drinking song with that title, which is not very scarce; there is one in the Roxburghe Ballads. $\frac{C. 20, f. 7}{298.}$

" Our man in the moon drinks Clarret,
With powder-beef, turnep, and carret;
If he doth so, why should not you
Drink until the sky looks blew?"

pleased them so that they said they were resolved to be sociable, and so called for each Man his Bottle to drink their Brothers Health in the Moon.

[93.] *George* (*Peele*) once had invited halfe a score of his friends to a great Supper, where they were passing merry, no cheere wanting, wine enough, musicke playing : the night growing on, & being upon departure, they call for a reckoning. *George* swears there is not a penny for them to pay. They, being men of good fashion, by no meanes would yeeld unto it, but every man throwes downe his money, some tenne shillings, some five, some more : protesting something they will pay. Well, quoth *George*, taking up all the money ; seeing you will be so wilfull you shall see what shall follow : he commands the musicke to play, and while they were skipping and dancing, *George* gets his Cloake, sends up two Pottles of Hypocrist, and leaves them and the reckoning to pay. They wondring at the stay of *George*, meant to be gone : but they were staide by the way, and before they went, forced to pay the reckoning anew.

[26.] A Vintner being broke, was, it seems, forc'd to set up an Ale house in the Suburbs, and being askt, why he did discredit himself so much, to leave off Wine, to sell Beer and Ale ? He told him the chief reason was because he lov'd a Countryman better than a stranger ; for Beer and Ale are my Countrymen, but Wine's a Stranger : but the Gentleman told him he did not well, for he must make much of any Stranger that comes within his gates : So will I that, says he, when I get it within my gates agen ; I'll make more of it than I did ; nay much more, because I would not break the Command.

[105.] On a time the Bishop would feast divers French Lords, and hee gave unto *Peter Achadus* (*Scogins* chamber fellow) twenty French Crownes to bestow at the Poulters, in Feasant, Partridge, Plover, Quaile, Woodcock, Larke, and such other : and because *Scogins* chamber fellow had great business to do, he wrote all such things as he would have bought in a bill, and desired *Scogin* to bestow the money, who was well contented. When *Scogin* had this money, he imagined in his mind how hee might deceive some Poulter, and so to have the money to himselfe. At last hee came to a Poulter in *Paris*, and said, sir, it is so that my Master the Abbot of *Spilding* doth feast a great many of his friends, and I must have so many of every sort of your wares as is mentioned in this bill, therefore I pray you lay them out quickly, and let the Bill be prised reasonably, and to morrow in the morning I will fetch them, and you shall have your money. The wares were laid out and prized, and the sum came to sixe pound and odde money, then on the morrow *Scogin* did come to the Poulter, and asked if everything were ready. Yea, said the Poulter, and here is your bill reasonably prized. Then said *Scogin*, let somebody goe with me for to receive your money : the Poulter said, my wife shal goe with you. *Scogin* went to *St. Peter's* Church, where there was a Priest that had on his Albe, and was ready to goe to Masse : *Scogin* went to the Priest, and said, Master, here is a woman that will not bee perswaded that her Husband ought to be her Head, and I have brought her to you, to the intent you should perswade her. The Priest said he would doe what he could. I thanke you, said *Scogin*. Then *Scogin* came to the woman, and said, if you will have your money, come to my Master, and hear what he doth say. Then *Scogin* came to the Priest, and said Master, here is the woman, will you dispatch her after Masse is done? Yea, said the Priest. Then said *Scogin* to the woman, you heare what my master doth say, therefore I pray you send me by some token, whereby I may receive the wares. The woman sent him by a true token, and then *Scogin* did hire two porters, and did fetch away all the wares from the Poulters house, and did carry it to his chamber : when masse was done, the Priest called the Poulters wife unto him, and asked why she would not acknowledge her husband to be her head? Why, said the woman, I cannot tarry to reason of such matters, therefore I pray you to pay me my money, that I were gone : Wherefore? said the Priest. The woman said, for wares that your man hath received. What man? said the Priest. He that spake to you when you went to masse. The Priest said, he is none of my man, and he said to me, that you would not bee perswaded that your husband ought to be your head. What, master Abbot, said the woman, you shal not mock me so, I must have 6 pound & 8 shillings of you for wares that your man hath received, for you promised to pay me when you went to masse. I am no Abbot, said the Priest, nor none of my men never received anything of you, nor I promised nothing when I went to masse, but that I would perswade you to obey your Husband, who ought to be your head, and so the Priest went his way. The woman perceiving that shee was deceived, went home to see if *Scogin* had received the ware, and he had received them, and was gone an houre before. Then both she and her husband sought for Scogin, but they could not find him.

[17.] A Citizen having married a Cockney, and he taking her with him into the Country, to see his Friends, as they were riding spyed a Willow tree on which abundance of Wants or Moles were hung : O dear, says she, Husband, look what a fine Tree here is ; I never knew how they grew till now ; for it is a Black Pudding tree.

[82.] A man was very angry with his maid, because his eggs were boyled too hard ; truly, said she, I have made them boyle a long houre, but the next you have, shall boyle two houres but they shall be tender enough.

[26.] A Man in a bitter cold Winter night was passing through the Street, and seeing all a Bed, and no Candle in any Window neither ; then bethought himself of this project ; for then he went up and down crying Fire, Fire, which made several come to the Windows : They askt him where ? where ? He told them that he did not know, for if he did, he would go to't to warm himself ; For, says he, I am devilish cold.

The Country-mans new care away.

To the Tune of, *Love will find out the way.*

[125.] If there were imployments
    for men, as have beene,
And Drummes, Pikes and Muskets
    in th' field to be seene,
And every worthy Souldier
    had truely their pay,
Then might they be bolder
    to sing, Care away.

If there were no Rooking,
    but plaine dealing used,
If honest Religion
    were no wayes abused,
If pride in the Country
    did not beare sway,
The Poore and the Gentry
    might sing, Care away.

If Farmers consider'd
    the dearenesse of graine,

·How honest poore Tradesmen
    their charge should maintaine,
And would bate the price on't
    to sing, Care away
We should not be nice on't
    of what we did pay.

If poore Tenants, Landlords
    would not racke their rents,
Which oft is the cause of
    their great discontents,
If, againe, good house-keeping
    in th' Land did beare sway,
The poore that sits weeping
    might sing, Care away.

If Spendthrifts were carefull
    and would leave their follies,
Ebriety hating
    Cards, Dice, Bowling-Alleyes,
Or with wantons to dally
    by night or by day,
Their wives might be merry,
    and sing, Care away.

If Children to Parents
    would dutifull be,
If Servants with Masters
    would deale faithfully,
If Gallants poore Tradesmen
    would honestly pay,
Then might they have Comfort
    to sing, Care away.

There is no contentment
    to a conscience that's cleare,
That man is most wretched
    a bad mind doth beare,

To wrong his poore Neighbour
   by night or by day,
He wants the true comfort
   to sing, Care away.

But he that is ready
   by goodnesse to labour,
In what he is able
   to helpe his poore Neighbour,
The Lord will ever blesse him
   by night and by day,
All ioyes shall possesse him
   to sing, Care away.

Would wives with their husbands,
   and husbands with wives
In love and true friendship
   would so lead their lives,
As best might be pleasing
   to God night and day,
Then they with hearts easing
   might sing, Care away.

No crosse can be greater
   unto a good mind,
Than a man to be matched
   with a woman unkind,
Whose tongue is never quiet
   but scolds night and day,
That man wants the comfort
   to sing, Care away.

A Vertuous woman
   a husband that hath,
That's given unto lewdnesse,
   to envy and wrath,
Who after wicked women
   does hunt for his prey,
That woman wants comfort
   to sing, Care away.

Like true subiects loyall,
    to God let us pray,
Our good king so Royall,
    to preserve night and day :
With the Queen, Prince and Nobles,
    the Lord blesse them aye,
Then may we have comfort
    to sing, Care away.

[82.] There was a lusty young Scholler preferred to a
Benefice in the Country, and commonly on Sundayes and
holy dayes after evening prayer hee would have a dozen bouts
at cudgels with the sturdiest youths in his parish : The Bishop
of the Diocesse hearing of it, sent for the parson, telling him
this beseemed not his profession and gravity, and if that he
did not desist from that unmeet kind of exercise, hee would
unbenefice him.   Good my Lord, (said the Parson) I beseech
you to conceive rightly of mee, and I doubt not but my
playing at cudgels will be counted tollerable ; for I doe it of
purpose to edifie the ruder sort of my people.   How so, said
the Bishop.   Marry, my Lord, (quoth the Parson) whatsoever
I do teach them at morning and evening prayer, I doe beat
soundly into their heads with cudgels afterward, for their better
remembrance.

[94.] He that buys a Horse in *Smithfield*, and does not
look upon him with a pair of Spectacles, before he buys him,
makes his Horse and himself a pair of sorrowful Spectacles for
others to look at.

[110.] Upon a time Maister *Hobson* lying in saint Albones,
there came certaine musitions to play at his chamber doore,
to the intent as they filled his eares with their musicke, he
should fil their purses with mony : whereupon he bad one of
the servants of the Inne (that waited upon him) to goe and
tell them that hee could not then indure to heare their musicke
for he mourned for the death of his mother, so the musitians
disapoynted of their purpose went sadly all away.   The fellow
heard him speake of mourning, asked him how long agoe it is
since he buried his mother ; truely (quoth maister *Hobson*) it

is now very neare forty yeares agoe. The fellow understanding his subtilty, and how wittily he sent away the musitians, laughed very hartely.

[52.] On a Winters evening a Country husband man went to fetch his wives kine home to milk, and driving them into the back side, hee forgot to shut the gate, and hee comes into the house, sits him down by the fire side. The kine finding the gate open, ranne trotting and lowing downe the durty lane, toward the field, and the mans daughter looking forth at the doore and seeing them, cries out to her mother, Faith my father is a fine man, I think the kine are gone to the devill, shall I goe after them ? No (quoth her mother) daughter, you are too forward : Let your father goe, he's fitter, he has his hie shoone on.

A Song.

[121.] Sir *Francis*, Sir *Francis*, Sir *Francis* his Son,
Sir *Robert* and eke Sir *William* did come,
And eke the good Earl of *Southampton*
March't on his way most gallantly ;
And then the Queen began to speak,
Youre welcome home Sir *Francis Drake*.
Then came my Lord Chamberlain, and with his white staffe,
And all the people began for to laugh.

The Queen's Speech.—

Gallants all of British bloud,
Why do ye not saile on th' Ocean flood ?
I protest ye'are not all worth a Philberd
Compared with Sir Humphrey Gilberd.

The Queen's Reason.

For he walkt forth in a rainy day,
To the new-found Land he took his way,
With many a gallant fresh and green ;
He never came home agen.[1]   God bless the Queen.

---

[1] Sir *Humphrey Gilbert* was half-brother to Sir *Walter Raleigh*, and was a famous navigator of Elizabeth's reign. In 1583 he took possession of Newfoundland, but his ship foundered on the voyage home, 9th September 1584.

[82.] A Justice of the Peace was very angry with a country yeoman, because hee came not to him at his first sending for him; and after he had bountifully bestowed two or three dozen of knaves upon him, hee said to him, Sirrah, I will make you know that the proudest knave that dwels under my command shall come before mee when I send for him. I beseech your worship said the man, to pardon mee, for I was afraid: afraid of what? said the Justice. Of your worship answered the fellow. Of mee? said the Justice, why wast thou afraid of mee? Because your worship lookes so like a Lyon, said the man. A Lyon? quoth the Justice, when didst thou see a Lyon? May it please your worship (the fellow replyde) I saw a Butcher bring one but yesterday to *Colebrooke* market, with a white face and his foure legs bound.

> This fellow was a knave, or foole, or both,
> Or else his wit was of but slender growth:
> He gave the white fac'd *Calfe* the Lyons stile,
> The Justice was a proper man the while.

[4.] One that was Born in the Parish of St Giles Cripplegate said: When I dye, I'll be Buried in Cripple Church Yard, an't please God I live.

[26.] A Notable Fellow, that, as 'tis said would not be drunk above seven days in the week; and when he was drunk was so besotted that he knew not what he did. Once his Prentice was sent by his Wife to fetch him home, and when he found him out, he found him reeling ripe also. And as they came down *Ludgate Hill*, in a Moon-shiny night, saw the reflection of the Bell-Savage sign post upon the ground, and it seems took it for a Block, and went to lift his Leg over it, his Prentice having him by the Arm for his supporter, askt what he meant by that? Why, says he, to go over this Block. He told him 'twas not a Block. What is it then? says he. 'Tis a Sign, says the Boy. What Sign, I prithee? Why Master 'tis a Sign you are drunk.

[17.] One who was deep in debt, and forced to keep within all day for fear of Serjeants and Bailiffs would yet at night adventure abroad in some back Lanes and Alleys. Passing one night through the Butchers Shambles, going in hast, one of the Tenter Hooks catcht hold of his cloak. He thinking it had been a Serjeant which had thus shoulder clapt him, looking back, said, *At whose Suit I pray you?*

[105.] When *Scogin* should ride home againe, his bootes were nought, and hee could not tell what shift to make. At last he devised what he might doe : whereupon he sent his man for a shoo-maker to bring him a paire of Bootes. The shoo-maker brought the bootes, and when hee had pulled on the right foot boote, and was pulling on the other boot, Scogin said, it was marvellous strait, and that it did pinch his leg : wherefore hee prayed him to carry it home, and set it on the laste an houre or two : for (quoth he) I have a thing to write that will hold mee two houres, and all that time I will sit and write, & keepe this other boote on my leg still untill that be ready. The shoomaker tooke the boot and went home, as Scogin had bidden him. When the shoo maker was gone, hee sent his man for another shoo maker, and caused one to pull off the boot which the first shoo maker had pulled on. When the other shoo maker was come, *Scogin* caused him to pull on the left boot, and when hee was pulling on the right foot boot, *Scogin* found fault with it, as he did with the first shoo maker, and sent him away in like sort. When he was gone, hee caused his man to make ready their horses, and hee pulled on the boot againe, which the first shoo maker had left behinde him, and so he rode away with the two bootes of two shoo makers : shortly after, the shoomakers came and enquired for *Scogin*, but hee and his man were gone, almost an houre before.

[82.] Two Playsterers being at worke for mee at my house in Southwarke, did many times patch and dawbe out part of their dayes labour with prating, which I, being digging in my garden did over heare that their chat was of their wives, and how that if I were able (quoth one) my wife should ride in pompe through London, as I saw a Countesse ride yesterday. Why, quoth the other, how did shee ride I pray? Marry, said hee, in state, in her *Horslitter*.   O base, quoth the other, *Horslitter :* I protest as poore a man as I am, I would have allowed my wife a three-peny trusse of cleane Straw.

[26.] *Henry Martin* the great Rumper, for you know all Martins are Birds, and he being so, flew so high before; but after the King's most happy Restauration, was brought so low, as to kneel at the Bar of the Lord's House; though 'tis thought he never came into the Lords House before, unless it were to see a handsome Girl there.   But at the Lords Bar he was askt what he could say, that Judgment should not pass upon him?   My Lords, says he, I understood that the King's Proclamation extended to favour of life, upon rendring myself, which I then did.   And, withal, my Lords, I do let you to know, and I do ingeniously confess it, that I never obey'd any of his Majesty's Proclamations before, but this; and I hope I shall not be hang'd for taking the King's word now.

[94.] One sitting by the Fire to take Tobacco, said the Fire was his friend, and presently spit into it : To which one replied, You do not well to quench your friends love by spitting in his face.

THE JOVIALL CREW.[1]

or

Beggars-Bush.

In which a Mad Maunder doth vapour and swagger
With praiseing the Trade of a bonney bold Beggar.

To the tune of, *From hunger and Cold.*

[126.]   A Beggar, a Beggar,
                       A Beggar I'le be,
          There's none leads a Life so jocond as hee ;
                       A Beggar I was,
                       And a Beggar I am,
          A Beggar I'le be, from a Beggar I came :

[1] For tune, see Appendix.

If (as it begins) our Trading do fall,
I fear (at the last) we shall be Beggars all.
Our Tradesmen miscarry in all their affayrs
And few men grow wealthy, but Courtiers and Players.

A Craver my father,
A Maunder my mother,
A Filer my sister, a Filcher my brother,
A Canter my Unckle,
That cared not for Pelfe,
A Lifter my aunt, a Beggar myselfe.

In white wheaten straw, when their bellies were full,
Then I was begot, between Tinker and Trul.
And therefore a Beggar, a Beggar I'le be,
For none hath a spirit so jocond as he.

When Boyes do come to us,
And that their intent is
To follow our Calling, we nere bind them Prentice,
Soon as they come too't,
We teach them to doo't,
And give them a Staff and a Wallet to boot.
We teach them their Lingua, to Crave and to Cant,
The devil is in them if then they can want.
If any are here that Beggars will bee,
We without Indentures will make them free.

We begg for our bread,
But sometimes it happens
We feast with Pigg, Pullet, Conny and Capons
For Churche's affairs
We are no Man-slayers
We have no religion, yet live by our prayers.
But if when we begg, Men will not draw their purses,
We charge and give fire, with a volley of curses,
The Devil confound your good Worship we cry,
And such a bold brazen fac'd Beggar am I.

London.   Printed for *W. Thackeray, T. Passenger,* and
W. Whitwood.

[82.] A Justice of the Peace committed a fellow to prison, and commanded him away three or foure times, but stil the fellow intreated him.   Sirrah, (said the Justice) must I bid you bee gone so many times, and will you not goe?   The fellow answered, Sir, if your worship had bidden mee to dinner or supper, I should in my poore manners not to have taken your offer under two or three biddings ; therefore I pray you blame me not if I looke for foure biddings to prison.

[26.] King James being in his Progress at Woodstock in Oxfordshire, the King, finding it to rain so one morning that he could not ride a hunting, had got some Nobility and Gentry together, resolving to be merry.   And one humour was, that the King having that morning a fine curvetting Horse given him, which kind of Horse he never lik'd in his life, told them that he that could tell the greatest lie should have that Horse. So one told one lie, and another, another : and several had told others, that there was great laughing ; and just in the midst of this mirth in comes a Country Fellow, complaining to the King that some of his Servants had wrong'd him : Well, well, says the King, we'll hear you of that anon ; come, come hither amongst us, and you must know that he that can tell the greatest lie shall have that horse.   Truly Sir, says he, an't please your Grace, I never told a lie in all my life.   With that says the King, Give him the Horse, give him the Horse, for I am sure that is the greatest lie that has been told to day.

[94.] A yong lascivious Gallant wanting money, could not with his credit sell anything; yet his father being but lately dead, at length was checkt by some of his friends for his loose and extravagant life, and withal told him he had base and beastly Associates that did draw him to ill houses. He, taking this opportunity, answered, Truly, Friends, your Counsel is very good, I will presently go sell my Coach and Horses.

[17.] One being desired to eat some Oysters, refused, saying they were ungodly meat, unchristianly meat, uncharitable meat, and unprofitable meat. And being demanded his reason why he said it, he answered, They were ungodly meat, because they were eaten without saying of Grace; unchristianly meat because the Creature was eaten alive; uncharitable meat, because they left no offal to the poor, and unprofitable meat, because most commonly there was more spent upon them than the Oysters cost.

[110.] Maister *Hobson*, and another of his neighbours, on a time walking to Southwarke faire, by chance drunke in a house which had the signe of Sa. *Christopher*, of the which signe the good man of the house gave this commendation; Saint *Christopher* (quoth he) when hee lived upon the earth bore the greatest burden that ever was, which was this, he bore Christ over a river. Nay there was one (quoth maister *Hobson*) that bore a greater burden; Who was that (quoth the in keeper). Mary, quoth Maister *Hobson*, the asse that bore both him and his mother: so was the Inne keeper called asse by Craft. After this, talking merely together, the aforsaid Inne keeper being a little whitled[1] with drinke, & his head so giddy that he fell into the fire, people standing by, ran sodainely and tooke him up; oh let him alone (quoth Maist. *Hobson*) a man may doe what he will in his owne house, and lie where so ever he listeth. The man having little hurt, with this sight grew immediately sober, and, after, foxed Maister *Hobson* and his neighbour so mightely, that comming over London bridge, being very late, ranne against one of the posts, which Maister *Hobson* thinking it to bee some man that had justled him, drew

[1] Intoxicated.

out his dodgion [1] dagger, and thrust it up into the very hilt into the hollow post; whereupon verely hee had thought hee had kil'd some man : so, running away, was taken by the watch, and so all the Jest was discovered.

[52.] A mad fellow newly married, had onely one young child by his wife, of some quarter old, whom he dearly and tenderly loved, but he was much given to good fellowship, and she altogether addicted to sparing, & good huswifery : still he used to come merry home from the taverne from his boone companions, to her great griefe, she being as sparing of her purse, as prodigall of her tongue, for she was little better than a Scold, would oft upbraid him with his expences of money, and time, and to be so often drunke was prejudiciall both to his estate and bodily health, and that it were far better to spend that at home in his house than in a Taverne ; with such Matron like speeches, always concluding her exhortations with a vow that if ever he came home again in the like pickle she would (happen what would come) fling the Child into the Moat (for the house was moted round.) It happned shortly after, that he revelling till late in a cold frosty Winter evening, she having intelligence by her scouts where hee was, made no doubt hee would come home flustred. She commands the Infant to bee convaied to the farther part of the house, and to wrap the Cat in the blankets, put it in the Cradle, and there sit and rocke it. Presently comes her Husband, she fals to her old lesson of quarrelling with him, and hee with her, ill words begot worse, much lewd language past betwixt them. The woman suddenly steps to the Cradle (having spied her advantage ;) I have long threatned thee a mischiefe, and that revenge I cannot worke on thee (come doggs, come devills) I will inflict on thy Brat in the Cradle ; instantly snatched it up in her armes, and ran with it to the Moat side, and flings it into the middle of the water : the poore man much affrighted, leaves to pursue her, and leaps into the water, up in mud and water to the very chinne, crying, Save, oh save the child. Now waded he in the Moat in a very bitter cold frost, till he brought out the Mantle, and with much paine and danger comes to the shore, and still

---

[1] A dudgeon dagger was one having a *boxwood* handle.

crying, Alas, my poore childe, opened the Cloathes : At length the frighted Cat cryed Mew, and being at liberty leapt from betwixt his armes, and ranne away.   The husband both amazed and vexed, the woman heartily laughed at her revenge, and the poore man was glad to reconcile the difference before she would either give him fire or dry linnen.

[26.] A dear and Loving wife, that always bore a great respect to her Husband, both in Sickness and in Health, and now did make it appear to the very last.   For when her dear Husband was, in *Essex*, condemned to die, for a small matter God knows, that is only for stealing four or five Horses, and breaking up as many Houses ; so this sweet loving Soul his wife, hearing where he was, came and gave him a visit.   Wife, says he, you see what I am come to now, prithee pray for me, and have a care to bring up our Children in the fear of God. Husband, says she, as soon as I heard of it, you see I came to you, and as you know I have always been loving to you, you shall now find it at the last.   Pray Husband, tell me, are we to be at the charge of a Rope, or they, for I would have all things ready to do you a kindness ; for here I have brought one forty Miles to do you a Courtesie, And so left the Rope with him.   Well, wife, says he, I thank you heartily, and pray go home, and look after the Children.   No, Husband, says she, I have not come so far, but a Grace a God I'll see you hang'd before I go.

[17.] A Countrey man passing by St Pauls Church, at such time as it was turn'd from a House of Prayer, to be a den of Thieves ; I mean, an unsanctified Guard of Souldiers : He seeing what manner of Cattle inhabited it, asked a Shopkeeper hard by, If that place were Noah's Ark ?   Being asked the reason of his demand, Because, said he, I see so many unclean beasts therein.

[105.] When *Scogin* and his man had ridden ten or twelve miles on their way, hee overtooke a Priest that was riding to London, to pay his first fruits, with whom he kept company untill he came to Stamford, and all that way as they rode, *Scogin* made the Priest very good cheere, and would let him

pay no money, so that *Scogin* had but two shillings left : and
riding betweene Stamford & Huntington, *Scogin* complayned
him to the Parson in this sort : I marvell master Parson (quoth
he) how men doe when they want money, to get it ? For when
I want money, I know not how to get any, except I should
steale. No, no, said the Priest, doe you not know that they
that serve God well, doe not want, and how that God promiseth,
that if you call upon him in your afflictions, that hee will helpe
you ? You say well, master Parson, said *Scogin*, and rode
before ; and when hee saw a faire place, hee kneeled downe
and lifted up his hands, and prayed to God, till Master
Parson and his man did overtake him, but nothing hee could
get. When they were come, hee told them he prayed, but
could get nothing. But (quoth he) I will try once againe, and
then if I can get nothing, both you, Master Parson and my
man shall helpe me to pray, for I doe not doubt but God will
helpe something, when hee heareth all our prayers. And then
Scogin did ride before againe, and when hee saw his place
convenient, hee alighted him from his horse and tied him to a
tree, and kneeled downe, and prayed as hee had done before,
until such time as they came to him. Then, said the Parson,
How do you now, Master *Scogin ?* By my troth, said he, I
can get nothing ; wherefore, alight, sirra, quoth he to his man,
and tie your horse to yonder tree, and then hee went to the
Parson, and took his horse by the bridle, and told him hee
must needes helpe him to pray. The Parson for feare durst
not say him nay, but alighted, and tooke his capcase[1] from the
saddle bow, wherein was fifty pounds. Then *Scogin* asked his
man how much money hee had in his purse ? He sayd, twenty
pence. By my troth, said *Scogin*, and I have but two shillings,
and how much have you Master Parson ? said hee. The
Parson thought that if he had told him all, hee would surely
have borrowed a good part of it, and he said, five pounds.
Well, let us pray hartily, said *Scogin*, and then they kneeled
downe, and prayed for the space of halfe an houre ; and *Scogin*
said, let us see whether God have heard our request, or no.
And then, he looked in his own purse, where was but two
shillings, and then he looked in his man's purse, where was

[1] A small leather travelling case.

but twenty pence. Then *Scogin* came to the Parson, and said, Now Master Parson, let us see what you have, for I doe not doubt but God hath heard our prayers; and tooke the Priests capcase and opened it, wherein was a bag with fifty Pounds in it, which the Parson should have paid for his first fruits. Then *Scogin* spread his cloake abroad, and poured out the money, and when hee had told it, hee said, By Lady, Master Parson, God hath heard our prayer; and then hee gave him five pounds, and said, Master Parson, here is the five pound that thou had before wee began to pray, and the rest we will have; for I see that you are so well acquainted with God, that with praying halfe an houre, you can get as much more : and this will doe us great pleasure, and it is but a small matter for you to pray halfe an houre. The Parson desired Scogin to let him have the rest of the money, for hee said that hee did ride to London to pay his first fruits. Well, said *Scogin*, then you must pray againe, for wee will have this, and so they rode away, and left the Priest behind them : and the Priest was faine to ride home againe for more money.

[82.] In Queene *Elizabeths* dayes there was a fellow that wore a brooch in his hat, like a tooth drawer, with a Rose and Crowne and two letters : this fellow had a warrant from the Lord Chamberlaine at that time to travell with an exceeding brave Ape which hee had; whereby hee gat his living from time to time at markets and fayres : his Ape did alwayes ride upon a mastiffe dog, and a man with a drum to attend him. It happened that these foure travellers came to a towne called *Looe* in *Cornwall*, where the Inne being taken, the drum went about to signifie to the people that at such an Inne was an Ape of singular vertue and quality, if they pleased to bestow their time and money to see him. Now the townsmen, being honest labouring Fishers, and other painfull functions, had no leasure to waste either time or coyne in *Ape tricks*, so that no audience came to the Inne, to the great griefe of *Jack an Apes* his Master; who, collecting his wits together, resolved to adventure to put a tricke upon the towne, whatsoever came of it ; whereupon hee took pen, inke, and paper and wrote a warrant to the Mayor of the towne as followeth.

These are to will and require you, and every of you, with your wives and families, that upon the sight hereof, you make your personall appearance before the Queenes Ape, for it is an Ape of ranke and quality, who is to be practised throughout her Majesties dominions, that by his long experience amongst her loving subjects, hee may bee the better enabled to doe her Majesty service hereafter ; and hereof faile you not, as you will answer the contrary. &c.

This warrant being brought to the Mayor, he sent for a shoomaker at the furthest end of the towne to read it ; which when he heard, hee sent for all his brethren, who went with him to the Towne Hall to consult upon this waighty businesse. Where after they had sate a quarter of an houre, no man saying any thing, nor any man knowing what to say ; at last a young man that never had borne any office, said, Gentlemen, if I were fit to speake, I thinke (without offence, under correction of the Worshipfull) that I should soone decide this businesse ; to whom the Mayor said, I pray good neighbour speake, for though you never did beare any office here, yet you may speake as wisely as some of us. Then sir, said the young man, my opinion is that this Ape carrier is a gybing scoffing knave, and one that doth purpose to make this towne a jesting mocking stocke throughout the whole Kingdome : for was it ever knowne that a fellow should be so impudent audacious, as to send a Warrant without either name or date, to a Mayor of a towne, to the Queenes Lieutenant, and that he with his brethren, their wives and families should be all commanded to come before a *Jack an Apes* ? My counsell is, that you take him and his Ape, with his man, and his dog, and whip the whole messe or murrinal[1] of them out of the towne, which I thinke will be much for your credit if you doe.

At which words a grave man of the towne being much moved, said, My friend, you have spoken little better than treason, for it is the Queene's *Ape*, and therefore beware what you say ; you say true, said master Mayor, I muse who bad

---

[1] Or all four of them. A corruption of murnival or mournival. The "Compleat Gamester" says, "A *Mournival* is either all the aces, the four kings, queens or knaves, and a *gleek* is three of any of the aforesaid."

that saucy fellow come into our Company, I pray thee, my
friend, depart; I thinke you long to have us all hanged. So
in briefe hee was put out of the doores, for they were no company for him. Well now, what is to bee done in this matter?
Marry (said another Senior) wee see by the Brooch in the
mans hat that hee is the Queenes man, and who knowes what
power a knave may have in the Court, to doe poore men
wrong in the Country, let us goe and see the *Ape*, it is but
two pence a peece, and no doubt but it will be well taken,
and if it come to the Queenes eare, shee will thinke us kinde
people that would shew so much duty to her *Ape*, what may
shee thinke wee would doe to her Beares if they came hither?
besides, it is above 200 miles to *London*, and if wee should
bee complained on and fetched up with Pursinants,[1] whereas
now every man may escape for his two pence, Ile warrant it
would cost us ten groats a peece at the least. This counsell
passed currant, and all the whole drove of the townsmen, with
wives and children, went to see the *Ape*, who was sitting on a
table with a chaine about his necke, to whom, master Mayor
(because it was the Queenes *Ape*) put off his hat, and made
a leg, but *Jacke* let him passe unregarded. But mistris
Mayoresse comming next in her cleane linnen, held her hands
before her belly, and like a woman of good breeding, made a
low curtsie, whilest Jacke, (still Court-like) although (he)
respected not the man, yet to expresse his courtesie to his
wife, hee put forth his paw towardes her, and made a mouth,
which the woman perceiving, said, Husband, I doe think in
my Conscience that the Queenes *Ape* doth mock mee: whereat Jacke made another mouth at her, which master Mayor
espying, was very angry, saying, Sirrah, thou *Ape*, I doe see
thy saucinesse, and if the rest of the courtiers have no more
manners than thou hast then they have all bin better fed than
taught: and I will make thee know before thou goest from
hence, that this woman is my wife, an ancient woman, and a
midwife, and one that might bee thy mother for age.

In this rage master Mayor went to the Inne doore, where
Jack an Apes tutor was gathering of money, to whom hee said,
Sir, doe you allow your *Ape* to abuse my Wife? No sir, quoth

---

[1] Pursuivants

the other, not by any meanes ; truly, said the Mayor, there is witnesse enough within that have seene him make mops and mowes at her, as if shee were not worthy to wipe his shooes, and I will not so put it up. *Jack's* tutor replyed, Sir, I will presently give him condigne punishment ; and straight hee tooke his Flanders blade, his Whip, and holdinge his *Ape* by the chaine, hee gave him halfe a dozen jerks, which made his teeth daunce in his head like so many Virginal Jackes :[1] Which master Mayor perceiving, ranne to him, and held his hands, saying, enough, enough, good Sir, you have done like a Gentleman, let mee intreat you not to give correction in your wrath ; and I pray you and your *Ape* after the Play is done, to come to my house and sup with mee and my wife.

[17.] King James keeping his Court at *Theobalds*,[2] in a time of some contagion, divers Constables with their watchmen were set at several places to hinder the concourse of people from flocking thither, without some necessary occasion : Amongst others, one Gentleman (being somewhat in the Garb of a Serving man) was examined what Lord he belonged unto ? To which he readily replyed, *To the Lord Jehovah:* which words being beyond the Constables understanding, he asked his Watchmen, if they knew any such Lord ? They replyed No— : However the Constable being unwilling to give distast, said, Well, let him pass, notwithstanding ; *I believe it is some Scottish Lord or other.*

[26.] A Gentleman having drank very hard at the Kings Head Tavern, came Reeling out up *Chancery Lane*, and

---

[1] A jack was usually made of pear tree, and rested on the back end of the key lever. It had a movable tongue of holly working in a centre and kept in its place by a bristle spring. A thorn or spike of crow quill projects at right angles from the tongue. On the key being depressed, the jack is forced upwards, and the quill is brought to the string, which it twangs in passing. Queen Elizabeth's virginal has fifty jacks and quills.

[2] Is in the parish of Cheshunt, co. Hertford. Was originally the seat of Lord Burleigh, whom Elizabeth frequently visited. It was used as a hunting lodge by James I., and Charles I. often resided there. William III. gave it to his friend Bentinck, Earl of Portland. In 1765 the remains of the old palace were pulled down, and the new mansion is now the seat of Sir Henry Meux, Bart.

chanced to Reel within the Rails of the Pump, and kept his motion round so long that he was tired; whereupon, leaning on the Rail he askt one that passed by, where he was; he told him over against the *Chancery.* I thought so (says he) and thats the Reason I think I shall never get out of this place.

[94.] A Welchman that had one of his own Countrey men waiting upon him, went to see a Comedy, and drawing out a Purse of gold and silver at the door, was espied by a Cut purse and dog'd, who seated himself close by him, his servant having all this while a careful eye towards his Master, and jealous of the Cut purse, so that whilest his Master was minding his sport, the Cheater got all his gold and silver out of his pocket, and was about to be gone. The little Welchman's blood rising at it, presently drew out his knife, and cut off his ear, which made the fellow startle, and troubled with the smart thereof, ask't what he meant by it? To whom the Welchman replied, shewing him his ear in his hand, No great harm friend, onely give hur Master hur purse, and I will give hur hur ear.

[105.] *Scogin* waxing sicker and sicker, his friends advertised him to make his Testament, and to shew where he would lye after hee was dead: Friends, said *Scogin*, when I came into this World, I brought nothing with me, and when I shall depart out of this world, I shall take nothing away but a sheet; take you the sheet, and let mee have the beginning againe naked. And if you cannot doe this for me, I pray you that I may be buried at the East side of Westminster, under one of the spouts of the leads, for I have ever loved good drinke all the dayes of my life, and there was he buried.

When the extreame pangs of death came upon *Scogin*, the holy Candle was put in his hand to blesse himselfe. When *Scogin* had done so, in surrendring thankes to God, hee said, Now the proverbe is fulfilled, that he that worst may shall hold the Candle, for ever the weakest is thrust to the wall.

On the syllable Con.

[17.] Dogs concurr, Steeples conspire wheels converse,

Lawyers contend, and Nurses can tend too, Foxes consent, Minors condescend, Women conceive, Apple mongers consider, Millstones contrive, Prisoners congeal, Rope makers concord, Scriveners condition, Faggotters combine, Jaylors confine, Sick men consume, Drums convene, and Scolds can vex, Commanders conduct, great Officers controul, Ducks can dive, Mourners condole, Clouds condense, great Schollars convince, Parishioners Congregate, Country Shoemakers contribute, viz Countrey boot, Gamesters are concise which does not much Conduce to their winning, grave Counsellors conceal, Cardinals conclave, School boys construe, Countrey fellows conjoble.[1] Judges condemn, Friars confess, Jesuites confute, and Friends conferr together. Politicians consult, Blind men connive, and Cutlers connive too. Proud men contemn, Disputants contest together, Landlords confirm, and their Tenants can farm any thing they let out ; Bells convoke, that is call Vokes together, Smiths contaminate, defile, that is do file, and I, like an Epilogue *conclude*.

FINIS.

[1] From *con*, together, and *jobbernol*, head. To concert, to settle, to discuss.

APPENDIX.

BIBLIOGRAPHICAL REFERENCE

TO THE SOURCES

WHENCE THIS BOOK WAS COMPILED.

[1.] C. 40, a. 11. The Sackfull of Newes. London. Printed by Andrew Clark, and are to be sold by Thomas Passenger,[1] at the Three Bibles upon London Bridge. 1673 (B.L.)

[2.] Additional MSS. 12,049. Epigrams &c of Sir John Harington, Knight.

[3.] E. 1617. Wit and Drollery, Jovial Poems. Never before Printed. By Sir J. M. Ja. S. Sir W. D. J. D.[2] And other admirable Wits— London. Printed for Nath Brook[3] at the Angel in Cornhill. 18 Jan. 1656 (? 1655 O.S.). Catalogued under P.(J.)

[4.] 12,316, a. 20. England's Jests Refin'd and Improv'd, being a Choice Collection of the Merriest Jests, Smartest Repartees, Wittiest Sayings, and most Notable Bulls, yet extant; with many New ones, never before Printed &c. 3rd Edition *London*. Printed for *John Harris*, at the *Harrow* in the *Poultry*. 1693. Catalogued H. C. (Humphrey Crouch).

[5.] 11,601, b.b. 23. Witts Recreations. Selected from the finest Fancies of Moderne Muses. With a Thousand out-Landish Proverbs. London. Printed for Humph. Blunden, at yᵉ Castle in Cornhill. 1640. Catalogued Wit.

[6.] 239, i. 25. Epigrams both Pleasant and Serious, *written by that All-Worthy Knight*, Sir Iohn Harrington, and never before Printed. London. Imprinted for *John Budge*,[4] and are to be sold at his shoppe at the south dore of *Pauls*, and at *Britaines Burse*[5] 1615.

---

[1] T. Passenger published between 1670 and 1682.
[2] Sir John Menzies, James Smith, Sir William Davenant, and John Dryden. The dedication and preface signed J.;P., *i.e.* John Playford, a publisher and writer of prefaces of that period.
[3] Nathaniel Brook published between 1661 and 1668.
[4] John Budge was in business in 1609, as one of the Roxburghe Ballads shows.
[5] Query, Royal Exchange.

[7.] $\frac{C.\ 20,\ f.\ 8}{534}$ Roxburghe Ballads.

[8.] Grenville, 10,381. Witty Apothegms delivered at Several Times and upon Several Occasions by King James King Charls, The Marquess of Worcester, Francis Lord Bacon, and Sir Thomas Moor. London. Printed for W. R. for *Matthew Smelt* and are to be sold at his Shop next to the *Castle* near *Moorgate* 1669.

[9.] Grenville, 10,374. Choice Chance and Change or Conceites in their Colours. Imprinted at London for *Nathaniell Fosbrooke*, and are to be sold at his shop in Pauls Churchyard at the signe of the Helmet, 1606.

[10.] $\frac{C.\ 20,\ f.\ 8}{554}$ Roxburghe Ballads.

[11.] $\frac{C.\ 20,\ f.\ 7}{158}$ Roxburghe Ballads.

[12.] 11,626, a. a. 36. Westminster Quibbles in verse : Being a MOCK to the *Crab* of the *Woood*, and to that Tune : or. a Miscellany of *Quibling*, *Catches*, *Joques* and Merriments. London. Printed for *William Cademan*,[1] at the Popes Head in the Lower Walk of the *New Exchange*. 1672.

[13.] Westminster Drollery, the Second Part, being a Compleat Collection of all the Newest and Choicest Songs and Poems at Court, and both the Theaters. By the *Author* of the First Part, never Printed before. London. Printed for *William Gilbert* at the Half Moon in *St Pauls* Church-yard, & *Tho. Sawbridge* at the three *Flower de Luces* in *Little Britain* 1672. (11,621, a. 45.)

[14.] Wits Interpreter the English Parnassus &c. The 3rd Edition with many new Additions By J. C(otgrave) London. 1671. (Grenville, 10,378.)

[15.] $\frac{C.\ 20,\ f.\ 8}{236.}$ Roxburghe Ballads.

[16.] The most Elegant and Wittie Epigrams of Sir John Harington Knight. Digested into foure Bookes.—London. Printed by George Miller 1633. $\left(\frac{638,\ k.\ 17}{2}\right)$

[17.] C. 40, b. 11. Oxford Jests Refined and Enlarged; being a Collection of Witty Jests, Merry Tales, & Pleasant Joques. Collected by Captain W. H.[2] Native of Oxford. London. Printed for Simon Miller, at the Star at the West End of St Paul's. 1684. Catalogued Hickes (W.)

[18.] Delight & Pastime or Pleasant Diversion for both sexes consisting of Good History &c &c—London. Printed for *J Sprint* at the *Bell*, and

---

[1] Cademan also published in 1675, as one of the Roxburghe Ballads bears that date.
[2] Nothing is known of Capt. Wm. Hickes, except as being the author of *Oxford Drolleries* and *Oxford Jests.*

G. Conyers at the *Gold Ring,* in *Little Britain,* over against the *Sugar Loaf.* 1697. Price 1/. Catalogued M.(G.)

[19.] $\frac{C.\ 20,\ f.\ 8}{226}$ Roxburghe Ballads.

[20.] $\frac{C.\ 20,\ f.\ 8}{227}$ Roxburghe Ballads.

[21.] $\frac{C.\ 22,\ c.\ 2}{110}$ A Collection of English Ballads.

[22.] $\frac{C.\ 20,\ f.\ 8}{279}$ Roxburghe Ballads.

[23.] $\frac{C.\ 20,\ f.\ 8}{359}$ Roxburghe Ballads.

[24.] C. 40, a. 1.   Wit Restor'd in severall select Poems not formerly publish't. London. Printed for *R. Pollard, N. Brooks* and *T. Dring,*[1] and are to be sold at the Old *Exchange,* and in *Fleet Street.* 1658. Catalogued Wit.

[25.] 1078, e. 2.   Norfolk Drollery, Or a Compleat Collection of the Newest Songs, Jovial Poems, and Catches &c—By the Author, M. *Stevenson. London.* Printed for *R. Reynolds,*[2] at the *Sun* and *Bible,* and *John Lutton* at the *Blue Anchor* in the *Poultry.* 1673. Catalogued Stevenson.

[26.] Coffee House Jests Refined and Enlarged. By the Author of the Oxford Jests. The Fourth Edition, with Large Additions. London. Printed for *Hen. Rhodes,* next door to the *Swan Tavern,* near *Bride Lane* in *Fleet Street.* 1686. Catalogued Coffee House Jests. 12,316, a. 15.

[27.] $\frac{816,\ m.\ 9}{31}$

[28.] $\frac{C.\ 20,\ f.\ 9}{74}$ Roxburghe Ballads.

[29.] $\frac{C.\ 20,\ f.\ 7}{42}$ Roxburghe Ballads.

[30.] $\frac{C.\ 20,\ f.\ 8}{51}$ Roxburghe Ballads.

[31.] $\frac{C.\ 20,\ f.\ 7}{340}$ Roxburghe Ballads.

[32.] C. 40, a. 6.   The Booke of Merry Riddles, together with proper Questions, and witty Proverbs, to make pleasant pastime. No lesse usefull than behoovefull for any young man or child, to know if he be quick witted, or no. London. Printed for *John Stafford,*[3] and *W.G,* and are to be sold at the *George* near *Fleetbridg.* 1660.

[33.] $\frac{660,\ f.\ 10}{99}$ Single Sheets.

---

[1] Published between 1650 and 1687.   [2] Rowland Reynolds published also in 1671.
[3] Published from 1631 to 1660. Mr. Halliwell reprinted this little book in 1866. He says, "It is believed to be unique. It is an edition with many variations of the old Book of Riddles alluded to by Slender." The copy in the British Museum has a pencil note, "Cost me ten pounds unbound." It is in black letter.

[34.] $\frac{669,\ f.\ 10}{106}$ Single Sheets.

[35.] $\frac{C.\ 20,\ f.\ 8}{112}$ The Roxburghe Ballads.

[36.] $\frac{E.\ 246}{23}$ A Dialogue or Rather a Parley betweene Prince *Ruperts* Dogge, whose name is PUDDLE and *Tobies* Dog whose name is PEPPER &c. Whereunto is added the Challeng which Prince *Griffins* Dogg called *Towzer* hath sent to Prince *Ruperts* Dogg Puddle, in the behalf of honest Pepper Tobies Dog. Moreover the said Prince *Griffin* is newly gone to Oxford to lay the Wager, and to make up the MATCH. Printed at London for I. Smith 1643.

[37.] $\frac{E.\ 99}{14}$ The Bloody Prince, or a declaration of the most cruell Practices of Prince Rupert, and the rest of the Cavaliers in fighting against God, and the true Members of His Church. By I. W. London. Printed 1643. Catalogued W. (I.)

[38.] 12,613 c. The History of the Blind Begger of Bednal Green.

[39.] $\frac{E.\ 92}{13}$ The Parliaments unspotted Bitch: in answer to Prince Roberts Dog called *Boy*, And his Malignant She Monkey. London. Printed for R. Jackson 1643.[1] Catalogued England.

[40.] $\frac{E.\ 96}{16}$ The Welsh Embassadour, Or the happy Newes his Worship hath brought to London, &c—Printed for *I. Underwood* 1643.[1]

[41.] 11,609, c. 6. The Works of Mr John Cleveland &c—London. Printed by *R Holt* for *Obadiah Blagrave* at the *Bear* and *Star*, over against the little North Door in St *Paul's* Church yard 1687.

[42.] $\frac{669,\ f.\ 11}{84}$ The Braggadocia Souldier: and the Civill Citizen. Printed for J. L. 1647.

[43.] $\frac{E.\ 3}{17}$ A Dogs Elegy, or Ruperts Tears[2] for the late Defeat given him at *Marston moore*, neer *York*, by the Three Renowned Generalls *Alexander Earl of* Leven, *Generall of the Scottish Forces*, Fardinando *Lord* Fairefax, *and the Earle of* Manchester Generalls of the English Forces in the North. Where his beloved Dog named BOY, was killed by a Valliant Souldier, who had skill in *Necromancy*. *Likewise the strange breed of this Shagg'd* Cavalier, *whelp'd of a Malignant* Water-witch; with all his tricks and feats.

> Sad Caveliers, *Rupert* invites you all
> That doe survive, to his Dogs Funerall.
> Close mourners are the Witch, Pope, & devill,
> That much lament yo'r late befallen evill.

Printed at *London* for G. B. July 27. 1644.

---

1 This, as far as I can learn, is the only year of his publishing.

2 These (said to be the invention of Prince Rupert) are small pear-shaped bubbles of glass, formed by dropping melted glass in water. They will bear a smart stroke on the thick end, but if the thin end is fractured, which is done very easily, they are resolved into a very fine powder, bursting with a slight explosion. These toys are easily procurable.

[44.] $\frac{E.3}{11}$ The Kingdomes Weekly Intelligencer. Catalogued P.P. London.

[45.] $\frac{E.3}{13}$ A CONTINUATION of Certain Speciall and Remarkable passages informed to the PARLIAMENT, and otherwise from divers parts of this Kingdome, from Wednesday the 10th of *July*, till Wednesday the 17. of *July*. 1644. Catalogued P. P. London. Special and Remarkable Passages.

[46.] $\frac{E.2}{24}$ Ruperts Sumpter, and Private Cabinet rifled. And a Discovery of his *Jewels* By way of Dialogue between Mercurius *Britannicus* and Mercurius *Aulicus*. London. Printed by J. Coe[1] A.D. 1644. Catalogued Rupert.

[47.] $\frac{E.4}{4}$ The Catholike's Petition to Prince *Rupert* showing The ground of their Griefe, The force of their Constancie, and their hopes of Recovery. With a Draught of a *Proclamation* presented to his Highnesse, for the more speedy Recruiting his Army, destroying the Protestants, and gaining a Crowne.

> Prince looke about thee, here is much adoe,
> 'Tis time to looke, and lay about thee too ;
> Send obstinate offenders to their graves.
> That neither will be Catholikes nor slaves.

Printed according to Order for G. B.[2] August 1. 1644. Catalogued Catholics.

[48.] $\frac{E.2}{1}$ A Continuation of true Intelligence from the *English* and *Scottish* Forces, in the North, for the service of King and Parliament, and now beleaguering York, from the 16th of June to Wednesday the 10th of *July*. 1644. Wherein is given a full and particular Accompt of the Battaile with Prince Rupert, and the Marquesse New Castle together with the successe thereof. By Sim. Ash. Chaplaine to the Earle of *Manchester*, and one of the Ministers of the Assembly. London. Printed for *Thomas Underhill*, at the Bible in Woodstreet. 1644.

[49.] $\frac{E.90}{25}$ An exact description of Prince *Rupert's* Malignant She-Monkey, a great Delinquent : Having approved herselfe a better servant, than his white Dog called *Boy*. Laid open in three particulars : 1. What she is in her owne shape. 2. What she doth figuratively signifie. 3. Her malignant tricks and qualities. Printed for *E. Johnson*. 1642 (a misprint for 1643). Catalogued Ruperts.

[50.] $\frac{E.93}{9}$ The Humerous Tricks and Conceits of Prince *Roberts* Malignant She-Monkey, discovered to the world before her marriage. Also the

---

[1] Jane Coe published between 1644 and 1647.
[2] Probably G. Bishop, who published from 1641 to 1644.

manner of her marriage to a Cavaleer, and how within three dayes space, she called him Cuckold to his face. London, printed for T. Cornish. (There is no date, but it must have been in the same year as [49.]) Catalogued Rupert. Prince.

[51.] C. 39, e. 58. Doctor Merry-man : or Nothing but Mirth. Written by S. R. London Printed for *Samuell Rand,* and are to be sold at his Shoppe neere Holborne bridge. 1616. Catalogued R.(s.)

[52.] C. 40, c. 33. Pasquil's Jests with the Merriments of Mother Bunch. Wittie pleasant, and delightfull. London. Printed by I. F, and are to be sold by *William Gilbertson*[1] at the signe of the Bible in Giltspur-street. (1650?)

[53.] $\frac{C. 20, f. 8}{254}$ Roxburghe Ballads.

[54.] 2044, g. Bartholomew Fayre : A Comedie, Acted in the Yeare 1614 By the Lady Elizabeths Servants, And then dedicated to King IAMES, of *most Blessed Memorie.* By the Author, Beniamin Johnson. London. Printed by I. B. for Robert Allot, and are to be sold at the signe of the *Beare,* in *Pauls* Church-yard. 1631.

[55.] $\frac{C. 20, f. 7}{214}$ Roxburghe Ballads.

[56.] $\frac{C. 20, f. 7}{325.}$ Roxburghe Ballads.

[57.] $\frac{C. 20, f. 7}{254.}$ Roxburghe Ballads.

[58.] $\frac{669, f. 10}{105}$ Single Sheets. 1646.

[59.] Harl. MSS. $\frac{5947}{166}$

[60.] $\frac{C. 20, f. 10}{76}$ Roxburghe Ballads.

[61.] 12,315, a. 11. Mirth in abundance. Set forth and made manifest in many Jests, upon severall occasions, full of Wit and Truth. Contriv'd to relieve the Melancholy, and rejoyce the Merry, to expell sorrow, and advance Jollity. All of them New and Noble, free from Rayling, Baudery, Blasphemy or Incivility. Collected and set together by a lover of lawfull Mirth and true hearted Society. London. Printed for *Francis Grove,* neere the Saracens Head on Snow Hill. 1659.

[62.] Harl. MSS. $\frac{5947}{167}$

[63.] $\frac{C. 20, f. 7}{384}$ Roxburghe Ballads.

[64.] $\frac{E. 1351}{2}$ The Astrologer's Bugg-beare : Being a briefe Description of many Pitthy Passages, which were brought to passe upon that day which the Astrologers pointed out for Black-Monday : Whereby wee may all see

---

1 Gilbertson published between 1640 and 1663.

and know that God's power is beyond man's expectation. Mark well and take notice, it is worth your observation. Written by L. P. London. Printed for *Sicnarf Seloe*, in the Yeare of the downfall of darke Astrology, and are to be sold in Country and City, by honest, harmlesse people, that love *England* and its Friends. Catalogued P.(L.)

[65.] 644. b. 56. The Alchemist written by Ben Ionson.

——Neque, me ut miretur turba, laboro :
Contentus paucis lectoribus.

London printed by *Thomas Snodham*[1] for *Walter Burre*,[2] and are sold by *John Stepneth* at the West End of Paules. 1612.

[66.] $\frac{C. 20, f. 8}{78}$ Roxburghe Ballads.

[67.] Ad. MSS. 15,227. Sir John Harringtons Epigrams.

[68.] $\frac{C. 20, f. 9}{212}$ Roxburghe Ballads.

[69.] $\frac{E. 135!}{5}$ No-Body his Complaint. Dialogue between Master No-Body, and Doctour Some-Body. A delightfull Discourse, by George Baron

No-Body *Why do'st thou father all thy Lies*
On me ? heaping Indignities
On one that never injur'd thee ?
Some-Body *My Words and Acts hurt* No-Body.
No-Body. Som-Body *hath belied me much,*
No-Body *sure hath cause to grutch.*

London. Printed by B. Alsop,[3] dwelling near the Upper-Pomp in Grub Street. 1652.

[70.] 2044, g. Ionson's Works. Vol. 1. Epigrammes. 1. Booke. The Author B. I.[4] London. 1616.[5]

[71.] $\frac{C. 20, f. 9}{88}$ Roxburghe Ballads.

[72.] Grenville, 16,427. Ar't asleepe Husband? A Boulster Lecture. Stored With all variety of Witty jeasts, merry Tales, and other pleasant passages; Extracted from the choicest flowers of Philosophy, Poesy, antient and moderne History. Illustrated with Examples of incomparable constancy, in the excellent History of *Philocles* and *Doriclea*. By *Philogenes Panedonius*. London, Printed by R. Bishop, for Richard Best, and are to be sold at his shop neare Graies-Inne-gate in Holeborne. 1646.

[73.] $\frac{C. 39, k. vol. 2}{171}$ Bagford Ballads.

1 Alias *East*, published between 1609 and 1612.   2 Certainly published in 1600.
3 Published between 1650 and 1652.   4 Ben Jonson.
5 I cannot find a separate edition of these Epigrams, although there is this entry in the Register of the Stationers Company: " John Stepneth. 15to Maii 1612. Entred for his Copy vnder th' (h)andes of master Nydd, and Th(e) wardens, A booke called, Ben Johnson his Epigrams. vj^d. "

[74] $\frac{E. 1640}{3}$ Here's Jack in a Box, that will Coniure the Fox, or a new List of the new Fashions now used in *London.*

> Come who buyes Jack in a Box,
> That will Cunjure the Fox,
> And move them to delight :
> It may serve as I may say,
> For to passe the time away,
> In the long Winter nights,
> To sit by a good fire,
> When the Season doth require,
> Your Body to keepe warme :
> This Booke of merriment
> Will yield you sweet content,
> And doe you no harme.
> This new merry Booke was newly Invented,
> But never before this time Imprinted.

Written by *Laurence Price* in the moneth of October. 1656.—London, Printed for *Tho. Vere*[1] at the *Angel* without *Newgate.*

[75.] Grenville, 11,163. The Wits, or Sport upon Sport. Being a curious Collection of several Drols and Farces, Presented and Shewn For the Merriment and Delight of Wise Men, and the Ignorant. As they have been sundry times Acted in Publique, and Private, In London at Bartholomew, In the Countrey at other Faires. In Halls and Taverns, On several Mountebancks Stages, at Charing Cross, Lincolns Inn Fields, and other places. By Several Stroleing Players, Fools, and Fidlers, and the Mountebancks Zainies with Loud Laughter, and great Applause. Written I know not when, by several Persons, I know not who, But now newly Collected by your Old Friend to please you. Francis Kirkman.[2] London, 1672.

[76.] $\frac{C. 20, f. 7}{343}$ Roxburghe Ballads.

[77.] 12,331, b. 42. Tarlton's Jests. Drawne into these three parts. 1. His Court Witty Iests. 2. His found City Iests. 3. His Countrey-pretty Iests. full of delight, Wit and honest Mirth. London. Printed by IH.[3] for Andrew Crook, and are to be sold in Pauls Church-yard, at the signe of the Beare. 1638.

[78.] C. 40, a. 22. Conceits, Clinches, Flashes, and Whimzies. Newly studied, with some Collections, but those never published before in this kinde. London. Printed by *R. Hodgkinsonne* for *Daniel Frere,* and are to be sold at the signe of the red *Bull* in *little Brittain.* 1639.

[79.] $\frac{669, f. 11}{121}$ (Single Sheets) 25 Jan. 1647.

[80.] $\frac{C. 22, e. 2}{153}$ A Collection of Ballads.

[81.] 11,623, a.a.a. 32. Epigrammes written on purpose to be read : with a Proviso that they may be understood by the Reader, being Ninety in Number : Besides two new made Satyres that attend them. By John

---

[1] He published from 1648 to 1680.   [2] Kirkman also published in 1661.
[3] In all probability Joseph Hunt in Bedlem, near Moore field gate, who printed in 1613.

Taylor,[1] at the Signe of the Poet's Head, in Phœnix Alley, neare the middle of Long Aker, or Covent Garden. London. Printed in the Yeare 1651.

[82.] **79, h. 22.** "Wit & Mirth" in "All the Workes of Iohn Taylor the Water poet being 63 in number, collected into one Volum by the Author with sundry new Additions, Corrected, Revised, and newly Imprinted. 1630.

[83.] $\frac{\text{C. 39, k. vol. 3}}{88}$ The Bagford Ballads.

[84.] $\frac{\text{C. 22, e. 2}}{210}$ A Collection of Ballads.

[85.] **1078, g. 15.** Covent Garden Drollery, or a Collection of all the Choice Songs, Poems, Prologues and Epilogues, Sung and Spoken at Courts and Theaters) never in Print before. Written by the refind'st Witts of the Age. And Collected by A(lexander) B(rome). London. Printed for James Magnes neer the Piazza in Russel Street. 1672. Catalogued B. (A.)

[86.] **12,316, a. 27.** Fragmenta Aulica, or Court and State Jests in Noble Drollery. True and Reall. Ascertained to their Times, Places and Persons. By T. S. Gent. London, Printed for H Marsh[2] at the Princes Armes in Chancery Lane near Fleet street; and Jos. Coniers[3] at the Black Raven in the long Walk near Christ Church. 1662. Catalogued S.(T. Gent.)

[87.] $\frac{\text{C. 20, f. 8}}{407}$ Roxburghe Ballads.

[88.] $\frac{\text{C. 22, e. 2}}{196}$ A Collection of Ballads.

[89.] $\frac{\text{C. 20, f. 7}}{36}$ Roxburghe Ballads.

[90.] $\frac{\text{C. 20, f. 7}}{28}$ Roxburghe Ballads.

[91.] **12,316, a.a. 7.** A Helpe to Discourse. Or A Misselany of Seriousnesse with Merriment. Consisting of witty Philosophicall, Gramaticall, and Astronomicall Questions and Answers. As also Of Epigrams, Epitaphs, Riddles, and Jests. Together with the Countrey-mans Counsellour, next his yearley Oracle or Prognostication to consult with. Contayning divers necessary Rules and Observations, of much use and consequence, *beeing knowne.* Now the sixt time published, and much inlarged by the former Authors W. B.[4] and E. P.[5] London. Printed by B. A. and T Fawcet, for Leonard Becket, and are to be sold at his shop in the Temple, neere the Church. 1627. Catalogued. B. (W.) and P. (E.)

---

1 The "Water Poet."   2 Published 1660, 1661.
3 Or Conyers, was also in Fetter Lane, Duck Lane, on Holborn Hill, and at the Anchor and Bible adjoining St. Peter's Alley, Cornhill, published 1682-1691.
4 William Basse.
5 Edward Phillips, author of Theatrum Poetarum, or a Compleat Collection of the Poets. Lond. 1675.

[92.] $\frac{C.\ 22,\ e.\ 2}{198}$ A Collection of Ballads.

[93.] C. 40, d. 38.   Merrie conceited Jests of George Peele[1] Gentle-man, sometimes a Student in Oxford.   Wherein is shewed the course of his life, how he lived ; a man very well knowne in the Citie of London, and elsewhere.

> Buy, reade and judge
> The price doe not grudge ;
> It will doe thee more pleasure,
> Than twice so much treasure.

London.   Printed by G. P. for F. Faulkner,[2] and are to be sold at his Shop in Southwarke, neere Saint Margarets Hill.   1627.

[94.] $\frac{1080,\ e.\ 28}{2}$ A choice Banquet of Witty Jests, Rare Fancies, and Pleasant Novels.   Fitted for all the Lovers of Wit, Mirth, and Eloquence. Being an Addition to *Archee's*[3] JESTS, taken out of his Closet ; but never publisht by him in his life time.   London.   Printed by T. J. and are to be sold by Peter Dring[4] at the Sun in the Poultry 1660.   Catalogued Armstrong (A.) Jester.

[95.] $\frac{669,\ f.\ 11}{127}$ Single Sheets.

[96.] $\frac{C.\ 20,\ f.\ 7}{138}$ Roxburghe Ballads.

[97.] 12,316, a. 43.   The Merry Dutch Miller and New Invented Wind-mill.   Wherewith he undertaketh to grind all sorts of Women, as the Old, Decreped, Wrinkled, Blear ey'd, Long Nosed, Blind, Lame, Scolds, Jealous, Angry, Poor, Drunkards, W——, Sluts, or all others what soever.   They shall come out of his Mill Young, Active, Pleasant, Hand-some, Wise, Loving, Vertuous and Rich ; Without any Deformity and just suteable to their Husband's Humours.

The Rich for Money, and the Poor for nothing.   Composed Dialogue wise, for the Recreation of all those that are inclined to be merry, and may serve to pass away an hour in a Cold winter night (without any great offence) by a good fire side.

> The Miller and the Mill you see
> How throng'd with Customers they be :
> Then bring your Wives unto the Mill,
> And Young for Old you shall have still

London.   Printed by E. Crowch,[5] for F. Coles,[6] T. Vere,[6] and J. Wright.[6] 1672.

---

[1] He was a dramatic author, and an acquaintance both of Shakespeare and Ben Jon-son. He led what we should term a somewhat "fast life."

[2] He lived "over against St. Margaret's Hill in Southwark," and published one of the Roxburghe ballads in 1631.

[3] Archie Armstrong, Court Jester to James I. and Charles I.

[4] There was another of this name, T. Dring, who lived in Fleet Street, and published between 1650 and 1687.   [5] Published from 1658 to 1674.

[6] Although separate publishers, they were occasionally partners, and as such pub-lished from 1655 to 1680.

[98.] $\frac{669,\ f.\ 26}{64\ 1}$ Single Sheets.

- [99.] $\frac{E.\ 451}{14}$ A Brown Dozen of Drunkards: (Ali-ass Drink-hards) Whipt, and shipt to the Isle of Guls: for their abusing of Mr *Malt* the bearded son, and *Barley-broth* the brainlesse daughter of Sir John Barley-corne. All joco-seriously descanted to our Wine drunk, Wrath drunk, Zeale drunk, staggering Times. By one that hath drunk at *St Patricks* [1] Well. London. Printed by Robert Austen on Addlin-hill. 1648.

[100.] $\frac{669,\ f.\ 10}{49}$ Single sheets.

[101.] $\frac{C.\ 20,\ f.\ 2}{12}$ Poetical Broadsides.

[102.] 1076, m. 2. Humors Ordinarie. Where a man may bee verie merrie, and exceeding well used for his six-pence. At London. Printed by Edward Allde, for William Firebrand, and are to bee sold at his Shoppe in the Popes head Alley, right over against the Taverne doore. 1607. Catalogued Rowlands. (s.)

[103.] 12,314, i. 31. Ingenii Fructus, or the Cambridge Jests, being Youths Recreation &c. By W. B. London printed for William Spiller, over against the Cross Keys in Red Lyon street, near the Fields, Holbourn, 1700. Price bound $\frac{s}{1/}$

[104.] $\frac{C.\ 39,\ vol.\ 2.}{111}$ Bagford Ballads.

[105.] 1080, e. 26. The First and best Part of Scoggins Jests. Full of witty mirth and pleasant shifts, done by him in France, and other places: being a preservative against melancholy. Gathered by Andrew Boord, Doctor of Physicke. London. Printed for Francis Williams 1626.

[106.] $\frac{669,\ f.\ 6}{12}$ Single Sheets.

[107.] $\frac{C.\ 22,\ e.\ 2}{5}$ English Ballads.

[108.] $\frac{C.\ 22,\ e.\ 2}{66}$ English Ballads.

[109.] $\frac{C.\ 22,\ e.\ 2}{69}$ English Ballads.

[110.] C. 39, d. 2. The Pleasant Conceites of Old Hobson the merry Londoner, full of humorous discourses, and witty merriments. Whereat the quickest wittes may laugh, and the Wiser sort take pleasure. Printed at London for John Wright, and are to be sold at his shoppe neere Christ Church gate, 1607. Catalogued Johnson (R.)

[111.] $\frac{C.\ 22,\ e.\ 2}{67}$ English Ballads.

[112.] $\frac{C.\ 22,\ e.\ 2}{141}$ English Ballads.

[113.] $\frac{669,\ f.\ 16}{66}$ Single Sheets—Sep. 1652.

[1] A cant Irish term for the best whisky.

[114.] $\frac{C.\ 22,\ e.\ 2}{43}$ English Ballads.

[115.] $\frac{C.\ 20,\ f.\ 4.\ vol.\ 2}{84}$ Luttrell Collection.

[116.] Newspapers, 1681, vol. 3. Heraclitus Ridens : at a Dialogue between Jest and Earnest, concerning the Times. Numb. 15. Tuesday May 10, 1681.

[117.] $\frac{816,\ m.\ 19}{38}$ An exact Accompt of the Receipts and Disbursements Expended by the Committee of Safety. Upon the Emergent Occasions of the Nation. Delivered in by Mr R. Secretary to the said Committee, to prevent false Reports, and prejudicate Censures. London Printed for Jer. Hanzen. 1660.

[118.] $\frac{C.\ 20,\ f.\ 4\ vol.\ 2}{103}$ (The Luttrell Collection) Inamorato and Misogamos ; or a Love Song Mock'd. London. Printed for H. Brome, at the Gun, at the West End of St Pauls. 1675.

[119.] $\frac{C.\ 39,\ k\ vol.\ 2}{61}$ Bagford Ballads.

[120.] $\frac{C.\ 22,\ e.\ 2}{82}$ English Ballads.

[121.] C. 39, b. 39. Wit and Drollery, Joviall Poems : Corrected and much amended with Additions, By Sir J. M. Ja. S. Sir W. D. J. D.[1] and the most refined Wits of the Age. London. Printed for Nath Brook, at the Angel in Cornhil, 1661. Catalogued M. (E.) (The Editor of this edition.)

[122.] $\frac{C.\ 22,\ e.\ 2}{52}$ English Ballads.

[123.] $\frac{669,\ f.\ 16}{13}$ Old Sayings and predictions verified.

[124.] $\frac{C.\ 20,\ f.\ 8}{376}$ Roxburghe Ballads.

[125.] $\frac{C.\ 20,\ f.\ 7}{34\ \ldots}$ Roxburghe Ballads.

[126.] $\frac{C.\ 39,\ k.\ vol.\ 2}{58}$ Bagford Collection.

[127.] 1078, e. 32. Wit and Mirth ; or Pills to purge Melancholy. Being a Collection of the best Merry Ballads and Songs, Old and New. Fitted to all Humours, having each there proper Tune for either Voice or Instrument, many of the Songs being a new Set. &c—London. Printed by Will. Pearson, for Henry Playford. at his Shop in the Temple Change. 1699.

[128.] $\frac{669,\ f.\ 10}{111}$ Catalogue of the severall Sects and Opinions in England and other Nations, With a briefe Rehearsall of their false and dangerous Tenents. Printed for R A 1647.

---

[1] See No. 3 and footnote.

SOME OF THE TUNES

noted

in this Book.

Sir Eglamore. *See p.* 9.

Come Lasses and Lads. *See p.* 23.

2 C

Sellenger's Round.   See p. 68.

Dumb, Dumb, Dumb.   See p. 99.

Sawney and Jockey.   See p. 116.

Stingo; or, the Oyle of Barley.   See p. 124.

Pegge of Ramsay ; or, Watton Town's End. See p. 142.

Upon a Summer's Day. See p. 159.

Shall I lye beyond thee ? or, Lulle me beyond thee. See p. 207.

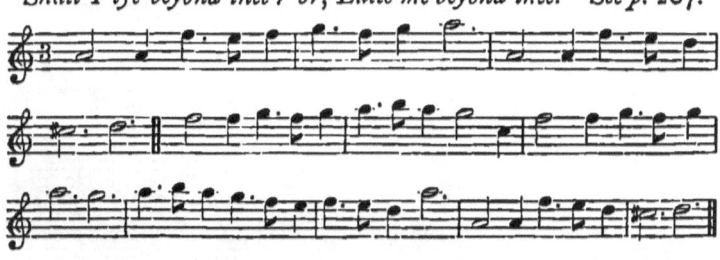

The Spinning Wheel. See p. 241.

Cuckolds all a Row.　See p. 255.

The Leather Bottel.　See p. 312.

Ragged and Torn.　See p. 327

There was a Jovial Beggar. *See p.* 386.

Ioan's Ale is New. *See p.* 399.

Love will find out the way. See p. 417.

The Joviall Crew; or,
A Beggar, a Beggar, a Beggar I'll be. See p. 424.

A List of Books

PUBLISHED BY

CHATTO & WINDUS,

214, Piccadilly, London, W.

Sold by all Booksellers, or sent post-free for the published price by the Publishers.

ABOUT.—THE FELLAH: An Egyptian Novel. By EDMOND ABOUT. Translated by Sir RANDAL ROBERTS. Post 8vo, illustrated boards, 2s.

ADAMS (W. DAVENPORT), WORKS BY.
A DICTIONARY OF THE DRAMA. Being a comprehensive Guide to the Plays, Playwrights, Players, and Playhouses of the United Kingdom and America. Crown 8vo half-bound, 12s. 6d. [*Preparing.*
QUIPS AND QUIDDITIES. Selected by W. D. ADAMS. Post 8vo, cloth limp, 2s. 6d.

AGONY COLUMN (THE) OF "THE TIMES," from 1800 to 1870. Edited, with an Introduction, by ALICE CLAY. Post 8vo, cloth limp, 2s. 6d.

AIDE (HAMILTON), WORKS BY. Post 8vo, illustrated boards, 2s. each.
CARR OF CARRLYON. | CONFIDENCES.

ALBERT.—BROOKE FINCHLEY'S DAUGHTER. By MARY ALBERT. Post 8vo, picture boards, 2s.; cloth limp, 2s. 6d.

ALDEN.—A LOST SOUL. By W. L. ALDEN. Fcap. 8vo, cl. bds., 1s. 6d.

ALEXANDER (MRS.), NOVELS BY. Post 8vo, illustrated boards, 2s. each.
MAID, WIFE, OR WIDOW? | VALERIE'S FATE.

ALLEN (F. M.).—GREEN AS GRASS. By F. M. ALLEN, Author of "Through Green Glasses." With a Frontispiece by JOSEPH SMYTH. Crown 8vo, cloth extra, 3s. 6d.

ALLEN (GRANT), WORKS BY. Crown 8vo, cloth extra, 6s. each.
THE EVOLUTIONIST AT LARGE. | COLIN CLOUT'S CALENDAR.
Crown 8vo, cloth extra, 3s. 6d. each; post 8vo, illustrated boards, 2s. each.
PHILISTIA. | BECKONING HAND. | THIS MORTAL COIL.
BABYLON. | FOR MAIMIE'S SAKE. | THE TENTS OF SHEM.
STRANGE STORIES. | IN ALL SHADES. | THE GREAT TABOO.
| THE DEVIL'S DIE.
Crown 8vo, cloth extra, 3s. 6d. each.
DUMARESQ'S DAUGHTER. | THE DUCHESS OF POWYSLAND. | BLOOD ROYAL.

AMERICAN LITERATURE, A LIBRARY OF, from the Earliest Settlement to the Present Time. Compiled and Edited by EDMUND CLARENCE STEDMAN and ELLEN MACKAY HUTCHINSON. Eleven Vols., royal 8vo, cloth extra, £6 12s.

ARCHITECTURAL STYLES, A HANDBOOK OF. By A. ROSENGARTEN. Translated by W. COLLETT-SANDARS. With 639 Illusts. Cr. 8vo, cl. ex., 7s. 6d.

ART (THE) OF AMUSING: A Collection of Graceful Arts, GAMES, Tricks, Puzzles, and Charades. By FRANK BELLEW. 300 Illusts. Cr. 8vo. cl. ex., 4s. 6d.

ARNOLD (EDWIN LESTER), WORKS BY.
THE WONDERFUL ADVENTURES OF PHRA THE PHŒNICIAN. With Introduction by Sir EDWIN ARNOLD, and 12 Illusts. by H. M. PAGET. Cr. 8vo, cl., 3s. 6d.
THE CONSTABLE OF ST. NICHOLAS. Crown 8vo, cloth, 3s. 6d. [*Shortly.*
BIRD LIFE IN ENGLAND. Crown 8vo, cloth extra, 6s.

ARTEMUS WARD'S WORKS: The Works of CHARLES FARRER BROWNE, better known as ARTEMUS WARD. With Portrait and Facsimile. Crown 8vo, cloth extra, **7s. 6d.**—Also a POPULAR EDITION, post 8vo, picture boards, **2s.**
THE GENIAL SHOWMAN: Life and Adventures of ARTEMUS WARD. By EDWARD P. HINGSTON. With a Frontispiece. Crown 8vo, cloth extra, **3s. 6d.**

ASHTON (JOHN), WORKS BY. Crown 8vo, cloth extra, **7s. 6d.** each.
HISTORY OF THE CHAP-BOOKS OF THE 18th CENTURY. With 334 Illusts.
SOCIAL LIFE IN THE REIGN OF QUEEN ANNE. With 85 Illustrations.
HUMOUR, WIT, AND SATIRE OF SEVENTEENTH CENTURY. With 82 Illusts.
ENGLISH CARICATURE AND SATIRE ON NAPOLEON THE FIRST. 115 Illusts.
MODERN STREET BALLADS. With 57 Illustrations.

BACTERIA.—A SYNOPSIS OF THE BACTERIA AND YEAST FUNGI AND ALLIED SPECIES. By W. B. GROVE, B.A. With 87 Illustrations, Crown 8vo, cloth extra, **3s. 6d.**

BARDSLEY (REV. C. W.), WORKS BY.
ENGLISH SURNAMES: Their Sources and Significations. Cr. 8vo, cloth, **7s. 6d.**
CURIOSITIES OF PURITAN NOMENCLATURE. Crown 8vo, cloth extra, **6s.**

BARING GOULD (S., Author of "John Herring," &c.), **NOVELS BY.**
Crown 8vo, cloth extra, **3s. 6d.** each; post 8vo, illustrated boards, **2s.** each.
RED SPIDER.   EVE.

BARRETT (FRANK, Author of "Lady Biddy Fane,") **NOVELS BY.**
Post 8vo, illustrated boards, **2s.** each; cloth, **2s. 6d.** each.
FETTERED FOR LIFE.   A PRODIGAL'S PROGRESS.
THE SIN OF OLGA ZASSOULICH.   JOHN FORD; and HIS HELPMATE.
BETWEEN LIFE AND DEATH.   A RECOILING VENGEANCE.
FOLLY MORRISON. | HONEST DAVIE. FOUND GUILTY.
LIEUT. BARNABAS.   FOR LOVE AND HONOUR.

BEACONSFIELD, LORD: A Biography. By T. P. O'CONNOR, M.P. Sixth Edition, with an Introduction. Crown 8vo, cloth extra, **5s.**

BEAUCHAMP.—GRANTLEY GRANGE: A Novel. By SHELSLEY BEAUCHAMP. Post 8vo, illustrated boards, **2s.**

BEAUTIFUL PICTURES BY BRITISH ARTISTS: A Gathering of Favourites from our Picture Galleries. beautifully engraved on Steel. With Notices of the Artists by SYDNEY ARMYTAGE, M.A. Imperial 4to, cloth extra, gilt edges, **21s.**

BECHSTEIN.—AS PRETTY AS SEVEN, and other German Stories. Collected by LUDWIG BECHSTEIN. With Additional Tales by the Brothers GRIMM, and 98 Illustrations by RICHTER. Square 8vo, cloth extra, **6s. 6d.;** gilt edges, **7s. 6d.**

BEERBOHM.—WANDERINGS IN PATAGONIA; or, Life among the Ostrich Hunters. By JULIUS BEERBOHM. With Illusts. Cr. 8vo, cl. extra, **3s. 6d.**

BENNETT (W. C., LL.D.), WORKS BY. Post 8vo, cloth limp, **2s.** each.
A BALLAD HISTORY OF ENGLAND. | SONGS FOR SAILORS.

BESANT (WALTER), NOVELS BY.
Cr. 8vo, cl. ex., **3s. 6d.** each; post 8vo, illust. bds., **2s.** each; cl. limp, **2s. 6d.** each.
ALL SORTS AND CONDITIONS OF MEN. With Illustrations by FRED. BARNARD.
THE CAPTAINS' ROOM, &c. With Frontispiece by E. J. WHEELER.
ALL IN A GARDEN FAIR. With 6 Illustrations by HARRY FURNISS.
DOROTHY FORSTER. With Frontispiece by CHARLES GREEN.
UNCLE JACK, and other Stories. | CHILDREN OF GIBEON.
THE WORLD WENT VERY WELL THEN. With 12 Illustrations by A. FORESTIER.
HERR PAULUS: His Rise, his Greatness, and his Fall.
FOR FAITH AND FREEDOM. With Illustrations by A. FORESTIER and F. WADDY.
TO CALL HER MINE, &c. With 9 Illustrations by A. FORESTIER.
THE BELL OF ST. PAUL'S.
THE HOLY ROSE, &c. With Frontispiece by F. BARNARD.
                          Crown 8vo, cloth extra, **3s. 6d.** each.
ARMOREL OF LYONESSE: A Romance of To-day. With 12 Illusts. by F. BARNARD.
ST. KATHERINE'S BY THE TOWER. With 12 page Illustrations by C. GREEN.
VERBENA CAMELLIA STEPHANOTIS, &c. Frontispiece by GORDON BROWNE.
FIFTY YEARS AGO. With 144 Plates and Woodcuts. Cheaper Edition, Revised, with a New Preface, &c. Crown 8vo, cloth extra, **5s.**
THE EULOGY OF RICHARD JEFFERIES. With Portrait. Cr. 8vo, cl. extra, **6s.**
THE ART OF FICTION. Demy 8vo, **1s.**
LONDON. With 124 Illustrations. Demy 8vo, cloth extra, **18s.**
THE IVORY GATE: A Novel. Three Vols., crown 8vo.

BESANT (WALTER) AND JAMES RICE, NOVELS BY.
Cr. 8vo, cl. ex., 3s. 6d. each; post 8vo, illust. bds., 2s. each; cl. limp, 2s. 6d. each.

READY-MONEY MORTIBOY.　　　　　BY CELIA'S ARBOUR.
MY LITTLE GIRL.　　　　　　　　　THE CHAPLAIN OF THE FLEET.
WITH HARP AND CROWN.　　　　　THE SEAMY SIDE.
THIS SON OF VULCAN.　　　　　　THE CASE OF MR. LUCRAFT, &c.
THE GOLDEN BUTTERFLY.　　　　　'TWAS IN TRAFALGAR'S BAY, &c.
THE MONKS OF THELEMA.　　　　　THE TEN YEARS' TENANT, &c.
　. There is also a LIBRARY EDITION of the above Twelve Volumes, handsomely
set in new type, on a large crown 8vo page, and bound in cloth extra. 6s. each.

BEWICK (THOMAS) AND HIS PUPILS. By Austin Dobson. With
95 Illustrations. Square 8vo, cloth extra, 6s.

BIERCE.—IN THE MIDST OF LIFE: Tales of Soldiers and Civilians.
By Ambrose Bierce. Crown 8vo, cloth extra, 6s.

BLACKBURN'S (HENRY) ART HANDBOOKS.
ACADEMY NOTES, separate years, from 1875-1887, 1889-1891, each 1s.
ACADEMY NOTES, 1892. With Illustrations. 1s.
ACADEMY NOTES, 1875-79. Complete in One Vol., with 600 Illusts. Cloth limp, 6s.
ACADEMY NOTES, 1880-84. Complete in One Vol. with 700 Illusts. Cloth limp, 6s.
GROSVENOR NOTES, 1877. 6d.
GROSVENOR NOTES, separate years, from 1878 to 1890, each 1s.
GROSVENOR NOTES, Vol. I., 1877-82. With 300 Illusts. Demy 8vo, cloth limp, 6s.
GROSVENOR NOTES, Vol. II., 1883-87. With 300 Illusts. Demy 8vo, cloth limp, 6s.
THE NEW GALLERY, 1888-1891. With numerous Illustrations, each 1s.
THE NEW GALLERY, 1892. With Illustrations. 1s.
THE NEW GALLERY, Vol. I., 1888-1892. With 250 Illusts. Demy 8vo, cloth, 6s.
ENGLISH PICTURES AT THE NATIONAL GALLERY. 114 Illustrations. 1s.
OLD MASTERS AT THE NATIONAL GALLERY. 128 Illustrations. 1s. 6d.
ILLUSTRATED CATALOGUE TO THE NATIONAL GALLERY. 242 Illusts. cl., 3s.
THE PARIS SALON, 1892. With Facsimile Sketches. 3s.
THE PARIS SOCIETY OF FINE ARTS, 1892. With Sketches. 3s. 6d.

BLAKE (WILLIAM): India-proof Etchings from his Works by William
Bell Scott. With descriptive Text. Folio, half-bound boards, 21s.

BLIND (MATHILDE). Poems by. Crown 8vo, cloth extra, 5s. each.
THE ASCENT OF MAN.
DRAMAS IN MINIATURE. With a Frontispiece by Ford Madox Brown.

BOURNE (H. R. FOX), WORKS BY.
ENGLISH MERCHANTS: Memoirs in Illustration of the Progress of British Com-
merce. With numerous Illustrations. Crown 8vo, cloth extra, 7s. 6d.
ENGLISH NEWSPAPERS: The History of Journalism. Two Vols., demy 8vo, cl., 25s.
THE OTHER SIDE OF THE EMIN PASHA RELIEF EXPEDITION. Crown 8vo,
cloth extra, 6s.

BOWERS.—LEAVES FROM A HUNTING JOURNAL. By George
Bowers. Oblong folio, half-bound. 21s.

BOYLE (FREDERICK), WORKS BY. Post 8vo, illustrated boards, 2s. each.
CHRONICLES OF NO-MAN'S LAND. |　　CAMP NOTES.
SAVAGE LIFE. Crown 8vo, cloth extra, 3s. 6d.; post 8vo, picture boards, 2s.

BRAND'S OBSERVATIONS ON POPULAR ANTIQUITIES; chiefly
illustrating the Origin of our Vulgar Customs, Ceremonies, and Superstitions. With
the Additions of Sir Henry Ellis, and Illustrations. Cr. 8vo, cloth extra, 7s. 6d.

BREWER (REV. DR.), WORKS BY.
THE READER'S HANDBOOK OF ALLUSIONS, REFERENCES, PLOTS, AND
STORIES. Fifteenth Thousand. Crown 8vo, cloth extra, 7s. 6d.
AUTHORS AND THEIR WORKS, WITH THE DATES: Being the Appendices to
"The Reader's Handbook," separately printed. Crown 8vo, cloth limp, 2s.
A DICTIONARY OF MIRACLES. Crown 8vo, cloth extra, 7s. 6d.

BREWSTER (SIR DAVID), WORKS BY. Post 8vo cl. ex. 4s. 6d. each.
MORE WORLDS THAN ONE: Creed of Philosopher and Hope of Christian. Plates.
THE MARTYRS OF SCIENCE: Galileo, Tycho Brahe, and Kepler. With Portraits.
LETTERS ON NATURAL MAGIC. With numerous Illustrations.

BRILLAT-SAVARIN.—GASTRONOMY AS A FINE ART. By Brillat-
Savarin. Translated by R. E. Anderson, M.A. Post 8vo, half-bound, 2s.

BRET HARTE, WORKS BY.

LIBRARY EDITION. In Seven Volumes, crown 8vo, cloth extra, **6s.** each.
BRET HARTE'S COLLECTED WORKS. Arranged and Revised by the Author.
Vol. I. COMPLETE POETICAL AND DRAMATIC WORKS. With Steel Portrait.
Vol. II. LUCK OF ROARING CAMP—BOHEMIAN PAPERS—AMERICAN LEGENDS.
Vol. III. TALES OF THE ARGONAUTS—EASTERN SKETCHES.
Vol. IV. GABRIEL CONROY. | Vol. V. STORIES—CONDENSED NOVELS, &c.
Vol. VI. TALES OF THE PACIFIC SLOPE.
Vol. VII. TALES OF THE PACIFIC SLOPE—II. With Portrait by JOHN PETTIE, R.A.

THE SELECT WORKS OF BRET HARTE, in Prose and Poetry With Introductory
Essay by J. M. BELLEW. Portrait of Author, and 50 Illusts. Cr. 8vo, cl. ex., **7s. 6d.**
BRET HARTE'S POETICAL WORKS. Hand-made paper & buckram. Cr. 8vo, **4s. 6d.**
THE QUEEN OF THE PIRATE ISLE. With 28 original Drawings by KATE
GREENAWAY, reproduced in Colours by EDMUND EVANS. Small 4to, cloth, **5s.**

Crown 8vo, cloth extra, **3s. 6d.** each.
A WAIF OF THE PLAINS. With 60 Illustrations by STANLEY L. WOOD.
A WARD OF THE GOLDEN GATE. With 59 Illustrations by STANLEY L. WOOD.
A SAPPHO OF GREEN SPRINGS, &c. With Two Illustrations by HUME NISBET.
COLONEL STARBOTTLE'S CLIENT, AND SOME OTHER PEOPLE. With a
Frontispiece by FRED. BARNARD.
SALLY DOWS, &c. With a Frontispiece.
SUSY: A Novel. With a Frontispiece. [Shortly.

Post 8vo, illustrated boards, **2s.** each.
GABRIEL CONROY. | THE LUCK OF ROARING CAMP, &c.
AN HEIRESS OF RED DOG, &c. | CALIFORNIAN STORIES.

Post 8vo, illustrated boards, **2s.** each; cloth limp, **2s. 6d.** each.
FLIP. | MARUJA. | A PHYLLIS OF THE SIERRAS.

Fcap. 8vo. picture cover, **1s.** each.
THE TWINS OF TABLE MOUNTAIN. | JEFF BRIGGS'S LOVE STORY.
SNOW-BOUND AT EAGLE'S.

BRYDGES.—UNCLE SAM AT HOME. By HAROLD BRYDGES. Post
8vo, illustrated boards, **2s.**; cloth limp, **2s. 6d.**

BUCHANAN'S (ROBERT) WORKS. Crown 8vo, cloth extra, **6s.** each.

SELECTED POEMS OF ROBERT BUCHANAN. With Frontispiece by T. DALZIEL.
THE EARTHQUAKE; or, Six Days and a Sabbath.
THE CITY OF DREAM: An Epic Poem. With Two Illustrations by P. MACNAB.
THE OUTCAST: A Rhyme for the Time. With 15 Illustrations by RUDOLF BLIND,
PETER MACNAB, and HUME NISBET. Small demy 8vo, cloth extra, **8s.**
ROBERT BUCHANAN'S COMPLETE POETICAL WORKS. With Steel-plate Por-
trait. Crown 8vo, cloth extra, **7s. 6d.**

Crown 8vo, cloth extra, **3s. 6d.** each; post 8vo, illustrated boards, **2s.** each.
THE SHADOW OF THE SWORD. | LOVE ME FOR EVER. Frontispiece.
A CHILD OF NATURE. Frontispiece. | ANNAN WATER. | FOXGLOVE MANOR.
GOD AND THE MAN. With 11 Illus- | THE NEW ABELARD.
trations by FRED. BARNARD. | MATT: A Story of a Caravan. Front.
THE MARTYRDOM OF MADELINE. | THE MASTER OF THE MINE. Front.
With Frontispiece by A. W. COOPER. | THE HEIR OF LINNE.

BURTON (CAPTAIN). — THE BOOK OF THE SWORD: Being a
History of the Sword and its Use in all Countries, from the Earliest Times. By
RICHARD F. BURTON. With over 400 Illustrations. Square 8vo, cloth extra, **32s.**

BURTON (ROBERT).

THE ANATOMY OF MELANCHOLY: A New Edition, with translations of the
Classical Extracts. Demy 8vo, cloth extra, **7s. 6d.**
MELANCHOLY ANATOMISED Being an Abridgment, for popular use, of BURTON'S
ANATOMY OF MELANCHOLY. Post 8vo, cloth limp, **2s. 6d.**

CAINE (T. HALL), NOVELS BY. Crown 8vo, cloth extra, **3s. 6d.** each;
post 8vo, illustrated boards, **2s.** each; cloth limp, **2s. 6d.** each.
SHADOW OF A CRIME. | A SON OF HAGAR. | THE DEEMSTER.

CAMERON (COMMANDER). — THE CRUISE OF THE "BLACK
PRINCE" PRIVATEER. By V. LOVETT CAMERON, R.N., C.B. With Two Illustrations by P. MACNAB. Crown 8vo, cloth extra, **5s.**; post 8vo, illustrated boards, **2s.**

CAMERON (MRS. H. LOVETT), NOVELS BY. Post 8vo, illust. bds., **2s.** each.
JULIET'S GUARDIAN. | DECEIVERS EVER.

CARLYLE (THOMAS) ON THE CHOICE OF BOOKS. With Life
by R. H. SHEPHERD, and Three Illustrations. Post 8vo, cloth extra, 1s. 6d.
THE CORRESPONDENCE OF THOMAS CARLYLE AND RALPH WALDO
EMERSON, 1834 to 1872. Edited by CHARLES ELIOT NORTON. With Portraits.
Two Vols., crown 8vo, cloth extra, 24s.

CARLYLE (JANE WELSH), LIFE OF. By Mrs. ALEXANDER IRELAND.
With Portrait and Facsimile Letter. Small demy 8vo, cloth extra, 7s. 6d.

CHAPMAN'S (GEORGE) WORKS. Vol. I. contains the Plays complete,
including the doubtful ones. Vol. II., the Poems and Minor Translations, with an
Introductory Essay by ALGERNON CHARLES SWINBURNE. Vol. III., the Translations
of the Iliad and Odyssey. Three Vols., crown 8vo, cloth extra, 6s. each.

CHATTO AND JACKSON.—A TREATISE ON WOOD ENGRAVING,
Historical and Practical. By WILLIAM ANDREW CHATTO and JOHN JACKSON. With
an Additional Chapter by HENRY G. BOHN, and 450 fine Illusts. Large 4to, hf.-bd., 28s.

CHAUCER FOR CHILDREN: A Golden Key. By Mrs. H. R. HAWEIS.
With 8 Coloured Plates and 30 Woodcuts. Small 4to, cloth extra, 6s.
CHAUCER FOR SCHOOLS. By Mrs. H. R. HAWEIS. Demy 8vo, cloth limp, 2s. 6d.

CLARE.—FOR THE LOVE OF A LASS: A Tale of Tynedale. By
AUSTIN CLARE. Post 8vo, picture boards, 2s.; cloth limp, 2s. 6d.

CLIVE (MRS. ARCHER), NOVELS BY. Post 8vo, illust. boards, 2s. each.
PAUL FERROLL. | WHY PAUL FERROLL KILLED HIS WIFE.

CLODD.—MYTHS AND DREAMS. By EDWARD CLODD, F.R.A.S.
Second Edition, Revised. Crown 8vo, cloth extra, 3s. 6d.

COBBAN.—THE CURE OF SOULS: A Story. By J. MACLAREN
COBBAN. Post 8vo, illustrated boards, 2s.

COLEMAN (JOHN), WORKS BY.
PLAYERS AND PLAYWRIGHTS I HAVE KNOWN. Two Vols., 8vo, cloth, 24s.
CURLY: An Actor's Story. With 21 Illusts. by J. C. DOLLMAN. Cr. 8vo, cl., 1s. 6d.

COLLINS (C. ALLSTON).—THE BAR SINISTER. Post 8vo, 2s.

COLLINS (MORTIMER AND FRANCES), NOVELS BY.
Crown 8vo, cloth extra, 3s. 6d. each; post 8vo, illustrated boards, 2s. each.
FROM MIDNIGHT TO MIDNIGHT. | BLACKSMITH AND SCHOLAR.
TRANSMIGRATION. | YOU PLAY ME FALSE. | A VILLAGE COMEDY.
Post 8vo, illustrated boards, 2s. each.
SWEET ANNE PAGE. | SWEET AND TWENTY.
A FIGHT WITH FORTUNE. | FRANCES.

COLLINS (WILKIE), NOVELS BY.
Cr. 8vo, cl. ex., 3s. 6d. each; post 8vo, illust. bds., 2s. each; cl. limp, 2s. 6d. each.
ANTONINA. With a Frontispiece by Sir JOHN GILBERT, R.A.
BASIL. Illustrated by Sir JOHN GILBERT, R.A., and J. MAHONEY.
HIDE AND SEEK. Illustrated by Sir JOHN GILBERT, R.A., and J. MAHONEY.
AFTER DARK. With Illustrations by A. B. HOUGHTON.
THE DEAD SECRET. With a Frontispiece by Sir JOHN GILBERT, R.A.
QUEEN OF HEARTS. With a Frontispiece by Sir JOHN GILBERT, R.A.
THE WOMAN IN WHITE. With Illusts. by Sir J. GILBERT, R.A., and F. A. FRASER.
NO NAME. With Illustrations by Sir J. E. MILLAIS, R.A., and A. W. COOPER.
MY MISCELLANIES. With a Steel-plate Portrait of WILKIE COLLINS.
ARMADALE. With Illustrations by G. H. THOMAS.
THE MOONSTONE. With Illustrations by G. DU MAURIER and F. A. FRASER.
MAN AND WIFE. With Illustrations by WILLIAM SMALL.
POOR MISS FINCH. Illustrated by G. DU MAURIER and EDWARD HUGHES.
MISS OR MRS.? With Illusts. by S. L. FILDES, R.A., and HENRY WOODS, A.R.A.
THE NEW MAGDALEN. Illustrated by G. DU MAURIER and C. S. REINHARDT.
THE FROZEN DEEP. Illustrated by G. DU MAURIER and J. MAHONEY.
THE LAW AND THE LADY. Illusts. by S. L. FILDES, R.A., and SYDNEY HALL.
THE TWO DESTINIES.
THE HAUNTED HOTEL. Illustrated by ARTHUR HOPKINS.
THE FALLEN LEAVES. | HEART AND SCIENCE. | THE EVIL GENIUS.
JEZEBEL'S DAUGHTER. | "I SAY NO." | LITTLE NOVELS.
THE BLACK ROBE. | A ROGUE'S LIFE. | THE LEGACY OF CAIN.
BLIND LOVE. With Preface by WALTER BESANT, and Illusts. by A. FORESTIER.

COLLINS (JOHN CHURTON, M.A.), BOOKS BY.
ILLUSTRATIONS OF TENNYSON. Crown 8vo, cloth extra, 6s.
A MONOGRAPH ON DEAN SWIFT. Crown 8vo, cloth extra, 8s.   [Shortly.

COLMAN'S HUMOROUS WORKS: "Broad Grins," "My Nightgown and Slippers," and other Humorous Works of GEORGE COLMAN. With Life by G. B. BUCKSTONE, and Frontispiece by HOGARTH. Crown 8vo, cloth extra, 7s. 6d.

COLMORE.—A VALLEY OF SHADOWS. By G. COLMORE, Author of "A Conspiracy of Silence." Two Vols., crown 8vo.

COLQUHOUN.—EVERY INCH A SOLDIER: A Novel. By M. J. COLQUHOUN. Post 8vo, illustrated boards, 2s.

CONVALESCENT COOKERY: A Family Handbook. By CATHERINE RYAN. Crown 8vo, 1s.; cloth limp, 1s. 6d.

CONWAY (MONCURE D.), WORKS BY.
DEMONOLOGY AND DEVIL-LORE. With 65 Illustrations. Third Edition. Two Vols., demy 8vo, cloth extra, 28s.
A NECKLACE OF STORIES. 25 Illusts. by W. J. HENNESSY. Sq. 8vo, cloth, 6s.
PINE AND PALM: A Novel. Two Vols., crown 8vo, cloth extra, 21s.
GEORGE WASHINGTON'S RULES OF CIVILITY Traced to their Sources and Restored. Fcap. 8vo, Japanese vellum, 2s. 6d.

COOK (DUTTON), NOVELS BY.
PAUL FOSTER'S DAUGHTER. Cr. 8vo, cl. ex., 3s. 6d.; post 8vo, illust. boards, 2s.
LEO. Post 8vo, illustrated boards, 2s.

CORNWALL.—POPULAR ROMANCES OF THE WEST OF ENG-LAND; or, The Drolls, Traditions, and Superstitions of Old Cornwall. Collected by ROBERT HUNT, F.R.S. Two Steel-plates by GEO.CRUIKSHANK. Cr. 8vo, cl., 7s. 6d.

COTES.—TWO GIRLS ON A BARGE. By V. CECIL COTES. With 44 Illustrations by F. H. TOWNSEND. Crown 8vo, cloth extra, 3s. 6d.

CRADDOCK.—THE PROPHET OF THE GREAT SMOKY MOUN-TAINS. By CHARLES EGBERT CRADDOCK. Post 8vo, illust. bds., 2s.; cl. limp, 2s. 6d.

CRIM.—ADVENTURES OF A FAIR REBEL. By MATT CRIM. With a Frontispiece by DAN. BEARD. Crown 8vo, cloth extra, 3s. 6d.

CROKER (B.M.), NOVELS BY. Post 8vo, 2s. each; cloth, 2s. 6d. each.
PRETTY MISS NEVILLE.	DIANA BARRINGTON.
A BIRD OF PASSAGE.	PROPER PRIDE.

A FAMILY LIKENESS. Three Vols., crown 8vo.

CRUIKSHANK'S COMIC ALMANACK. Complete in TWO SERIES: The FIRST from 1835 to 1843; the SECOND from 1844 to 1853. A Gathering of the BEST HUMOUR of THACKERAY, HOOD, MAYHEW, ALBERT SMITH, A'BECKETT, ROBERT BROUGH, &c. With numerous Steel Engravings and Woodcuts by CRUIK-SHANK, HINE, LANDELLS, &c. Two Vols., crown 8vo, cloth gilt, 7s. 6d. each.
THE LIFE OF GEORGE CRUIKSHANK. By BLANCHARD JERROLD. With 84 Illustrations and a Bibliography. Crown 8vo, cloth extra, 7s. 6d.

CUMMING (C. F. GORDON), WORKS BY. Demy 8vo, cl. ex., 8s. 6d. each.
IN THE HEBRIDES. With Autotype Facsimile and 23 Illustrations.
IN THE HIMALAYAS AND ON THE INDIAN PLAINS. With 42 Illustrations.
VIA CORNWALL TO EGYPT. With Photogravure Frontis. Demy 8vo, cl., 7s. 6d.

CUSSANS.—A HANDBOOK OF HERALDRY; with Instructions for Tracing Pedigrees and Deciphering Ancient MSS., &c. By JOHN E. CUSSANS. With 408 Woodcuts, Two Coloured and Two Plain Plates. Crown 8vo, cloth extra, 7s. 6d.

CYPLES(W.)—HEARTS of GOLD. Cr. 8vo, cl. 3s. 6d.; post 8vo, bds., 2s.

DANIEL.—MERRIE ENGLAND IN THE OLDEN TIME. By GEORGE DANIEL. With Illustrations by ROBERT CRUIKSHANK. Crown 8vo, cloth extra, 3s. 6d.

DAUDET.—THE EVANGELIST; or, Port Salvation. By ALPHONSE DAUDET. Crown 8vo, cloth extra, 3s. 6d.; post 8vo, illustrated boards, 2s.

DAVENANT.—HINTS FOR PARENTS ON THE CHOICE OF A PRO-FESSION FOR THEIR SONS. By F. DAVENANT, M.A. Post 8vo, 1s.; cl., 1s. 6d.

DAVIES (DR. N. E. YORKE-), WORKS BY.
Crown 8vo, 1s. each; cloth limp, 1s. 6d. each.
ONE THOUSAND MEDICAL MAXIMS AND SURGICAL HINTS.
NURSERY HINTS: A Mother's Guide in Health and Disease.
FOODS FOR THE FAT: A Treatise on Corpulency, and a Dietary for its Cure.
AIDS TO LONG LIFE. Crown 8vo, 2s.; cloth limp, 2s. 6d.

DAVIES' (SIR JOHN) COMPLETE POETICAL WORKS, for the first time Collected and Edited, with Memorial-Introduction and Notes, by the Rev. A. B. GROSART, D.D. Two Vols., crown 8vo, cloth boards, **12s.**

DAWSON.—THE FOUNTAIN OF YOUTH: A Novel of Adventure. By ERASMUS DAWSON, M.B. Edited by PAUL DEVON. With Two Illustrations by HUME NISBET. Crown 8vo, cloth extra, **3s. 6d.**

DE GUERIN.—THE JOURNAL OF MAURICE DE GUERIN. Edited by G. S. TREBUTIEN. With a Memoir by SAINTE-BEUVE. Translated from the 20th French Edition by JESSIE P. FROTHINGHAM. Fcap, 8vo, half-bound, **2s. 6d.**

DE MAISTRE.—A JOURNEY ROUND MY ROOM. By XAVIER DE MAISTRE. Translated by HENRY ATTWELL. Post 8vo, cloth limp, **2s. 6d.**

DE MILLE.—A CASTLE IN SPAIN. By JAMES DE MILLE. With a Frontispiece. Crown 8vo, cloth extra, **3s. 6d.**; post 8vo, illustrated boards, **2s.**

DERBY (THE).—THE BLUE RIBBON OF THE TURF: A Chronicle of the RACE FOR THE DERBY, from Diomed to Donovan. With Brief Accounts of THE OAKS. By LOUIS HENRY CURZON. Crown 8vo, cloth extra, **6s.**

DERWENT (LEITH), NOVELS BY. Cr. 8vo, cl., **3s.6d.** ea.; post 8vo, bds., **2s.** ea.
OUR LADY OF TEARS. | CIRCE'S LOVERS.

DICKENS (CHARLES), NOVELS BY. Post 8vo, illustrated boards, **2s.** each.
SKETCHES BY BOZ. | NICHOLAS NICKLEBY.
THE PICKWICK PAPERS. | OLIVER TWIST.
THE SPEECHES OF CHARLES DICKENS, 1841–1870. With a New Bibliography. Edited by RICHARD HERNE SHEPHERD. Crown 8vo, cloth extra, **6s.**—Also a SMALLER EDITION, in the *Mayfair Library*, post 8vo, cloth limp, **2s. 6d.**
ABOUT ENGLAND WITH DICKENS. By ALFRED RIMMER. With 57 Illustrations by C. A. VANDERHOOF, ALFRED RIMMER, and others. Sq. 8vo, cloth extra, **7s. 6d.**

DICTIONARIES.
A DICTIONARY OF MIRACLES: Imitative, Realistic, and Dogmatic. By the Rev. E. C. BREWER, LL.D. Crown 8vo, cloth extra, **7s. 6d.**
THE READER'S HANDBOOK OF ALLUSIONS, REFERENCES, PLOTS, AND STORIES. By the Rev. E. C. BREWER, LL.D. With an ENGLISH BIBLIOGRAPHY Fifteenth Thousand. Crown 8vo, cloth extra, **7s. 6d.**
AUTHORS AND THEIR WORKS, WITH THE DATES. Cr. 8vo, cloth limp, **2s.**
FAMILIAR SHORT SAYINGS OF GREAT MEN. With Historical and Explanatory Notes. By SAMUEL A. BENT, A.M. Crown 8vo, cloth extra, **7s. 6d.**
SLANG DICTIONARY: Etymological, Historical, and Anecdotal. Cr. 8vo, cl., **6s. 6d.**
WOMEN OF THE DAY: A Biographical Dictionary. By F. HAYS. Cr. 8vo, cl., **5s.**
WORDS, FACTS, AND PHRASES: A Dictionary of Curious, Quaint, and Out-of-the-Way Matters. By ELIEZER EDWARDS. Crown 8vo, cloth extra, **7s. 6d.**

DIDEROT.—THE PARADOX OF ACTING. Translated, with Annotations, from Diderot's "Le Paradoxe sur le Comédien," by WALTER HERRIES POLLOCK. With a Preface by HENRY IRVING. Crown 8vo, parchment, **4s. 6d.**

DOBSON (AUSTIN), WORKS BY.
THOMAS BEWICK & HIS PUPILS. With 95 Illustrations. Square 8vo, cloth, **6s.**
FOUR FRENCHWOMEN: MADEMOISELLE DE CORDAY; MADAME ROLAND; THE PRINCESS DE LAMBALLE; MADAME DE GENLIS. Fcap. 8vo, hf.-roxburghe, **2s. 6d.**
EIGHTEENTH CENTURY VIGNETTES. Crown 8vo, cloth extra, **6s.** [*Preparing.*

DOBSON (W. T.), WORKS BY. Post 8vo, cloth limp, **2s. 6d.** each.
LITERARY FRIVOLITIES, FANCIES, FOLLIES, AND FROLICS.
POETICAL INGENUITIES AND ECCENTRICITIES.

DONOVAN (DICK), DETECTIVE STORIES BY.
Post 8vo, illustrated boards, **2s.** each; cloth limp, **2s. 6d.** each.
THE MAN-HUNTER. | WANTED! | A DETECTIVE'S TRIUMPHS.
CAUGHT AT LAST! | IN THE GRIP OF THE LAW.
TRACKED AND TAKEN. | FROM INFORMATION RECEIVED.
WHO POISONED HETTY DUNCAN?
THE MAN FROM MANCHESTER. With 23 Illustrations. Crown 8vo, cloth extra, **3s. 6d.**; post 8vo, illustrated boards, **2s.**
TRACKED TO DOOM. With 6 full-page Illustrations by GORDON BROWNE. Crown 8vo, cloth extra, **3s. 6d.**

DOYLE (CONAN).—THE FIRM OF GIRDLESTONE. By A. CONAN DOYLE, Author of "Micah Clarke." Crown 8vo, cloth extra, **3s. 6d.**

DRAMATISTS, THE OLD. With Vignette Portraits. Cr. 8vo, cl. ex., **6s.** per Vol.
BEN JONSON'S WORKS. With Notes Critical and Explanatory, and a Bio-
graphical Memoir by WM. GIFFORD. Edited by Col. CUNNINGHAM. Three Vols.
CHAPMAN'S WORKS. Complete in Three Vols. Vol. I. contains the Plays
complete; Vol. II., Poems and Minor Translations, with an Introductory Essay
by A. C. SWINBURNE ; Vol. III., Translations of the Iliad and Odyssey.
MARLOWE'S WORKS. Edited, with Notes, by Col. CUNNINGHAM. One Vol.
MASSINGER'S PLAYS. From GIFFORD's Text. Edit by Col.CUNNINGHAM. OneVol.

DUNCAN (SARA JEANNETTE), WORKS BY.
Crown 8vo, cloth extra, **7s. 6d.** each.
A SOCIAL DEPARTURE: How Orthodocia and I Went round the World by Our-
selves. With 111 Illustrations by F. H. TOWNSEND.
AN AMERICAN GIRL IN LONDON. With 80 Illustrations by F. H. TOWNSEND.
THE SIMPLE ADVENTURES OF MEM SAHIB. Numerous Illusts. [*Preparing.*

DYER.—THE FOLK-LORE OF PLANTS. By Rev. T. F. THISELTON
DYER, M.A. Crown 8vo, cloth extra, **6s.**

EARLY ENGLISH POETS. Edited, with Introductions and Annota-
tions, by Rev. A. B. GROSART, D.D. Crown 8vo, cloth boards, **6s.** per Volume.
FLETCHER'S (GILES) COMPLETE POEMS. One Vol.
DAVIES' (SIR JOHN) COMPLETE POETICAL WORKS. Two Vols.
HERRICK'S (ROBERT) COMPLETE COLLECTED POEMS. Three Vols.
SIDNEY'S (SIR PHILIP) COMPLETE POETICAL WORKS. Three Vols.

EDGCUMBE.—ZEPHYRUS : A Holiday in Brazil and on the River Plate.
By E. R. PEARCE EDGCUMBE. With 41 Illustrations. Crown 8vo, cloth extra, **5s.**

EDWARDES (MRS. ANNIE), NOVELS BY:
A POINT OF HONOUR. Post 8vo, illustrated boards, **2s.**
ARCHIE LOVELL. Crown 8vo, cloth extra, **3s. 6d.** ; post 8vo, illust. boards, **2s.**

EDWARDS (ELIEZER).—WORDS, FACTS, AND PHRASES: A
Dictionary of Curious, Quaint, and Out-of-the-Way Matters. By ELIEZER EDWARDS.
Crown 8vo, cloth extra, **7s. 6d.**

EDWARDS (M. BETHAM-), NOVELS BY.
KITTY. Post 8vo, illustrated boards, **2s.**; cloth limp, **2s. 6d.**
FELICIA. Post 8vo, illustrated boards, **2s.**

EGERTON.—SUSSEX FOLK & SUSSEX WAYS. By Rev. J. C. EGERTON.
With Introduction by Rev. Dr. H. WACE, and 4 Illustrations. Cr. 8vo, cloth ex., **5s.**

EGGLESTON (EDWARD).—ROXY : A Novel. Post 8vo, illust. bds., **2s.**

EMANUEL.—ON DIAMONDS AND PRECIOUS STONES: Their
History, Value, and Properties; with Simple Tests for ascertaining their Reality. By
HARRY EMANUEL, F.R.G.S. With Illustrations, tinted and plain. Cr. 8vo, cl. ex., **6s.**

ENGLISHMAN'S HOUSE, THE: A Practical Guide to all interested in
Selecting or Building a House; with Estimates of Cost, Quantities, &c. By C. J.
RICHARDSON. With Coloured Frontispiece and 600 Illusts. Crown 8vo, cloth, **7s. 6d.**

EWALD (ALEX. CHARLES, F.S.A.), WORKS BY.
THE LIFE AND TIMES OF PRINCE CHARLES STUART, Count of Albany
(THE YOUNG PRETENDER). With a Portrait. Crown 8vo, cloth extra, **7s. 6d.**
STORIES FROM THE STATE PAPERS. With an Autotype. Crown 8vo, cloth, **6s.**

EYES, OUR : How to Preserve Them from Infancy to Old Age. By
JOHN BROWNING, F.R.A.S. With 70 Illusts. Eighteenth Thousand. Crown 8vo, **1s.**

FAMILIAR SHORT SAYINGS OF GREAT MEN. By SAMUEL ARTHUR
BENT, A.M. Fifth Edition. Revised and Enlarged. Crown 8vo, cloth extra, **7s. 6d.**

FARADAY (MICHAEL), WORKS BY. Post 8vo, cloth extra, **4s. 6d.** each.
THE CHEMICAL HISTORY OF A CANDLE: Lectures delivered before a Juvenile
Audience. Edited by WILLIAM CROOKES. F.C.S. With numerous Illustrations.
ON THE VARIOUS FORCES OF NATURE, AND THEIR RELATIONS TO
EACH OTHER. Edited by WILLIAM CROOKES, F.C.S. With Illustrations.

FARRER (J. ANSON), WORKS BY.
MILITARY MANNERS AND CUSTOMS. Crown 8vo, cloth extra, **6s.**
WAR: Three Essays, reprinted from "Military Manners." Cr. 8vo, **1s.**; cl., **1s. 6d.**

FENN (MANVILLE).—THE NEW MISTRESS : A Novel. By G. MAN-
VILLE FENN, Author of "Double Cunning," &c. Crown 8vo, cloth extra, **3s. 6d.**

FIN-BEC.—THE CUPBOARD PAPERS: Observations on the Art of Living and Dining. By FIN-BEC. Post 8vo, cloth limp, **2s. 6d.**

FIREWORKS, THE COMPLETE ART OF MAKING; or, The Pyrotechnist's Treasury. By THOMAS KENTISH. With 267 Illustrations. Cr. 8vo, cl., **5s.**

FITZGERALD (PERCY, M.A., F.S.A.), WORKS BY.
THE WORLD BEHIND THE SCENES. Crown 8vo, cloth extra, **3s. 6d.**
LITTLE ESSAYS: Passages from Letters of CHARLES LAMB. Post 8vo, cl., **2s. 6d.**
A DAY'S TOUR: Journey through France and Belgium. With Sketches. Cr. 4to, **1s.**
FATAL ZERO. Crown 8vo, cloth extra, **3s. 6d.**: post 8vo, illustrated boards, **2s.**
Post 8vo, illustrated boards, **2s.** each.
BELLA DONNA. | LADY OF BRANTOME. | THE SECOND MRS. TILLOTSON.
POLLY. | NEVER FORGOTTEN. | SEVENTY-FIVE BROOKE STREET.
LIFE OF JAMES BOSWELL (of Auchinleck). With an Account of his Sayings, Doings, and Writings; and Four Portraits. Two Vols., demy 8vo, cloth, **24s.**

FLAMMARION.—URANIA: A Romance. By CAMILLE FLAMMARION. Translated by AUGUSTA RICE STETSON. With 87 Illustrations by DE BIELER, MYRBACH, and GAMBARD. Crown 8vo, cloth extra, **5s.**

FLETCHER'S (GILES, B.D.) COMPLETE POEMS: Christ's Victorie in Heaven, Christ's Victorie on 'Earth, Christ's Triumph over Death, and Minor Poems. With Notes by Rev. A. B. GROSART, D.D. Crown 8vo, cloth boards, **6s.**

FLUDYER (HARRY) AT CAMBRIDGE: A Series of Family Letters. Post 8vo, picture cover, **1s.**; cloth limp, **1s. 6d.**

FONBLANQUE (ALBANY).—FILTHY LUCRE. Post 8vo, illust. bds., **2s.**

FRANCILLON (R. E.), NOVELS BY.
Crown 8vo, cloth extra, **3s. 6d.** each; post 8vo, illustrated boards, **2s.** each.
ONE BY ONE. | QUEEN COPHETUA. | A REAL QUEEN. | KING OR KNAVE?
OLYMPIA. Post 8vo, illust. bds., **2s.** | ESTHER'S GLOVE. Fcap. 8vo, pict. cover, **1s.**
ROMANCES OF THE LAW. Crown 8vo, cloth, **6s.**; post 8vo, illust. boards, **2s.**

FREDERIC (HAROLD), NOVELS BY.
SETH'S BROTHER'S WIFE. Post 8vo, illustrated boards, **2s.**
THE LAWTON GIRL. With Frontispiece by F. BARNARD. Cr. 8vo, cloth ex., **6s.**
post 8vo, illustrated boards, **2s.**

FRENCH LITERATURE, A HISTORY OF. By HENRY VAN LAUN. Three Vols., demy 8vo, cloth boards, **7s. 6d.** each.

FRERE.—PANDURANG HARI; or, Memoirs of a Hindoo. With Preface by Sir BARTLE FRERE. Crown 8vo, cloth, **3s. 6d.**; post 8vo, illust. bds., **2s.**

FRISWELL (HAIN).—ONE OF TWO: A Novel. Post 8vo, illust. bds., **2s.**

FROST (THOMAS), WORKS BY. Crown 8vo, cloth extra, **3s. 6d.** each.
CIRCUS LIFE AND CIRCUS CELEBRITIES. | LIVES OF THE CONJURERS.
THE OLD SHOWMEN AND THE OLD LONDON FAIRS.

FRY'S (HERBERT) ROYAL GUIDE TO THE LONDON CHARITIES.
Showing their Name, Date of Foundation, Objects, Income, Officials, &c. Edited by JOHN LANE. Published Annually. Crown 8vo, cloth, **1s. 6d.**

GARDENING BOOKS. Post 8vo, **1s.** each; cloth limp, **1s. 6d.** each.
A YEAR'S WORK IN GARDEN AND GREENHOUSE: Practical Advice as to the Management of the Flower, Fruit, and Frame Garden. By GEORGE GLENNY.
HOUSEHOLD HORTICULTURE. By TOM and JANE JERROLD. Illustrated.
THE GARDEN THAT PAID THE RENT. By TOM JERROLD.
OUR KITCHEN GARDEN: The Plants we Grow, and How we Cook Them. By TOM JERROLD. Crown 8vo, cloth, 1s. 6d.
MY GARDEN WILD, AND WHAT I GREW THERE. By FRANCIS G. HEATH. Crown 8vo, cloth extra, gilt edges, **6s.**

GARRETT.—THE CAPEL GIRLS: A Novel. By EDWARD GARRETT. Crown 8vo, cloth extra, **3s. 6d.**; post 8vo, illustrated boards, **2s.**

GENTLEMAN'S MAGAZINE, THE. 1s. Monthly. In addition to the Articles upon subjects in Literature, Science, and Art, for which this Magazine has so high a reputation, "TABLE TALK" by SYLVANUS URBAN appears monthly.
*** Bound Volumes for recent years kept in stock, **8s. 6d.** each; Cases for binding, **2s.**

GENTLEMAN'S ANNUAL, THE. Published Annually in November. 1s. The 1892 Annual, written by T. W. Speight, is entitled "**THE LOUDWATER TRAGEDY.**"

GERMAN POPULAR STORIES. Collected by the Brothers Grimm and Translated by Edgar Taylor. With Introduction by John Ruskin, and 22 Steel Plates after George Cruikshank. Square 8vo. cloth, 6s. 6d.; gilt edges, 7s. 6d.

GIBBON (CHARLES), NOVELS BY, Crown 8vo, cloth extra, 3s. 6d. each; post 8vo, illustrated boards, 2s. each.

ROBIN GRAY. | LOVING A DREAM.	THE GOLDEN SHAFT.
THE FLOWER OF THE FOREST.	OF HIGH DEGREE.

Post 8vo, illustrated boards, 2s. each.

THE DEAD HEART.	IN LOVE AND WAR.
FOR LACK OF GOLD.	A HEART'S PROBLEM.
WHAT WILL THE WORLD SAY?	BY MEAD AND STREAM.
FOR THE KING. | A HARD KNOT.	THE BRAES OF YARROW.
QUEEN OF THE MEADOW.	FANCY FREE. | IN HONOUR BOUND.
IN PASTURES GREEN.	HEART'S DELIGHT. | BLOOD-MONEY.

GIBNEY (SOMERVILLE).—SENTENCED! Cr. 8vo, 1s. ; cl., 1s. 6d.

GILBERT (WILLIAM), NOVELS BY. Post 8vo, illustrated boards, 2s. each.
DR. AUSTIN'S GUESTS. | JAMES DUKE, COSTERMONGER.
THE WIZARD OF THE MOUNTAIN. |

GILBERT (W. S.), ORIGINAL PLAYS BY. Two Series, 2s. 6d. each. The First Series contains: The Wicked World—Pygmalion and Galatea—Charity—The Princess—The Palace of Truth—Trial by Jury. The Second Series: Broken Hearts—Engaged—Sweethearts—Gretchen—Dan'l Druce—Tom Cobb—H.M.S. " Pinafore "—The Sorcerer—Pirates of Penzance.

EIGHT ORIGINAL COMIC OPERAS written by W. S. Gilbert. Containing: . The Sorcerer—H.M.S. "Pinafore—Pirates of Penzance—Iolanthe—Patience—Princess Ida—The Mikado—Trial by Jury. Demy 8vo, cloth limp, 2s. 6d.
THE "GILBERT AND SULLIVAN" BIRTHDAY BOOK: Quotations for Every Day in the Year, Selected from Plays by W. S. Gilbert set to Music by Sir A. Sullivan. Compiled by Alex. Watson. Royal 16mo, Jap. leather, 2s. 6d.

GLANVILLE (ERNEST), NOVELS BY.
THE LOST HEIRESS: A Tale of Love, Battle and Adventure. With 2 Illusts. by Hume Nisbet. Cr. 8vo, cloth extra, 3s. 6d. ; post 8vo, illustrated boards, 2s.
THE FOSSICKER: A Romance of Mashonaland. With Frontispiece and Vignette by Hume Nisbet. Second Edition. Crown 8vo, cloth extra, 3s. 6d.

GLENNY.—A YEAR'S WORK IN GARDEN AND GREENHOUSE: Practical Advice to Amateur Gardeners as to the Management of the Flower, Fruit, and Frame Garden. By George Glenny. · Post 8vo, 1s.; cloth limp, 1s. 6d.

GODWIN.—LIVES OF THE NECROMANCERS. By William Godwin. Post 8vo, cloth limp, 2s.

GOLDEN TREASURY OF THOUGHT, THE: An Encyclopædia of Quotations. Edited by Theodore Taylor. Crown 8vo, cloth gilt, 7s. 6d.

GOODMAN.—THE FATE OF HERBERT WAYNE. By E. J. Goodman, Author of "Too Curious." Crown 8vo, cloth, 3s. 6d.

GOWING.—FIVE THOUSAND MILES IN A SLEDGE : A Midwinter Journey Across Siberia. By Lionel F. Gowing. With 30 Illustrations by C. J. Uren, and a Map by E. Weller. Large crown 8vo, cloth extra, 8s. ·

GRAHAM. — THE PROFESSOR'S WIFE: A Story By Leonard Graham. Fcap. 8vo, picture cover, 1s.

GREEKS AND ROMANS, THE LIFE OF THE, described from Antique Monuments. By Ernst Guhl and W. Koner. Edited by Dr. F. Hueffer. With 545 Illustrations. Large crown 8vo, cloth extra, 7s. 6d.

GREENWOOD (JAMES), WORKS BY. Cr. 8vo. cloth extra, 3s. 6d. each.
THE WILDS OF LONDON. | LOW-LIFE DEEPS.

GREVILLE (HENRY), NOVELS BY:
NIKANOR. Translated by Eliza E. Chase. With 8 Illustrations. Crown 8vo, cloth extra, 6s.; post 8vo, illustrated boards, 2s.
A NOBLE WOMAN. Crown 8vo, cloth extra, 5s.; post 8vo. illustrated boards, 2s.

GRIFFITH.—CORINTHIA MARAZION : A Novel. By Cecil Griffith, Author of "Victory Deane," &c. Crown 8vo, cloth extra, 3s. 6d.

HABBERTON (JOHN, Author of "Helen's Babies"), NOVELS BY.
Post 8vo, illustrated boards **2s.** each; cloth limp, **2s. 6d.** each.
BRUETON'S BAYOU. | COUNTRY LUCK.

HAIR, THE : Its Treatment in Health, Weakness, and Disease. Translated from the German of Dr. J. PINCUS. Crown 8vo, **1s.**

HAKE (DR. THOMAS GORDON), POEMS BY. Cr. 8vo, cl. ex., **6s.** each.
NEW SYMBOLS. | LEGENDS OF THE MORROW. | THE SERPENT PLAY.
MAIDEN ECSTASY. Small 4to, cloth extra, **8s.**

HALL.—SKETCHES OF IRISH CHARACTER. By Mrs. S. C. HALL.
With numerous Illustrations on Steel and Wood by MACLISE, GILBERT, HARVEY, and
GEORGE CRUIKSHANK. Medium 8vo, cloth extra, **7s. 6d.**

HALLIDAY (ANDR.).—EVERY-DAY PAPERS. Post 8vo, bds., **2s.**

HANDWRITING, THE PHILOSOPHY OF. With over 100 Facsimiles
and Explanatory Text. By DON FELIX DE SALAMANCA. Post 8vo, cloth limp, **2s. 6d.**

HANKY-PANKY : A Collection of Very Easy Tricks, Very Difficult
Tricks, White Magic, Sleight of Hand. &c. Edited by W. H. CREMER. With 200
Illustrations. Crown 8vo, cloth extra, **4s. 6d.**

HARDY (LADY DUFFUS).—PAUL WYNTER'S SACRIFICE. By
Lady DUFFUS HARDY. Post 8vo, illustrated boards, **2s.**

HARDY (THOMAS).—UNDER THE GREENWOOD TREE. By
THOMAS HARDY, Author of "Far from the Madding Crowd." With Portrait and 15
Illustrations. Crown 8vo, cloth extra, **3s. 6d.**; post 8vo, illustrated boards, **2s.**

HARPER.—THE BRIGHTON ROAD : Old Times and New on a Classic
Highway. By CHARLES G. HARPER. With a Photogravure Frontispiece and 90 Illustrations. Demy 8vo, cloth extra, **16s.**

HARWOOD.—THE TENTH EARL. By J. BERWICK HARWOOD. Post
8vo, illustrated boards, **2s.**

HAWEIS (MRS. H. R.), WORKS BY. Square 8vo, cloth extra, **6s.** each.
THE ART OF BEAUTY. With Coloured Frontispiece and 91 Illustrations.
THE ART OF DECORATION. With Coloured Frontispiece and 74 Illustrations.
CHAUCER FOR CHILDREN. With 8 Coloured Plates and 30 Woodcuts.
THE ART OF DRESS. With 32 Illustrations. Post 8vo, **1s.**; cloth, **1s. 6d.**
CHAUCER FOR SCHOOLS. Demy 8vo, cloth limp, **2s. 6d.**

HAWEIS (Rev. H. R., M.A.).—AMERICAN HUMORISTS : WASHINGTON
IRVING, OLIVER WENDELL HOLMES, JAMES RUSSELL LOWELL, ARTEMUS WARD,
MARK TWAIN, and BRET HARTE. Third Edition. Crown 8vo, cloth extra, **6s.**

HAWLEY SMART.—WITHOUT LOVE OR LICENCE : A Novel. By
HAWLEY SMART. Crown 8vo, cloth extra, **3s. 6d.**; post 8vo, illustrated boards, **2s.**

HAWTHORNE.—OUR OLD HOME. By NATHANIEL HAWTHORNE.
Annotated with Passages from the Author's Note-book, and Illustrated with 31
Photogravures. Two Vols., crown 8vo, buckram, gilt top, **15s.**

HAWTHORNE (JULIAN), NOVELS BY.
Crown 8vo, cloth extra, **3s. 6d.** each; post 8vo, illustrated boards, **2s.** each.
GARTH. | ELLICE QUENTIN. | BEATRIX RANDOLPH. | DUST.
SEBASTIAN STROME. | DAVID POINDEXTER.
FORTUNE'S FOOL. | THE SPECTRE OF THE CAMERA.
             Post 8vo, illustrated boards, **2s.** each.
MISS CADOGNA. | LOVE—OR A NAME.
MRS. GAINSBOROUGH'S DIAMONDS. Fcap. 8vo, illustrated cover, **1s.**

HEATH.—MY GARDEN WILD, AND WHAT I GREW THERE.
By FRANCIS GEORGE HEATH. Crown 8vo, cloth extra, gilt edges, **6s.**

HELPS (SIR ARTHUR), WORKS BY. Post 8vo, cloth limp, **2s. 6d.** each.
ANIMALS AND THEIR MASTERS. | SOCIAL PRESSURE.
IVAN DE BIRON : A Novel. Cr. 8vo, cl. extra, **3s. 6d.**; post 8vo, illust. bds., **2s.**

HENDERSON.—AGATHA PAGE : A Novel. By ISAAC HENDERSON.
Crown 8vo, cloth extra, **3s. 6d.**

HERMAN.—A LEADING LADY. By HENRY HERMAN, joint-Author
of "The Bishops' Bible." Post 8vo, illustrated boards, **2s.**; cloth extra, **2s. 6d.**

HERRICK'S (ROBERT) HESPERIDES, NOBLE NUMBERS, AND COMPLETE COLLECTED POEMS. With Memorial-Introduction and Notes by the Rev. A. B. GROSART, D.D.; Steel Portrait, &c. Three Vols., crown 8vo, cl. bds., 18s.

HERTZKA.—FREELAND : A Social Anticipation. By Dr. THEODOR HERTZKA. Translated by ARTHUR RANSOM. Crown 8vo, cloth extra, 6s.

HESSE-WARTEGG.—TUNIS : The Land and the People. By Chevalier ERNST VON HESSE-WARTEGG. With 22 Illustrations. Cr. 8vo, cloth extra, 3s. 6d.

HILL.—TREASON-FELONY : A Novel. By JOHN HILL. Two Vols.

HINDLEY (CHARLES), WORKS BY.
TAVERN ANECDOTES AND SAYINGS: Including Reminiscences connected with Coffee Houses, Clubs, &c. With Illustrations. Crown 8vo, cloth, 3s. 6d.
THE LIFE AND ADVENTURES OF A CHEAP JACK. By ONE OF THE FRA-TERNITY. Edited by CHARLES HINDLEY. Crown 8vo, cloth extra, 3s. 6d.

HOEY.—THE LOVER'S CREED. By Mrs. CASHEL HOEY. Post 8vo, 2s.

HOLLINGSHEAD (JOHN).—NIAGARA SPRAY. Crown 8vo, 1s.

HOLMES.—THE SCIENCE OF VOICE PRODUCTION AND VOICE PRESERVATION. By GORDON HOLMES, M.D. Crown 8vo, 1s.; cloth, 1s. 6d.

HOLMES (OLIVER WENDELL), WORKS BY.
THE AUTOCRAT OF THE BREAKFAST-TABLE. Illustrated by J. GORDON THOMSON. Post 8vo, cloth limp, 2s. 6d.—Another Edition, in smaller type, with an Introduction by G. A. SALA. Post 8vo, cloth limp, 2s.
THE PROFESSOR AT THE BREAKFAST-TABLE. Post 8vo, cloth limp, 2s.

HOOD'S (THOMAS) CHOICE WORKS, in Prose and Verse. With Life of the Author, Portrait, and 200 Illustrations. Crown 8vo, cloth extra, 7s. 6d.
HOOD'S WHIMS AND ODDITIES. With 85 Illustrations. Post 8vo, printed on laid paper and half-bound, 2s.

HOOD (TOM).—FROM NOWHERE TO THE NORTH POLE: A Noah's Arkæological Narrative. By TOM HOOD. With 25 Illustrations by W. BRUNTON and E. C. BARNES. Square 8vo, cloth extra, gilt edges, 6s.

HOOK'S (THEODORE) CHOICE HUMOROUS WORKS; including his Ludicrous Adventures, Bons Mots, Puns, and Hoaxes. With Life of the Author, Portraits, Facsimiles, and Illustrations. Crown 8vo, cloth extra, 7s. 6d.

HOOPER.—THE HOUSE OF RABY : A Novel. By Mrs. GEORGE HOOPER. Post 8vo, illustrated boards, 2s.

HOPKINS.—"'TWIXT LOVE AND DUTY :" A Novel. By TIGHE HOPKINS. Post 8vo, illustrated boards, 2s.

HORNE. — ORION : An Epic Poem. By RICHARD HENGIST HORNE. With Photographic Portrait by SUMMERS. Tenth Edition. Cr. 8vo, cloth extra, 7s.

HORSE (THE) AND HIS RIDER : An Anecdotic Medley. By "THOR-MANBY." Crown 8vo, cloth extra, 6s.

HUNGERFORD (MRS.), Author of "Molly Bawn," NOVELS BY.
Post 8vo, illustrated boards, 2s. each.
A MAIDEN ALL FORLORN. | IN DURANCE VILE. | A MENTAL STRUGGLE.
MARVEL. | A MODERN CIRCE.

HUNT.—ESSAYS BY LEIGH HUNT : A TALE FOR A CHIMNEY CORNER, &c. Edited by EDMUND OLLIER. Post 8vo, printed on laid paper and half-bd., 2s.

HUNT (MRS. ALFRED), NOVELS BY.
Crown 8vo, cloth extra, 3s. 6d. each; post 8vo, illustrated boards, 2s. each.
THE LEADEN CASKET. | SELF-CONDEMNED. | THAT OTHER PERSON.
THORNICROFT'S MODEL. Post 8vo, illustrated boards, 2s.
MRS. JULIET. Three Vols., crown 8vo.

HUTCHISON.—HINTS ON COLT-BREAKING. By W. M. HUTCHISON. With 25 Illustrations. Crown 8vo, cloth extra, 3s. 6d.

HYDROPHOBIA : An Account of M. PASTEUR'S System ; Technique of his Method, and Statistics. By RENAUD SUZOR, M.B. Crown 8vo, cloth extra, 6s.

IDLER (THE) : A Monthly Magazine. Edited by JEROME K. JEROME and ROBERT E. BARR. Profusely Illustrated. Sixpence Monthly.—Vol. I. now ready, cloth extra, price 5s.; Cases for Binding, 1s. 6d.

INGELOW (JEAN).—FATED TO BE FREE. With 24 Illustrations by G. J. PINWELL. Cr. 8vo, cloth extra, **3s. 6d.**; post 8vo, illustrated boards, **2s.**

INDOOR PAUPERS. By ONE OF THEM. Crown 8vo, **1s.**; cloth, **1s. 6d.**

IRISH WIT AND HUMOUR, SONGS OF. Collected and Edited by A. PERCEVAL GRAVES. Post 8vo, cloth limp, **2s. 6d.**

JAMES.—A ROMANCE OF THE QUEEN'S HOUNDS. By CHARLES JAMES. Post 8vo, picture cover, **1s.**; cloth limp, **1s. 6d.**

JANVIER.—PRACTICAL KERAMICS FOR STUDENTS. By CATHERINE A. JANVIER. Crown 8vo, cloth extra, **6s.**

JAY (HARRIETT), NOVELS BY. Post 8vo, illustrated boards, **2s.** each.
THE DARK COLLEEN. | **THE QUEEN OF CONNAUGHT.**

JEFFERIES (RICHARD), WORKS BY. Post 8vo, cloth limp, **2s. 6d.** each.
NATURE NEAR LONDON. | **THE LIFE OF THE FIELDS.** | **THE OPEN AIR.**

THE EULOGY OF RICHARD JEFFERIES. By WALTER BESANT. Second Edition. With a Photograph Portrait. Crown 8vo, cloth extra, **6s.**

JENNINGS (H. J.), WORKS BY.
CURIOSITIES OF CRITICISM. Post 8vo, cloth limp, **2s. 6d.**
LORD TENNYSON: A Biographical Sketch. With a Photograph. Cr. 8vo, cl., **6s.**

JEROME.—STAGELAND. By JEROME K. JEROME. With 64 Illustrations by J. BERNARD PARTRIDGE. Square 8vo, picture cover, **1s.**; cloth limp, **2s.**

JERROLD.—THE BARBER'S CHAIR; & THE HEDGEHOG LETTERS. By DOUGLAS JERROLD. Post 8vo, printed on laid paper and half-bound, **2s.**

JERROLD (TOM), WORKS BY. Post 8vo, **1s.** each; cloth limp, **1s. 6d.** each.
THE GARDEN THAT PAID THE RENT.
HOUSEHOLD HORTICULTURE: A Gossip about Flowers. Illustrated.
OUR KITCHEN GARDEN: The Plants, and How we Cook Them. Cr. 8vo, cl., **1s. 6d.**

JESSE.—SCENES AND OCCUPATIONS OF A COUNTRY LIFE. By EDWARD JESSE. Post 8vo, cloth limp, **2s.**

JONES (WILLIAM, F.S.A.), WORKS BY. Cr. 8vo, cl. extra, **7s. 6d.** each.
FINGER-RING LORE: Historical, Legendary, and Anecdotal. With nearly 300 Illustrations. Second Edition, Revised and Enlarged.
CREDULITIES, PAST AND PRESENT. Including the Sea and Seamen, Miners, Talismans, Word and Letter Divination, Exorcising and Blessing of Animals, Birds, Eggs, Luck, &c. With an Etched Frontispiece.
CROWNS AND CORONATIONS: A History of Regalia. With 100 Illustrations.

JONSON'S (BEN) WORKS. With Notes Critical and Explanatory and a Biographical Memoir by WILLIAM GIFFORD. Edited by Colonel CUNNINGHAM. Three Vols., crown 8vo, cloth extra, **6s.** each.

JOSEPHUS, THE COMPLETE WORKS OF. Translated by WHISTON. Containing "The Antiquities of the Jews" and "The Wars of the Jews." With 52 Illustrations and Maps. Two Vols., demy 8vo, half-bound, **12s. 6d.**

KEMPT.—PENCIL AND PALETTE : Chapters on Art and Artists. By ROBERT KEMPT. Post 8vo, cloth limp, **2s. 6d.**

KERSHAW. — COLONIAL FACTS AND FICTIONS : Humorous Sketches. By MARK KERSHAW. Post 8vo, illustrated boards, **2s.**; cloth, **2s. 6d.**

KEYSER. — CUT BY THE MESS: A Novel. By ARTHUR KEYSER. Crown 8vo, picture cover, **1s.**; cloth limp, **1s. 6d.**

KING (R. ASHE), NOVELS BY. Cr. 8vo, cl., **3s. 6d.** ea.; post 8vo, bds., **2s.** ea.
A DRAWN GAME. | **"THE WEARING OF THE GREEN."**
Post 8vo, illustrated boards, **2s.** each.
PASSION'S SLAVE. | **BELL BARRY.**

KNIGHTS (THE) OF THE LION : A Romance of the Thirteenth Century. Edited, with an Introduction, by the MARQUESS of LORNE, K.T. Cr. 8vo, cl. ex., **6s.**

KNIGHT.—THE PATIENT'S VADE MECUM : How to Get Most Benefit from Medical Advice. By WILLIAM KNIGHT, M.R.C.S., and EDWARD KNIGHT, L.R.C.P. Crown 8vo, 1s.; cloth limp, 1s. 6d.

LAMB'S (CHARLES) COMPLETE WORKS, in Prose and Verse, including "Poetry for Children" and "Prince Dorus." Edited, with Notes and Introduction, by R. H. SHEPHERD. With Two Portraits and Facsimile of a page of the "Essay on Roast Pig." Crown 8vo, half-bound, 7s. 6d.
THE ESSAYS OF ELIA. Post 8vo, printed on laid paper and half-bound, 2s.
LITTLE ESSAYS: Sketches and Characters by CHARLES LAMB, selected from his Letters by PERCY FITZGERALD. Post 8vo, cloth limp, 2s. 6d.
THE DRAMATIC ESSAYS OF CHARLES LAMB. With Introduction and Notes by BRANDER MATTHEWS, and Steel-plate Portrait. Fcap. 8vo, hf.-bd., 2s. 6d.

LANDOR.—CITATION AND EXAMINATION OF WILLIAM SHAKS-
PEARE, &c., before Sir THOMAS LUCY, touching Deer-stealing, 19th September, 1582. To which is added, A CONFERENCE OF MASTER EDMUND SPENSER with the Earl of Essex, touching the State of Ireland, 1595. By WALTER SAVAGE LANDOR. Fcap. 8vo, half-Roxburghe, 2s. 6d.

LANE.—THE THOUSAND AND ONE NIGHTS, commonly called in England THE ARABIAN NIGHTS' ENTERTAINMENTS. Translated from the Arabic, with Notes, by EDWARD WILLIAM LANE. Illustrated by many hundred Engravings from Designs by HARVEY. Edited by EDWARD STANLEY POOLE. With a Preface by STANLEY LANE-POOLE. Three Vols., demy 8vo, cloth extra, 7s. 6d. each.

LARWOOD (JACOB), WORKS BY.
THE STORY OF THE LONDON PARKS. With Illusts. Cr. 8vo, cl. extra, 3s. 6d.
ANECDOTES OF THE CLERGY: The Antiquities, Humours, and Eccentricities of the Cloth. Post 8vo, printed on laid paper and half-bound, 2s.

Post 8vo, cloth limp, 2s. 6d. each.
FORENSIC ANECDOTES. | THEATRICAL ANECDOTES.

LEIGH (HENRY S.), WORKS BY.
CAROLS OF COCKAYNE. Printed on hand-made paper, bound in buckram, 5s.
JEUX D'ESPRIT. Edited by HENRY S. LEIGH. Post 8vo, cloth limp, 2s. 6d.

LEYS (JOHN).—THE LINDSAYS : A Romance. Post 8vo, illust. bds., 2s.

LIFE IN LONDON; or, The History of JERRY HAWTHORN and COR-
INTHIAN TOM. With CRUIKSHANK'S Coloured Illustrations. Crown 8vo, cloth extra, 7s. 6d.   [New Edition preparing.

LINTON (E. LYNN), WORKS BY. | Post 8vo, cloth limp, 2s. 6d. each.
WITCH STORIES. | OURSELVES: ESSAYS ON WOMEN.

Crown 8vo, cloth extra, 3s. 6d. each; post 8vo, illustrated boards, 2s. each.
SOWING THE WIND. | UNDER WHICH LORD?
PATRICIA KEMBALL. | "MY LOVE!" | IONE.
ATONEMENT OF LEAM DUNDAS. | PASTON CAREW, Millionaire & Miser.
THE WORLD WELL LOST.

Post 8vo, illustrated boards, 2s. each.
THE REBEL OF THE FAMILY. | WITH A SILKEN THREAD.
FREESHOOTING : Extracts from the Works of Mrs. LYNN LINTON. Post 8vo, cloth, 2s. 6d.

LONGFELLOW'S POETICAL WORKS. With numerous Illustrations on Steel and Wood. Crown 8vo, cloth extra, 7s. 6d.

LUCY.—GIDEON FLEYCE : A Novel. By HENRY W. LUCY. Crown 8vo, cloth extra, 3s. 6d.; post 8vo, illustrated boards, 2s.

LUSIAD (THE) OF CAMOENS. Translated into English Spenserian Verse by ROBERT FFRENCH DUFF. With 14 Plates. Demy 8vo, cloth boards, 18s.

MACALPINE (AVERY), NOVELS BY.
TERESA ITASCA, and other Stories. Crown 8vo, bound in canvas, 2s. 6d.
BROKEN WINGS. With 6 Illusts. by W. J. HENNESSY. Crown 8vo, cloth extra, 6s.

MACCOLL (HUGH), NOVELS BY.
MR. STRANGER'S SEALED PACKET. Second Edition Crown 8vo, cl. extra, 5s.
EDNOR WHITLOCK. Crown 8vo, cloth extra, 6s.

MACDONELL.—QUAKER COUSINS : A Novel. By AGNES MACDONELL. Crown 8vo, cloth extra, 3s. 6d.; post 8vo, illustrated boards, 2s.

McCARTHY (JUSTIN, M.P.), WORKS BY.

A HISTORY OF OUR OWN TIMES, from the Accession of Queen Victoria to the General. Election of 1880. Four Vols. demy 8vo, cloth extra, **12s.** each.—Also a POPULAR EDITION, in Four Vols., crown 8vo, cloth extra, **6s.** each.—And a JUBILEE EDITION, with an Appendix of Events to the end of 1886, in Two Vols., large crown 8vo, cloth extra, **7s. 6d.** each.

A SHORT HISTORY OF OUR OWN TIMES. One Vol., crown 8vo, cloth extra, **6s.** —Also a CHEAP POPULAR EDITION, post 8vo, cloth limp, **2s. 6d.**

A HISTORY OF THE FOUR GEORGES. Four Vols. demy 8vo, cloth extra, **12s.** each. [Vols. I. & II. *ready.*

Crown 8vo, cloth extra, **3s. 6d.** each; post 8vo, illustrated boards, **2s.** each.

THE WATERDALE NEIGHBOURS.	**MISS MISANTHROPE.**
MY ENEMY'S DAUGHTER.	**DONNA QUIXOTE.**
A FAIR SAXON.	**THE COMET OF A SEASON.**
LINLEY ROCHFORD.	**MAID OF ATHENS.**
DEAR LADY DISDAIN.	**CAMIOLA:** A Girl with a Fortune.

"THE RIGHT HONOURABLE." By JUSTIN McCARTHY, M.P., and Mrs. CAMPBELL-PRAED. Fourth Edition. Crown 8vo, cloth extra, **6s.**

McCARTHY (JUSTIN H., M.P.), WORKS BY.

THE FRENCH REVOLUTION. Four Vols., 8vo, **12s.** each. [Vols. I. & II. *ready.*
AN OUTLINE OF THE HISTORY OF IRELAND. Crown 8vo, **1s.**; cloth, **1s. 6d.**
IRELAND SINCE THE UNION: Irish History, 1798-1886. Crown 8vo, cloth, **6s.**
HAFIZ IN LONDON: Poems. Small 8vo, gold cloth, **3s. 6d.**
HARLEQUINADE: Poems. Small 4to, Japanese vellum, **8s.**
OUR SENSATION NOVEL. Crown 8vo, picture cover, **1s.**; cloth limp, **1s. 6d.**
DOOM! An Atlantic Episode. Crown 8vo, picture cover, **1s.**
DOLLY: A Sketch. Crown 8vo, picture cover, **1s.**; cloth limp, **1s. 6d.**
LILY LASS: A Romance. Crown 8vo, picture cover, **1s.**; cloth limp, **1s. 6d.**
THE THOUSAND AND ONE DAYS: Persian Tales. Edited by JUSTIN H. McCARTHY. With 2 Photogravures by STANLEY L. WOOD. Two Vols., crown 8vo, half-bound, **12s.**

MACDONALD (GEORGE, LL.D.), WORKS BY.

WORKS OF FANCY AND IMAGINATION. Ten Vols., cl. extra, gilt edges, in cloth case, **21s.** Or the Vols. may be had separately, in grolier cl., at **2s. 6d.** each.

Vol. I. WITHIN AND WITHOUT.—THE HIDDEN LIFE.
„ II. THE DISCIPLE.—THE GOSPEL WOMEN.—BOOK OF SONNETS.—ORGAN SONGS.
„ III. VIOLIN SONGS.—SONGS OF THE DAYS AND NIGHTS.—A BOOK OF DREAMS.—ROADSIDE POEMS.—POEMS FOR CHILDREN.
„ IV. PARABLES.—BALLADS.—SCOTCH SONGS.
„ V. & VI. PHANTASTES: A Faerie Romance. | Vol. VII. THE PORTENT.
„ VIII. THE LIGHT PRINCESS.—THE GIANT'S HEART.—SHADOWS.
„ IX. CROSS PURPOSES.—THE GOLDEN KEY.—THE CARASOYN.—LITTLE DAYLIGHT
„ X. THE CRUEL PAINTER.—THE WOW O' RIVVEN.—THE CASTLE.—THE BROKEN SWORDS.—THE GRAY WOLF.—UNCLE CORNELIUS.

THE POETICAL WORKS OF DR. GEORGE MACDONALD. Collected and arranged by the Author. 2 vols., crown 8vo, buckram, **12s.** [*Shortly.*
A THREEFOLD CORD. Poems by Three Friends. Edited by Dr. GEORGE MACDONALD. Post 8vo, cloth, **5s.**
HEATHER AND SNOW: A Novel. 2 vols., crown 8vo. [*Shortly.*

MACGREGOR. — PASTIMES AND PLAYERS: Notes on Popular Games. By ROBERT MACGREGOR. Post 8vo, cloth limp, **2s. 6d.**

MACKAY.—INTERLUDES AND UNDERTONES; or, Music at Twilight. By CHARLES MACKAY, LL.D. Crown 8vo, cloth extra, **6s.**

MACLISE PORTRAIT GALLERY (THE) OF ILLUSTRIOUS LITER-ARY CHARACTERS: 85 PORTRAITS; with Memoirs — Biographical, Critical, Bibliographical, and Anecdotal—illustrative of the Literature of the former half of the Present Century, by WILLIAM BATES, B.A. Crown 8vo, cloth extra, **7s. 6d.**

MACQUOID (MRS.), WORKS BY. Square 8vo, cloth extra, **7s. 6d.** each.

IN THE ARDENNES. With 50 Illustrations by THOMAS R. MACQUOID.
PICTURES AND LEGENDS FROM NORMANDY AND BRITTANY. With 34 Illustrations by THOMAS R. MACQUOID.
THROUGH NORMANDY. With 92 Illustrations by T. R. MACQUOID, and a Map.
THROUGH BRITTANY. With 35 Illustrations by T. R. MACQUOID, and a Map.
ABOUT YORKSHIRE. With 67 Illustrations by T. R. MACQUOID.

Post 8vo, illustrated boards, **2s.** each.
THE EVIL EYE, and other Stories. | **LOST ROSE.**

MAGIC LANTERN, THE, and its Management: including full Practical Directions for producing the Limelight, making Oxygen Gas, and preparing Lantern Slides. By T. C. HEPWORTH. With 10 Illustrations. Cr. 8vo, **1s.**; cloth, **1s. 6d.**

MAGICIAN'S OWN BOOK, THE: Performances with Cups and Balls, Eggs, Hats, Handkerchiefs, &c. All from actual Experience. Edited by W. H. CREMER. With 200 Illustrations. Crown 8vo, cloth extra, **4s. 6d.**

MAGNA CHARTA: An Exact Facsimile of the Original in the British Museum, 3 feet by 2 feet, with Arms and Seals emblazoned in Gold and Colours, **5s.**

MALLOCK (W. H.), WORKS BY.
THE NEW REPUBLIC. Post 8vo, picture cover, **2s.**; cloth limp, **2s. 6d.**
THE NEW PAUL & VIRGINIA: Positivism on an Island. Post 8vo, cloth, **2s. 6d.**
POEMS. Small 4to, parchment, **8s.**
IS LIFE WORTH LIVING? Crown 8vo, cloth extra, **6s.**
A ROMANCE OF THE NINETEENTH CENTURY. Crown 8vo, cloth, **6s.** [Shortly.

MALLORY'S (SIR THOMAS) MORT D'ARTHUR: The Stories of King Arthur and of the Knights of the Round Table. (A Selection.) Edited by B. MONTGOMERIE RANKING. Post 8vo, cloth limp, **2s.**

MARK TWAIN, WORKS BY. Crown 8vo, cloth extra, **7s. 6d.** each.
THE CHOICE WORKS OF MARK TWAIN. Revised and Corrected throughout by the Author. With Life, Portrait, and numerous Illustrations.
ROUGHING IT, and INNOCENTS AT HOME. With 200 Illusts. by F. A. FRASER.
MARK TWAIN'S LIBRARY OF HUMOUR. With 197 Illustrations.
A YANKEE AT THE COURT OF KING ARTHUR. With 220 Illusts. by BEARD.
Crown 8vo, cloth extra (illustrated), **7s. 6d.** each; post 8vo, illust. boards, **2s.** each.
THE INNOCENTS ABROAD; or, New Pilgrim's Progress. With 234 Illustrations. (The Two-Shilling Edition is entitled MARK TWAIN'S PLEASURE TRIP.)
THE GILDED AGE. By MARK TWAIN and C. D. WARNER. With 212 Illustrations.
THE ADVENTURES OF TOM SAWYER. With 111 Illustrations.
A TRAMP ABROAD. With 314 Illustrations.
THE PRINCE AND THE PAUPER. With 190 Illustrations.
LIFE ON THE MISSISSIPPI. With 300 Illustrations.
ADVENTURES OF HUCKLEBERRY FINN. With 174 Illusts. by E. W. KEMBLE.
MARK TWAIN'S SKETCHES. Post 8vo, illustrated boards, **2s.**
THE STOLEN WHITE ELEPHANT, &c. Cr. 8vo, cl., **6s.**; post 8vo, illust. bds., **2s.**
THE AMERICAN CLAIMANT. With 81 Illustrations by HAL HURST and DAN BEARD. Crown 8vo, cloth extra, **3s. 6d.**

MARLOWE'S WORKS. Including his Translations. Edited, with Notes and Introductions, by Col. CUNNINGHAM. Crown 8vo, cloth extra, **6s.**

MARRYAT (FLORENCE), NOVELS BY. Post 8vo, illust. boards, **2s.** each.
A HARVEST OF WILD OATS. | FIGHTING THE AIR.
OPEN! SESAME! | WRITTEN IN FIRE.

MASSINGER'S PLAYS. From the Text of WILLIAM GIFFORD. Edited by Col. CUNNINGHAM. Crown 8vo, cloth extra, **6s.**

MASTERMAN.—HALF-A-DOZEN DAUGHTERS: A Novel. By J. MASTERMAN. Post 8vo, illustrated boards, **2s.**

MATTHEWS.—A SECRET OF THE SEA, &c. By BRANDER MATTHEWS. Post 8vo, illustrated boards, **2s.**; cloth limp, **2s. 6d.**

MAYHEW.—LONDON CHARACTERS AND THE HUMOROUS SIDE OF LONDON LIFE. By HENRY MAYHEW. With Illusts. Crown 8vo, cloth, **3s. 6d.**

MENKEN.—INFELICIA: Poems by ADAH ISAACS MENKEN. With Illustrations by F. E. LUMMIS and F. O. C. DARLEY. Small 4to, cloth extra, **7s. 6d.**

MERRICK.—THE MAN WHO WAS GOOD. By LEONARD MERRICK, Author of "Violet Moses," &c. Post 8vo, illustrated boards, **2s.** [Shortly.

MEXICAN MUSTANG (ON A), through Texas to the Rio Grande. By A. E. SWEET and J. ARMOY KNOX. With 265 Illusts. Cr. 8vo, cloth extra, **7s. 6d.**

MIDDLEMASS (JEAN), NOVELS BY. Post 8vo, illust. boards, **2s.** each.
TOUCH AND GO. | MR. DORILLION.

MILLER.—PHYSIOLOGY FOR THE YOUNG; or, The House of Life: Human Physiology, with its application to the Preservation of Health. By Mrs. F. FENWICK MILLER. With numerous Illustrations. Post 8vo, cloth limp, **2s. 6d.**

MILTON (J. L.), WORKS BY. Post 8vo, 1s. each; cloth, 1s. 6d. each.
THE HYGIENE OF THE SKIN. With Directions for Diet, Soaps, Baths, &c.
THE BATH IN DISEASES OF THE SKIN.
THE LAWS OF LIFE, AND THEIR RELATION TO DISEASES OF THE SKIN.
THE SUCCESSFUL TREATMENT OF LEPROSY. Demy 8vo, 1s.

MINTO (WM.)—WAS SHE GOOD OR BAD? Cr. 8vo, 1s. ; cloth, 1s. 6d.

MOLESWORTH (MRS.), NOVELS BY.
HATHERCOURT RECTORY. Post 8vo, illustrated boards, 2s.
THAT GIRL IN BLACK. Crown 8vo, cloth, 1s. 6d.

MOORE (THOMAS), WORKS BY.
THE EPICUREAN; and ALCIPHRON. Post 8vo, half-bound, 2s.
PROSE AND VERSE, Humorous, Satirical, and Sentimental, by THOMAS MOORE;
    with Suppressed Passages from the MEMOIRS OF LORD BYRON. Edited by R.
    HERNE SHEPHERD. With Portrait. Crown 8vo, cloth extra, 7s. 6d.

MUDDOCK (J. E.), STORIES BY.
STORIES WEIRD AND WONDERFUL. Post 8vo, illust. boards, 2s.; cloth, 2s. 6d.
THE DEAD MAN'S SECRET; or, The Valley of Gold. With Frontispiece by
    F. BARNARD. Crown 8vo, cloth extra, 5s.; post 8vo, illustrated boards, 2s.
MAID MARIAN AND ROBIN HOOD: A Romance of Old Sherwood Forest. With
    12 Illustrations by STANLEY L. WOOD. Crown 8vo, cloth extra, 5s.

MURRAY (D. CHRISTIE), NOVELS BY.
    Crown 8vo, cloth extra, 3s. 6d. each; post 8vo, illustrated boards, 2s. each.

A LIFE'S ATONEMENT.	HEARTS.	BY THE GATE OF THE SEA.
JOSEPH'S COAT.	WAY OF THE WORLD	A BIT OF HUMAN NATURE.
COALS OF FIRE.	A MODEL FATHER.	FIRST PERSON SINGULAR.
VAL STRANGE.	OLD BLAZER'S HERO.	CYNIC FORTUNE.

BOB MARTIN'S LITTLE GIRL. Three Vols., crown 8vo.   [Sept.

MURRAY (D. CHRISTIE) & HENRY HERMAN, WORKS BY.
ONE TRAVELLER RETURNS. Cr. 8vo, cl. extra, 6s.; post 8vo, illust. bds., 2s.
    Crown 8vo, cloth extra, 3s. 6d. each; post 8vo, illustrated boards, 2s. each.
PAUL JONES'S ALIAS. With 13 Illustrations by A. FORESTIER and G. NICOLET.
THE BISHOPS' BIBLE.

MURRAY (HENRY), NOVELS BY.
A GAME OF BLUFF. Post 8vo, illustrated boards, 2s.; cloth, 2s. 6d.
A SONG OF SIXPENCE. Post 8vo, cloth extra, 2s. 6d.

NEWBOLT.—TAKEN FROM THE ENEMY. By HENRY NEWBOLT.
Fcap. 8vo, cloth boards, 1s. 6d.

NISBET (HUME), BOOKS BY.
"BAIL UP!" A Romance of BUSHRANGERS AND BLACKS. Cr. 8vo, cl. ex., 3s. 6d.
LESSONS IN ART. With 21 Illustrations. Crown 8vo, cloth extra, 2s. 6d.
WHERE ART BEGINS. With 27 Illusts. Square 8vo, cloth extra, 7s. 6d. [Shortly.

NOVELISTS.—HALF-HOURS WITH THE BEST NOVELISTS OF
THE CENTURY. Edit. by H. T. MACKENZIE BELL. Cr. 8vo, cl., 3s. 6d. [Preparing.

O'HANLON (ALICE), NOVELS BY. Post 8vo, illustrated boards, 2s. each.
    THE UNFORESEEN. | CHANCE? OR FATE?

OHNET (GEORGES), NOVELS BY.
DOCTOR RAMEAU. 9 Illusts. by E. BAYARD. Cr. 8vo, cl., 6s.; post 8vo, bds., 2s.
A LAST LOVE. Crown 8vo, cloth, 5s.; post 8vo, boards, 2s.
A WEIRD GIFT. Crown 8vo, cloth, 3s. 6d.; post 8vo, boards, 2s.

OLIPHANT (MRS.), NOVELS BY. Post 8vo, illustrated boards, 2s. each.
THE PRIMROSE PATH. | THE GREATEST HEIRESS IN ENGLAND
WHITELADIES. With Illustrations by ARTHUR HOPKINS and HENRY WOODS,
    A.R.A. Crown 8vo, cloth extra, 3s. 6d.; post 8vo, illustrated boards, 2s.

O'REILLY (HARRINGTON).—FIFTY YEARS ON THE TRAIL: Adventures of JOHN Y. NELSON. 100 Illusts. by P. FRENZENY. Crown 8vo, 3s. 6d.

O'REILLY (MRS.).—PHŒBE'S FORTUNES. Post 8vo, illust. bds., 2s.

O'SHAUGHNESSY (ARTHUR), POEMS BY.
LAYS OF FRANCE. Crown 8vo, cloth extra, 10s. 6d.
MUSIC AND MOONLIGHT. Fcap. 8vo, cloth extra, 7s. 6d.
SONGS OF A WORKER. Fcap. 8vo, cloth extra, 7s. 6d.

OUIDA, NOVELS BY. Cr. 8vo, cl., **3s. 6d.** each; post 8vo, illust. bds., **2s.** each.

HELD IN BONDAGE.
TRICOTRIN.
STRATHMORE.
CHANDOS.
CECIL CASTLEMAINE'S GAGE.
IDALIA.
UNDER TWO FLAGS.
PUCK.

FOLLE-FARINE.
A DOG OF FLANDERS.
PASCAREL.
TWO LITTLE WOODEN SHOES.
SIGNA.
IN A WINTER CITY.
ARIADNE.
FRIENDSHIP.

MOTHS.
PIPISTRELLO.
A VILLAGE COMMUNE.
IN MAREMMA.
BIMBI. | SYRLIN.
WANDA.
FRESCOES. | OTHMAR.
PRINCESS NAPRAXINE.
GUILDEROY. | RUFFINO.

BIMBI. Presentation Edition, with Nine Illustrations by EDMUND H. GARRETT. Square 8vo, cloth, **5s.**
SANTA BARBARA, &c. Second Edition. Square 8vo, cloth, **6s.**; cr. 8vo, **3s. 6d.**
WISDOM, WIT, AND PATHOS, selected from the Works of OUIDA by F. SYDNEY MORRIS. Post 8vo, cloth extra, **5s.** CHEAP EDITION, illustrated boards, **2s.**

PAGE (H. A.), WORKS BY.
THOREAU: His Life and Aims. With Portrait. Post 8vo, cloth limp, **2s. 6d.**
ANIMAL ANECDOTES. Arranged on a New Principle. Crown 8vo, cloth extra, **5s.**

PARLIAMENTARY ELECTIONS AND ELECTIONEERING, A HISTORY OF, from the Stuarts to Queen Victoria. By JOSEPH GREGO. A New Edition, with 93 Illustrations. Demy 8vo, cloth extra, **7s. 6d.**

PASCAL'S PROVINCIAL LETTERS. A New Translation, with Historical Introduction and Notes by T. M'CRIE, D.D. Post 8vo, cloth limp, **2s.**

PAUL.—GENTLE AND SIMPLE. By MARGARET A. PAUL. With Frontispiece by HELEN PATERSON. Crown 8vo, cloth, **3s. 6d.**; post 8vo, illust. boards, **2s.**

PAYN (JAMES), NOVELS BY.
Crown 8vo, cloth extra, **3s. 6d.** each; post 8vo, illustrated boards, **2s.** each.

LOST SIR MASSINGBERD.
WALTER'S WORD.
LESS BLACK THAN WE'RE PAINTED.
BY PROXY.
HIGH SPIRITS.
UNDER ONE ROOF.
A CONFIDENTIAL AGENT.

A GRAPE FROM A THORN.
FROM EXILE.
THE CANON'S WARD.
THE TALK OF THE TOWN.
HOLIDAY TASKS.
GLOW-WORM TALES.
THE MYSTERY OF MIRBRIDGE.
THE WORD AND THE WILL.

Post 8vo, illustrated boards, **2s.** each.

HUMOROUS STORIES.
THE FOSTER BROTHERS.
THE FAMILY SCAPEGRACE.
MARRIED BENEATH HIM.
BENTINCK'S TUTOR.
A PERFECT TREASURE.
A COUNTY FAMILY.
LIKE FATHER, LIKE SON.
A WOMAN'S VENGEANCE.
CARLYON'S YEAR. | CECIL'S TRYST.
MURPHY'S MASTER.
AT HER MERCY.
THE CLYFFARDS OF CLYFFE.

FOUND DEAD.
GWENDOLINE'S HARVEST.
A MARINE RESIDENCE.
MIRK ABBEY. | SOME PRIVATE VIEWS.
NOT WOOED, BUT WON.
TWO HUNDRED POUNDS REWARD.
THE BEST OF HUSBANDS.
HALVES. | THE BURNT MILLION.
FALLEN FORTUNES.
WHAT HE COST HER.
KIT: A MEMORY.
FOR CASH ONLY.
A PRINCE OF THE BLOOD.

Crown 8vo, cloth extra, **3s. 6d.** each.

IN PERIL AND PRIVATION: Stories of MARINE ADVENTURE. With 17 Illusts.
SUNNY STORIES, and some SHADY ONES. Frontispiece by FRED. BARNARD.
NOTES FROM THE "NEWS." Crown 8vo, portrait cover, **1s.**; cloth, **1s. 6d.**

PENNELL (H. CHOLMONDELEY), WORKS BY. Post 8vo, cl., **2s. 6d.** each.
PUCK ON PEGASUS. With Illustrations.
PEGASUS RE-SADDLED. With Ten full-page Illustrations by G. DU MAURIER.
THE MUSES OF MAYFAIR. Vers de Société, Selected by H. C. PENNELL.

PHELPS (E. STUART), WORKS BY. Post 8vo, **1s.** each; cloth, **1s. 6d.** each.
BEYOND THE GATES. By the Author of "The Gates Ajar."
AN OLD MAID'S PARADISE.
BURGLARS IN PARADISE.

JACK THE FISHERMAN. Illustrated by C. W. REED. Cr. 8vo, **1s.**; cloth, **1s. 6d.**

PIRKIS (C. L.), NOVELS BY.
TROOPING WITH CROWS. Fcap. 8vo, picture cover, **1s.**
LADY LOVELACE. Post 8vo, illustrated boards, **2s.**

PLANCHE (J. R.), WORKS BY.

THE PURSUIVANT OF ARMS; or, Heraldry Founded upon Facts. With Coloured Frontispiece, Five Plates, and 209 Illusts. Crown 8vo, cloth, **7s. 6d.**

SONGS AND POEMS, 1819-1879. Introduction by Mrs. MACKARNESS. Cr. 8vo, cl., **6s.**

PLUTARCH'S LIVES OF ILLUSTRIOUS MEN. Translated from the Greek, with Notes Critical and Historical, and a Life of Plutarch, by JOHN and WILLIAM LANGHORNE. With Portraits. Two Vols., demy 8vo, half-bound, **10s. 6d.**

POE'S (EDGAR ALLAN) CHOICE WORKS, in Prose and Poetry. Introduction by CHAS. BAUDELAIRE, Portrait, and Facsimiles. Cr. 8vo, cloth, **7s. 6d.**

THE MYSTERY OF MARIE ROGET, &c. Post 8vo, illustrated boards, **2s.**

POPE'S POETICAL WORKS. Post 8vo, cloth limp, 2s.

PRICE (E. C.), NOVELS BY.

Crown 8vo, cloth extra, **3s. 6d.** each; post 8vo, illustrated boards, **2s.** each.

VALENTINA. | **THE FOREIGNERS.** | **MRS. LANCASTER'S RIVAL.**

GERALD. Post 8vo, illustrated boards, **2s.**

PRINCESS OLGA.—RADNA; or, The Great Conspiracy of 1881. By the Princess OLGA. Crown 8vo, cloth extra, **6s.**

PROCTOR (RICHARD A., B.A.), WORKS BY.

FLOWERS OF THE SKY. With 55 Illusts. Small crown 8vo, cloth extra, **3s. 6d.**

EASY STAR LESSONS. With Star Maps for Every Nigh in the Year, Drawings of the Constellations, &c. Crown 8vo, cloth extra, **6s.**

FAMILIAR SCIENCE STUDIES. Crown 8vo, cloth extra, **6s.**

SATURN AND ITS SYSTEM. With 13 Steel Plates. Demy 8vo, cloth ex., **10s. 6d.**

MYSTERIES OF TIME AND SPACE. With Illustrations. Cr. 8vo, cloth extra, **6s.**

THE UNIVERSE OF SUNS. With numerous Illustrations. Cr. 8vo, cloth ex., **6s.**

WAGES AND WANTS OF SCIENCE WORKERS. Crown 8vo, **1s. 6d.**

PRYCE.—MISS MAXWELL'S AFFECTIONS. By RICHARD PRYCE, Author of "No Impediment." With a Frontispiece by HAL LUDLOW. Crown 8vo, cloth extra, **3s. 6d.**

RAMBOSSON.—POPULAR ASTRONOMY. By J. RAMBOSSON, Laureate of the Institute of France. With numerous Illusts. Crown 8vo, cloth extra, **7s. 6d.**

RANDOLPH.—AUNT ABIGAIL DYKES: A Novel. By Lt.-Colonel GEORGE RANDOLPH, U.S.A. Crown 8vo, cloth extra, **7s. 6d.**

READE (CHARLES), NOVELS BY.

Crown 8vo, cloth extra, illustrated, **3s. 6d.** each; post 8vo, illust. bds., **2s.** each.

PEG WOFFINGTON. Illustrated by S. L. FILDES, R.A.—Also a POCKET EDITION, set in New Type, in Elzevir style, fcap. 8vo, half-leather, **2s. 6d.**

CHRISTIE JOHNSTONE. Illustrated by WILLIAM SMALL.—Also a POCKET EDITION, set in New Type, in Elzevir style, fcap. 8vo, half-leather, **2s. 6d.**

IT IS NEVER TOO LATE TO MEND. Illustrated by G. J. PINWELL.

THE COURSE OF TRUE LOVE NEVER DID RUN SMOOTH. Illustrated by HELEN PATERSON.

THE AUTOBIOGRAPHY OF A THIEF, &c. Illustrated by MATT STRETCH.

LOVE ME LITTLE, LOVE ME LONG. Illustrated by M. ELLEN EDWARDS.

THE DOUBLE MARRIAGE. Illusts. by Sir JOHN GILBERT, R.A., and C. KEENE.

THE CLOISTER AND THE HEARTH. Illustrated by CHARLES KEENE.

HARD CASH. Illustrated by F. W. LAWSON.

GRIFFITH GAUNT. Illustrated by S. L. FILDES, R.A., and WILLIAM SMALL.

FOUL PLAY. Illustrated by GEORGE DU MAURIER.

PUT YOURSELF IN HIS PLACE. Illustrated by ROBERT BARNES.

A TERRIBLE TEMPTATION. Illustrated by EDWARD HUGHES and A. W. COOPER.

A SIMPLETON. Illustrated by KATE CRAUFURD.

THE WANDERING HEIR. Illustrated by HELEN PATERSON, S. L. FILDES, R.A., C. GREEN, and HENRY WOODS, A.R.A.

A WOMAN-HATER. Illustrated by THOMAS COULDERY.

SINGLEHEART AND DOUBLEFACE. Illustrated by P. MACNAB.

GOOD STORIES OF MEN AND OTHER ANIMALS. Illustrated by E. A. ABBEY, PERCY MACQUOID, R.W.S., and JOSEPH NASH.

THE JILT, and other Stories. Illustrated by JOSEPH NASH.

A PERILOUS SECRET. Illustrated by FRED. BARNARD.

READIANA. With a Steel-plate Portrait of CHARLES READE.

BIBLE CHARACTERS: Studies of David, Paul, &c. Fcap. 8vo, leatherette, **1s.**

SELECTIONS FROM THE WORKS OF CHARLES READE. With an Introduction by Mrs. ALEX. IRELAND, and a Steel-Plate Portrait. Crown 8vo, buckram, **6s.**

RIDDELL (MRS. J. H.), NOVELS BY.
Crown 8vo, cloth extra, 3s. 6d. each: post 8vo, illustrated boards, 2s. each.
THE PRINCE OF WALES'S GARDEN PARTY. | **WEIRD STORIES.**

Post 8vo, illustrated boards, 2s. each.
THE UNINHABITED HOUSE. | **HER MOTHER'S DARLING.**
MYSTERY IN PALACE GARDENS. | **THE NUN'S CURSE.**
FAIRY WATER. | **IDLE TALES.**

RIMMER (ALFRED), WORKS BY. Square 8vo, cloth gilt, 7s. 6d. each.
OUR OLD COUNTRY TOWNS. With 55 Illustrations.
RAMBLES ROUND ETON AND HARROW. With 50 Illustrations.
ABOUT ENGLAND WITH DICKENS. With 58 Illusts. by C. A. VANDERHOOF, &c.

RIVES (Amélie).—BARBARA DERING. By AMÉLIE RIVES, Author
of "The Quick or the Dead?" Two Vols., crown 8vo.

ROBINSON CRUSOE. By DANIEL DEFOE. (MAJOR'S EDITION.) With
37 Illustrations by GEORGE CRUIKSHANK. Post 8vo, half-bound, 2s.

ROBINSON (F. W.), NOVELS BY.
WOMEN ARE STRANGE. Post 8vo, illustrated boards, 2s.
THE HANDS OF JUSTICE. Crown 8vo, cloth extra, 3s. 6d.; post 8vo, illustrated
boards, 2s.

ROBINSON (PHIL), WORKS BY. Crown 8vo, cloth extra, 7s. 6d. each.
THE POETS' BIRDS. | **THE POETS' BEASTS.**
THE POETS AND NATURE: REPTILES, FISHES, INSECTS. [Preparing.

ROCHEFOUCAULD'S MAXIMS AND MORAL REFLECTIONS. With
Notes, and an Introductory Essay by SAINTE-BEUVE. Post 8vo, cloth limp, 2s.

ROLL OF BATTLE ABBEY, THE : A List of the Principal Warriors
who came from Normandy with William the Conqueror, and Settled in this Country,
A.D. 1066-7. With Arms emblazoned in Gold and Colours. Handsomely printed, 5s.

ROWLEY (HON. HUGH), WORKS BY. Post 8vo, cloth, 2s. 6d. each.
PUNIANA: RIDDLES AND JOKES. With numerous Illustrations.
MORE PUNIANA. Profusely Illustrated.

RUNCIMAN (JAMES), STORIES BY. Post 8vo, bds., 2s. ea.; cl., 2s. 6d. ea.
SKIPPERS AND SHELLBACKS. | **GRACE BALMAIGN'S SWEETHEART.**
SCHOOLS AND SCHOLARS.

RUSSELL (W. CLARK), BOOKS AND NOVELS BY :
Crown 8vo, cloth extra, 6s. each; post 8vo, illustrated boards, 2s. each.
ROUND THE GALLEY-FIRE. | **A BOOK FOR THE HAMMOCK.**
IN THE MIDDLE WATCH. | **MYSTERY OF THE "OCEAN STAR."**
A VOYAGE TO THE CAPE. | **THE ROMANCE OF JENNY HARLOWE.**

Crown 8vo, cloth extra, 3s. 6d. each; post 8vo, illustrated boards, 2s. each.
AN OCEAN TRAGEDY. | **MY SHIPMATE LOUISE.**
ALONE ON A WIDE WIDE SEA. Crown 8vo, cloth extra, 3s. 6d.
ON THE FO'K'SLE HEAD. Post 8vo, illustrated boards, 2s.

SAINT AUBYN (ALAN), NOVELS BY.
A FELLOW OF TRINITY. With a Note by OLIVER WENDELL HOLMES and a
Frontispiece. Crown 8vo, cloth extra, 3s. 6d.; post 8vo, illust. boards, 2s.
THE JUNIOR DEAN. Crown 8vo, cloth extra, 3s. 6d.

Fcap. 8vo, cloth boards, 1s. 6d. each.
THE OLD MAID'S SWEETHEART. | **MODEST LITTLE SARA.**

SALA (G. A.).—GASLIGHT AND DAYLIGHT. Post 8vo, boards, 2s.

SANSON.—SEVEN GENERATIONS OF EXECUTIONERS : Memoirs
of the Sanson Family (1688 to 1847). Crown 8vo, cloth extra, 3s. 6d.

SAUNDERS (JOHN), NOVELS BY.
Crown 8vo, cloth extra, 3s. 6d. each; post 8vo, illustrated boards, 2s. each.
GUY WATERMAN. | **THE LION IN THE PATH.** | **THE TWO DREAMERS.**
BOUND TO THE WHEEL. Crown 8vo, cloth extra, 3s. 6d.

SAUNDERS (KATHARINE), NOVELS BY.
Crown 8vo, cloth extra, 3s. 6d. each; post 8vo, illustrated boards, 2s. each.
MARGARET AND ELIZABETH. | **HEART SALVAGE.**
THE HIGH MILLS. | **SEBASTIAN.**

JOAN MERRYWEATHER. Post 8vo, illustrated boards, 2s.
GIDEON'S ROCK. Crown 8vo, cloth extra, 3s. 6d.

SCIENCE-GOSSIP : An Illustrated Medium of Interchange for Students and Lovers of Nature. Edited by Dr. J. E. TAYLOR, F.L.S., &c. Devoted to Geology, Botany, Physiology, Chemistry, Zoology, Microscopy, Telescopy, Physiography, Photography, &c. Price **4d.** Monthly; or **5s.** per year, post-free. Vols. I. to XIX. may be had, **7s. 6d.** each; Vols. XX. to date, **5s.** each. Cases for Binding, **1s. 6d.**

SECRET OUT, THE : One Thousand Tricks with Cards; with Entertaining Experiments in Drawing-room or "White Magic." By W. H. CREMER. With 300 Illustrations. Crown 8vo, cloth extra, **4s. 6d.**

SEGUIN (L. G.), WORKS BY.
THE COUNTRY OF THE PASSION PLAY (OBERAMMERGAU) and the Highlands of Bavaria. With Map and 37 Illustrations. Crown 8vo, cloth extra, **3s. 6d.**
WALKS IN ALGIERS. With 2 Maps and 16 Illusts. Crown 8vo, cloth extra, **6s.**

SENIOR (WM.).—BY STREAM AND SEA. Post 8vo, cloth, **2s. 6d.**

SHAKESPEARE FOR CHILDREN : LAMB'S TALES FROM SHAKE-
SPEARE. With Illustrations, coloured and plain, by J. MOYR SMITH. Cr. 4to, **6s.**

SHARP.—CHILDREN OF TO-MORROW : A Novel. By WILLIAM SHARP. Crown 8vo, cloth extra, **6s.**

SHARP (LUKE).—IN A STEAMER CHAIR. By LUKE SHARP (R. E. BARR). With Two Illusts. by DEMAIN HAMMOND. Crown 8vo, cloth extra, **3s. 6d.**

SHELLEY.—THE COMPLETE WORKS IN VERSE AND PROSE OF
PERCY BYSSHE SHELLEY. Edited, Prefaced, and Annotated by R. HERNE SHEPHERD. Five Vols., crown 8vo, cloth boards, **3s. 6d.** each.
POETICAL WORKS, in Three Vols.:
Vol. I. Introduction by the Editor; Posthumous Fragments of Margaret Nicholson; Shelley's Correspondence with Stockdale; The Wandering Jew; Queen Mab, with the Notes; Alastor, and other Poems; Rosalind and Helen; Prometheus Unbound; Adonais, &c.
Vol. II. Laon and Cythna : The Cenci; Julian and Maddalo; Swellfoot the Tyrant; The Witch of Atlas; Epipsychidion; Hellas.
Vol. III. Posthumous Poems; The Masque of Anarchy; and other Pieces.
PROSE WORKS, in Two Vols.:
Vol. I. The Two Romances of Zastrozzi and St. Irvyne; the Dublin and Marlow Pamphlets; A Refutation of Deism; Letters to Leigh Hunt, and some Minor Writings and Fragments.
Vol. II. The Essays; Letters from Abroad; Translations and Fragments, Edited by Mrs. SHELLEY. With a Bibliography of Shelley, and an Index of the Prose Works.

SHERARD.—ROGUES : A Novel. By R. H. SHERARD. Crown 8vo, picture cover, **1s.** ; cloth, **1s. 6d.**

SHERIDAN (GENERAL). — PERSONAL MEMOIRS OF GENERAL
P. H. SHERIDAN. With Portraits and Facsimiles. Two Vols., demy 8vo, cloth, **24s.**

SHERIDAN'S (RICHARD BRINSLEY) COMPLETE WORKS. With
Life and Anecdotes. Including his Dramatic Writings, his Works in Prose and Poetry, Translations, Speeches and Jokes. 10 Illusts. Cr. 8vo, hf.-bound, **7s. 6d.**
THE RIVALS, THE SCHOOL FOR SCANDAL, and other Plays. Post 8vo, printed on laid paper and half-bound. **2s.**
SHERIDAN'S COMEDIES : THE RIVALS and THE SCHOOL FOR SCANDAL. Edited, with an Introduction and Notes to each Play, and a Biographical Sketch, by BRANDER MATTHEWS. With Illustrations. Demy 8vo, half-parchment, **12s. 6d.**

SIDNEY'S (SIR PHILIP) COMPLETE POETICAL WORKS, including all those in "Arcadia." With Portrait, Memorial-Introduction, Notes, &c. by the Rev. A. B. GROSART, D.D. Three Vols., crown 8vo, cloth boards, **18s.**

SIGNBOARDS : Their History. With Anecdotes of Famous Taverns and Remarkable Characters. By JACOB LARWOOD and JOHN CAMDEN HOTTEN. With Coloured Frontispiece and 94 Illustrations. Crown 8vo, cloth extra, **7s. 6d.**

SIMS (GEORGE R.), WORKS BY.
Post 8vo, illustrated boards, **2s.** each; cloth limp, **2s. 6d.** each.
ROGUES AND VAGABONDS.	MARY JANE MARRIED.
THE RING O' BELLS.	TALES OF TO-DAY.
MARY JANE'S MEMOIRS.	DRAMAS OF LIFE. With 60 Illustrations.
TINKLETOP'S CRIME. With a Frontispiece by MAURICE GREIFFENHAGEN.
ZEPH : A Circus Story, &c.
Crown 8vo, picture cover, **1s.** each; cloth, **1s. 6d.** each.
HOW THE POOR LIVE; and HORRIBLE LONDON.
THE DAGONET RECITER AND READER : being Readings and Recitations in Prose and Verse, selected from his own Works by GEORGE R. SIMS.
DAGONET DITTIES. From the *Referee*.
THE CASE OF GEORGE CANDLEMAS.

SISTER DORA: A Biography. By MARGARET LONSDALE. With Four Illustrations. Demy 8vo, picture cover, **4d.**; cloth, **6d.**

SKETCHLEY.—A MATCH IN THE DARK. By ARTHUR SKETCHLEY. Post 8vo, illustrated boards, **2s.**

SLANG DICTIONARY (THE): Etymological, Historical, and Anecdotal. Crown 8vo, cloth extra, **6s. 6d.**

SMITH (J. MOYR), WORKS BY.
THE PRINCE OF ARGOLIS. With 130 Illusts. Post 8vo, cloth extra, **3s. 6d.**
TALES OF OLD THULE. With numerous Illustrations. Crown 8vo, cloth gilt, **6s.**
THE WOOING OF THE WATER WITCH. Illustrated. Post 8vo, cloth, **6s.**

SOCIETY IN LONDON. By A FOREIGN RESIDENT. Crown 8vo, **1s.**; cloth, **1s. 6d.**

SOCIETY IN PARIS: The Upper Ten Thousand. A Series of Letters from Count PAUL VASILI to a Young French Diplomat. Crown 8vo. cloth, **6s.**

SOMERSET. — SONGS OF ADIEU. By Lord HENRY SOMERSET. Small 4to, Japanese vellum, **6s.**

SPALDING.—ELIZABETHAN DEMONOLOGY: An Essay on the Belief in the Existence of Devils. By T. A. SPALDING, LL.B. Crown 8vo, cloth extra, **5s.**

SPEIGHT (T. W.), NOVELS BY.
Post 8vo, illustrated boards, **2s.** each.

THE MYSTERIES OF HERON DYKE.	HOODWINKED; and THE SANDY-
BY DEVIOUS WAYS, &c.	CROFT MYSTERY.
THE GOLDEN HOOP.	BACK TO LIFE.

Post 8vo, cloth limp, **1s. 6d.** each.

A BARREN TITLE.	WIFE OR NO WIFE?

THE SANDYCROFT MYSTERY. Crown 8vo, picture cover, **1s.**

SPENSER FOR CHILDREN. By M. H. TOWRY. With Illustrations by WALTER J. MORGAN. Crown 4to, cloth gilt, **6s.**

STARRY HEAVENS (THE): A POETICAL BIRTHDAY BOOK. Royal 16mo, cloth extra, **2s. 6d.**

STAUNTON.—THE LAWS AND PRACTICE OF CHESS. With an Analysis of the Openings. By HOWARD STAUNTON. Edited by ROBERT B. WORMALD. Crown 8vo, cloth extra, **5s.**

STEDMAN (E. C.), WORKS BY.
VICTORIAN POETS. Thirteenth Edition. Crown 8vo. cloth extra, **9s.**
THE POETS OF AMERICA. Crown 8vo, cloth extra, **9s.**

STERNDALE. — THE AFGHAN KNIFE: A Novel. By ROBERT ARMITAGE STERNDALE. Cr. 8vo, cloth extra, **3s. 6d.**; post 8vo, illust. boards, **2s.**

STEVENSON (R. LOUIS), WORKS BY. Post 8vo, cl. limp, **2s. 6d.** each.
TRAVELS WITH A DONKEY. Seventh Edit. With a Frontis. by WALTER CRANE.
AN INLAND VOYAGE. Fourth Edition. With a Frontispiece by WALTER CRANE.

Crown 8vo, buckram, gilt top, **6s.** each.
FAMILIAR STUDIES OF MEN AND BOOKS. Sixth Edition.
THE SILVERADO SQUATTERS. With a Frontispiece. Third Edition.
THE MERRY MEN. Third Edition. | UNDERWOODS: Poems. Fifth Edition.
MEMORIES AND PORTRAITS. Third Edition.
VIRGINIBUS PUERISQUE, and other Papers. Seventh Edition. | BALLADS.
ACROSS THE PLAINS, with other Memories and Essays.

NEW ARABIAN NIGHTS. Eleventh Edition. Crown 8vo, buckram, gilt top, **6s.**; post 8vo, illustrated boards, **2s.**
THE SUICIDE CLUB; and THE RAJAH'S DIAMOND. From NEW ARABIAN NIGHTS. With Six Illustrations by J. BERNARD PARTRIDGE. Crown 8vo, cloth extra, **5s.**
PRINCE OTTO. Sixth Edition. Post 8vo, illustrated boards, **2s.**
FATHER DAMIEN: An Open Letter to the Rev. Dr. Hyde. Second Edition Crown 8vo, hand-made and brown paper, **1s.**

STODDARD. — SUMMER CRUISING IN THE SOUTH SEAS. By C. WARREN STODDARD. Illustrated by WALLIS MACKAY. Cr. 8vo, cl. extra, **3s. 6d.**

STORIES FROM FOREIGN NOVELISTS. With Notices by HELEN and ALICE ZIMMERN. Crown 8vo, cloth extra, **3s. 6d.**; post 8vo, illustrated boards, **2s.**

STRANGE MANUSCRIPT (A) FOUND IN A COPPER CYLINDER.
With 19 Illustrations by GILBERT GAUL. Third Edition. Crown 8vo, cloth extra, **5s.**

STRANGE SECRETS. Told by CONAN DOYLE, PERCY FITZGERALD, FLORENCE MARRYAT, &c. Cr. 8vo, cl. ex., Eight Illusts., **6s.**; post 8vo, illust. bds., **2s.**

STRUTT'S SPORTS AND PASTIMES OF THE PEOPLE OF ENGLAND; including the Rural and Domestic Recreations, May Games, Mummeries, Shows, &c., from the Earliest Period to the Present Time. Edited by WILLIAM HONE. With 140 Illustrations. Crown 8vo, cloth extra, **7s. 6d.**

SUBURBAN HOMES (THE) OF LONDON : A Residential Guide. With a Map, and Notes on Rental, Rates, and Accommodation. Crown 8vo, cloth, **7s. 6d.**

SWIFT'S (DEAN) CHOICE WORKS, in Prose and Verse. With Memoir, Portrait, and Facsimiles of the Maps in "Gulliver's Travels." Cr. 8vo, cl., **7s. 6d.**
GULLIVER'S TRAVELS, and A TALE OF A TUB. Post 8vo, half-bound, **2s.**
A MONOGRAPH ON SWIFT. By J. CHURTON COLLINS. Cr. 8vo, cloth, **8s.** [*Shortly.*

SWINBURNE (ALGERNON C.), WORKS BY.

SELECTIONS FROM POETICAL WORKS OF A. C. SWINBURNE. Fcap. 8vo, **6s.**
ATALANTA IN CALYDON. Crown 8vo, **6s.**
CHASTELARD: A Tragedy. Cr. 8vo. **7s.**
NOTES ON POEMS AND REVIEWS. Demy 8vo, **1s.**
POEMS AND BALLADS. FIRST SERIES. Crown 8vo or fcap. 8vo, **9s.**
POEMS AND BALLADS. SECOND SERIES. Crown 8vo or fcap. 8vo, **9s.**
POEMS AND BALLADS. THIRD SERIES. Crown 8vo, **7s.**
SONGS BEFORE SUNRISE. Crown 8vo, **10s. 6d.**
BOTHWELL: A Tragedy. Crown 8vo, **12s. 6d.**
SONGS OF TWO NATIONS. Cr. 8vo, **6s.**

GEORGE CHAPMAN. (*See* Vol. II. of G. CHAPMAN's Works.) Crown 8vo, **6s.**
ESSAYS AND STUDIES. Cr. 8vo, **12s.**
ERECHTHEUS: A Tragedy. Cr. 8vo, **6s.**
SONGS OF THE SPRINGTIDES. Crown 8vo, **6s.**
STUDIES IN SONG. Crown 8vo, **7s.**
MARY STUART: A Tragedy. Cr. 8vo, **8s.**
TRISTRAM OF LYONESSE. Cr. 8vo, **9s.**
A CENTURY OF ROUNDELS. Sm. 4to, **8s.**
A MIDSUMMER HOLIDAY. Cr. 8vo, **7s.**
MARINO FALIERO: A Tragedy. Crown 8vo, **6s.**
A STUDY OF VICTOR HUGO. Cr. 8vo, **6s.**
MISCELLANIES. Crown 8vo, **12s.**
LOCRINE: A Tragedy. Cr. 8vo, **6s.**
A STUDY OF BEN JONSON. Cr. 8vo, **7s.**
THE SISTERS: A Tragedy. Cr. 8vo, **6s.**

SYMONDS.—WINE, WOMEN, AND SONG : Mediæval Latin Students' Songs. With Essay and Trans. by J. ADDINGTON SYMONDS. Fcap. 8vo, parchment, **6s.**

SYNTAX'S (DR.) THREE TOURS : In Search of the Picturesque, in Search of Consolation, and in Search of a Wife. With ROWLANDSON'S Coloured Illustrations, and Life of the Author by J. C. HOTTEN. Crown 8vo, cloth extra, **7s. 6d.**

TAINE'S HISTORY OF ENGLISH LITERATURE. Translated by HENRY VAN LAUN. Four Vols., small demy 8vo, cl. bds., **30s.**—POPULAR EDITION, Two Vols., large crown 8vo, cloth extra. **15s.**

TAYLOR'S (BAYARD) DIVERSIONS OF THE ECHO CLUB: Burlesques of Modern Writers. Post 8vo, cloth limp, **2s.**

TAYLOR (DR. J. E., F.L.S.), WORKS BY. Cr. 8vo, cl. ex., **7s. 6d.** each.
THE SAGACITY AND MORALITY OF PLANTS: A Sketch of the Life and Conduct of the Vegetable Kingdom. With a Coloured Frontispiece and 100 Illustrations.
OUR COMMON BRITISH FOSSILS, and Where to Find Them. 331 Illustrations.
THE PLAYTIME NATURALIST. With 366 Illustrations. Crown 8vo, cloth, **5s.**

TAYLOR'S (TOM) HISTORICAL DRAMAS. Containing "Clancarty," "Jeanne Darc," "'Twixt Axe and Crown," "The Fool's Revenge," "Arkwright's Wife," "Anne Boleyn," "Plot and Passion." Crown 8vo, cloth extra, **7s. 6d.**
*** The Plays may also be had separately, at **1s.** each.

TENNYSON (LORD): A Biographical Sketch. By H. J. JENNINGS. With a Photograph-Portrait. Crown 8vo, cloth extra, **6s.**

THACKERAYANA : Notes and Anecdotes. Illustrated by Hundreds of Sketches by WILLIAM MAKEPEACE THACKERAY. Crown 8vo, cloth extra, **7s. 6d.**

THAMES.—A NEW PICTORIAL HISTORY OF THE THAMES. By A. S. KRAUSSE. With 340 Illustrations. Post 8vo, **1s.**; cloth, **1s. 6d.**

THOMAS (BERTHA), NOVELS BY. Cr. 8vo, cl., **3s. 6d.** ea.; post 8vo, **2s.** ea.
THE VIOLIN-PLAYER. | PROUD MAISIE.
CRESSIDA. Post 8vo, illustrated boards, **2s.**

THOMSON'S SEASONS, and CASTLE OF INDOLENCE. With Introduction by ALLAN CUNNINGHAM, and 48 Illustrations. Post 8vo, half-bound, 2s.

THORNBURY (WALTER), WORKS BY. Cr. 8vo, cl. extra, 7s. 6d. each.
THE LIFE AND CORRESPONDENCE OF J. M. W. TURNER. Founded upon Letters and Papers furnished by his Friends. With Illustrations in Colours.
HAUNTED LONDON. Edit. by E. WALFORD, M.A. Illusts. by F. W. FAIRHOLT, F.S.A.

Post 8vo, illustrated boards, 2s. each.
OLD STORIES RE-TOLD. | TALES FOR THE MARINES.

TIMBS (JOHN), WORKS BY. Crown 8vo, cloth extra, 7s. 6d. each.
THE HISTORY OF CLUBS AND CLUB LIFE IN LONDON: Anecdotes of its Famous Coffee-houses, Hostelries, and Taverns. With 42 Illustrations.
ENGLISH ECCENTRICS AND ECCENTRICITIES: Stories of Delusions, Impostures, Sporting Scenes, Eccentric Artists, Theatrical Folk, &c. 48 Illustrations.

TROLLOPE (ANTHONY), NOVELS BY.
Crown 8vo, cloth extra, 3s. 6d. each; post 8vo, illustrated boards, 2s. each.
THE WAY WE LIVE NOW. | MARION FAY.
KEPT IN THE DARK. | MR. SCARBOROUGH'S FAMILY.
FRAU FROHMANN. | THE LAND-LEAGUERS.

Post 8vo, illustrated boards, 2s. each.
GOLDEN LION OF GRANPERE. | JOHN CALDIGATE. | AMERICAN SENATOR.

TROLLOPE (FRANCES E.), NOVELS BY.
Crown 8vo, cloth extra, 3s. 6d. each; post 8vo, illustrated boards, 2s. each.
LIKE SHIPS UPON THE SEA. | MABEL'S PROGRESS. | ANNE FURNESS.

TROLLOPE (T. A.).—DIAMOND CUT DIAMOND. Post 8vo, illust. bds., 2s.

TROWBRIDGE.—FARNELL'S FOLLY: A Novel. By J. T. TROWBRIDGE. Post 8vo, illustrated boards, 2s.

TYTLER (C. C. FRASER-).—MISTRESS JUDITH: A Novel. By C. C. FRASER-TYTLER. Crown 8vo, cloth extra, 3s. 6d.; post 8vo, illust. boards, 2s.

TYTLER (SARAH), NOVELS BY.
Crown 8vo, cloth extra, 3s. 6d. each; post 8vo, illustrated boards, 2s. each.
THE BRIDE'S PASS. | BURIED DIAMONDS.
NOBLESSE OBLIGE. | LADY BELL. | THE BLACKHALL GHOSTS.

Post 8vo, illustrated boards, 2s. each.
WHAT SHE CAME THROUGH. | BEAUTY AND THE BEAST.
CITOYENNE JACQUELINE. | DISAPPEARED.
SAINT MUNGO'S CITY. | THE HUGUENOT FAMILY.

VILLARI.—A DOUBLE BOND. By LINDA VILLARI. Fcap. 8vo, picture cover, 1s.

WALT WHITMAN, POEMS BY. Edited, with Introduction, by WILLIAM M. ROSSETTI. With Portrait. Cr. 8vo, hand-made paper and buckram, 6s.

WALTON AND COTTON'S COMPLETE ANGLER; or, The Contemplative Man's Recreation, by IZAAK WALTON; and Instructions how to Angle for a Trout or Grayling in a clear Stream, by CHARLES COTTON. With Memoirs and Notes by Sir HARRIS NICOLAS, and 61 Illustrations. Crown 8vo, cloth antique, 7s. 6d.

WARD (HERBERT), WORKS BY.
FIVE YEARS WITH THE CONGO CANNIBALS. With 92 Illustrations by the Author, VICTOR PERARD, and W. B. DAVIS. Third ed. Roy. 8vo, cloth ex., 14s.
MY LIFE WITH STANLEY'S REAR GUARD. With a Map by F. S. WELLER, F.R.G.S. Post 8vo, 1s.; cloth, 1s. 6d.

WARNER.—A ROUNDABOUT JOURNEY. By CHARLES DUDLEY WARNER. Crown 8vo, cloth extra, 6s.

WARRANT TO EXECUTE CHARLES I. A Facsimile, with the 59 Signatures and Seals. Printed on paper 22 in. by 14 in. 2s.
WARRANT TO EXECUTE MARY QUEEN OF SCOTS. A Facsimile, including Queen Elizabeth's Signature and the Great Seal. 2s.

WASSERMANN.—THE DAFFODILS: A Novel. By LILLIAS WASSERMANN. Crown 8vo, 1s.; cloth, 1s. 6d.

WATSON.—THE MARQUIS OF CARABAS: A Novel. By AARON WATSON and LILLIAS WASSERMANN. 3 vols., crown 8vo.

WALFORD (EDWARD, M.A.), WORKS BY.
WALFORD'S COUNTY FAMILIES OF THE UNITED KINGDOM (1892). Containing the Descent, Birth, Marriage, Education, &c., of 12,000 Heads of Families, their Heirs, Offices, Addresses, Clubs, &c. Royal 8vo, cloth gilt, **50s.**
WALFORD'S WINDSOR PEERAGE, BARONETAGE, AND KNIGHTAGE (1892). Crown 8vo, cloth extra, **12s. 6d.**
WALFORD'S SHILLING PEERAGE (1892). Containing a List of the House of Lords, Scotch and Irish Peers, &c. 32mo. cloth, **1s.**
WALFORD'S SHILLING BARONETAGE (1892). Containing a List of the Baronets of the United Kingdom, Biographical Notices, Addresses, &c. 32mo, cloth, **1s.**
WALFORD'S SHILLING KNIGHTAGE (1892). Containing a List of the Knights of the United Kingdom, Biographical Notices, Addresses, &c. 32mo, cloth, **1s.**
WALFORD'S SHILLING HOUSE OF COMMONS (1892). Containing a List of all Members of the New Parliament, their Addresses. Clubs, &c. 32mo, cloth, **1s.**
WALFORD'S COMPLETE PEERAGE, BARONETAGE, KNIGHTAGE, AND HOUSE OF COMMONS (1892). Royal 32mo, cloth extra, gilt edges, **5s.**
TALES OF OUR GREAT FAMILIES. Crown 8vo, cloth extra, **3s. 6d.**

WEATHER, HOW TO FORETELL THE, WITH POCKET SPEC-TROSCOPE. By F. W. CORY. With 10 Illustrations. Cr. 8vo. **1s.;** cloth, **1s. 6d.**

WESTALL (William).—TRUST-MONEY. Three Vols., crown 8vo.

WESTROPP.—HANDBOOK OF POTTERY AND PORCELAIN. By HODDER M. WESTROPP. With Illusts. and List of Marks. Cr. 8vo, cloth, **4s. 6d.**

WHIST.—HOW TO PLAY SOLO WHIST. By ABRAHAM S. WILKS and CHARLES F. PARDON. Crown 8vo, cloth extra, **3s. 6d.**

WHISTLER'S (MR.) TEN O'CLOCK. Cr. 8vo, hand-made paper, **1s.**

WHITE.—THE NATURAL HISTORY OF SELBORNE. By GILBERT WHITE, M.A. Post 8vo, printed on laid paper and half-bound, **2s.**

WILLIAMS (W. MATTIEU, F.R.A.S.), WORKS BY.
SCIENCE IN SHORT CHAPTERS. Crown 8vo, cloth extra, **7s. 6d.**
A SIMPLE TREATISE ON HEAT. With Illusts. Cr. 8vo, cloth limp, **2s. 6d.**
THE CHEMISTRY OF COOKERY. Crown 8vo, cloth extra, **6s.**
THE CHEMISTRY OF IRON AND STEEL MAKING. Crown 8vo, cloth extra, **9s.**

WILLIAMSON (MRS. F. H.).—A CHILD WIDOW. Post 8vo, bds., **2s.**

WILSON (DR. ANDREW, F.R.S.E.), WORKS BY.
CHAPTERS ON EVOLUTION. With 259 Illustrations. Cr. 8vo, cloth extra, **7s. 6d.**
LEAVES FROM A NATURALIST'S NOTE-BOOK. Post 8vo, cloth limp, **2s. 6d.**
LEISURE-TIME STUDIES. With Illustrations. Crown 8vo, cloth extra, **6s.**
STUDIES IN LIFE AND SENSE. With numerous Illusts. Cr. 8vo, cl. ex., **6s.**
COMMON ACCIDENTS: HOW TO TREAT THEM. Illusts. Cr. 8vo, **1s.;** cl., **1s. 6d.**
GLIMPSES OF NATURE. With 35 Illustrations. Crown 8vo, cloth extra, **3s. 6d.**

WINTER (J. S.), STORIES BY. Post 8vo, illustrated boards, **2s.** each.
CAVALRY LIFE. | **REGIMENTAL LEGENDS.**
A SOLDIER'S CHILDREN. With 34 Illustrations by E. G. THOMSON and E. STUART HARDY. Crown 8vo, cloth extra, **3s. 6d.**

WISSMANN.—MY SECOND JOURNEY THROUGH EQUATORIAL AFRICA. By HERMANN VON WISSMANN. With 92 Illusts. Demy 8vo, **16s.**

WOOD.—SABINA: A Novel. By Lady WOOD. Post 8vo, boards, **2s.**

WOOD (H. F.), DETECTIVE STORIES BY. Cr. 8vo, **6s.** ea.; post 8vo. bds. **2s.**
PASSENGER FROM SCOTLAND YARD. | **ENGLISHMAN OF THE RUE CAIN.**

WOOLLEY.—RACHEL ARMSTRONG; or, Love and Theology. By CELIA PARKER WOOLLEY. Post 8vo, illustrated boards, **2s.;** cloth, **2s. 6d.**

WRIGHT (THOMAS), WORKS BY. Crown 8vo, cloth extra, **7s. 6d.** each.
CARICATURE HISTORY OF THE GEORGES. With 400 Caricatures, Squibs, &c.
HISTORY OF CARICATURE AND OF THE GROTESQUE IN ART, LITERATURE, SCULPTURE, AND PAINTING. Illustrated by F. W. FAIRHOLT, F.S.A.

WYNMAN.—MY FLIRTATIONS. By MARGARET WYNMAN. With 13 Illustrations by J. BERNARD PARTRIDGE. Crown 8vo, cloth extra, **3s. 6d.**

YATES (EDMUND), NOVELS BY. Post 8vo, illustrated boards, **2s.** each.
LAND AT LAST. | **THE FORLORN HOPE.** | **CASTAWAY.**

ZOLA.—THE DOWNFALL. By EMILE ZOLA. Translated by E. A. VIZETELLY. Crown 8vo cloth, **3s. 6d.**

LISTS OF BOOKS CLASSIFIED IN SERIES.

* *For fuller cataloguing, see alphabetical arrangement, pp. 1-25.*

THE MAYFAIR LIBRARY.   Post 8vo, cloth limp, 2s. 6d. per Volume.

A Journey Round My Room. By XAVIER DE MAISTRE.
Quips and Quiddities. By W. D. ADAMS.
The Agony Column of "The Times."
Melancholy Anatomised: Abridgment of "Burton's Anatomy of Melancholy."
The Speeches of Charles Dickens.
Literary Frivolities, Fancies, Follies, and Frolics. By W. T. DOBSON.
Poetical Ingenuities. By W. T. DOBSON.
The Cupboard Papers. By FIN-BEC.
W. S. Gilbert's Plays. FIRST SERIES.
W. S. Gilbert's Plays. SECOND SERIES.
Songs of Irish Wit and Humour.
Animals and Masters. By Sir A. HELPS.
Social Pressure. By Sir A. HELPS.
Curiosities of Criticism. H. J. JENNINGS.
Holmes's Autocrat of Breakfast-Table.
Pencil and Palette. By R. KEMPT.

Little Essays: from LAMB's Letters.
Forensic Anecdotes. By JACOB LARWOOD.
Theatrical Anecdotes. JACOB LARWOOD.
Jeux d'Esprit. Edited by HENRY S. LEIGH.
Witch Stories. By E. LYNN LINTON.
Ourselves. By E. LYNN LINTON.
Pastimes & Players. By R. MACGREGOR.
New Paul and Virginia. W.H.MALLOCK.
New Republic. By W. H. MALLOCK.
Puck on Pegasus. By H. C. PENNELL.
Pegasus Re-Saddled. By H. C. PENNELL.
Muses of Mayfair. Ed. H. C. PENNELL.
Thoreau: His Life & Aims. By H. A. PAGE.
Puniana. By Hon. HUGH ROWLEY.
More Puniana. By Hon. HUGH ROWLEY.
The Philosophy of Handwriting.
By Stream and Sea. By WM. SENIOR.
Leaves from a Naturalist's Note-Book.
By Dr. ANDREW WILSON.

THE GOLDEN LIBRARY.   Post 8vo, cloth limp, 2s. per Volume.

Bayard Taylor's Diversions of the Echo Club.
Bennett's Ballad History of England.
Bennett's Songs for Sailors.
Godwin's Lives of the Necromancers.
Pope's Poetical Works.
Holmes's Autocrat of Breakfast Table.

Holmes's Professor at Breakfast Table.
Jesse's Scenes of Country Life.
Leigh Hunt's Tale for a Chimney Corner.
Mallory's Mort d'Arthur: Selections.
Pascal's Provincial Letters.
Rochefoucauld's Maxims & Reflections.

THE WANDERER'S LIBRARY.   Crown 8vo, cloth extra, 3s. 6d. each.

Wanderings in Patagonia. By JULIUS BEERBOHM. Illustrated.
Camp Notes. By FREDERICK BOYLE.
Savage Life. By FREDERICK BOYLE.
Merrie England in the Olden Time. By G. DANIEL. Illustrated by CRUIKSHANK.
Circus Life. By THOMAS FROST.
Lives of the Conjurers. THOMAS FROST.
The Old Showmen and the Old London Fairs. By THOMAS FROST.
Low-Life Deeps. By JAMES GREENWOOD.

Wilds of London. JAMES GREENWOOD.
Tunis. Chev. HESSE-WARTEGG. 22 Illusts.
Life and Adventures of a Cheap Jack.
World Behind the Scenes. P.FITZGERALD.
Tavern Anecdotes and Sayings.
The Genial Showman. By E.P. HINGSTON.
Story of London Parks. JACOB LARWOOD.
London Characters. By HENRY MAYHEW.
Seven Generations of Executioners.
Summer Cruising in the South Seas. By C. WARREN STODDARD. Illustrated.

POPULAR SHILLING BOOKS.

Harry Fludyer at Cambridge.
Jeff Briggs's Love Story. BRET HARTE.
Twins of Table Mountain. BRET HARTE.
Snow-bound at Eagle's. By BRET HARTE.
A Day's Tour. By PERCY FITZGERALD.
Esther's Glove. By R. E. FRANCILLON.
Sentenced! By SOMERVILLE GIBNEY.
The Professor's Wife. By L. GRAHAM.
Mrs. Gainsborough's Diamonds. By JULIAN HAWTHORNE.
Niagara Spray. By J. HOLLINGSHEAD.
A Romance of the Queen's Hounds. By CHARLES JAMES.
The Garden that Paid the Rent. By TOM JERROLD.
Cut by the Mess. By ARTHUR KEYSER.
Our Sensation Novel. J. H. MCCARTHY.
Doom! By JUSTIN H. MCCARTHY, M.P.
Dolly. By JUSTIN H. MCCARTHY, M.P.

Lily Lass. JUSTIN H. MCCARTHY, M.P.
Was She Good or Bad? By W. MINTO.
Notes from the "News." By JAS. PAYN.
Beyond the Gates. By E. S. PHELPS.
Old Maid's Paradise. By E. S. PHELPS.
Burglars in Paradise. By E. S. PHELPS.
Jack the Fisherman. By E. S. PHELPS.
Trooping with Crows. By C. L. PIRKIS.
Bible Characters. By CHARLES READE.
Rogues. By R. H. SHERARD.
The Dagonet Reciter. By G. R. SIMS.
How the Poor Live. By G. R. SIMS.
Case of George Candlemas. G. R. SIMS.
Sandycroft Mystery. T. W. SPEIGHT.
Hoodwinked. By T. W. SPEIGHT.
Father Damien. By R. L. STEVENSON.
A Double Bond. By LINDA VILLARI.
My Life with Stanley's Rear Guard. By HERBERT WARD.

HANDY NOVELS.   Fcap. 8vo, cloth boards, 1s. 6d. each.

The Old Maid's Sweetheart. A.ST.AUBYN.
Modest Little Sara. ALAN ST. AUBYN.

Taken from the Enemy. H. NEWBOLT.
A Lost Soul. By W. L. ALDEN.

THE PICCADILLY NOVELS.
LIBRARY EDITIONS OF NOVELS BY THE BEST AUTHORS, many Illustrated, crown 8vo, cloth extra, **3s. 6d.** each.

THE PICCADILLY (3/6) NOVELS—*continued.*

By CHARLES GIBBON.

Robin Gray. | The Golden Shaft.
Loving a Dream. | Of High Degree.
The Flower of the Forest.

By E. GLANVILLE.

The Lost Heiress.
The Fossicker.

By CECIL GRIFFITH.

Corinthia Marazion.

By THOMAS HARDY.

Under the Greenwood Tree.

By BRET HARTE.

A Waif of the Plains.
A Ward of the Golden Gate.
A Sappho of Green Springs.
Colonel Starbottle's Client.

By JULIAN HAWTHORNE.

Garth. | Dust.
Ellice Quentin. | Fortune's Fool.
Sebastian Strome. | Beatrix Randolph.
David Poindexter's Disappearance.
The Spectre of the Camera.

By Sir A. HELPS.

Ivan de Biron.

By ISAAC HENDERSON.

Agatha Page.

By Mrs. ALFRED HUNT.

The Leaden Casket. | Self-Condemned.
That other Person.

By JEAN INGELOW.

Fated to be Free.

By R. ASHE KING.

A Drawn Game.
"The Wearing of the Green."

By E. LYNN LINTON.

Patricia Kemball. | Ione.
Under which Lord? | Paston Carew.
"My Love!" | Sowing the Wind.
The Atonement of Leam Dundas.
The World Well Lost.

By HENRY W. LUCY.

Gideon Fleyce.

By JUSTIN McCARTHY.

A Fair Saxon. | Donna Quixote.
Linley Rochford. | Maid of Athens.
Miss Misanthrope. | Camiola.
The Waterdale Neighbours.
My Enemy's Daughter.
Dear Lady Disdain.
The Comet of a Season.

By AGNES MACDONELL.

Quaker Cousins.

By D. CHRISTIE MURRAY.

Life's Atonement. | Val Strange.
Joseph's Coat. | Hearts.
Coals of Fire. | A Model Father.
Old Blazer's Hero.
By the Gate of the Sea.
A Bit of Human Nature.
First Person Singular.
Cynic Fortune.
The Way of the World.

By MURRAY & HERMAN.

The Bishops' Bible.
Paul Jones's Alias.

By HUME NISBET.

"Bail Up!"

By GEORGES OHNET.

A Weird Gift.

By Mrs. OLIPHANT.

Whiteladies.

THE PICCADILLY (3/6) NOVELS—*continued.*

By OUIDA.

Held in Bondage. | Two Little Wooden
Strathmore. | Shoes.
Chandos. | In a Winter City.
Under Two Flags. | Ariadne.
Idalia. | Friendship.
CecilCastlemaine's | Moths. | Ruffino.
Gage. | Pipistrello.
Tricotrin. | Puck. | A Village Commune
Folle Farine. | Bimbi. | Wanda.
A Dog of Flanders. | Frescoes.| Othmar.
Pascarel. | Signa. | In Maremma.
Princess Naprax- | Syrlin.| Guilderoy.
ine. | Santa Barbara.

By MARGARET A. PAUL.

Gentle and Simple.

By JAMES PAYN.

Lost Sir Massingberd.
Less Black than We're Painted.
A Confidential Agent.
A Grape from a Thorn.
In Peril and Privation.
The Mystery of Mirbridge.
The Canon's Ward.
Walter's Word. | Talk of the Town
By Proxy. | Holiday Tasks.
High Spirits. | The Burnt Million.
Under One Roof. | The Word and the
From Exile. | Will.
Glow-worm Tales. | Sunny Stories.

By E. C. PRICE.

Valentina. | The Foreigners.
Mrs. Lancaster's Rival.

By RICHARD PRYCE.

Miss Maxwell's Affections.

By CHARLES READE.

It is Never Too Late to Mend.
The Double Marriage.
Love Me Little, Love Me Long.
The Cloister and the Hearth.
The Course of True Love.
The Autobiography of a Thief.
Put Yourself in his Place.
A Terrible Temptation.
Singleheart and Doubleface.
Good Stories of Men and other Animals.
Hard Cash. | Wandering Heir.
Peg Woffington. | A Woman-Hater.
Christie Johnstone. | A Simpleton.
Griffith Gaunt. | Readiana.
Foul Play. | The Jilt.
A Perilous Secret.

By Mrs. J. H. RIDDELL.

The Prince of Wales's Garden Party.
Weird Stories.

By F. W. ROBINSON.

Women are Strange.
The Hands of Justice.

By W. CLARK RUSSELL.

An Ocean Tragedy.
My Shipmate Louise.
Alone on a Wide Wide Sea.

By JOHN SAUNDERS.

Guy Waterman. | Two Dreamers.
Bound to the Wheel.
The Lion in the Path.

By KATHARINE SAUNDERS.

Margaret and Elizabeth.
Gideon's Rock. | Heart Salvage.
The High Mills. | Sebastian,

CHEAP EDITIONS OF POPULAR NOVELS.

Post 8vo, illustrated boards, 2s. each.

TWO-SHILLING NOVELS—*continued.*

By WILKIE COLLINS.

Armadale.	My Miscellanies.
After Dark.	Woman in White.
No Name.	The Moonstone.
Antonina. | Basil.	Man and Wife.
Hide and Seek.	Poor Miss Finch.
The Dead Secret.	The Fallen Leaves.
Queen of Hearts.	Jezebel's Daughter
Miss or Mrs?	The Black Robe.
New Magdalen.	Heart and Science.
The Frozen Deep.	"I Say No."
Law and the Lady.	The Evil Genius.
The Two Destinies.	Little Novels.
Haunted Hotel.	Legacy of Cain.
A Rogue's Life.	Blind Love.

By M. J. COLQUHOUN.
Every Inch a Soldier.

By DUTTON COOK.
Leo. | Paul Foster's Daughter.

By C. EGBERT CRADDOCK.
Prophet of the Great Smoky Mountains.

By B. M. CROKER.
Pretty Miss Neville.
A Bird of Passage.
Diana Barrington.
Proper Pride.

By WILLIAM CYPLES.
Hearts of Gold.

By ALPHONSE DAUDET.
The Evangelist; or, Port Salvation.

By JAMES DE MILLE.
A Castle in Spain.

By J. LEITH DERWENT.
Our Lady of Tears. | Circe's Lovers.

By CHARLES DICKENS.
Sketches by Boz. | Oliver Twist.
Pickwick Papers. | Nicholas Nickleby.

By DICK DONOVAN.
The Man-Hunter. | Caught at Last!
Tracked and Taken.
Who Poisoned Hetty Duncan?
The Man from Manchester.
A Detective's Triumphs.
In the Grip of the Law.

By Mrs. ANNIE EDWARDES.
A Point of Honour. | Archie Lovell.

By M. BETHAM-EDWARDS.
Felicia. | Kitty.

By EDWARD EGGLESTON.
Roxy.

By PERCY FITZGERALD.
Bella Donna. | Polly.
Never Forgotten. | Fatal Zero.
The Second Mrs. Tillotson.
Seventy-five Brooke Street.
The Lady of Brantome.

By PERCY FITZGERALD
and others.
Strange Secrets.

ALBANY DE FONBLANQUE.
Filthy Lucre.

By R. E. FRANCILLON.
Olympia. | Queen Cophetua.
One by One. | King or Knave?
A Real Queen. | Romances of Law.

By HAROLD FREDERIC.
Seth's Brother's Wife.
The Lawton Girl.

Pref. by Sir BARTLE FRERE.
Pandurang Hari.

TWO-SHILLING NOVELS—*continued.*

By HAIN FRISWELL.
One of Two.

By EDWARD GARRETT.
The Capel Girls.

By CHARLES GIBBON.

Robin Gray.	In Honour Bound.
Fancy Free.	Flower of Forest.
For Lack of Gold.	Braes of Yarrow.
What will the	The Golden Shaft.
World Say?	Of High Degree.
In Love and War.	Mead and Stream.
For the King.	Loving a Dream.
In Pastures Green.	A Hard Knot.
Queen of Meadow.	Heart's Delight.
A Heart's Problem.	Blood-Money.
The Dead Heart.	

By WILLIAM GILBERT.
Dr. Austin's Guests. | James Duke.
The Wizard of the Mountain.

By ERNEST GLANVILLE.
The Lost Heiress.

By HENRY GREVILLE.
A Noble Woman. | Nikanor.

By JOHN HABBERTON.
Brueton's Bayou. | Country Luck.

By ANDREW HALLIDAY.
Every-Day Papers.

By Lady DUFFUS HARDY.
Paul Wynter's Sacrifice.

By THOMAS HARDY.
Under the Greenwood Tree.

By J. BERWICK HARWOOD.
The Tenth Earl.

By JULIAN HAWTHORNE.

Garth.	Sebastian Strome.
Ellice Quentin.	Dust.
Fortune's Fool.	Beatrix Randolph.
Miss Cadogna.	Love—or a Name.
David Poindexter's Disappearance.	
The Spectre of the Camera.	

By Sir ARTHUR HELPS.
Ivan de Biron.

By HENRY HERMAN.
A Leading Lady.

By Mrs. CASHEL HOEY.
The Lover's Creed.

By Mrs. GEORGE HOOPER.
The House of Raby.

By TIGHE HOPKINS.
'Twixt Love and Duty.

By Mrs. HUNGERFORD.
A Maiden all Forlorn.
In Durance Vile. | A Mental Struggle.
Marvel. | A Modern Circe.

By Mrs. ALFRED HUNT.
Thornicroft's Model. | Self-Condemned.
That Other Person. | Leaden Casket.

By JEAN INGELOW.
Fated to be Free.

By HARRIETT JAY
The Dark Colleen.
The Queen of Connaught.

By MARK KERSHAW.
Colonial Facts and Fictions.

By R. ASHE KING.
A Drawn Game. | Passion's Slave.
"The Wearing of the Green."
Bell Barry.

Two-Shilling Novels—*continued.*

By JOHN LEYS.
The Lindsays.

By E. LYNN LINTON.
Patricia Kemball. | Paston Carew.
World Well Lost. | "My Love!"
Under which Lord? | Ione.
The Atonement of Leam Dundas.
With a Silken Thread.
The Rebel of the Family.
Sowing the Wind.

By HENRY W. LUCY.
Gideon Fleyce.

By JUSTIN McCARTHY.
A Fair Saxon. | Donna Quixote.
Linley Rochford. | Maid of Athens.
Miss Misanthrope. | Camiola.
Dear Lady Disdain.
The Waterdale Neighbours.
My Enemy's Daughter.
The Comet of a Season.

By AGNES MACDONELL.
Quaker Cousins.

KATHARINE S. MACQUOID.
The Evil Eye. | Lost Rose.

By W. H. MALLOCK.
The New Republic.

By FLORENCE MARRYAT.
Open! Sesame! | Fighting the Air.
A Harvest of Wild Oats.
Written in Fire.

By J. MASTERMAN.
Half-a-dozen Daughters.

By BRANDER MATTHEWS.
A Secret of the Sea.

By LEONARD MERRICK.
The Man who was Good.

By JEAN MIDDLEMASS.
Touch and Go. | Mr. Dorillion.

By Mrs. MOLESWORTH.
Hathercourt Rectory.

By J. E. MUDDOCK.
Stories Weird and Wonderful.
The Dead Man's Secret.

By D. CHRISTIE MURRAY.
A Model Father. | Old Blazer's Hero.
Joseph's Coat. | Hearts.
Coals of Fire. | Way of the World.
Val Strange. | Cynic Fortune.
A Life's Atonement.
By the Gate of the Sea.
A Bit of Human Nature.
First Person Singular.

By MURRAY and HERMAN.
One Traveller Returns.
Paul Jones's Alias.
The Bishops' Bible.

By HENRY MURRAY.
A Game of Bluff.

By ALICE O'HANLON.
The Unforeseen. | Chance? or Fate?

Two-Shilling Novels—*continued.*

By GEORGES OHNET.
Doctor Rameau. | A Last Love.
A Weird Gift. |

By Mrs. OLIPHANT.
Whiteladies. | The Primrose Path
The Greatest Heiress in England.

By Mrs. ROBERT O'REILLY.
Phœbe's Fortunes.

By OUIDA.
Held in Bondage. | Two Little Wooden
Strathmore. | Shoes.
Chandos. | Friendship.
Under Two Flags. | Moths.
Idalia. | Pipistrello.
CecilCastlemaine's | A Village Com-
Gage. | mune.
Tricotrin. | Bimbi.
Puck. | Wanda.
Folle Farine. | Frescoes.
A Dog of Flanders. | In Maremma.
Pascarel. | Othmar.
Signa. | Guilderoy.
Princess Naprax- | Ruffino.
ine. | Syrlin.
In a Winter City. | Ouida's Wisdom,
Ariadne. | Wit, and Pathos.

MARGARET AGNES PAUL.
Gentle and Simple.

By JAMES PAYN.
Bentinck's Tutor. | £200 Reward.
Murphy's Master. | Marine Residence.
A County Family. | Mirk Abbey.
At Her Mercy. | By Proxy.
Cecil's Tryst. | Under One Roof.
Clyffards of Clyffe. | High Spirits.
Foster Brothers. | Carlyon's Year.
Found Dead. | From Exile.
Best of Husbands. | For Cash Only.
Walter's Word. | Kit.
Halves. | The Canon's Ward
Fallen Fortunes. | Talk of the Town.
Humorous Stories. | Holiday Tasks.
Lost Sir Massingberd.
A Perfect Treasure.
A Woman's Vengeance.
The Family Scapegrace.
What He Cost Her.
Gwendoline's Harvest.
Like Father, Like Son.
Married Beneath Him.
Not Wooed, but Won.
Less Black than We're Painted.
A Confidential Agent.
Some Private Views.
A Grape from a Thorn.
Glow-worm Tales.
The Mystery of Mirbridge.
The Burnt Million.
The Word and the Will.
A Prince of the Blood.

By C. L. PIRKIS.
Lady Lovelace.

By EDGAR A. POE.
The Mystery of Marie Roget.

By E. C. PRICE.
Valentina. | The Foreigners.
Mrs. Lancaster's Rival.
Gerald.

TWO-SHILLING NOVELS—continued.

By CHARLES READE.
It is Never Too Late to Mend.
Christie Johnstone.
Put Yourself in His Place.
The Double Marriage.
Love Me Little, Love Me Long.
The Cloister and the Hearth.
The Course of True Love.
Autobiography of a Thief.
A Terrible Temptation.
The Wandering Heir.
Singleheart and Doubleface.
Good Stories of Men and other Animals.

Hard Cash.	A Simpleton.
Peg Woffington.	Readiana.
Griffith Gaunt.	A Woman-Hater.
Foul Play.	The Jilt.

A Perilous Secret.

By Mrs. J. H. RIDDELL.

Weird Stories.	Fairy Water.

Her Mother's Darling.
Prince of Wales's Garden Party.
The Uninhabited House.
The Mystery in Palace Gardens.

The Nun's Curse.	Idle Tales.

By F. W. ROBINSON.
Women are Strange.
The Hands of Justice.

By JAMES RUNCIMAN.
Skippers and Shellbacks.
Grace Balmaign's Sweetheart.
Schools and Scholars.

By W. CLARK RUSSELL.
Round the Galley Fire.
On the Fo'k'sle Head.
In the Middle Watch.
A Voyage to the Cape.
A Book for the Hammock.
The Mystery of the "Ocean Star."
The Romance of Jenny Harlowe.
An Ocean Tragedy.
My Shipmate Louise.

GEORGE AUGUSTUS SALA.
Gaslight and Daylight.

By JOHN SAUNDERS.

Guy Waterman.	Two Dreamers.

The Lion in the Path.

By KATHARINE SAUNDERS.

Joan Merryweather.	Heart Salvage.
The High Mills.	Sebastian.

Margaret and Elizabeth.

By GEORGE R. SIMS.
Rogues and Vagabonds.
The Ring o' Bells.
Mary Jane's Memoirs.
Mary Jane Married.

Tales of To-day.	Dramas of Life.

Tinkletop's Crime.
Zeph: A Circus Story.

By ARTHUR SKETCHLEY.
A Match in the Dark.

By HAWLEY SMART.
Without Love or Licence.

By T. W. SPEIGHT.
The Mysteries of Heron Dyke.

The Golden Hoop.	By Devious Ways.
Hoodwinked, &c.	Back to Life.

TWO-SHILLING NOVELS—continued.

By R. A. STERNDALE.
The Afghan Knife.

By R. LOUIS STEVENSON.

New Arabian Nights.	Prince Otto.

BY BERTHA THOMAS.

Cressida.	Proud Maisie.

The Violin-player.

By WALTER THORNBURY.
Tales for the Marines.
Old Stories Re-told.

T. ADOLPHUS TROLLOPE.
Diamond Cut Diamond.

By F. ELEANOR TROLLOPE.
Like Ships upon the Sea.

Anne Furness.	Mabel's Progress.

By ANTHONY TROLLOPE.

Frau Frohmann.	Kept in the Dark.
Marion Fay.	John Caldigate.

The Way We Live Now.
The American Senator.
Mr. Scarborough's Family.
The Land-Leaguers.
The Golden Lion of Granpere.

By J. T. TROWBRIDGE.
Farnell's Folly.

By IVAN TURGENIEFF, &c.
Stories from Foreign Novelists.

By MARK TWAIN.
A Pleasure Trip on the Continent.
The Gilded Age.
Mark Twain's Sketches.

Tom Sawyer.	A Tramp Abroad.

The Stolen White Elephant.
Huckleberry Finn.
Life on the Mississippi.
The Prince and the Pauper.

By C. C. FRASER-TYTLER.
Mistress Judith.

By SARAH TYTLER.

The Bride's Pass.	Noblesse Oblige.
Buried Diamonds.	Disappeared.
Saint Mungo's City.	Huguenot Family.
Lady Bell.	Blackhall Ghosts.

What She Came Through.
Beauty and the Beast.
Citoyenne Jaqueline.

By Mrs. F. H. WILLIAMSON.
A Child Widow.

By J. S. WINTER.

Cavalry Life.	Regimental Legends

By H. F. WOOD.
The Passenger from Scotland Yard.
The Englishman of the Rue Cain.

By Lady WOOD.
Sabina.

CELIA PARKER WOOLLEY.
Rachel Armstrong; or, Love & Theology.

By EDMUND YATES.

The Forlorn Hope.	Land at Last.

Castaway.

OGDEN, SMALE AND CO., LIMITED, PRINTERS, GREAT SAFFRON HILL, LONDON, E.C.